Edward Greey

Blue Jackets, or, the Adventures of J. Thompson, A.B.

Edward Greey

Blue Jackets, or, the Adventures of J. Thompson, A.B.

ISBN/EAN: 9783337048778

Printed in Europe, USA, Canada, Australia, Japan

Cover: Foto ©Andreas Hilbeck / pixelio.de

More available books at **www.hansebooks.com**

BLUE JACKETS;

OR,

THE ADVENTURES OF J. THOMPSON, A. B.

AMONG "THE HEATHEN CHINEE."

A NAUTICAL NOVEL.

BY

EDWARD GREEY,

(SUNG-TIE.)

IN ONE VOLUME.

———◆◆———

BOSTON:

J. E. TILTON & CO.

1871.

Shanley & Lynch, Print, 39 Vesey St., N. Y.

PREFACE

THE most cruel and ignominious punishment man can inflict upon his fellow men, is still enforced in the English Naval Service; though many indignantly deny it, and stigmatize this story as "a libel on the British Navy." Unfortunately for "Blue Jackets" this is not so, and the novel is founded on facts, as I have been in the service, and, on many occasions, seen sailors subjected to most painful degradation at the caprice of those, who, because they were officers, seemed to forget that the men possessed feelings in common with them. As facts are the best proofs, I quote the "London Daily News," November 7, 1870, which records that on October 30, 1870, a scene, similar in barbarity to the one described in the fifth chapter, occurred in Plymouth Sound, England, on board the "Vanguard" (Captain E. H. G. Lambert), "within hearing of a large number of women and children, who were waiting permission to go on board the iron-clad."

It may interest readers to know, that the adventures of J. Thompson, A. B., among "The Heathen Chinee," are not entirely fictitious, the descriptions of the peculiar habits of "The Coming Man" being from personal observation during a lengthened sojourn in China.

EDWARD GREEY.

NEW YORK, *January* 1, 1871.

CONTENTS.

CONTENTS.

BLUE JACKETS;

OR, THE ADVENTURES OF

J. THOMPSON, A. B., AMONG "THE HEATHEN CHINEE."

CHAPTER I.

THE big bell of Woolwich Dockyard had just commenced its deafening announcement that "dinner time" had arrived, producing at its first boom, a change from activity to rest in every department of that vast establishment.

Burly convicts, resembling in their brown striped suits human zebras, upon hearing the clang, immediately threw down their burdens, and, followed by the severe-looking pensioners who acted as their guards, sauntered carelessly towards the riverside, where they knew boats waited to convey them on board the hulks. As these scowling outcasts drifted along, they here and there passed parties of perspiring sailors still toiling under the direction of some petty officer; noticing which, the convicted ones would grin and nudge each other, glad to find that while they could cease their labour at the first stroke of the bell, there were free men who dared not even think of relaxing their hands until ordered to do so by their superiors; and many of the rogues turned their forbidden quids, and thanked their stars that they were convicted felons, and not men-of-wars's men.

In the smithies, at the first welcome stroke of the bell, hammers, which were then poised in the air, were dropped with a gentle thud upon the fine iron scales with which the floor was covered; the smiths, like all other artisans, having the greatest disinclination to work for the Government one second beyond the time for which they were paid. The engines kept up their din a few moments after all other sounds had ceased, but finding themselves deserted gave it up, and, judging by the way they jerked the vapour from their steam pipes, appeared to be taking a quiet smoke on their own account.

From forge, workshop, factory, mast-pond, saw-mill, store, and building shed—from under huge ships propped up in dry-dock, or towering grandly on their slips,—from lofty tops and dark holds,—out of boat and lighter,—from every nook and corner swarmed mechanics and labourers,—all these uniting in one eager mob, elbowed and jostled their way towards the gate, like boys leaving school.

The dockyard was bounded by a high wall upon the side nearest the town; whilst its river frontage was guarded by sentries, who not only protected the Queen's property, but prevented her jolly tars from taking boat in a manner not allowed upon Her Majesty's service.

The doors of the great gate were thrown wide open, and the crowd poured through as if quite ignoring the presence of a number of detectives, who were posted near it, to prevent deserters from the ships of war from passing out with the workpeople; special precaution being taken at that time, as the country required every sailor she could muster, to man the ships then being fitted out for service against the Russians.

When the rush was at its height a sailor disguised in the sooty garb of a smith emerged from behind a stack of timber, piled near the main entrance, and joining a party of workmen, who evidently recognized him, was forced on with them towards the gate, the man walking as unconcernedly as any ordinary labourer. As they neared the detectives the attention of the latter was suddenly distracted by the noise of a passing circus procession, and for a moment the officials were off their guard.

"Keep your face this way, mate, and look careless at the peelers," whispered one of the party to the deserter, and the man so warned did as he was directed, although he scarcely breathed as he brushed by them, the very buttons on their uniforms seeming to spy him out, and to raise a fear in his breast that he would find a hand rudely laid upon his collar, and hear the words, "You're a prisoner?" However, they did not even look at him, and in another moment he found himself free.

The deserter was an able seaman named Tom Clare, a sober, excellent sailor, and the devoted husband of a worthy girl to whom he had been but a few weeks united. Tom had not long before arrived home from the China Station in H. M. S. Porpoise, and finding some property bequeathed to him, had applied to the Admiralty for his discharge, but his application was refused ; and although he offered to provide one or more substitutes, his petition was returned to him, with orders to proceed at once to the ship to which he had been drafted, under penalty of being arrested as a deserter. Tom found, to his sorrow, there was no alternative. If he stayed, the authorities would at once arrest him, as they were notified of his whereabouts. He knew England had just entered upon a tremendous struggle with Russia; so, hoping it would soon be over, and the demand for seamen decrease, he determined to face his misery, and proceed to Woolwich to join the Stinger, that ship being rapidly fitted out for foreign service.

As it was customary to allow the men leave to go on shore at least twice a week, Clare was accompanied to the port by his wife, his only request being that she should never attempt to visit him on board his ship, to which she reluctantly agreed, but thought it very hard that her husband should make such a stipulation. Leaving her in respectable lodgings, he walked down to the docks, was directed to his ship, and in a few moments found himself before the first lieutenant. This officer, by name Howard Crushe, was a tall cadaverous-looking man, with a face upon which meanness and cruelty were plainly depicted. Clare knew him at once, Crushe having been the second lieutenant of his last ship, and as such having twice endeavoured to get him flogged.

"Come on board to jine, if you please, sir," said the seaman.

"Oh! that's you, Mr. Clare, is it?" sneered this ornament of the navy.

"Yes, sir," replied Tom, putting a cheerful face on it, and endeavouring to appear rather pleased than otherwise to see his old officer.

"Do you remember I promised you four dozen when you sailed with me in the Porpoise, eh? Well, my fine fellow, mind your p's and q's, or you'll find I shall keep my word. I remember! You're the brute who objected to my kicking a whelp of a boy. All right! I'm glad you have been drafted to my ship, as I can make it a little heaven for you."

Clare remembered the circumstance to which Crushe alluded, he having once interfered to save a poor boy from brutal treatment at the hands of that officer, and now he was in his power he knew he was a marked man.

The lieutenant called for Mr. Shever, the boatswain, and told him to put the sailor in the starboard-watch, at the same time privately informing that warrant officer of his dislike to the man.

"Leave him to me, sir. I knows him. He is a werry good man, but has them high-flown notions," was the reply of the boatswain.

Tom was taken forward and put to work; and when the dinner pipe went, proceeded on board the receiving hulk with the rest of the Stinger's, having fully made up his mind to be civil, and do his duty, in spite of the depressing aspect of the future. "Perhaps he'll not try and flake me, arter all," he thought. "If I does my best and don't answer him sassy, he can't be such a cold-blooded monster as to do what he ses. I suppose he only wanted to frighten me." As the sailor pondered over this, his face showed that although he endeavoured to argue himself into the belief that all would come right, still his mind was filled with alarm at the prospect before him.

The Stinger was, according to the Navy-List, commanded by Captain Puffeigh, a short, fat, vulgar, fussy little man; but in reality Crushe, who had married the captain's niece, had sole control of ⬤ ship, Puffeigh merely coming on board once a week, and staying just long enough to throw the first lieutenant's plans into confusion. The crew knew there was a captain belonging to the ship, but probably not two of their number could tell who he was. Crushe was the officer they looked to, and all of them soon found out that he was a Tartar. His first act of despotism towards Clare was to stop his leave to go on shore; and this he did on the day the man joined the ship.

"Please, sir, do let me go ashore to see my wife," pleaded the sailor.

"Let your fancy come off with the other girls," was the lieutenant's brutal rejoinder.

Tom bit his lips, and turned away disgusted and almost mad, knowing it would not do to show what he felt. He thought, "of course the lieutenant imagines all women who have anything to do with sailors are bad; he don't know how good *she* is. I wish I could have him face to face on shore, I'd cram them ere words down his lean throat, I would."

Tom's leave had been stopped for over a fortnight, and all his appeals met with insults from Crushe, when one morning, the crew having been transferred from the hulk to the Stinger, Captain Puffeigh visited the ship; and after a superficial survey, desired the first lieutenant to muster the men, observing, "I think it's time they should know who I am." The fact was, he began to be a little jealous of his lieutenant's power, and thought it best to show his authority.

After much piping and shouting on the part of Shever and his mates, the men were mustered upon the quarter-deck, and they certainly were "a motley crew." There was the usual proportion of petty-officers, all old men-of-war's men; able seamen, principally volunteers from the merchant service; ordinary seamen, mostly outcasts driven by dire necessity to join the navy; and first and second class boys. The latter were, with a few exceptions, workhouse-bred, and imagined themselves in clover. They served their country by doing all the dirty work of the ship from 4 A.M. until 6 P.M., after which time, until piped to rest, the lads amused themselves by learning to drink and smoke, or by listening to the intellectual conversation and songs of the gentlemanly outcasts before mentioned. Men like Clare felt rather disgusted upon finding themselves ranked with such fellows; although had this collection of human beings been under the guidance of a humane commander and first lieutenant, they might after a time

have been moulded into a good crew. Of course they were a rough lot, as the Queen's
service offered, at that time, but few inducements to decent sailors.

Puffeigh walked up and down the line, scanning the faces of the men with anything
but a pleasant expression upon his countenance. He picked out the sailors at a glance,
and spoke to them, asking the usual question, were they satisfied with their ship?
When he came to Clare he stopped for a moment, and observed to Crushe, "What a
fine fellow that is!"

"One of the worst characters in the fleet," replied the first lieutenant.

However, the captain questioned him as he had done the others, upon which Tom
briefly and respectfully asked the commander for permission to go on shore, like the
rest of the men.

"Speak to Lieutenant Crushe about that. I leave those things to him entirely."

Tom was about to reply that he had done so, when the captain cut him short with,
"There, my man, discipline must be maintained," and then gave the order to "pipe
down."

The dignified Puffeigh strutted aft, and Lieutenant Crushe, calling Clare to him,
said, between his teeth, "You sweep! I'll keep my word with you as soon as we get
into blue water."

Tom knew full well what that meant: he was to be flogged; so he determined to
desert, and get out of the country. His country required his services, but no man could
stand such treatment. His mind was made up, and he wrote to his wife as follows:

H. M. Stinger, Woolwich doc-yard, 12 *October,* ———

"DEAR POLLY,

"Come aborde at dinner time on Sunday. Mind you are not laite.

"Your loving husband,

"TOM CLARE."

His wife had not seen him since the day he joined the ship, although she had several
times been tempted to go on board; but remembering his earnest wish, was obliged to
content herself with the letters he sent her; and the poor fellow often went without a
meal in order to find time to write her a line. He could not bear to have his fair young
wife herded upon the wharf with the degraded creatures who daily swarmed down to
the ship, but come she must now, as it was the only chance by which he could escape
from his hateful bondage.

On the appointed day Polly went down, and was one of the first to be passed on
board by the ship's-corporal. Tom's lips quivered as he saw her descend the gangway
ladder, and soon he was by her side. There was no loud demonstration, but the fervant
pressure of their hands showed how happy they were to meet again, even in that place.
By a fortunate accident, the boatswain was absent, and his cabin left in charge of
a good-natured A. B., by name Jerry Thompson.

When Polly was descending the main hatchway ladder, Jerry, who knew all about
Crushe's behaviour towards Clare, stepped forward, saying, "This way, mum," and, to
the delight of the couple, they were shown into Mr. Shever's cabin, and thus enabled to
have four hours' uninterrupted chat; the sailor going off, after placing before them his
own dinner and allowance of grog. Jerry had a susceptible heart, and would do any
thing to serve a woman.

Tom rapidly ran over his reasons for attempting to escape, and you may be sure
Polly agreed and sympathized with him in everything.

"What a shame," she exclaimed, "to keep you on board, when even the boys get as
much leave as they choose to ask for!"

"Never mind, my dear," he replied. "I'll not ask 'em for leave this day week, if all goes well."

Polly left the ship in good spirits, and was gallantly escorted to the dock-gates by the kind-hearted A. B., who said to her on parting,

"Mum, if ever Tom wants a friend, I'll do my best for him, for the sake of his wife. You see, mum, I'm not a married man myself, but I can feel for them as is."

"God bless you, sir, for your kindness," sobbed Polly.

"Jerry, mum, not *sir*; we ain't allowed that rate in a man-o'-war."

Polly laughed through her tears, and nodding to the sailor, passed quickly through the turnstile, and was soon out of sight.

Before the week was over she had made all the arrangements for her husband's flight; having smuggled off a complete suit of well-worn smith's clothes, and paid the men from whom she obtained them a sum of money to assist Tom in getting through the gate.

As we have described, Clare played his part well, and passed the detectives without the slightest suspicion on their part that a deserter had escaped before their eyes.

On leaving the men who had assisted him, Clare turned to the left, keeping with the crowd as much as possible. All along the foot of the wall were crouched anxious wives and children, waiting with "father's dinner," in order to save him a long walk. Many of these watchers peered into his face, and some of the little ones would clap their hands and cry, "Here's daddy!"

Tom walked on for a few moments, hardly able to realize he was free, when suddenly Polly, who had followed him from the dock-gate, caught him by the arm.

"For heaven's sake, Polly, don't draw notice on me; walk on ahead, dear, I'll follow you; but don't look behind you, unless you would have me took."

Poor Tom! The loving taunt of that speech was understood by his wife. She have him taken! Why, he knew the poor girl would die for him.

Away she walked, quite in a different direction from that of her old lodgings; up one street and down another, until they were fairly out in the country, she praying all the time that her love might never be retaken, and thanking God her husband was now free. The footfall behind her was delightful music; while he, devouring her with his eyes, and longing once more to clasp her to his heart, thanked heaven in his own rough sailor style.

"Am I dreaming?" he muttered. "No, there she is, the beauty—there she is—thank the good God who guards her always—I am awake—it's real—I ain't asleep."

He imagined that walk the longest he had ever taken.

"Will she never bring to?" he thought.

At last she stopped before a neat cottage, and lifting the latch, darted in. Her husband was not long after her, and she was soon clasped in his arms.

"Polly, dear heart! Wife! look at me!" he almost sobbed as he tenderly pressed her to his heart. "Bear up, my pretty one! I'm here, and all safe, and never going away again."

But the poor girl was too happy to reply, and a flood of tears gave relief to her feelings, ere she was composed enough to talk about his plans of escape. When her agitation had somewhat abated, Polly produced a suit of farmer's clothes; and after Tom had shaved off his whiskers, she cut the curly locks from his head, although it very much grieved her to do so. When the process was complete, she called in her father and mother, who had come up from Kingsdown to assist their girl in her trouble. Clare had taken a seat by the fire, and his disguise was so complete, that the good old people could not, until he spoke to them, make out who he was.

"That beant you, Tom, be it?"

"Yes, it's me, father."

"Why, you do puzzle me. I don't know you a bit. You looks like the young squire."

Many were the congratulations which passed between them, and when the old fisherman handed Tom a passage ticket for himself and Polly, by which Clare found he could leave Liverpool for New York on the following Wednesday, he caught the old man in his arms and fairly hugged him.

It was settled they should leave the house about six o'clock P.M., and as the police were sure to be on the alert, a cart was procured in which they were to be conveyed to London, it being arranged that a brother of their kind hostess was to act as driver, while Tom and Polly were to lie down in the straw until they arrived in the big city. Once there, they might walk to the railway station. If all went well they would reach Liverpool the next day, where they could remain unmolested, until the ship sailed for America.

"Come, Tom," said the old woman, "you must be hungry, lad. I warrant you, a bit of meat and a drop o' beer won't come amiss," upon which she bustled about; and, with the assistance of Polly, a meal was prepared and placed upon the table.

Tom sat by the window, keenly watching the few stragglers who passed by, when suddenly he started back and turned pale, as a corporal of marines walked up, looked suspiciously at the cottage, and then crossing the road, questioned an old fellow, who was breaking stones.

Clare could not make out what he said, but imagined from the motions of the corporal that he was inquiring who lived in the cottage. Tom called Polly and told her his suspicion,—it was a moment of great anxiety for both of them. At length, however, the corporal turned upon his heel, and retraced his steps down the lane. Their landlady was sent for; and as the good creature knew all about her lodgers' plans, they freely imparted their fears to her, begging she would call the old stone-breaker in-doors, and ascertain what questions the petty officer had put to him, Tom and his wife retreating to the stairs, where they overheard the following conversation:

"I say, master, who was that speaking to ye this minute?"

"Don't know, missis; but I expects he be a perlice."

"What did he say to you, master?"

"'Well,' he says to me, ses he, 'do you know,' he ses, 'who lives over there?' he ses; that's what he ses to me, missis, as near as I can recollect."

"What did you tell him?"

"Why, I says, ses I, 'Look here! what do you want to know for?' I says."

"Well, go on, go on! What else did he ask you?"

"'Well,' ses he, 'have you seen any one go in there this morning,' he ses. 'Yes!' ses I. 'Who?' he ses. 'Well,' ses I, 'I seed Missis Drake, I ses, and her lodger, I ses, and a man,' I ses."

"You old foo—! Excuse me, Master Noyce, but you did not see no man come in but my lodger. There, go away! You allus was a stupid, and I'm sure of it now."

"Come, missis! I don't want no blowin' up. You axed me civil, and I gave you an answer," retorted the old man, turning sulkily away.

"Yes! you ses, and you ses, and you've been and gone and done it, you wooden-headed old post!" whimpered the good-natured woman, after she had closed the door upon him. "You've done it this time, you donkey!" whereupon she sat down in a chair, and had a good cry.

Tom and his wife came out of their place of concealment, and begged she would not take on so, as it was no fault of hers that the man had given the information; but the kind creature was with difficulty assured "it might all turn out to be nothing." She felt that, after all the poor fellow's trouble, he would be captured and flogged, and their arguments only increased her sympathy for the unfortunate couple. However, the afternoon passed away with no more signs of the corporal, and by six o'clock everything was in readiness. The old folks had embraced their girl, and poor Tom was leading her out, when suddenly a party of marines rushed into the house, and the corporal in charge laid hands on Clare, and told him he was his prisoner.

Polly clung to her husband's arm, not fully realizing the dreadful truth; but soon she saw all, and that Tom was about to be torn from her. Rushing between the corporal and her husband, and endeavouring to force him from the former's grasp, she raved like a mad woman.

"You dare touch him! Take your hands away, you wretch! Do you hear? Leave go!"

Clare was about to speak to her, when the corporal said with a sneer, "Pull that thing away, and gag her if she gives any more of her talk. She need not make such a fuss; she'll soon find another feller."

These words had hardly passed his lips before Tom had the speaker down upon the floor, with both his hands tightly clutching the soldier's windpipe.

"You brute, I'll kill you!" he yelled. And he seemed likely to carry out his threat. However, the marines threw themselves upon the deserter, who, after a desperate struggle, was beaten senseless, handcuffed, and dragged away.

When the old fisherman, his wife's father, saw how brutally they ill-treated Tom, he seized a stick and endeavoured to assist him, but was overpowered and beaten, until he, too, lay like a dead man, the corporal encouraging his men "to pitch into the old scoundrel."

Polly and her mother were happily unconscious of the last part of the outrage, both having fainted when Clare seized upon the soldier. Some neighbours, aroused by the screams of their landlady, came to the assistance of the women, who after a short time were restored to their senses.

When Polly became somewhat composed, she asked for her husband.

"Where is my love? Where is my brave, handsome husband? Gone? Have those wretches taken him? You coward, father, to let them take my Tom! O God! They'll flog him! I can't bear it! Let me go! I shall go mad!"

And the poor girl had fit after fit, until they feared she would die of exhaustion. The heart-broken old people watched her through the night, thinking and almost praying that death would come to her relief.

The prisoner was conveyed on board his ship, and taken aft upon the quarter-deck, where he was reported to the officer of the watch, a mate named Cravan, derisively called by the midshipman "Nosey," and that officer being a creature of the first lieutenant's, took upon himself to reprimand the man.

"So you have caught him, eh?"

"Yes, sir," replied the corporal with a military flourish, "but we had no end of trouble. He were in a low den outside the town, along with a lot of vimen, and ven I arrested him, he werry nigh killed me."

"I were with my *wife*, sir," pleaded the prisoner.

" Your *wife*, of course ! Any trollop is your *wife*. It is a very convenient relation-ship," sneered the bully.

Roused by this coarse speech, and not caring for consequences, Clare raised his manacled hands, and dealt the brutal speaker a blow between the eyes, which stretched him upon the deck. The sailor was about following up the attack, but was prevented by the marines, who after a desperate struggle secured him, and stopped further violence on his part.

" Put him in irons ? " yelled Cravan, rising to his feet. " And," added he, as the prisoner was dragged from his presence, " you hound ! your woman will bring you to the gratings yet ! "

Clare was taken below, heavily ironed, and thrown into the ship's prison. There, bruised in body and sick at heart, he watched away the weary night. He almost regretted he had not killed the mate. No doubt this was wrong and horrible ; but we must remember he had been driven nearly mad, and knew full well the punishment for the attack upon Cravan would be death—or a worse fate to a man of feeling—a flogging.

Once during the night he was visited by a midshipman who evidently pitied him. Tom's wrists were raw and bleeding, so the youngster tore up his handkerchief, and bound it round the handcuffs, the sentry who accompanied the officer holding the light, and laughing to himself all the time to think any one could be so "soft." James Ryan—this was the middy's name—was a warm-hearted Irish lad, and would never allow a man to be treated like a dog, if he had power to prevent it. Clare did not say anything when the boy had completed his task of mercy ; in fact, it was almost impossible for him to speak, so overcome was he by the kindness. When the door was closed upon him, he heard the sentry say, with a chuckle,

" Didn't seem to thank ye for it much, sir ? "

" Perhaps he felt all the more," replied the generous boy. This was true, as Tom thanked him in his heart.

Few who do not know the service can understand the goodness of the middy, who was laughed at for weeks afterwards for his act of mercy. If any one lost his hand-kerchief, he was directed to Ryan for it, with the remark that " possibly he had given it to some deserter."

Mr. Cravan submitted his bruises to the inspection of a sympathizing assistant-surgeon, and then went to bed, or, as sailors term it, " turned in," determined to be revenged on the man who had so violently attacked him. " He's safe for four dozen, anyhow," he murmured, as he arranged the bandage over his aching eyes, " and it will do the brute good."

The next day he received the condolence of Puffeigh and Crushe ; but Lieutenant Ford and the rest of the ward-room officers did not conceal the disgust they felt at his behaviour, and he also found himself cut by many of his mess-mates in the gun-room.

A few evenings after this he went to a ball, and as only one or two of those present knew the facts of the case, he received many sympathizing inquiries. The poor fellow who had so nearly been killed by a brute of a deserter was an object of great attention to many present, and " Nosey " Cravan for once experienced little difficulty in obtaining partners. He was, however, not a little piqued by the reply of the belle of the evening, to his request to honour him with her hand for the next waltz. Bending towards him, and smiling as if she were conveying a complimentary reply, she whispered, " No, sir, I cannot dance with such a hero."

This young lady was a cousin of Lieutenant Ford's, and had heard from her relation that Mr. Cravan had grossly insulted the man who attacked him ; therefore, when elated with his success among the ladies, the mate ventured to solicit her as a partner, she quietly put him down.

"She never can mean to snub me because I spoke rather roughly to the fellow. Well, I suppose Ford has told them his version of the affair. She's a deuced peculiar sort of a girl, and probably thinks the man ought not to be flogged for his infernal conduct, and has romantic ideas that the fellow has feelings like ours," thought Cravan. He, however, wandered into the supper-room, and finding a vacant place, was soon too far gone in champagne to trouble himself what people thought of him, under any circumstances whatever.

CHAPTER II.

The Stinger being nearly ready for sea, the boatswain's wife determined to give a party in honour of the event, and suggested that Mr. Shever should ask a few of his men. Now, this was certainly very contrary to all that warrant officer's ideas of propriety.

"What! ask blue jackets? why, my dear, it is against all precedent," he exclaimed.

"Bother your president," said the good natured woman. "Ask a few of the poor fellows; I warrant you they will behave well; then, knowing me, if ever you are sick, they will look after you."

After many pros and cons the husband as usual, yielded to his wife's persuasion, and agreed to invite Gummings, a quartermaster, Price, a boatswain's mate, and the tender-hearted Jerry Thompson.

Jerry was of middle height, well built and active, with good-looking oval face bronzed by exposure in many climes, dark eyes, and curly chestnut-coloured hair. Frank, generous and good natured to a fault, he was liked by every man and boy in the ship,—while his respectfully cheeky manner was tolerated by his officers, who passed over his freedom of speech and action.

At various times Jerry had determined to give up the sea and settle on shore, but after a few month's trial his roving propensities would get the better of him, and in spite of the lamentations of the children and regrets of his numerous circle of lady friends, he would pack his chest and be off to sea again.

Previous to joining the Stinger he had for some months been employed as a super at the Surrey Theatre ; but growing weary of that life, and the country being at war, he joined the navy, as he remarked, "from patriotic motives of a hard-up description." This was his first trial of a man-of-war's life, he being, to all intents and purposes, a merchant-service sailor, which will account for his want of reverence for the authorities and traditions of H. M. Navy.

Mr. Shever was serving out spun yarn one morning, when Jerry came to him for orders. Giving directions as to the business on which the seaman had consulted him, the boatswain, after a short pause, suddenly asked "if he had ever been to a party?"

"Many a one," replied the sailor, "The last one of any importance was with my Lord Buckingham."

"Come, now," growled the boatswain, "I wants no chaff. I knows a lady who intends giving a party, and probably she may ask you."

Jerry at once saw how the land lay, and assured the official that, "in case of his being a favored one, he would be on his best behavior."

"None of your—" (here the boatswain lifted his hand as if in the act of imbibing some intoxicating fluid). "You know I don't allow none of that sort of goings on in my house; and," added he, "the party breaks up when I pipes down; that will be your signal."

Mr. Shever was somewhat doubtful in his own mind whether Jerry was sufficiently sedate for admission to such a select company as his wife had asked; but, as she had set her mind upon it, come he must, or a family difficulty might arise, in which case

Mr. Shever would as usual, come off second best. His idea of "piping down" when he thought his visitors should depart was both novel and nautical.

He merely stated to the other sailors that he wanted them to take a cup of tea at his house on a certain day; they were old and tried men, and he knew they would not be any trouble to him.

Whenever the boatswain had an opportunity he would put a few questions to Jerry, or ask his advice on important points of the coming entertainment. Mr. Shever was of the opinion that "tea and shrimps, with a song afterwards, was the correct sort of thing;" while Jerry suggested tea and muffins, with a dance to follow,—the whole to wind up with a glass of punch." On this coming to Mrs. Shever's ears, she at once adopted the idea as an entirely original plan of her own, and declared "if Mr. Shever did not order a fiddler and a harpist, she would forthwith pack up, visit her mother, and remain there until the Stinger had sailed."

Jerry looked forward with pleasure to the entertainment, and determined to show the natives a few of his most elaborate steps in the hornpipe line, being sure he would be called upon to amuse the company in that way.

At last the day arrived, and at about six o'clock P.M. Thompson was on his way to the boatswain's house. His companions were dressed in their very best, and looked as unhappy as two baboons who had tried on a suit of clothes for the first time. On the road he endeavoured to instil a little cheerfulness into them, but it proved a total failure.

"We mustn't chew, and we mustn't get tight, and we mustn't smoke," growled Gummings.

"We've got to stay until he pipes down, and then all the publics will be shut," muttered Price.

Mr. Shever walked slowly home, keeping the party always at a respectable distance from him. What would people say if they knew he had invited such strange guests? You see even H. M. boatswains are afraid of Mrs. Grundy.

Mrs. Shever had stationed a small girl at the front door to let in visitors, so that when Jerry touched the bell the door was promptly opened and they were shown into the parlour. Here, enthroned upon the sofa-bedstead, sat the good lady, waiting to receive her company. By her side was seated her sister, a plump jolly girl, about eighteen years of age, who, when she saw the sailors, giggled and bashfully hid her face behind a turkey-feather fan.

The three men walked into the room, and stood looking at the ladies like shy children.

In a few moments Mrs. Shever recovered her composure, which had been slightly disturbed by the sudden entrance of the sailors, although all three of them were well known to her, and addressing Jerry, said, "Good-evening, Thompson, I'm proud to see you; and you too, Price and Gummings." Jerry, not at all abashed after the ice was broken, advanced towards the ladies, and politely inquired after their health. The two sailors looked around with a bewildered air, pulled their forelocks, mumbled, "Service to ye missis," and then retired to a bench behind the door, from which place they did not emerge until tea commenced.

Thompson was soon quite at home; and as one corner of the sofa was vacant, he requested permission to take it. His amusing stories quickly won the young girl's attention, and a formal introduction took place, Mrs. Shever giving him what he termed a handle to his name, by saying, "Miss Mary Ann Roes, permit me to introjuce you to Mr. Thompson." When she rose to bow, the artful fellow seized the opportunity, and

sat down between the ladies; and as they did not ask him to move, he made the most
of his position.

Soon after this Mr, Shever arrived, and seeing Thompson ensconsed so snugly, tried
to catch his eye, to show him that he did not quite approve of his freedom. But it was of
no use. Jerry was oblivious of winks and nods, or returned them as witty and artful
exchanges to the bewildered boatswain, At last, upon the arrival of Mrs. Shever's
mother and father and two of her cousins with their respective young men in waiting.
Mr. Shever requested Jerry to " move off that 'ere sofa, and let the girls sit down,"
upon which his wife told the aforesaid girls to "sit on chairs by the fire, as Mr.
Thompson was getting on nicely," and forthwith ordered her husband to go into the
kitchen, and help the girl to toast the muffins, adding, " she thought they could spare
him well enough."

This flattering sentiment was fully indorsed by Jerry, who declared " he often saw
too much of the boatswain," a remark which was received as a real joke by all
present excepting the two sailors, who were fast asleep when it was made. They woke
up, however, in time to join in the laugh that follwed, after which they again sweetly
slumbered.

Mr. Shever stood in the passage between the parlour and kitchen until the laughter
died away, and, we are sorry to state, said anything but his prayers. " Bless his
impudence to sit on the sofa between 'Melia and Mary Ann, and to wink at me like
that there, and he only a common sailor. For two pins I'd pipe down now."

Another peal of laughter followed just then, as Jerry had finished relating a joke,
the fun of which was torture to the boatswain. The latter seized his call, and putting
it to his lips, blew the shrill signal, known on board ship as " pipe down."

" What's that ? " exclaimed Mrs. Shever.

" Do you keep a canary ? " innocently inquired Thompson. Upon which the boatswain gave another blast of the pipe, and this time it was much louder.

Mrs. Shever rang the bell, and when the servant appeared told her " to inform Mr.
Shever if he wanted to amuse himself in that way he'd better wait until he got on
board his ship," and added, " I suppose he don't want *me* to come out to him."

As he did not repeat the noise, it may be presumed he felt as if his wife was just as
well where she was ; so holding his peace, he turned his attention to toasting the
muffins, and winking at the servant girl, which combination of amusement and labour
at last made him recover his temper, and by the time he had finished he became quite
cheerful again.

" If you please mem, tea's aready in the back bedroom," said the servant.

Mrs. Shever darted a look of displeasure at the girl, but without otherwise
noticing the *faux pas*, invited her visitors to the room above, which was indeed
usually devoted to the purpose described by the maid.

The boatswain had what he called "rigged the tea table" after the fashion common on
board ship, when the sailors make an effort to entertain some distinguished visitor. In
the centre was a huge earthenware jug, filled with choice flowers ; and the decorations
on this article being of a gorgeous and somewhat eccentric nature, we will briefly
describe them. On one side was depicted H. M. S. Bluefire, which with brown sails,
red masts and rigging, and blue hull, was bounding over a yellow and black sea, in
company with some purple and brown boats. On the reverse side was a representation
of the Sailor's Farewell, showing how a gallant tar in a blue suit, scarlet face, and
goggle eyes, takes leave of a young woman dressed in a yellow gown, cut very low to
show off her pea-green complexion. The said jug was a relic of Mrs. Shever's girlish
days ; and being a present to her from a sweetheart, who was lost in an Artic expedition,

was looked upon as an ornament of great value, and as such only brought out on state occasions, like the present.

The table presented a somewhat crowded appearance, as the boatswain had piled up the eatables until there was not room to set another tea-cup. As they had only eleven chairs, he rigged a seat by the window, and when the visitors entered the room, he endeavored to allot this to Jerry.

"Well, mum," said the unabashed sailor, "you have done the thing hansom; ellow me—" upon which he handed the delighted woman to her place at the head of the table. He next installed Mary Ann; and taking a seat between them, cheerfully observed that, "the company had better fall to."

The silent sailors being somewhat modest, were still standing in the passage, and there were two vacant places at the table. The boatswain was about availing himself of one of these, when his wife exclaimed, "Mr. Shever, where's your manners? the visitors are not all accommodated."

Shever brought in the two sailors, who seated themselves upon the extreme edge of their chairs, and looked around at the festive party like infants suddenly led into a confectioner's and left to their own resources.

The unfortunate boatswain had no alternative but to take the seat by the window, from which he was presently drawn to hand round the muffins; this occupation calling forth from Jerry the witty remark that, "Mr. Shever seemed quite in his element," the point of which was utterly lost upon that worthy.

Thompson related some of his most amusing yarns, which were received with roars of laughter by all present, with the exception of the host and the two seamen. The latter, finding themselves behind a heap of bread and butter, were busily employed in reducing the level of the same, varying their banquet with a few pinches of shrimps, which they swallowed whole, utterly oblivious of heads or tails, washing down any little obstacle with tea, which they imbibed from pint mugs, Mrs. Shever knowing it was useless to tickle their palates with ordinary quantities.

"Oh, you funny man!" screamed Mary Ann; "I never heard the likes of you before."

Jerry received this as a direct avowal of admiration on the part of the young lady, and redoubled his exertions to amuse her.

The boatswain was boiling over with rage; and as he dared not object before his wife, was obliged to nurse his wrath, his only relief being to go outside the room, and "pipe down" softly in the passage, or to wink at the servant whenever he could do so with safety.

The ladies pressed Thompson to eat, saying "he had not done justice to the fare. This brought forth an avowal from him, "that to his idea their company was more delightful than the choicest viands." Upon this sentence being explained to Mrs. Shever's mother, who was a deaf old lady, the latter signified her appreciation by hammering on the table with a fork, and crying "braywo," which being looked upon as a genteel proceeding and part of the ceremony by the silent sailors, was immediately adopted by them, and a round of hearty applause followed. The boatswain, seizing this opportunity, placed his call to his lips and "piped belay," a feat which he accomplished without being detected by his wife; although the seamen understood it, and ceased their knocking at once.

The company descended to the parlour, which they cleared for dancing; after this the seamen took up their old positions behind the door, where, like two well-gorged boaconstrictors, they curled themselves up and went to sleep.

As a sort of opening exercise, one of the young men in waiting volunteered a song, which was chiefly on "wiolets." This he bellowed out in a high tone, turning up his eyes to the ceiling all the while, until, in rendering the more powerful notes, he strongly resembled a blind man.

Jerry listened very attentively, until the last verse was sung, when, attracting Mary Ann's eye, he turned up his optics exactly as the singer was doing. This was too much for her, and she laughed outright; the rest of the company following suit, until the fellow began to think he was singing a comic song instead of a floral howl; and catching the infection himself, laughed louder than any of the party.

The boatswain now introduced the fiddler, who, apologizing for the absence of the harpist, who, he stated, was suffering from a headache, fell to tuning his violin.

Thompson was uncertain whether to ask the hostess or Mary Ann to dance with him. He was about to speak to Mrs. Shever, when she said good-humouredly, " Now, Mr. Thompson, *don't* neglect Mary Ann !" upon which he led the blushing girl out, and in a few moments they were "hard at it," this being the only term we can apply to their exertions, Mrs. Shever dancing with her husband, who was about as active as a half-trained elephant.

Jerry was in great favour. His frank manner and amusing stories delighted every one ; he danced with all the ladies in succession, and quite won the heart of the oldest one by asking her twice, although there was little danger of her accepting him the second time, as he had completely exhausted her for the evening during the first ; nevertheless, the old lady was charmed with him, and declared he was "quite a ʾentleman."

His best efforts were, however, reserved for his performance with Mary Ann and his hostess. with whom he was, as the boatswain remarked, "as much at home as if the house belonged to him." He amused them during the intervals of the dances with choice songs of a pathetic kind ; and, as he possessed a good voice and style, the women were several times melted to tears.

About ten o'clock the hostess produced a steaming bowl of punch, upon which the silent sailors immediately woke up, and received a liberal allowance of the liquid. Carefully holding their mugs, as if anxious that none of the nectar should escape they retreated to their corner, and two sponges could not have absorbed the fluid more expeditiously or quietly than they did. After a time they emerged from their conceal- ment, and finding no one was looking, helped each other to another dose of the delicious beverage, then sank back into their former retirement, this manœuvre being repeated several times during the evening.

Under the influence of Mrs. Shever's brewing the party had become quite noisy, and Thompson had danced his last hornpipe before they found the time had arrived to separate. The boatswain decided to walk a short distance with the seamen ; and Price and Gummings after many declarations that "Misshis Sheaver was a dutchessh, and Missir Sheaver wast a perfetchs shentleman, and they never had enjoyshed themselves so much afore," were with the assistance of Jerry, at last fairly got out of the house.

When at some distance from his residence the boatswain suddenly stopped, and drawing forth his pipe, blew the well-known " pipe down ; " then assuming his naval authority, he ordered the sailors to go their ways. Upon turning to speak to Jerry, with whom he wished to have an explanation, he found that individual had vanished ; thinking it might be from fear of his anger, he did not trouble himself, knowing he could talk to him at a future time, when the sailor would be a little more respectful. Mr. Shever then walked about with his hat off, until his mind was thoroughly com- posed, when he retired to the bosom of his family.

Jerry had quietly returned to bid Mary Ann good-bye, and entering the house, found the two ladies busily engaged in putting their hair in paper, preparatory to retiring up-stairs.

"Law, Jerry, how you did frighten me," exclaimed Mary Ann.

As the effects of love at first sight were somewhat increased by the punch he had imbibed, Thompson was not at all hurt at being called Jerry, but he advanced towards the blushing maiden, and saying she looked like an angel, proceeded to kiss her in a vigorous manner.

"For shame!" said the delighted girl. "Have done now, Jerry, or I'll scream."

"You rogue, you," observed Mrs. Shever. "Why you'd kiss me if I didn't stop you. I wish Shever would come in."

The active sailor proceeded at once to demonstrate his admiration of the latter speaker, evidently having little fear of the boatswain's returning just then, and a loud smack on the face, administered "more in sorrow than in anger" announced the completion of the outrage.

"There never was such a shocking man," giggled the matron.

"Don't you try it on again!" cried Mary Ann, in a most provoking manner.

Despite her pleading, Jerry renewed his attention, and as they parted, boldly declared that "he'd have her if she'd have him."

Mary Ann saw him out of the house, and as he kissed her for the last time, quietly murmured, "Jerry, dear, I'll marry you whenever you are ready."

Happy pair! they had now a bright future to anticipate: both could dream of it. It was a pleasant and inexpensive luxury, and about as likely to be realized as such visions usually are. However, "they've done it now," as the boatswain observed, when his wife informed him of the fact of Mary Ann's engagement. "That's what comes of introducing people of low manners into society. There'll be a 'mess-alliance,' and all the parties will be sorry for it when it's too late." Mr. Shever was evidently of opinion that Jerry was far beneath Mary Ann's notice, and possibly forgot that when he married her sister he was only what he now termed a common sailor; while his wife, seeing in Thompson, a good-hearted, merry fellow, woman-like, favoured his suit.

CHAPTER III.

The day after Clare's arrest the Stinger was hauled out of dock, and towed down to Greenhythe, in order to hoist in her powder and heavy stores. After a few days' delay she proceeded to the German Ocean, where she cruised about, while her commander endeavoured to work the ship's company into something like man-of-war shape.

Tom was all this time kept a close prisoner below, as he would have to be tried by court-martial. The ship being on the Home Station, and immediately under the Admiralty, it would hardly do to decide his case in the usual style afloat, viz. by a court, the judge and jury of which are one person, the captain of the ship. Commander Puffeigh was annoyed at the trouble and delay that must ensue before Clare could be punished, and observed to Crushe, "What a pity it is we have not been sent off to a foreign station at once; we could then have settled that scoundrel's business in ten minutes, without the fuss and worry of a court-martial."

One morning, when the crew were at breakfast, Clare was paraded on the quarter-deck, and Captain Puffeigh heard the preliminary evidence against him, which was duly taken down by the ship's clerk, and on that statement a court-martial was applied for, and granted on the ship's return to England. When Tom came on deck he looked careworn and pale; but seeing Mr. Cravan, his face flushed. This was noticed by the captain, who observed to the first lieutenant that "the fellow was case-hardened," an opinion which Crushe at once confirmed.

Mr. Cravan gave his evidence, which was duly recorded by the clerk, and then Crushe charged Clare with having used mutinous language to him before his arrest. Everything that could be brought against the man was stated in the report, which, on being completed, was read over to the prisoner, who was then asked if he had anything to say.

Tom looked at the commander with astonishment, and replied.

"Captain, one half of that 'ere writing aint true, and the other is exaggerated out of all shape."

Upon hearing this bold statement, the gallant Puffeigh at once cried, "Silence! you mutinous fellow; that's enough. I hope you will get your deserts on our return to England. If I had my will, I'd hang all such as you!"

Clare was then taken below again, and put in irons.

The Stinger continued her cruise, until her commander had what he termed "toned his crew down." In this artistic occupation he found a valuable ally in Crushe, who gave full vent to his cowardly nature, and proved himself a bully of the first water. Suffice it to say, by the time the ship reached Portsmouth the first lieutenant was detested by nearly all the officers, and thoroughly feared and hated by the whole of the crew.

On her arrival in port, the ship was at once docked, and Clare sent on board the flag-ship Victory, where he was very fairly treated, as her commander did not understand that the man should be considered a felon until he was tried and convicted.

Polly came off to the ship, and was allowed to spend a few moments with him, in the presence of the master-at-arms. Tom saw, with sorrow, that his situation and their separation were telling fearfully on his wife's health; he tried to cheer her up, and even joked about his prospects, but without avail, and it was with difficulty she could repress her feelings.

His wife used every argument she could think of to induce him to accept a lawyer's services for his defence, but he would not consent to it, saying, "I'll stand up and tell 'em what I did, and own what was wrong. If so be they turn agin my true defence, they wont believe the lies of a long-shore lawyer."

Like many other sailors, the unfortunate fellow had a dread of the legal profession; and trusting to the mercy of the court, and the facts of the case coming out on his trial, determined to defend himself.

Clare's friends also urged him to alter his determination, but in vain; and with great reluctance they gave up their pleading, and were compelled to abandon him to his own resources.

There was great excitement on the Common Hard at Portsmouth, on the morning when the signal gun from the Victory announced the holding of a court-martial on Clare's case. Crowds of what are termed "the lower orders" were assembled all along the portion of the Hard off which the flag-ship was moored, their object being to witness the embarkation of the officers of the court, who were to be conveyed on board in boats specially detailed for the duty. Every one was in full dress, and the handsome blue and gold uniforms of the officers contrasted strongly with the squalid appearance of the crowd who swarmed around them.

As each member of the court left his carriage at the end of the wharf, he found, to his disgust, that he had to walk between a line of these "lower orders," who, unabashed by his grand air and dazzling uniform, passed remarks upon any one who happened to be unpopular, in a manner more free than pleasant. Not having any fear of the lash, they gave their thoughts free vent.

"There goes lanky Jack, who flogged a boat's crew because his wife ran away with a sojer officer," screamed a woman in the crowd, as Captain Curt, a well-known advocate for the lash, walked down and entered the boat.

"Lord help Tom Clare if there's many more like *him* in the court," said another lady.

Some commanders were more popular, particularly with the Irish women, who formed no small part of the crowd; and gratuitous advice, such as, "Be aisy wid the poor boy, captain, aroon," or, "Say a good word for poor Tom, for the love of the mother of yez," were freely offered on all sides.

The spectators up to this time were, excepting in their observations, tolerably quiet. But when Commander Puffeigh, Lieutenant Crushe, Mr. Cravan, Mr. Shever, and the other witnesses, came down to the wharf, a loud yell of hatred broke from the people, and several stones were thrown at the officers. Unfortunately on their arrival at the end of the pier, they found no boat to receive them, and for ten minutes had to bear the insults of the mob.

Puffeigh was resplendent in a bran new uniform, which fitted him like a tight pair of boots; in fact, he was so well tailored, that he could scarcely breathe.

"Isn't that a picture for a tax-payer?" cried a voice.

"I say, don't Puffeigh look like old Stiff the beadle this morning?"

"That long beast of a lieutenant is the cove wot drove Tom to desert," roared a costermonger. Upon which a policeman who was near tried to arrest him, but he was hustled away from his grasp, and the man escaped.

At this moment a stone, thrown by some one at the back of the crowd, struck Crushe on the cheek. Turning round, his face livid with rage, he found himself confronted by an amazon, who coolly putting her arms akimbo, sneeringly asked him "if he would like to strike a woman?"

Shever, who knew the lady, thinking to curry favour, turned to her and said sharply, "I'm surprised at you, Mrs. Holloway."

"Keep your breath for lying at the court-martial, and dry up, or I'll serve you as your wife does," retorted the dame.

Mr. Shever looked at her fiercely for a moment; then, probably thinking she might slap his face if he gazed too intently on her, turned away, and embarked with the officers in a boat, which had at that moment opportunely arrived from the Victory.

The mob yelled and screamed like demons, and several stray stones and oyster-shells went flying after the boat. The captain, imagining these favours were from Clare's friends, expressed his opinion that "he trusted all present would endeavour to get Tom what he deserved;" a gentle hint, which was not lost upon Shever and the sailors who were going on board as witnesses. On arrival alongside the flag-ship, Captain Puffeigh was received with naval honours, ending with a doleful wail on the boatswain's pipe. Fortified by this, and feeling once more safe, he reported himself to the officer of the court. The proceedings immediately commenced, Puffeigh's clerk first identifying Clare as belonging to the Stinger, his name being upon the ship's books. It was noticed by the spectators that the prisoner wore two war medals, and the Royal Humane Society's medal.

Then followed the examination of the witnesses for the prosecution, all of whom had been already primed as to their evidence by Captain Puffeigh, who as is usual, acted the part of prosecutor.

The court was composed of naval officers of rank, and undoubtedly was a fair tribunal, if we could shut our eyes to the fact that many of them had been brought up in a school which denied a blue jacket the common rights possessed by the most wretched outcast on shore. The president was an old and feeble officer, who thought the whole affair a bore, and he remarked to another veteran,

"Ah! formerly every commander tried his own men, unless in very extraordinary cases, and we got on well enough. Now every fellow who requires the lash must be tried by a court-martial if the ship is in a port or near a flag-ship. The service is going to the deuce."

Lieutenant Crushe was the first witness called; and his deposition which was taken down in writing by the Judge advocate, was in substance as follows, Captain Puffeigh being allowed to put a most unwarrantable amount of leading questions.

Having deposed that he was first lieutenant of the Stinger, and identified the prisoner as an able seaman, belonging to her, the following questions were asked by the prosecutor:

"You know the prisoner?"

"Yes."

"About what length of time?"

"About four years. He served with me in my last ship."

"Has his character been good, or bad?"

"Unquestionably bad. But he is a good seaman, and knows his duty."

"You had to find fault with him soon after he was drafted to the ship? State to the court what then occurred."

"I was obliged to stop his leave for insolence, the very day he joined the Stinger; and though I spoke kindly to him, he continued this line of conduct, barely doing the work he was appointed to, and that in a sullen, disrespectful manner."

"He deserted from the Stinger, did he not?"

"He did."

" Knowing his chara... r, you were obliged to send a strong force to bring him on board, were you not ? "

" Yes. I sent an armed party of marines, as I was aware that, being a desperate man, he would offer resistance."

" Where was he found secreted by the non-commissioned officer ? "

Here the president assumed a grave air and informed Puffeigh that he could not put the last question, as Lieutenant Crushe could not testify to hearsay. The examination then proceeded.

" You had other reasons for sending an armed party to secure the prisoner ? Please state them."

" Yes. I was aware that he consorted with people of the worst character."

" Some of them had visited him on board the Stinger, I believe. State if that be so."

" Yes, a young woman, whose conduct while on board led me to suppose that she had come for no good. She came down with some of the worst characters in Woolwich. He was afterwards arrested in her company."

When Crushe stated that the man was arrested in the company of bad people, Clare bit his lips, and tried to address the court, when he was informed that "he would have an opportunity of asking questions at a later period, but at present he must remain silent."

Upon receiving this rebuke his face flushed with shame, seeing which, the members of the court, who took it for a sign of passion and rebellion, looked at each other, as much as to say, " See what a ruffian the prisoner is."

The corporal was the next witness. With a military salute that concise individual stated his name and rank, and was thus examined by Puffeigh.

" You received orders to arrest the prisoner, and take a strongly-armed party with you ? "

" I did " (with a salute).

"State to the court what occurred on that occasion."

(Saluting) " Well, sir, you see, being a corporal of the Rile Marine division at Woolwich, I knowed that where the prisoner wor a hiding wor a werry bad place, so I went prepared."

" The prisoner showed a determined resistance, I understand ? In fact nearly killed you."

(Saluting) " That he did, sir, and the other willings with him,"

" There were women in the house ? "

(Saluting) " Yes, sir, a regler bad lot—speshilly one on them—his gal, who used awful langevage. I were expostulatin' with her about it in a werry perlite manner, ven the prisoner sudden seized me by the stock, my back being turned to him, and would have killed me but for my men."

(President) " How many men had you ? "

(Saluting) " Twenty."

" All armed ? "

(Saluting) " Yes, sir."

(Puffeigh) " Do you know any reason for the prisoner's attack upon you ? "

" None in the verld, sir."

Here Tom Clare's face flushed again, but remembering the hint he had shortly before received, he held his peace.

The next witness called was Cravan, who, after the usual preliminary question, thus testified—

"You were the officer of the watch when the prisoner was brought on board as a deserter?"

"Yes, and being kindly disposed towards the man, I expressed my regret at seeing him in such a position."

"What then occurred?"

"He struck me a violent blow with his clenched hands, injuring me severely."

(President) "And this without any provocation on your part?"

"Yes. I had spoken to him in the mildest manner."

"Can you in any way account for this conduct; was the man drunk?"

"No, sir; I believe it was premeditated."

Here Tom could restrain his feelings no longer, but exclaimed,

"It ain't true, gentlemen; he's swearing away my life."

Having been with difficulty quieted, he was asked if he had any questions to put, but Clare declined to cross-examine witnesses, whom he had heard boldly perjuring themselves, and who were encouraged, and evidently instructed what to say, by Captain Puffeigh.

Price and Gummings were next called, their testimony going to show that Clare had told them "he'd run away as soon as he could get a chance;" that his language was mutinous; and that he had declared his intention "of dropping a marlin spike on Lieutenant Crushe's head when he got a chance." Price swearing he had said that "it would be a first rate end for the brute," meaning the first lieutenant. "He said it would be considered justifiable homicide, or words to that effect;" and that when the witness asked him "if he wished to be hanged," the prisoner had laughed and said, "he would be let off." Both witnesses hypocritically tried to put in some words of condolence for their "unfortinit shipmate," but were silenced by the court.

"Mr. Shever, the boatswain, was then examined by Captain Puffeigh. After the warrant-officer had corroborated the other evidence, the examination proceeded as follows:

"Have you any idea what led the prisoner to desert?"

"No, sir; but I thought, from the first day he jined the Stinger, that he would desert whenever he got the chance."

"What led you to suppose so?"

"Well, sir, you see he belongs to a low lot, and wor always that mutinous and discontented. He is one of them as is always speakin' about rights. I could make no good on him, although he's a fust-rate sailor."

"The prisoner gave you a great deal of trouble, did he not, Mr. Shever?"

"Yes, sir; and when he left I missed a palm and needle, which some woman has since brought aboard, and left in my cabin."

The president here again interfered, as the examination had been allowed to stray from the charges upon which Clare was being tried.

Puffeigh then said there were some questions he would like to submit to the president and court, which, though they did not bear on the charges upon which the prisoner was being tried, certainly would have some effect upon the sentence of the Honorable Court, should they find the prisoner guilty

The court was then cleared, and after some time, it being again opened, the president informed Captain Puffeigh that the questions could be put.

"Are you aware, Mr. Shever, who the mob were who insulted myself and my officers coming aboard?"

"Yes, sir; they wos friends of the prisoner's. (Sensation in the court.) I believe one on 'em wos his mother." (Great sensation.)

"State to the court the treatment we received."

"They throwed stones at us and dirt, and cut the first lieutenant's face with a large flint. (Immense sensation in the court.) They also mobbed us down, and abused us shameful."

Mr. Shever then went on to state that he had often heard the prisoner say "that he would be cautious what he did." This the worthy boatswain construed into a threat against the first lieutenant. "He considered Clare a dangerous man. Never had seen him drunk, but believed he drank considerable when he had a chance."

We must observe, with regret, that the foregoing evidence of the boatswain was entirely fictitious in its most important portions; in fact, Mr. Shever did on that occasion commit what is commonly called perjury, and the evidence of the seamen was very much of the same unblushing kind. The boatswain knew that if the lieutenant could trust him, and depend upon him to say anything that would carry out his plans, he could do pretty much as he liked with the men, who would not dare to complain of his treatment. His first officer was his model; and being somewhat of a cur, he did not mind swearing to any falsehood that would injure Tom, provided he could curry favour with his superiors.

The prisoner was then asked if he had any questions to put to the witnesses, upon which he replied,

"No, your honour. I've heard 'em say too much already."

This answer was looked upon by the court as evidence of the man's mutinous and dangerous disposition, it being, of course, entirely misconstrued.

Clare was then called upon for his defence. Usually when a sailor is tried this is prepared for him in writing by his counsel, and handed to the Judge advocate, who reads it to the court; but Clare availed himself of the privilege of reading his own defence, and standing up with his earnest face fixed upon the president, he spoke as follows, having committed what he had written to memory:

"Your honors and gentlemen, I bows to you respectfully and begs to be allowed to say a few words in defence of this 'ere crime. I was drove to desert, regler drove, your honors. I jined my ship, intendin' to serve out my time, and if needs be, fight agin the Roosians, and give my life for my country. But that was not to be. Lieutenant Crushe drove me to desert; 'twas him wot hounded me on, and him wot caused me to be here this day a prisoner. Your honors, I could stand it no longer. I have a wife—a good gal—not a common gal—I love her, and I wanted to see her. Yet, gentlemen, knowin' that, and probable that if we went on a furrin station I might never see my wife again, Lieutenant Crushe deliberate stopped my leave, and hounded me on to desert. Says he to me one day, "I'll give you a flakin', as soon as I gets you into blue water," or words to that effect, and then I took it into my mind to escape, and not afore that time. I throws myself on the mercy of the court, with regard to striking Mr. Cravan. Your honours, I love my wife. You, surely, who are married love your wives, although I suppose you may think a sailor can't love as you does. I love my poor girl, and they have called her vile names, and said she used bad language. Gentlemen, that's false! Prisoner as I am, and at your mercy, I say that is a lie; she never uttered a bad word in her life. Allow *I* am bad—a mutineer—a deserter. I won't defend myself agin all that; but I can't hear them lies, and not say a word. If I am wrong, I begs your honors' pardon, but let my wife be cleared from such falsehoods. I struck Mister Cravan because he spoke of my wife as I would not, and could not bear to hear her spoken of. I was mad, possibly; but I am sorry, and pleads guilty, gentlemen, and throws myself upon the mercy of the court, who I beg will look over my discharge papers from eleven of Her Majesty's ships, in all of which my character stands "*very good.*"

Clare warmed in his defence when he spoke about his wife, until he no longer looked the prisoner. He uttered every word with a peculiarly expressive manner, which would have moved the hearts of most men. But the officers who composed the court heard only in his speech the words of mutiny and sedition. As to his love for the woman he called his wife, that was to them a subject of the most sublime indifference. During his defence, eloquent in its naïve pathos, few of them really appeared to be listening to him. One dozed as if half asleep, and another read a letter, while others again wrote their opinions on certain passages of his speech, and pushed the scraps of paper across to their opposite neighbours.

When Clare ceased speaking, he bowed respectfully to the court; then having signed his defence, handed the paper to the Judge-advocate, after which the court was cleared for deliberation.

The members having consulted for a few moments, now resumed their cocked hats, which up to that time had reposed upon the table before them, and thus decorated, in grim silence, awaited the arrival of the prisoner, who was shortly afterwards brought in.

The Judge-advocate then read the finding of the court, which declared him guilty on both charges,—first of "desertion," and secondly of "striking his superior officer," and the sentence of *death* was passed upon him for the latter offence. But in consideration of his former services and the very good certificates of character produced by him, the court mercifully commuted the sentence of death, and awarded the punishment of flogging. He would be taken on board H.M.S. Stinger and kept in irons until the day Commander Puffeigh fixed upon as being most convenient for the execution of his sentence, which was, "that he should receive upon his bare back fifty lashes with the cat-o'-nine-tails."

The prisoner, who seemed quite overcome by the sentence, was then taken away and sent on board his ship, to be closely guarded and heavily ironed until the sentence was carried out. As he left the Victory many of her crew who had been his shipmates cast pitying looks upon him but not one of them dared openly to express his opinion.

Clare saw wife for one moment, as he was entering the dock-yard on his way to the ship, and upon being allowed to speak, told her "to bear up, as his punishment would soon be over, and it was lighter than he expected," &c., &c. In fact, he said all he could to cheer her. Polly, who had thrown her arms around his neck, was then torn from him by the police, who would not allow her to enter the dock gate with the prisoner; and when Tom saw her for the last time, she was being carried away by her grief-stricken father, in whose arms she had fainted.

CHAPTER IV.

LIEUTENANT CRUSHE gave the crew to understand that in future only those men who pleased him would be allowed leave to go on shore, consequently the "liberty list" of H.M.S. Stinger was a short one.

As the time drew near for leaving the dock, the number of favored ones grew less every day, few being bold enough to go aft and face the lieutenant for the purpose of asking leave of absence. However, Thompson who was not afraid of Crushe, determined to try what he could do; and one evening he, with two other seamen, walked aft, stood between two guns on the port side of the quarter-deck, and waited patiently until that gallant officer condescended to notice them. After keeping the men for some time in a pleasant state of expectation, Crushe suddenly seemed aware of their presence, and with a ghastly twist of his visage, which he intended for a grin, asked the sailors "if they wanted four dozen a-piece? if not, they had better go forward."

"Please, sir," pleaded one of the men, "may I go on shore?"

"What for?" demanded the bully.

"My little gal is sick," said the sailor.

"Come, my fine fellow, that won't do. Go forward, and tell that to the marines."

The man addressed slunk away like a beaten hound. It was true his child was ill, but he was obnoxious to Crushe, so he contented himself with vowing vengeance, and on going forward procured some rank poison in the shape of gin, which he forthwith imbibed, and went to sleep. His little girl died during the night. The poor mother wondered why father did not come home; and it was a bitter grief to her, upon visiting the ship the next morning, to find her husband under punishment for being intoxicated the night before.

"Tell him I'm ashamed of him! and little Carrie so bad!" said the indignant woman to the ship's corporal, who had informed her of her husband's disgrace. "Tell him the dear little angel cried for him till she got too weak, and wanted so to see him before she died; and," added the poor creature, in a low, dreamy voice, "he drunk when he ought to have been with her!"

Bursting into tears, the desolate mother was led away by a sympathizing spectator, to ponder over what she thought her husband's brutality.

When the news was given him by the callous ship's corporal, that "his kid was dead," the man, who was not perfectly sober, smiled and said, "Thank God! she is now better off;" then, crouching down, with his hands tightly pressed to his forehead, wept bitterly.

But we must return to the sailors whom we left standing before the lieutenant on the quarter-deck.

"What do *you* want leave for?" demanded Crushe, as Jerry, with his face elongated in a most doleful way, touched his forelock to attract the officer's attention.

"Leave to visit my widowed mother, who is werry ill," replied the scamp.

As he said this, his visage relaxed for a moment, and in his endeavour to work it back into a solemn cast, he presented such a serio-comic appearance, that the lieutenant laughed outright; and telling the impudent fellow to go on shore and be hanged to him, turned to the other sailor, to whom he granted the same privilege.

Of course the illness of Jerry's mother existed only in his fertile imagination, and he afterwards remarked to the boatswain that he had obtained leave through a pious fraud, which he trusted would not be chalked down agin him up aloft.

Since the night of the memorable tea-party at her sister's, Mary Ann had become the lady's-maid of Mrs. Captain Puffeigh, who was residing with a relative at Portsea, near Portsmouth. Thompson heard the ship was to be sent to the Cape of Good Hope, and determined to say good-bye to his lady-love, who had written to inform him, "the captain and ladies would be absent from home that evening, and if he did not come and see her, she would forever discard him."

After rigging himself in his best suit, he was, with the other sailor, paraded before first lieutenant, who gave them the comforting assurance that if they were not on board by six o'clock the following morning, they would both be looked upon as deserters, then allowed them to depart, the ship's corporal passing them through the dock gates. Jerry now wished to get rid of his companion, who, on his part seemed determined to stick by him, in spite of hints, and even of the pointed remark "that his absence would not be felt." At last, being somewhat annoyed by the patient way in which his companion took his rebuffs, Thompson suddenly stopped before the door of a private residence, and taking the bell-handle, as if about to ring, told his shipmate "that his mother was in there dangerously ill," and curtly bade him good-night.

When the man was out of sight, Jerry pulled forth a small bag, suspended by a string around his neck, and took from it a black ribbon, which had formerly encircled the slender waist of Mary Ann. He first looked round in order to ascertain if any one was watching him, when, noticing a smartly-dressed girl at an attic window, he waved the belt triumphantly towards her, and then pressed it to his heart. The damsel affected the greatest indignation, though in reality she was highly delighted with his impudent manner, and giving him several scornful and withering glances, intended as "finishers," withdrew behind the curtain, through a hole in which she watched him, wishing all the while "that heaven had made her such a man."

He pulled off his hat, removed a ribbon, bearing in letters of gold the word "Stinger," and tied Mary Ann's gift in its place; or, as he termed it "flew her pennant." This, also, prevented any one knowing the name of his ship, and subsequent events proved the wisdom of the precaution. With a true nautical twist, he jerked the hat upon the back of his head, then blowing a few sounding kisses in the direction of the hidden one, shaped his course for Portsea.

Being on a mission of love, he steered clear of refreshment bars and other allurements, liquid and solid, vowing "not to touch a drop of beer until he received the same from the hands of his own Mary Ann;" but alas! poor human nature,—at the first temptation he gave in.

Upon being so pointedly cut, the sailor who accompanied Jerry on shore left him with the full determination of finding a kindred spirit; but not meeting one, retraced his steps, and, as a matter of course, came full tilt upon his shipmate. Here was a fix for the latter. If he ran, the sailor would give chase; if he put on a bold face and spoke to him, drink he must; he dare not refuse if invited, and he knew he would be asked.

As the men approached, Thompson assumed an appearance of the deepest dejection, winking very hard, as if to keep back the tears, and with his lips trembling and working like those of a person who endeavours to be calm while suffering great agony, he walked slowly until they were face to face.

The sailor not being very sober, was quite taken aback; and speech for the moment failing him, contented himself with grasping his shipmate's hand and gazing profoundly in his face. Hereupon Jerry pulled from his pocket an article, which at first glance might have been taken for a small sail, but was in reality a genuine bandana handkerchief. With this he slowly rubbed his eyes, until his friend became a little more coherent.

"Whatsh the mattersh, Jerry?"

"Mother's gone off the hooks."

"What! dead, d-e-d?" spelt the man, as if to make quite sure.

"Made sail about an hour ago," said Jerry, again burying his face in the bandana.

The sympathetic tar took his friend by the sleeve and led him into the nearest public-house, where, calling for two tankards of half and half, he placed one before his mate, and took the other himself; remarking as he did so, that "as they could not bring the old woman to life again, he'd wish her every happiness and prosperity."

The position was a very trying one for Jerry, the liquor being cool and tempting, but—he had made a vow.

"Did the old woman get under weigh sudden?" said the convivial one.

Fixing his eyes upon his interrogator, and mechanically grasping the tankard, which was thrust into his hand, Jerry, with most dejected countenance and in a whisper, replied,

"Sudden? I rayther think she did. She went off like—" Saying this he heaved a deep sigh, looked resignedly at the half and half, blew off the froth and gulped it down; then directing his shipmate's attention to a distant part of the bar, he seized the opportunity and made off.

The convivial sailor bawled after him to come back; but finding it a useless proceeding, returned to the bar, and calling together a host of generous spirits, ordered the landlord to supply them with unlimited beer. This was done until the sailor became unruly, when the honest landlord thrashed him severely, emptied his pockets, and kicked him into the street, whence he was conveyed to the station-house, where "he enjoyed his liberty" all night.

It being somewhat late the next morning before the magistrate released him, he was, upon leaving the police-court, arrested as a deserter by the ship's corporal, and when he arrived on board, Lieutenant Crushe informed him "that his grog was stopped for a month, and three pounds sterling would be deducted from his wages, the same to be paid over to the ship's corporal for arresting him." This double-barrelled style of punishment was not much to the man's taste; but knowing it would be useless to say a word in defence, he pulled his forelock and left the quarter-deck, vowing he'd never go ashore agin as long as he belonged to the Stinger.

Jerry soon found out the house where Captain Puffeigh was visiting; but in his uncertainty whether the family were out, he steered clear of the front door, and dived down a lane which ran to the back of the premises. Now, it was a very easy matter to tell the right house by the front, as the name "Portland Villa" was marked upon the gate; but the back doors were provokingly alike, and the poor fellow was sorely puzzled to know at which to knock.

In vain he tried to make out the form of his lady-love at one of the windows. He saw several very pretty girls, who evidently would not have objected to a little flirtation, but he dared not even wink at one of them, fearing Mary Ann might detect him in the act, or subsequently hear of it. It was almost as great a temptation as the half and half; and had it been a closer one, he might have yielded as easily.

Finding an empty barrel near one of the doors, he seated himself on it; and lighting his pipe, waited for the appearance of some one who would give him the information he required. Over the door was clustered a mass of ivy; and as he presently heard a voice which strongly reminded him of his girl's, he kicked off his shoes, and clambering up, soon found himself in a position to ascertain if his conjecture was correct.

Judge his horror and astonishment, when this feat revealed to him Mary Ann—his *own* Mary Ann—actually kissing a sergeant of the line. The sight nearly took away his breath. He rubbed his eyes, chewed a leaf of ivy to ascertain if he were awake, found from the flavour that he was, looked again, and saw her kiss him a second time (on this occasion the salute was returned by the military man), then with a smothered groan he relaxed his grasp of the ivy, and lowered himself into the lane. For some moments he could hardly credit it was a reality ; but the flavour of the ivy lingering upon his palate, proved to him it was not a vision.

"Blame his imperdince ; and to think my gal could kiss a soger!" he cried. However—there was no good in lamenting over it, revenge was his next idea ; so he walked up and down the lane, now and then stopping to square off at imaginary soldiers, by way of relieving his pent-up rage, until his rival should make his appearance.

After the lapse of a short time, which seemed hours to the irate sailor, the door was cautiously opened, and the military gentleman stepped forth, whistling as he came the well-known air "The girl I left behind me," and swaggering along in the inoffensive manner peculiar to the regular army.

Jerry planted himself before the astonished son of Mars, and fiercely demanded if he considered himself a man. The suddenness of the attack for a moment bewildered the sergeant, who said, by way of reply, "Wot's the matter with *you*, Jack ?" Delivering a tremendous blow under the chin of his opponent, and knocking him clean off his feet, the sailor proceeded to dance around his foe, exclaiming, "That's wot's the matter, my Mormon elder ; that's *my* answer, my cherry garden duke." The soldier quickly got up, and squared off at him, upon which Jerry again sailed into the enemy. Quite a lively encounter ensued, and the combatants being both active and much enraged, the "Regular Army" and the "Royal Navy" made it pretty tropical for each other.

Mary Ann did not look into the lane when she let the sergeant out, but returned to the kitchen, and informed the cook "that it was nearly time her sweetheart arrived." She was about leaving the apartment when her attention was arrested by a noise in the lane. Thinking it might be her admirer, she ran to the back-door, and opened it just in time to see Jerry in the act of flooring the sergeant with a well-directed blow on the nose. Glancing proudly upon her brave but excited lover, and uttering a scream, she rushed into his arms, and endeavoured to clasp him round the neck, but failed to do so, as he waved her off with a gloomy, sorrowful air.

The noise brought out the cook, who seeing her lover, the sergeant, extended on the grass as if dead, rushed to him, knelt by his side, and, like another "Thisbe," endeavoured to re-animate his manly form, declaring all the while that " the sailor was a brute, who ought to be given into the custody of the perlice."

Thompson was keeping Mary Ann at arm's length, his eyes flashing and body quivering with excitement, as he vainly endeavoured to get at his foe, every attempt being thwarted by his girl.

Upon hearing the cook's observations, Mary Ann turned quickly round, and exclaimed,

" Perlice, indeed, Amelia ! Why this is my own dear Jerry !"

" Who's that ere soger?" demanded her lover, upon which she made another attempt to clasp him to her heart. Waving her off with a dignified and injured air, he exclaimed,

"Mary Ann, tell me—who is that soger? Tell me, Mary Ann—or I'll kill him!"

With this he again tried to rush at his foe.

"Will you kill him?" screamed the cook, letting fall the sergeant's head, which she was tenderly supporting, and darting towards his opponent. "Will you, you willin?"

"Oh dear! oh dear! what shall I do with these mad folks?" exclaimed the lady's maid. "Jerry, dear, that sergeant is my own brother Alfred; however did you come for to fight him?"

"I'll let you know, young man," screamed the cook; but her attention was suddenly attracted by the sergeant, who, staggering to his feet, requested some one to inform him where they had buried the sailor he had killed, and upon seeing the latter he was about to rush upon him, when he found himself locked in the arms of his lady-love.

It was some time before the ladies succeeded in making their excited lovers understand matters, and during the first part of the negotiation the men were with difficulty restrained from renewing the combat. As it was, they glowered at each other, over the shoulders of their respective ladies, like infuriated mastiffs.

However, as the facts dawned upon them, their anger gave place to merriment.

"I'm proud to know you, sergeant-major."

"And I'm equally proud to know you, commodore."

And the heroes continued to compliment each other in the most extravagant style for some moments, until their vocabulary of honorary titles became exhausted.

Mary Ann was delighted with her lover's spirit, although after the reconciliation she declared "that Jerry was a horrid fellow to hurt her brother, and vowed she would never permit him to kiss her again." We regret to record she immediately broke her word. We are sorry, but it was so, another proof of the vanity of vows in general, and those of lovers in particular.

The party then adjourned to the servants' hall, where, after a merry time over a cup of tea, Thompson was called upon to entertain the company with imitations of celebrated tragic actors. The hall table was pushed against the wall, and an Indian screen, borrowed from the drawing-room, placed thereon. As if by previous invitation, a number of ladies and gentlemen in the same rank of life as their entertainers, shortly arrived, and the servants' hall at "Portland Villa" was soon densely crowded. Among the visitors of distinction were Mr. Noble, the "young man from the painter's," William, from the grocer's, Mr. Slab, the fishmonger, and several good-looking domestics from the adjoining houses, with their "shadows," the latter being young men of mild and obedient dispositions, who were sometimes allowed to bask in the sunshine of their smiles.

The sergeant, who was by this time quite reconstructed, agreed to act as Jerry's dresser and general assistant during the performance. The house was rummaged for properties, and the heap piled up behind the screen somewhat puzzled Thompson, who dressed and redressed four or five times before he quite made up his mind which selection would become him best.

Every available chair in the house was brought into the hall, and when the supply in that direction failed, some were fetched in from the neighbouring residences by the obedient "shadows."

The band consisted of a violin and flute, assisted by the sergeant, who operated upon a snare drum, which some lunatic had brought from the attic. As the space was limited, the musicians were stowed away behind the screen, much to the annoyance of

Thompson, who could hardly turn when dressing, and their din prevented the sergeant hearing his directions.

Precisely as the hall clock struck nine the band was "taken worse." The overture was rather peculiar. First the "shadow" who played the violin called out, "The Red, White, and Blue," and then proceeded to indulge the company with a "spiral agony," which sounded very much like the Old Hundredth played in jerks. After getting well warmed to his work, he was suddenly stopped by a prolonged roll on the drum, put in by the sergeant, who, thinking the air was becoming "thready," came to his assistance. The flutist now essayed "The last Rose of Summer," delivered note by note in a laboured and painful manner. He also was assisted by the military; and when the latter found "he was going it seriously, and didn't mean to stop," he finished him off with a ran-tan-tan upon the drum, which quite electrified the audience, and a hearty round of applause followed.

When the last sound had died away the sergeant unslung the drum, marched from behind the screen, stood at attention, made the orthodox military salute, and spoke as follows:—

"Ladies and gents, a talented gent will oblige this evening with imitations of actors, giving Macready as Macbeth, Kean as Hamlet, and Creswick as Romeo ; " then, with another salute, he faced half-round and gravely marched behind the screen. This speech being considered quite enchanting by the lady portion of the audience, several of whom cried "enkéore," the soldier was prevailed upon to come forward again, which he did in the same automatic manner as before; but being called upon for a third time, he looked over the screen, and said, "Not if I knows it! hold your row," upon which the company quieted down, and awaited the entrance of the hero of the hour.

In order to produce "soft music," Jerry hit upon the novel idea of throwing a blanket over the band, who thus, extinguished, had to feel their way through the intricacies of the well-known minstrel air "Mary Blane." This deadening process was so effectual, that at times the music could not be heard at all, upon which Thompson would call out in a voice quite audible to the spectators, "Come, fiddler ; more steam, old man."

Loud was the applause when Macbeth slowly emerged from behind the screen, gliding along as if he ran on wheels. He bowed low, and winking at Mary Ann, proceeded at once to business. His costume defies description, and any one not well posted would have imagined he was personating one of the witches.

The sergeant officiated as ghost, being no less ludicrously got up. Upon his elaborately floured head was tied a tight night-cap, his face was chalked, and his body enveloped in a night-habit, which must have been made for a short, fat woman, as it only reached to his knees, leaving his striped trousers visible, and presenting anything but a spectral appearance. Whenever he blundered, Macbeth prompted him *sotto voce*, and stage directions, such as—"I say, Stripey, mind your eye, or you'll be off the table," to which the ghost of Banquo would reply, "All right, Jerry, old man; you're wurry near the edge yourself," were received by the audience as comic interludes, and as such brought down the house.

In the second representation Thompson appeared in long black cotton hose, borrowed from the cook, an old Zouave jacket, and black cloak. He had on his head a high felt hat, with a brim of the broadest kind, and fastened to the gigantic buckle of this article was a bunch of feathers. His *tout emsemble* was a kaleidoscopic combination of Beppo, a primitive African, Captain Kidd the pirate, and a Pilgrim Father. We omitted to mention that dangling from his side was the dress sword of Captain Puffeigh, which clanked and got in his way in a most uncomfortable fashion.

The sergeant again appeared as a spirit, but was on this occasion draped in white muslin, several skirts formed of that material being wound about him, in an artistic manner. When he marched on, he could not be induced to glide, one of the audience took him for a "vestal virgin," and remarked the same to a neighbour, upon which the cook corrected him with the stinging observation that "any donkey might see it was a ghost," this sage remark producing a murmur of confirmation from her friends.

The greatest sensation of the evening was the third and last portion of the entertainment; and when the violinist appeared to announce that, "by special desire a young lady would support Mr. Thompson as Juliet," everybody rose and applauded. A sharp discussion among the audience followed, some imagining Jerry was to undertake the part of Juliet, assisted by a young lady, while to others the somewhat enigmatical speech was as plain as possible; however, the conversation served to pass away the time, and it brought forward some startling opinions.

If Thompson's rendering was correct, there must have been a wonderful similarity of voice and style between the distinguished tragedians. Be this as it may, he succeeded in delighting his audience. The fishmonger, who declared he was very intimate with the three great actors—he had seen them in the street—loudly asserting that "to his mind Jerry was more life-like than the originals." Of course, after this further criticism was superfluous.

Mary Ann had on one or two occasions, assisted at some parlour theatricals, and liked the fun immensely; so when her lover, who in her eyes appeared a greater hero than ever, requested her to take the part of "Juliet," she declared "she knew every word of it," and was dressed in a few moments.

Romeo certainly presented a most comical appearance. His lower limbs were encased in salmon-coloured hose, short blue trousers, fastened at the knee with green ribbon, purple doublet slashed with white, short cloak, and the before-mentioned dress sword. Upon his head was a lady's Leghorn hat—one of the old broad-brim period—attached to this being a crushed ostrich feather, which sometimes tilted over his eyes, and at others stuck bolt upright, his face being "got up" in a most alarming style, with cork wrinkles, moustache, and imperial.

Mary Ann being added to the company, the musicians were ordered to take up their positions on the stairs, from which elevated place they slaughtered "See the Conquering Hero comes," sandwiched artistically with "Auld Lang Syne," their numbers being strengthened by the addition of a young gentleman in stand-up collar and weak eyes, who performed on the "paperophonicon," and a fat man who was great on the drum and tea-tray. The overture to this piece strongly resembled a musical rendering of an earthquake.

Jerry made his entrance, and flattering was the greeting he received. His gorgeous costume quite took the audience by surprise, and the ladies unanimously declared "he was a duck."

After he had shouted the words "He jests at scars that never felt a wound," this being delivered in a tone of voice suitable to a deaf audience, Mary Ann, who was dressed in a lovely white silk robe, with a muslin veil fastened mantilla-like to her head, rose from behind the screen, placed her arm gingerly upon it, rested her cheek upon her hand, and at the proper time replied, "Ah, me!" in a very pathetic and creditable manner. After which she turned to her brother, who was holding her as she stood upon the chair, and observed, "Don't joggle the chair so, Alfred dear, or I shall slip off."

The performance went off splendidly. Sergeant Ross held Mary Ann quite firmly, and prompted her from a copy of Shakespeare, procured for the occasion from the library. Everything was lovely, and loud the applause that followed the delivery of each period.

Juliet had made her exit, or rather had been assisted off her perch by her brother, and Romeo was repeating the well-known lines, "Oh blessed, blessed night! I am afeard, being in night, all this is but a dream," when he suddenly stopped, gaped, made a grimace, and shouting, "Look out there!" rushed behind the screen, rapidly stripped off his costume, and resumed his sailor's attire. The audience seeing his agile exit, took it as a portion of the performance, and screamed with delight, when suddenly they were aware of the presence of an unwelcome visitor, as some one in the doorway said, "You'll find it isn't a dream, my fine fellow. Where's the cook?"

"Turn him out!" cried several of the audience.

"Where's the cook?" demanded the angry voice.

"Gone to the play," returned a wag.

"Who's that taking my name in vain?" inquired that lady. As she said this she turned round, and beheld the fiery visage of Captain Puffeigh, who had returned to fetch something for his wife, and to tell the servants "they need not sit up."

Upon seeing him she screamed out, "Oh! my! it's the capting!" and immediately went into violent hysterics.

The place was soon cleared, and Puffeigh about to depart, when a movement at the end of the hall arrested his attention. He walked to the table, and pulled the screen on one side; beholding as he did so, a tableau which nearly brought on an apoplectic fit. Mary Ann was seated in a chair, sobbing as if her heart would break. Supporting her on either side were the sergeant and Thompson, who looked at the captain as if he were a transparent substance, and could be seen through.

"Who the deuce are you?" said the captain.

The soldier saluted and the sailor smiled.

"You—you—who are you?"

The sergeant saluted again.

"Bless you! you red coated puppy! what's your name?"

This only brought forth another mechanical salute from the military man.

Being baffled by the tactics of the "regular army," Puffeigh next tackled the sailor. What with cork wrinkles and other facial decorations, it would have been somewhat a puzzle for his mother to have identified Jerry, who looked his officer full in the face, and bowed rapidly, saying,

"Service to ye, sir."

"What ship do you belong to?" demanded the captain.

"Wictory, yer honour."

"What's your name?" bullied Puffeigh.

"Jemmy Green, sir."

"It's a deuced good job for you that I leave England a few days, or I'd call in a policeman and give you in charge. Clear out! you fellow, it's a blessing you don't belong to my ship, or I'd give you four dozen lashes for this evening's amusement." Saying this the noble commander strutted fiercely out of the hall.

Thompson waited until his superior officer was fairly up stairs, when he bawled after him, "Pleasant voyage to you, captain. I'm glad we ain't aboard the Stinger," and then vanished out-of-doors with his lady.

The lovers lingered long at the gate, and bade each other good-bye a hundred times.

"I'll never look at any one else again, Jerry dear," sobbed Mary Ann.

"And I'll be as true as steel, s' help me, I will," replied the ardent lover.

The girl saw him to the end of the lane, and then bade him good-bye, upon which he vowed he must see her safely back again. This little amusement they repeated a great many times, until the cook came out, with her apron over her head, and declared "they were both fools; and if Mary Ann didn't come in, she would lock her out." This announcement brought them to their senses; so, resigning his love to the care of her sympathetic fellow-servant, he, with something very much like a groan, tore himself away.

One of the housemaids lingered upon the stairs to hear how the lovers parted, and when the cook gave her the particulars, she exclaimed "*Poor* Mary Ann! *poor* Jerry! especially poor Mary Ann!" And in this sentiment, peculiar as it is, we cordially agree.

CHAPTER V.

A HEAVY raw fog hung about the ships anchored off Spithead on the morning appointed for Clare's punishment. Aurora seemed to have an inkling that man was about to do a very mean action ; and not being able to prevent the outrage, endeavoured, woman-like, to veil it.

The officer of the watch was leaning upon the capstan on the quarter-deck of H. M. S. Stinger. He was wet, cold and miserable, and wished himself anywhere else. Lounging there, with the fog collecting in silvery drops upon his uniform, he wondered how his god-father and god-mother, after having among other impossible vows, promised that "he should renounce the devil and all his works," could have used their utmost endeavour to get him into the navy, where he was called upon to assist Zamiel in such fiend-like business as the one in which he was then engaged. Lieutenant Ford having lately belonged to a ship commanded by a man who could govern sailors without bombast, and threatening every slight offence with the punishment of the lash, the preparations for torturing a sailor under the pretence of administering justice, disgusted him. He knew full well that the carpenter's mates had quietly brought aft two capstan bars, and lashed them securely to the ship's side, just abaft the starboard gangway; he was aware they had fastened two gratings to these vertical bars, and perfectly conscious of the boatswain's yeoman having brought aft a bag containing a number of the whips called " cats," and the necessary canvas bands or seizings by which the prisoner was to be seized, or lashed to the gratings. Lieutenant Ford knew all this, but he never turned his eyes in that direction, or appeared to be aware of the proceedings.

At the appointed time he gave the necessary instructions to the boatswain, upon receipt of which, Mr. Shever walked to the main hatchway, and stooping down so that the sound might reach the cell where Clare was confined, blew a shrill blast upon his call, waited until the same was repeated by his mates between decks, then bellowed forth, with all the force of his powerful lungs, "Lash up hammocks, rouse out; rouse out, all of ye."

Slipping his call into his vest pocket, he darted down the hatchway, and running forward, worried the men out of their hammocks, administering a kick, curse, or blow, as his playful fancy or the defenceless positions of his victims dictated. Small boys were there who turned out of their warm beds into the raw air with a gulph, as if suddenly seized with ague chills. These white, shivering forms were fair marks for Shever, who, snatching a piece of line from the hand of one of his assistants, soon demonstrated to the unlucky urchins how skilfully he could manipulate a rope's end, their howls showing that every stroke had raised what he jocosely termed " a mark that would give 'em some trouble to rub out."

With the active assistance of the boatswain's mates there was soon an empty line of hammocks dangling between decks. The late occupants dressed, lashed up their nautical beds, took them on deck, and placed them in the nettings, after which some skulked in out-of-the-way places and smoked ; while others, who had been the recipients of the boatswain's gentle attentions, collected in groups about the foremost guns, and scowled at each other, as if anxious to be revenged upon some one. None of them prayed; indeed, very many of the Stingers looked upon prayer as an admiralty ordinance served out to them on Sundays along with the articles of war and other luxuries.

The kindly Shever and his assistants soon cleared between decks of all the sailors, and sentries were placed over each hatchway, to prevent the men going below again until punishment was over. None of the crew seemed inclined to go aft, but kept as far forward as possible.

A few of the men mentioned Clare's name, and expressed a wish "he might get off easily;" others, who under different circumstances would have still been in their hammocks, abused the prisoner in round terms, and "trusted the fool might get what he asked for." One gentleman, who had formerly been an eminent sneak-thief (but finding the land too warm, had betaken himself to the water), blessed the service collectively and individually, from the first lord of the admiralty to the last captured sailor, offering up a specially fervent appeal for the welfare of all the Stingers both now and hereafter. He continued in this strain until his remarks became personal to another gentlemen, whereupon the latter knocked him down and jumped upon him, after which he held his peace.

It may be gathered from these occurrences that Clare's shipmates did not exhibit much sympathy for him, the truth being, no one could tell when his own turn would arrive to taste the lash; and not looking forward to receiving much condolence themselves, they did not display any for the victim on this occasion. Some of the boys, thinking by the light manner in which the idea of flogging was treated by one or two of the crew, that it would be a capital joke to see a man tied up and tortured, were squabbling about places, one imp offering "sixpence and two plugs of tobacco to any cove who would shove him into a good place to see;" several of the men kept their eyes on that lad with a view to receiving this reward.

Crushe, resplendent with gold lace, cocked hat on head, his sword resting on his arm, was lounging about the quarter-deck in conversation with Cravan, and seeing Mr. Shever standing forward, sent for him. When that worthy came aft and touched his cap, Crushe walked over to the gratings, and asked him if he knew anything of his mate's capabilities in the flogging line. Shever replied that "one of them was a first-rate hand with the cats, and the other would do his duty;" and added, "I seed to them before I left between decks," by which he implied that the bottle of brandy sent to his cabin by the generous Crushe had been shared with these mates, who, like the boatswain, were now far from sober.

"Of course *you* know how to do your duty, Shever?" observed the lieutenant in a patronizing tone. "No nervousness about you, eh?"

Shever looked at his interrogator, and replied in a somewhat injured manner, "Lieutenant Crushe, you trust me, I won't leave a bit of cheek in the feller. Wot with my cat and the raw air he'll be quiet enough before he gets his allowance."

Crushe smiled approvingly, and ordered the warrant officer "to send the hands aft."

The boatswain staggered forward; and putting his call to his mouth, the sharp vindictive notes, proper on the occasion, echoed through the ship, his assistants repeating the same in a more imperfect manner.

The sounds having died away, Shever, with hoarse voice and congested visage, roared out, " All ha-nds,—to punishment;" then with the assistance of his mates and the ship's corporal, he drove the crew aft to the port side of the quarter-deck, and reported "all aft" to Crushe.

Shortly after this, the officers came up from below, all being in full uniform: the surgeon and his assistant, the paymaster and clerk, the lieutenants, mates, midshipmen. and engineers, were all compelled to be present, although many of them were disgusted with the duty. As they came on deck the ship's boys thought "how beautiful the show was, and wondered what would come next." Notwithstanding the fog, Cravan had donned his best full dress, the prospect seeming to light up his visage with a glow of satisfaction. We must mention that the midshipmen, who had less gold lace upon their uniforms than the other officers, were in the greatest stew about their bullion being tarnished, their principal occupation being to discover which officer gave most shelter, and when found, to avail themselves of the same.

A body of those water soldiers known in H. M. navy as "Rile Marines" now slowly ascended the main hatchway, and fell into line before the crew, on the port side of the quarter-deck. In heavy marching order, and knapsack on shoulder, they manœuvred as nimbly as snails.

These military evolutions struck terror into the hearts of the second-class boys, who shut their eyes, and prepared for the worst.

Clare was escorted on deck by two marines, between whom he walked with a quiet, unassuming air: there was no sign of fear in his face, nor the slightest trace of braggadocio in his manner.

The captain now made his appearance, and was saluted by the officers and crew, the marines presenting arms, after being ordered to do so in a frantic manner by the sergeant.

Noticing that the ship's boys were completely hidden by the marines, Puffeigh, in order that the imposing ceremony might have due effect, directed that the lads should be ranged in front of the capstan before them, remarking, "they will be able fully to understand what flogging is like;" and truly they were placed in a position where none of the horrors would be missed by them.

"Strip!" cried the commander, as if directing the movements of a dog.

The prisoner removed his serge and flannel, and stood before his fellows a very model of a man. In spite of his fortitude, the cold air made him shiver. It was one of those piercing fogs which seem to absorb all the warmth from the body, and charge it in lieu with rheumatic pains; as if in very spite and wantonness it seized on Clare's muscular form, and tortured it into blueness in a few seconds.

"Seize him up!" continued the commander.

The ship's corporal advanced with two quarter-masters, and they were about to lay hands on Clare, but he, divining their intentions, without the slightest hesitation, walked to the grating, and held out his wrists. One of the quarter-masters took his right hand, and having passed a canvas seizing twice round it, fastened it to the capstan bar just above where the upper grating was lashed, his companion doing the same with the other wrist on the adjoining bar; after which they placed bands round his neck and loins, and lashed his knees to the lower grating, the man now being what sailors term "spread-eagled."

His flannel shirt was laid across his shoulders, and the men who had seized him up retired, upon which Captain Puffeigh proceeded to read the warrant for punishment. This was a formal document which, with many "now wherefores" and "now whereases," recapitulated the finding of the court-martial. A portion of the articles of war was also read, the crew standing bareheaded all the while.

At this moment the sentry reported, "Boat right alongside, sir."

"See who it is," bawled the commander.

"It's a woman as wants to see you, sir," shouted the sentry from the gangway, "and she's a coming up the gangway ladder, sir."

Upon this Puffeigh directed Cravan to tell her she could not come on board.

Cravan returned in a few moments, and with a grin upon his face, reported that "it was the prisoner's wife, who wished to speak with the captain."

"Is she in her boat?" demanded Puffeigh.

"Yes, sir! I promised if she would get off the ladder and let her watermen pull clear away from the side, that I'd tell you what she wanted," replied the officer.

"Tell her if her watermen come near the ship I will have a cold shot thrown into their boat, and that all her whining won't save her man, who will shortly get what she has helped him to."

Upon hearing this, the crew uttered a yell of disgust, one fierce roar, and then all was silent; hardened as some of them were, this was too much for them. Puffeigh was almost mad with rage, and he screamed, "Open your mouths like that once again, and I'll order the marines to fire amongst you, you mutinous hounds," and the marines looked as if they would like to carry out such a humane command.

When the gallant Cravan had reported "that the woman was gone," and added, for the edification of the prisoner, "that when he last saw her she was lying all of a heap in the stern of the boat," the captain called to the boatswain, and said, "Mr. Shever, do your duty," upon which the ship's corporal removed the shirt from Clare's back, and retired a few paces to the right.

Tom heard all that passed about his wife, but he "ate his heart," and showed no sign of his terrible torture.

Shever took a cat-o'-nine-tails from under his jacket, walked to the left side of the prisoner, grasped the handle firmly in his right, and separated the cords with the fingers of his left hand; then with a rapid swish raised the weapon high above his head, and brought the cruel lashes savagely across the naked back of the helpless victim.

"One!" calls the ship's corporal.

"Two!"

"Three!" and now a number of blue lines crept across the man's back.

"Four!" They changed to red, beaded with the blood of the poor wretch, who trembled, yet bore the pain without uttering a word.

"Five!" "Six!" "Seven!" What is that staining the boatswain's fingers? Blood, my Christian friends!

"Eight!" "Nine!" "Ten!" More blood! Think of that, parents who give your sons to the service of their country!

"Eleven!" Blood, which no longer stains the cat alone, for specks fly off and dot the blanched faces of the terror-stricken lads who had been so fiendishly stationed near by the gallant commander.

"Twelve!" called the ship's corporal, who then advanced and offered the trembling victim some water, which he refused.

Price, the boatswain's mate, now took up his position in the place vacated by Mr. Shever, and at the words, "Boatswain's mate, do your duty," laid on the lash with savage, nervous energy.

"One!" "Two!" "Three!" "Four!" "Five!" "Six!" The man's back showed a number of broad, blue lines, and two raw patches blushed upon his blade bones.

"Seven!" "Eight!" "Nine!" "Ten!" "Eleven!" "Twelve!" The brandy with which the savage had been plied was doing its devil's work, and he seemed desirous of adding a thirteenth blow, but was stopped by the commander.

At the last stroke Clare threw back his head, and gasped for water, which was immediately supplied him by the ship's corporal.

The boatswain resumed his position; and now fully warmed to his work, lashed away at the shuddering mass with great ferocity. 'Twas no longer blood alone that clung to the cats, but at every stroke he stripped off more solid cuttings from poor humanity. See how the thirty-sixth lash has calmed the poor wretch! There was little sign of insubordination in the man when the ship's corporal sprinkled his face and held the water to his lips after the boatswain had retired.

Another boatswain's mate stepped forward, and being somewhat inexperienced, is cautioned by the captain "not to miss his man." With an awkward sweep he brought his lash across the loins of the prisoner, who writhed in agony from this new torture, the protecting hand having become displaced. But what cared the operator as long as the captain failed to notice it? and stroke followed stroke with clumsy rapidity.

"O God!" cried the poor victim, "flog lower," as at the "eleventh" blow the cat flew stinging round his head and across his eyes. At the "fourteenth" the prisoner threw back his head in agony, and became quite rigid.

When the last of the fifty lashes had been delivered, and properly told off by the ship's corporal, Tom Clare hung motionless from the grating, a sight so pitiful that many of the officers were visibly affected.

"Cast him off!" directed the commander.

In a few moments the prisoner was released and supported below, where the surgeon did his best to mitigate the man's sufferings.

Puffeigh turned to the crew and addressed them as follows :— "I have among you some more fellows like the man who has just received punishment. Now, mark my words, my fine fellows, if any of you give me the slightest trouble you will soon find yourselves *there*" (pointing towards the gratings) "Some of you have got the idea that you have rights, and ought to be treated like officers. Dismiss all such ideas of equality from your minds. You were never intended to be put on a level with your superiors. We're going on a foreign station, and I'll keep you in your places. Now, look you! respect your superior officers, do as you are ordered, and thank God that you are under a man who will give you four dozen as soon as look at you."

The effect of this speech upon the crew may be better imagined than described. The marines stared straight before them, and did not seem to be affected in any way, but the sailors looked askance, and whispered to each other, "Won't the ship be a heaven afloat arter this?"

"Pipe down," ordered the commander, as he watched the faces of the crew, in order to note the dissatisfied among them; "and," added he, "Mr. Crushe, you may have them piped to breakfast."

When Clare had somewhat recovered he was ordered up to the quarter-deck, and placed aft under the charge of a sentry until sunset, when the ship's corporal informed him he was free.

Doubtless, justice was satisfied.

Puffeigh went on shore, and boasted that he had conquered his men.

Crushe hugged himself to think how well he had kept his word.

Cravan, not knowing any better, imagined he was revenged.

And the devil was delighted with the whole business.

CHAPTER VI.

THE day after Clare's punishment the matter was almost forgotten in the hurry incident to preparation for sea. By 5 P.M. the ship was perfectly ready, and every one at his post, in immediate anticipation of getting under weigh, when the signal midshipman announced, " Our pennant's flying, sir." Up went the rolls of bunting, threading their way aloft until they reached the mast-heads of the flag-ship, when they broke and unfolded themselves to the breeze. Their purport being ascertained, Captain Puffeigh was informed that the Stinger was to remain at anchor until sunrise the next morning. Upon receiving this order the commander directed "the engine-room fires to be banked, and the crew piped to dance and skylark ; " thus giving the officers and men an opportunity of writing farewells to their friends.

Captain Puffeigh retired to his cabin, called for a supply of pens, ink, paper, and old crusted port, and proceeded to torture himself into letter-writing condition. In a short time he worked his ideas up to literary red-heat, and produced the following extraordinary effusion, during the manufacture of which he had blessed the paper, execrated his spectacles, and, in fact, blamed everything, but his own dull brains. Mrs. Puffeigh being young and pretty, we fear did not see much to admire in her husband, and was not at all sorry to be once more free from his oriental attentions.

> " H. M. S. Stinger, off Spithead,
> " 16 November, ——.

" ROBBY'S OWN PET,

" I am sorry I cannot come on shore to say one more good-bye to my Tooty. I know that horrid Captain Dasher will be with you at the pic-nic about this time ; but my pet will keep him at a distance. Don't give the dog too much meat, and discharge that ——cy maid of yours, find out if you can to what ship her fellow belongs, his name is James Green.

" I almost cry when I think how lonely you must be, poor Tooty, keep up your spirits. Tell the gardener to discharge his boys, and send all the peaches to the fruiterers. Keep the cellar key yourself, and if my brother visits you, give him bin three, port, it is good enough for a curate. How will my pet get on without me. Keep up your music, and don't paint your dear little face, don't you remember how people laughed at me at the archery meeting, when I wiped Tooty's face and the stuff came off.

" Pretend to be gay, and show the envious ones that you are happy—don't waltz, darling pet. Doctor Muddle says, *it's the very worst exercise you can take,* slow dances are *not so bad.* I hope you will visit your relations as much as possible, *particularly those who do not wish you to invite them in return.*

" I have a pair of your dear little bootikins, which stand in my cabin, I look at them with tears in my eyes.

" Put the servants on board wages when you are absent.

" With a billion kisses from your own doting

" ROBERT PUFFEIGH."

Tooty screamed with delight when she read this letter, but followed her own inclinations in spite of its warnings.

The lieutenants and other commissioned officers were in their respective cabins, emulating their captain's example in letter-writing. Crushe scrawled two epistles which ran as follows:—

"Stinger, at Spithead,
"16 November.

"My Beloved Aunt,

"Providence has ordained that I shall be chastened by being separated from those I love. I kiss the rod, and submit with resignation.

"You will be happy to hear, my dear aunt, that I am in a ship where the voice is raised in supplication, and where we can meet, when we choose, for mutual improvement. One of our officers, named Cravan, is seriously seeking, and I trust will become a shining light. I gave your beautiful tracts to our boatswain, a most worthy young inquirer, who, I doubt not, will make good use of them. He remarked, "if he had ten times as many they would be acceptable," which gratified me exceedingly. We were obliged to flog that wretched man, Clare, yesterday. I did all I could for him, but he was hardened, and refused a tract offered him by the boatswain. I enclose my mite towards the Reverend Mr. Bulpurp's chapel, give it him, with my humble prayers for the cause.

"My poor wife still refuses to join our blessed band, and therefore will not visit you. I am much concerned about her hereafter. She refused to read that excellent book you gave me for her special perusal. You may remember it was called "Beauty a Sin;" pray for her, dear aunt, and for your unworthy nephew,

"Howard Crushe."

(No date.)

"Dear Mary,

"Another of your weak compositions has reached me; how foolish you are to waste your time in endeavouring to make me believe you care for me. I have no money to send you. Ask your *doting* father for some. So you still refuse to visit my aunt, and assist me to secure her money.

"*Very good;* until you do this I shall not answer another of your letters.

"Your afft. husband,

"Howard Crushe."

When Crushe's aunt perused her letter she wiped her eyes, declared "he was too good a husband for such a wife," and sitting down wrote an order for one hundred pounds, which she forwarded to his agents, with directions to place the same to her nephew's account.

His wife read hers with a sad heart, and when she had received its last keen stab, cried bitterly, and wished the grave might soon be her resting-place.

The manly fellow who wrote them anticipated these results.

LIEUTENANT FORD TO MISS ———.

"Dearest Florence,

"I have but a few seconds in which to scratch farewell. Your letter of yesterday reached me. I did not know that Clare's wife had been your maid. Tell her I will get him into my watch, and do all I can for him, *for your dear sake.* He bore his punishment nobly, and even his enemies must have admired his courage. Cravan (you know, the man who made himself so ridiculous at the archery meeting) is in our ship. I never speak to him except on duty. Your sweet miniature shall never be parted from me until I claim you as my wife.

"I told Clare that you knew his wife, and had interested yourself about him, and he seemed thoroughly to appreciate your good action.

"With love to Kate and Reg. and Chin-chin to Mamma and Papa, believe me to be ever your devotedly attached

"ERNEST.

"*H. M. S. 'Stinger,' Spithead,* 16th *November.*"

The gun-room was a scene of the most lively disorder. Most of the lads were leaving home for the first time, and consequently had a great deal to communicate to their friends, yet every now and then they would cease writing, and turn their attention to squabbling with their neighbours about desk room.

The questions of boundary lines and elbow rights being settled, these combative bantams would challenge each other "to cut for glasses round." The article divided for was by them facetiously termed "stout;" a cask of this cholera-mixture being on tap under the mess-table. Affixed to the bulk-head was a notice, running as follows:—

"In future, any officer ordering stout, must attend to the following: When the steward stoops under the table, he must whistle, and continue at this exercise until his head is again upon a level with the mess-table. In default of which, boots and other blunt weapons may be used.

"(Signed) PALGRAVE BROWN,

"Caterer."

This stringent regulation was the result of a tendency on the part of their steward to remain unnecessarily long under the table, when ordered to draw the delectable beverage for his superiors.

The said steward was a hang-dog looking object, who had bolted from servitude under a parish undertaker, and sought peace on board a man-of-war, yet found it not, having exchanged one weak tyrant for several bullying, inconsistent, savage little Neros. Some of the youngsters, taking their cue from Crushe, seemed to think the only way they could show their authority was by domineering over the wretched servant; and in spite of Ryan and other gentlemen, would vent their spleen upon the poor fellow, treating him as if he were destitute of feelings.

Between decks forward the crew took leave of their friends according to their various temperaments; some yawned, and told of faithful and faithless loves, vowing one good-bye was enough for most women, while they never would cease to remember others with whom they had consorted. A few stretched themselves out on the bags in the rack forward, and dropped off into a broken sleep, from which they would start with a wondering air, observing to those around them that they "was werry near off that time."

Seated near the cook's galley was a careworn-looking sailor, cheek on hand, evidently so deeply buried in thought as to be quite unconscious of the babel around him. He was thinking of the past, when, in spite of mother's prayers and father's warning, he determined to leave his home and enter the navy. Bitterly he regretted the unspoken compliance which rose to his lips, when his mother begged him "not to go to sea, but stay to comfort her in her old age," and, angered by the silence of his father, he steeled his heart against them, and the words, "Father, I'm wrong; forgive me," were never uttered.

He remembered how, when leaving their cottage, he heard the old man angrily refuse to call him back, saying, " He don't mean it, and will be home again in a few days." He nearly faltered then, but dreaded the kindly laugh which would follow if he returned. Brave heart to face the lash and degradation, rather than submit to the will of one who loved him, although he was a little harsh at times.

He left them in anger, and never afterwards communicated his whereabouts, or sent them a word of comfort; but he was never out of *their* thoughts, and their last years were racked with torturing anxiety on his account. After a long absence, he returned to England, and bent his steps towards his native village, thinking with the gold he had earned to cheer his aged parents, and heal their bruised hearts—wondering, as he passed along the streets, why the people stared so; mistaking children for their parents, and taking young men for old, in his eager desire to be recognized by some one. The very ale-house sign was cold in its appearance, and swung lazily on its hinges, as if to wave him off. " I don't know you," said the children. " I don't know you," echoed the trees—and the whole place seemed to enter a protest against his re-appearance among them. " Well, never mind! mother will know me," he thought; "and father will be glad to see me, I dare say;" and he turned down the lane in which stood his home. An old woman was in the porch. He shouted to her, "Mammy, here's Joe," upon which she tottered in and closed the door.

"What!" he bawled, " up to your old tricks, mammy, hiding again? Come, let me in, I'm real glad to see you." As he said this, he reached the threshold and rapped playfully, to hasten her re-appearance.

As no answer was given, he lifted the latch and walked into the house, where he was confronted by the woman, who ordered him to " begone and not worrit her." He gazed on the old crone in speechless amazement, until she again urged him to depart, upon which he mumbled something about "*her*" not being his mother."

The woman, finding he was much affected, tendered him a seat, and he soon learned that his father was sleeping calmly by the side of his faithful spouse, in the village churchyard. He got up and walked to that place like one in a dream. When he stood by their neglected graves the choke rose in his throat, and bitterly he repented the sad consequences of his rash step.

The old sexton seeing some one at the graves, thought possibly he might be a relation of those buried there; so he hobbled to his side, and with parrot-like volubility told him, " there lies two good old folks, who died broken-hearted because their boy left them to go to sea, and was never again heard of; " and the sailor felt his utter loneliness, that he was an outcast, a very dog, with no one in the world to love or care for him.

These thoughts came crowding into his brain, and he writhed under the magic of their influence. However, after a time they left him, when he arose, and preluding the transformation with an oath, became once more a rough, callous fellow, "a daring, reckless sailor."

A knot of ordinary seamen and boys were collected around one old tar, who was evidently "a man of mark among them." This ancient mariner did not impart choice moral instructions to his audience; far from it, he was what they called "yarning," and his reminiscences savoured of back slums and low dens, but were not on that account less interesting to those about him. When he laughed they followed suit, and woe betide the man who dared contradict "Old Jemmy," or for one moment doubt the veracity of his "tough ones:" while instant squashment would be the doom of any boy who did not laugh louder or believe more implicitly than the men. Offerings of grog and tobacco were made by his obsequious admirers, and he was in that condition graphically described by sailors as "werry tight."

"Does any o' you remember Limpin Lew?" demanded this old man, adding par thetically, "I suppose none of *you* ever knowed *her*, though."

"I knowed her rayther!" squeaked a small boy, who was standing on a shot rack, so as to get a full view of the old Tycoon's face.

"Did you?" mumbled the ancient mariner. "I should like to know how the likes of *you* became ack-vainted with sich an elegant field-male?" saying which this oracle placed a plug of tobacco between his toothless jaws, and looked round until he spied out the small boy, who, being thus challenged, retorted—

"Vy shouldn't I know her, vhen she drinked herself to death at my fauther's?"

"*Your* father's! who's *your* father?" growled the patriarch.

"Bill Jordun, wot keeps the Blue Postes at Portsea—he's as good a man as you, anyhow."

Much to the astonishment of the spectators, the daring child was not slain, or maimed for life; but with a look of the most profound admiration, the hoary sinner drew forth his tobacco box, which he tendered to the lad, requesting him to "help hisself," remarking as he did so, "Wot! the kid of my old chum Bill? Lord love you, sit down along side of me, vy, I've been as tight as an owl at your old man's many's the time. I'll be as good as a father to you, my boy; see if I don't"

The ancient mariner religiously kept his word—*with a rope's end*—and the lad repeatedly had occasion to "anything but bless" the memory of "that elegant field-male Limpin Lew."

A few of the men were seated at their mess-tables, scrawling off their epistolary farewells. Tom Clare was one of these—crippled as he was, he managed to write to his wife.

H. M. S. Stinger,
Nov. 16, ——

"DEAR POLLY,

"We leave in a few hours for a foreign station, it is now all past, and I am wot they cal a free man once again. Tell her, the angell as you knows,—I menshun no name for fear of accident,—that I thank her for her kindness to you. I wait patient until I see you again. Love to Mother and Father. I have you always in my hart until death do us part, God bless my wife.

"From Thomas Clare, A. B., to Mrs. Clare, care of Mrs. Morks, 41, John Street, Portsmouth, or if not there, to Mrs. Clare, Kingsdown, near Deal, Kent.

"Write soon, she will tell you were too,

"TOM CLARE."

Mr. Thompson not only wrote to Mary Ann, but also in consideration of sundry glasses of grog, acted as amanuensis to several of his shipmates. The letter to his intended running thus:—

Pentonville, afloat off Spithead.

"DEAR MISS MARY ANN ROSS, Perfection in Wimen,

"This comes opin to find you well as leafs me at present with a full intenshun to bolt as soon as i gets harf a chans.

"I am sorry to ad your brother in lawer is a brute, i knowed he were a mene kus but i did not think 'im wishous, being a perfec tyerant.

"He gave us a trete a flakin pore T. Clare, i was horri-fied and his pore wife a faintin over the ship's side, and the skipper as hard as a stone, which i hope she will bolt with some good looking feller and drive him into a lunatic a-sylum.   T. Clare behaved like a bric—but enuf of those melancholy subjex which I dismiss with love to Mrs. Shever and wishin her a better husband that i feels as if i would like to punch his edd.

   " P. S. Give my love to your cousin Amelia, alsow to that red-ed-ded gal the cook next door, if so be you don't objex, she avin a bligh of my sister Fanne in Australia.

   " P. S. Remember me, Horatio, to the sarjunt, but don't allow no other soljar nere your lips, ders Mary Ann.

   " P. S. P. S. Minde you keep clear of that young Carpenter who is after no goode.

   " P. S. If this should meat the high of the cook, give her my love, also a kiss if you don't objex.

   " P. S. S. S. S. S. We are going to the Cape of Good ope tomorro before breakfast, so dri your tears, dispell your fears, for true you'll always find me i must and will return again to the girl i left behind me.

   " JERRY THOMPSON, A. B. on board H. M. Ship Stinger.   Seamen's Letter bag."

Mr. Price, the boatswain's mate, not being able to write to his good lady himself, had captured a bull-headed boy and under threat of dire torment compelled him to write to his dictation. The lad was directed to "chalk down" every word his persecutor uttered, and he followed his instructions with Chinese exactness.

   Every now and then the bull-headed one would thrust out his tongue, square his elbows and settle close to the paper, until there seemed every probability of his resting his cheek upon the letter and indulging in a short slumber. When Price saw the closely-cropped poll inclining paperwards, he would seize his victim by the scruff of the neck with his left hand, while his right would be operating upon the person of the secretary with a motion which rapidly took the kink out of his vertebra, and made him sit as upright as a soldier: " If you goes a kissin of the paper again I'll rope's end you! " said Price, after having jerked his clerk into position for the tenth time.

   This is the result of Price's system.

   " 16 Nov. — Mind your i am going to write a few lines hold up your head you d—ear Eliza we are going to leave for a furrin, isn't so I say it is, furrin station to-morrow. Now then keep up my half pay note is given to the paymaster you infernal little f—ond lins. All my clothes was right but a nod sock right on the paper none of your lip and the ditty box lid was broke you young warmint. I'll give you something to wake you up in love to Meryar hold your jaw also my respects to Mister Mage wot keeps the Red Lion.—keep up and be — also to all inquirin friends lay down again and I'll give you this rope's end which you knows. We flaked Tha. Clare and I hurt my wrist a so doing and will give you just the same if you don't mind your high. If you can write me W. Price boatswains mate starboard watch H. M. S. Stinger Cape of Good ope or elsewear to be forwarded if left till called for, lord bless you all I'll cut you in halves if you go a kissin agin like that, your lovely husband,   BILL PRICE."

   (Mrs. Price was somewhat puzzled with the foregoing, but finding the half-pay came in regularly, she consoled herself with that, and telling her neighbours " that her Bill was off his chump.")

   On the morning of the 17th November the Stinger got under weigh, and after saluting the flag of Admiral * * *, steamed slowly down the British Channel.

   The last link of the chain, supposed to bind folks to their native land, having been severed the Stingers turned their faces towards the future, and their more immediate attention to matters connected with securing boats and anchors.

The screw continued its music, and rattled away at a tune which lasted, with intervals, until the ship returned to England. It was an auxilliary screw—a noisy, bumptious, mad little article—going off with a bang, as if desirous of giving every one a headache; after which it would undergo a paroxysm, and worry at a great rate—at first free and strong, then gradually quieting down to a dead strain, like a blind man's dog when held in by its owner. Thus people who did not know the secret of its weakness would imagine it a very powerful, hard-working auxiliary.

Sometimes it stopped dead, or jingled like a tambourine, when Mr. Sniff, the chief engineer, gravely doctored it with pantomime property forceps, which operation would somewhat relieve it, and start it clattering on its way again. When the wind freshened it would drag after the ship in a lazy, sulky manner, leaving a curve of bubbles to mingle in her wake as if in silent protest against the superior force of its rival. But let the breeze fall light, with a sudden kick it would throw off the water, rattle, and rush; and when thus excited, had been known to propel the Stinger at the dizzy rate of six knots an hour.

After they were out two days the commander opened his despatches, and informed his officers that "they were bound for the Cape of Good Hope," which they already knew, although not officially.

"Going to the Cape of Good Hope! hurrah!" cried Jerry Thompson, who had not scrupled to listen to the communication made by Puffeigh to the first lieutenant. "Going to the Cape, my boys; hurrah for fat-tailed sheep and Cape smoke!" It seems Thompson had been there before.

Clare was placed in Lieutenant Ford's watch. He went about his work in a quiet, unassuming manner, and became a prime favourite of that officer. No one interfered with him, and he would never trouble his shipmates except on matters of duty.

Captain Puffeigh took a great fancy to Thompson; and one day called him, and questioned him as to his antecedents. "Have you not sailed with me somewhere, my man?" demanded the commander. "It's my brother you know, sir," replied the scamp. "We're so werry much alike, that our mother don't know us." This remark partly satisfied Puffeigh, who thereupon rated Jerry to be his coxswain. "I know I've seen you somewhere, though, he repeated. "My eyesight isn't first-rate, but I seem to remember your features."

It was probably a very good thing for the coxswain that Puffeigh's vision was imperfect.

The Stinger made the best of her way Capewards, and Crushe relieved the dullness of the passage by experimenting on the endurance of the crew. Five times the gratings were rigged, and the disgraceful farce of justice enacted, five men broken into obedience, or rendered worse demons than before.

The ship, however, in due time arrived in Simon's Bay, and proceeded to refit. The first order given being "no leave allowed to any one while we are in this place."

Commander Puffeigh accepted the hospitality of one of the merchant houses, and took Jerry on shore to act as his valet. While there an adventure befell them, which we will narrate in the next chapter.

CHAPTER VII.

BEING appointed captain's coxswain and valet suited Thompson to a nicety, and it was amusing to see how he adapted himself to his new position, as from a merry wag he suddenly quieted down into a solemn-looking fellow. We hardly need say this was all assumption on his part, but "quiet dignity tinged with a slight shade of melancholy" he considered the correct sort of thing for the *role*, and no one who saw him recognized the gay and festive youth of old times.

"Promotion's ruined Thompson," said the boatswain to Price. "He ain't hisself. I shouldn't wonder if he goes into a consumption."

"I wish he would," feelingly replied the boatswain's mate, "provided the captain would give *me* a chance to ketch the complaint arter him."

Commander Puffeigh had shipped as his steward a young and aspiring cockney, who entered the service with the full determination of becoming an admiral, but finding his chances in that particular direction rather few, gave up the idea, and devoted his attention to the acquirement of grand words. The doctor was his great fountain-head; and when that gentleman dined with the captain, Mr. Boyldwyte would be on the alert, and listen to every word which fell from the medico's lips.

The appointment of Jerry in a double capacity annoyed the steward. He did not mind the sailor attending to his master when on board ship, but to be taken on shore, and regularly installed as captain's valet, was rather too much of a good thing. Whenever, therefore, the grave face of Mr. Thompson appeared at his pantry door, the steward forthwith would stand on the offensive. The sailor knew this, and aggravated his opponent accordingly.

The ship had been anchored in Simon's Bay about twenty-four hours, and Puffeigh was comfortably quartered on shore, before the coxswain made his appearance on board again. After delivering letters and messages to the first lieutenant, he proceeded to the steward's pantry, where he found Mr. Boyldwyte deep in the mystery of plate cleaning, and evidently not in the very best temper.

"Good morning, Mister Biled-up," whispered the sailor.

The steward took up a spoon and leathered away as if quite unconscious of the coxswain's presence.

"Mr. Biled right! I begs your pardon," insinuated the mischievous Jerry. "Im come from the captain with orders, Mr. B."

"Cuss your Mr. B., you infernal collyoptera!" retorted the now thoroughly-roused flunkey. "My name is Boyldwyte! Yes, sir, Boyld—wyte. I want none of your cheek! Speak to me on duty, sir! Yes, sir!—on duty. I don't belong to your class of society." Having thus delivered himself, he stared hard at Thompson, and breathed defiantly, as much as to say, "I'm ready for you,—come on."

The coxswain-valet smiled, unhooked the half-door, walked into the pantry, and took a seat beside the ferocious one, who immediately turned his back upon him. When his anger had evaporated the steward demanded what the sailor required, and added, "Why didn't you tell me when you come in?"

"My dear Mister B., wot with your colly-wotshisnames and other blowings up, I haven't had a chance of getting a word in edgeways. Please don't use such teatotal long words; I ain't got a pocket jaxionaiary with me, you know."

"Did the captain give you any instructions for my guidance, Mr. Thompson?"

"Yes, Mr. B.."

"What was they, Mr. Thompson?"

"Well, he says to me, says he, 'Jerry, that infernal fool of mine—meaning you—ain't worth his salt, ses he, and for two pins I'd sack him and take you in his place.'"

"The captain made use of *that* observation, did he, Mr. Thompson?"

"He did, Mister B."

"He were not speaking anamgretically, were he, Mr. Thompson?"

"I dont know what you means by adamgratoolly. Is it one of your French ragonts, Mister B.?"

"No, it ain't; I forgot I was talking to a man of no education," replied the steward. "We'd better drop the subject."

"Come, don't be put out, old man; I was only joking—the fact was—now this is truth. The captain says, 'give my regards to Broiled-tight—beg your pardon, Mister Boyldwyte,—and tell him to give you all the little extras we require.'"

"We! who's *we*, Mr. Thompson?"

Jerry did not notice him, but went on. "We have lots of shirts and other linen, but we want more private brandy and some solder water, as ours is all out."

"Mister Thompson, I won't stand by and hear the likes of you, a person in your position in society, say we in eproximation with the name of our noble commander. I wont stand it, sir."

"Then," replied the sailor, "sit down to it, my pretty fellow, and hold your helloquence, or I'll call myself Co., there now."

This was a finisher for Mr. Boyldwyte, who thereupon procured the stores, and got rid of his tormentor. When the latter received the packages he asked if "there was anything in the message line for the captain."

The steward did not condescend to reply, so Thompson helped him to a parting shot.

"I say, Mr. B., can't you chuck in one of them long words of yours? One on 'em would be enough to give all the fellers ashore the colic," saying which his face resumed its melancholy cast; and waving a farewell to his victim, he went on shore.

There was more meaning in the word *we* than Thompson cared to explain, as during the day time he fortified himself with sundry nips of the captain's private brandy, and after dismissal in the evening would array himself in his master's plain clothes, in which he called upon his acquaintances; so the terms We and Co. were correctly used by him when speaking to the steward.

The domestics of the shore establishment in which they were located were coloured persons, the only exception being the housekeeper, an old Irish woman named Maggy, who, although a great admirer of Thompson, was much too aged a party for him to think of. However, in twenty-four hours he had made the acquaintance of every good-looking girl in the place, and in eight-and-forty was head-over-heels in love with a saffron-headed damsel of the heavy Teutonic order of architecture, by name Wallburg Pferdscreptern.

This young lady was the only child of a sturdy German, who dealt in flour, axes, pork, dumb-bells, cheese, ales, coffins, wine, fresh beef, hides, soft-bread, fat-tailed sheep, and other luxuries required by the men-of-war frequenting the place, and as labour was considered honourable in Simon's Bay, the fraulein attended to the sale department of her papa's store.

Wallburg's beauty was without a crease. Her very dimples had long ago given out, like the seat of a spring chair when the tyings snap; she was one harmonious whole, and nobody for a moment imagined she would ever fall in love. Great was the excitement in the Bay when her mother announced, "tae fraulein Wallburg vas in lofs mit ter matrose Scherry."

Thus it came about: Puffeigh, who possessed most of old Falstaff's weaknesses, had, on the day of his arrival, spied out the lovely fraulein, and marked her as his own. Quite taken in with his coxswain's quiet manner, he ordered him to carry a note down to her. Jerry did so—went, saw, and fell in love right away. The young lady soon explained matters in her most choice English, and they determined to take advantage of the old man's foolishness, and have a good time generally. It was love at first sight on the part of the maiden,—she had never been smitten before; but Cupid had fixed her this time, and in spite of "vater or mutter," she declared she would have her way or perish.

Four or five times a day was the coxswain sent to the German's store, where he delivered the billet-doux of the amorous Puffeigh. When he had read those charming epistles to the mädchen, he would write a suitable reply, and take it back to the delighted old fellow, his master.

"Was she pleased to get my letter?" demanded Puffeigh on one occasion; "did she look delighted?"

"Yes, sir. Ses she, ' Yaw, yaw, tell dem alten narren I loaf him very much.' "

"What's alten narren, my man?"

"It means splendid gentleman, sir, in English."

"You're picking up German very fast."

"Yes, sir; it's a picking me up, sir. I'm learning fast, sir; so as to be useful to you, sir."

This quite satisfied Puffeigh, who began to look upon his new coxswain as a treasure, and a very model of circumspection and perfection in his line.

Jerry, on his part, would invent the most astonishing yarns to get sent down to the store. Sometimes it was, "her father was in the last time, and he could not get a chance to speak to her;" at others "her mother was there."

"What is her mother like?" demanded Puffeigh.

"She's more fatter and bigger than the young lady," replied Thompson. The captain did not ask further questions.

The coxswain's courtship was conducted upon peculiar principles. He knew the fraulein disliked to exert herself, so, upon entering the little parlour at the back of the store where he usually found her calmly reclining in a rocking-chair, he would at once proceed to kiss her in a most vigorous manner. She, not at all disliking his attention, gazed upon him with a calmly-tickled air; and when he was tired would playfully slap him on the face, and declare he "vos ein goot veller."

After a pause, he proceeded again to salute her, showering the kisses with sounding smack upon her wax-like features, when a smile would extend over her visage like a ripple of air on a pan of oil, and she would ejaculate, "Scherry, mein hubscher matrose, runs away vrom der schips und marrys me," to which Jerry would reply with another consignment of kisses,—"Yaw, yaw, Wall-ker;" from this the fraulein imagined he would desert, and marry her when the ship was gone. "I loves you vorse den nopodys else, Scherry," gurgled his fair seducer. This was the signal for more kisses, and a fervent avowal of affection on the part of the coxswain.

One morning Captain Puffeigh informed his valet, in great confidence that "their destination on leaving the Cape would be the East Indies:" so during the day Jerry broke the news to his enslaver, and declared it would be madness for him to attempt to run away.

The information was a tremendous blow to Miss Wallburg, who replied, "I veels so pad at ter news, that I almost bust with deers." This catastrophe was averted by a scientific application of kisses on the part of her lover.

Miss Pferdscreptern was very desirous of knowing all about India,—how far off it was, &c., &c., the following conversation taking place upon the subject:

"India crate vays vrom here, Scherry?"

"Werry long way, Wallbug."

"Plack mans, Caffres, dere too, Scherry?"

Thompson was quite posted, so he replied, "Well, they're coppery like, Wallbug—coppery like, my gal."

"How don't dey know much dere, Scherry?"

"Well, Wallbug, you see, being uncivilized, they're savage; and being savage, they sometimes kills and eats each other." Jerry began to suspect she wanted to follow him, so he invented this to frighten her.

"Does dey have no rights to do dat?" gasped the fraulein, who was immensely interested with the replies of her Othello. "Does dey have no rights to do noting vot dey never does?"

This was rather a puzzler for the sailor, who replied, "You see as how it's somewhat like flogging; they hasn't no right to do it always as they does, but they do it nevertheless." After delivering this opinion Jerry refreshed himself with a few kisses of a choice and deliberate kind.

When she had recovered from the effects of the attack, the mädchen sadly observed, "Ach, Scherry, dere's beeples all over der vorld dat does dem sort of tings vot dey never ought to did."

Whether she referred to the East Indians or Thompson we know not, but the latter cut short all further remarks by another and more frantic attack upon her ruby lips.

Wallburg's papa was very little seen at the store, his chief duty being to board the ships when they came into the bay, bask in the sun while they remained there, and collect his money from them on their departure. No one informed him of his daughter's indiscretion for some time; and when they did, upon his mildly expostulating with her, he was told to "mind his own business;" he accordingly did so, but at the same time determined to be revenged upon the fellow who was causing his little one to be so lightly spoken of, and he observed to a friend, "Schust vait dill I kets hold of der veller, I vil kiv him vits." Jerry was too smart, however; and the whole time the ship was in port the parent never set eyes on him.

The day before the Stinger departed Puffeigh determined, come what might, to risk an interview with the charming girl who had written so many loving letters to him. In vain his coxswain represented the danger to be great, and the chance of seeing her alone very small: go he would.

He dressed himself in his most killing uniform, and in about three P.M. walked gently down to the store. Seeing the fair fraulein seated upon a bale of goods waiting for a customer, he thought the coast was clear, and boldly marched in.

Considering the numerous loving passages in her letters, the young lady's reception was rather a cool one. He, however, smiled on her, bowed, and said, "I'm Captain Puffeigh of Her Majesty's ship Stinger."

"You Captain Buffy? Ye-as?" interrogated the lady.

"Yes, my dear, I am he who has so often been delighted with your—" Here he advanced, and was about to grasp her plump hand, when she gave a little scream, and exclaimed, "Gott in Himmel. Mein vater!"

"What? Your father? The deuce!" exclaimed Puffeigh, looking round him with a bewildered air; upon which Miss Pferdscreptern, springing from her seat with a vivacity she rarely evinced, pointed to a narrow door, which the gallant captain hurriedly dashed open, darting into what proved to be a flour-shoot, the young lady immediately turning the button which fastened it.

There was no help for it. Puffeigh could "brave the raging of the sea, but not an angry father." Soon he heard the guttural voice of old Pferdscreptern, who loudly demanded of his daughter "vere vos dat tam sailor who vos schust gome into der store?" The commander trembled, not from fear, of course, so it must have been from the effects of the flour.

The old German was upon the rampage for some time, until at last, being assured by his "kind" "dat the man vos not dere," he quieted down, and calling for his pipe, was soon lost to view in a cloud of smoke.

About a quarter of an hour elapsed, when the lovely fraulein, finding her father asleep, proceeded to mount up into the loft, where, with the ready help of Jerry, who had been there all the time, she raised the board which usually covered the shoot, and having untied a sack of flour, she shot the contents down upon the imprisoned captain.

Half-choked, blinded, and mad, he burst the latch and staggered into the store. Up jumped the parent Pferdscreptern, seized a cowhide, and laid it right vigorously across the whitened figure. The flour flew all over the place, and the captain darted about like a man playing blind-man's buff, his assailant holding on to his coat-tails during the last part of the exercise, and occasionally varying the programme with a well-directed kick. At length, becoming somewhat exhausted, he let his victim go, upon which Puffeigh gasped out, "Wa! what the deuce is all this outrage for, sir? Do you know who I am?"

"You—schust—kit—out, and tousent—gifs—no—more—scheck!" panted the irate Teuton. "Let me catch you mit my kind agin and I vill make it much hotter dan it vas not dis time, mine friend. I tousant care ein heller who you ist. Shust you kit out, dat's all; I'm capden of dis schanty."

Puffeigh left the store a wiser and more subdued man. As he passed the cause of his trouble he imagined she was crying, her apron being thrown over her head and her shoulders heaving as if with grief. But Wallburg did not cry. The strong convulsion moving her frame was not that of woe; and when her father came to her and spoke kindly, she threw off the covering, and fairly roared—with laughter.

When the commander reached his quarters he found no one about, so slipped up to his bed-room, where Jerry was sitting on a chair as if fast asleep.

"Lord bless us!" said the valet, "has it been a spowtn'?"

Muttering something about "being attacked and nearly killed," Puffeigh directed his man to get a change of clothes. When he was comfortably arranged he turned to his coxswain and asked him "if he could keep a secret?"

"Any amount of 'em, sir," replied the sailor.

"Then forget you have ever seen me in such a pickle, my man. The day you remember it will be a bad one for you. There's a shilling for you."

"You're too generous, sir," said the amused valet.

The next morning Puffeigh announced to his host that he must at once take up his residence on board ship; and much to his man's sorrow, he ordered him "to pack his traps and take them on board."

It was nearly sunset before Jerry got off, and the traps were packed in anything but a neat manner. The truth was, the coxswain lingered with the fair Wallburg, and had almost made up his mind not to go at all, but a little calculation determined him. "If she weighs one hundred and ninety pounds when she is nineteen years old, what will she turn when she's thirty-eight?" thought he. This and his snug berth of coxswain outweighed her tempting offer, and with one last fond kiss, somewhere about the ten-thousandth, the distracted lover tore himself away.

There was the usual hard work going on in the ship during the time they remained in the bay: the men slaved all day, and sang or fished in the evening. After a lapse of four days the Stinger slipped from her moorings and proceeded out to sea. They left Simon's Bay with little regret, and as the land grew dim in their vision there was but one man on board who wished himself back.

"I shall never have such a big chance again," Jerry observed to Mr. Boyldwyte, as they strained their eyes in the direction of the land.

"What chance do you elude to, Mr. Thompson?"

"Ah, cockney, wouldn't you like to know?"

We regret this inconstancy to his old love, Mary Ann, on the part of Jerry. Our only explanation is, that he had an accommodating heart, and was a sailor who

> "In every mess would find a friend,
> In every port a wife."

CHAPTER VIII.

The Stinger made the best of her way towards the East Indies, it being rumoured that a portion of the Russian fleet was sailing in that direction, having been shut out of Sebastopol by the rapid action of the allied fleets of France and England.

The day after leaving the Cape, Puffeigh was taken seriously ill, his sickness proving to be brain fever, doubtless caused by the severe treatment received at the hands of the old German. Thompson acted as his nurse; and although he took quite as great care of himself as he did of his patient, Jerry's appointment was not an agreeable one. The commander did not leave his bed until they arrived in Singapore, and the ship was more than ever under the despotic control of Crushe.

It must not be imagined that the first lieutenant tyrannized over every one of his crew,—he was far too prudent to do that. By countenancing a few of the most brutal of the men, he kept himself posted with regard to those who had received cruel treatment by his orders. Again, if his misdeeds came to the knowledge of the press at any port they might visit, he thought it would be as well to have a number of trusty men he could send on shore, who would be a living advertisement for him, and prove by word and deed what jolly fellows the Stingers all were; so he promoted the fiends among the crew, and flogged those who showed a particle of manly feeling or self-respect. Shever was his right-hand man, being perfectly willing to testify to anything at his bidding; and between the Cape and Singapore many a man was brought to the gratings.

The crew were teased and worried until several of them became mutinous, upon which they were reported and flogged, the number of lashes awarded the victims varying from twenty-four to thirty-six, according to the caprice of Crushe; and very few of those not in the first lieutenant's favour escaped with unscarred backs. The boatswain and his mates were often the worse for liquor, and this, when the unjust lieutenant was punishing men for being intoxicated, upon the false testimony of Shever.

Puffeigh signed all the warrants, and would compliment Crushe upon the excellent state of discipline into which he was bringing the crew. "Flog the brutes now you are away from the station, and when in port stop the leave of all those mutinous dogs who ask for their rights, and you will soon have a good crew," commented the commander one day when requested to sanction a brace of warrants for punishment. Thompson, who handed him the pen with which he signed the atrocious orders, uttered a silent prayer that the old Tartar might never be able to sign any others.

Cravan and Crushe were greater friends than ever, and the former gloated over the spectacle of seeing Englishmen enjoy one of their naval privileges—the Lash.

Lieutenant Ford was pained and disgusted, and with the doctor, master, and pay-master, showed his contempt for the first lieutenant by cutting him in every way, and only speaking to him on duty.

They knew that there was no remedy. If either of them were rash enough to report matters to the senior officer, on their arrival at Singapore a court of inquiry would follow. What that would result in they knew but too well; Crushe, having creatures enough at his command ready to swear to anything, would be exonerated, while in all probability the officer who made the complaint would be sent home in disgrace. Moreover, it is considered ungentlemanly for officers to report each other.

One morning the ship was steaming in a dead calm, with Cravan in charge of the deck, the first lieutenant having ceased to keep regular watch, in consequence of the captain's illness. Midshipman Ryan had mustered the watch and idlers, and found one of the number absent.

"Who is the infernal sweep," demanded Nosey.

Upon this Mr. Shever, who was standing by, reported, "It's Dunstable, sir."

"Fetch him up—rouse him out—don't spare him, Mr. Shever; cut him down, curse him!"

Dunstable was a weak-minded fellow, who had one day before he went to sea stolen a loaf of bread to keep life in his body, and therefore had been a thief according to the law of the land. A humane magistrate gave him the alternative of "entering a man-of-war, or going to prison for a month." The poor idiot chose the freedom of the sea to a lodging in Pentonville palace, and was in due time drafted to the Stinger as an ordinary seaman; probably being, in the words of the facetious boatswain, "about as ordinary a seaman as he'd ever set eyes on." Crushe imagined the idiotic expression of the fellow's face was assumed to induce the commander to dismiss him from the service as useless; but this was not so—the man was weak-minded,—and any one with a particle of humanity in his heart would have been gentle with the "softy."

While at the Cape, Dunstable had tried to desert, so the day after they left that place he was brought to the gratings and received two dozen lashes, which destroyed the little sense he originally possessed; and some of the crew, finding the first lieutenant down upon the poor fellow, played him all manner of tricks. Wet swabs were dropped upon the "mad un," his grog stolen or diluted with vinegar, and pipes charged with powder were lent him by pretended sympathizers; who, knowing their superior officer disliked the man, vented their spleen upon him without fear of consequences.

Shever found Dunstable coiled up in his hammock, pretending to snooze. With the grin of a demon he took out his knife, cut the clews, and let the man down crash upon his head, then grasped him by the hair, and found he had received a severe scalp wound.

Rousing out one of the men who was sleeping near, and who proved to be Tom Clare, Shever told him to call the assistant-surgeon, adding, "Don't you call that cursed meddler, the old doctor;" and giving him a caution not to say anything to the latter, the worthy warrant-officer went on deck.

By some extraordinary accident the senior surgeon was called, we strongly suspect by Clare—although the doctor declared he came forward by accident. Dunstable's wound was sewed up, and the unfortunate fellow told "that he was on the sick list," but as the surgeon left the man the latter got up, and in spite of Clare's persuasions, walked on deck, where he went aft and reported himself ready for duty.

Crushe had just turned out, and was walking the starboard side of the quarter-deck, conversing with Cravan about Dunstable, when the latter made his appearance. Crossing over to the port side, he cursed the smiling idiot as a "useless thing"—" a dirty, beastly hound "—" a son of a dog, unfitted to live;" and turning to Cravan, asked what there was against the fellow.

"Absence from muster, skulking below in his watch on deck, insulting his superior officer (the boatswain), and not going on deck when directed by his superior officer," saying which Cravan pointed to the grinning object, as he would to some loathsome reptile, and added, "Yes, and the beast is filthy, and wants holy stoning."

Crushe then indulged in a flow of shameful abuse. His victim—fool as he was—clenched his fists, ground his teeth, and replied in language no less foul; but after a time he faltered, and wound up with, " Well, thank goodness for everything ! "

What did you say, you yahoo ? " roared Crushe.

" I said, Thank goodness for everything, amen. Can't I say my prayers in a man-o'-war ? "

" Mr. Shever, give this hound a scrubbing with sand and canvas, and clean his mouth out with it," said the gallant officer and gentleman.

Unable to keep his tongue quiet, and not realizing the purport of the cruel order Dunstable replied, " You're too good to me, sir ; thank goodness again ! who'd have thought I'd have found such a good friend in a man-o'-war ?" However, seeing Shever advance to seize him, the imbecile began to yell, and tried to run forward, but was quickly secured by the boatswain and his mates, with whom the poor fellow bit and fought in very desperation.

"Let me go, you brutes! I won t bother you again if you let me go! I'll take a good long drink if you'll only let me go ! "

He would have jumped overboard, if they had released him then, but there was no fear of that,—the business they had in hand was too congenial to their taste for them to let him drown himself, so he was bundled and worried about until his few clothes were stripped off, when, to prevent any further noise on his part, Mr. Shever roughly thrust a gag in his mouth.

The wash deck tub was filled with salt water, a grating laid across, and Dunstable's hands made fast to it behind, so that he could not rise or struggle without injuring his wrists. The boatswain called for a bucket of coarse sand, took a piece of hard sail-cloth, wetted it, dipped it in the sand, and himself commenced to inflict the scandalous torture known as " scrubbing with sand and canvas.' His mates fell to with zeal, and those fiends in human shape rubbed and excoriated the person of the wretched Dunstable from head to foot. The sand was mixed with shells, which cut like knives, while the salt water pickled and stung until the victim almost fainted, upon which they cut his hands adrift and ducked him in the water.

The watch and idlers knocked off work " to see the sport," and encouraged by the countenance of Crushe and Cravan, shouted with delight whenever the idiot uttered a groan or writhed in agony. There had lately been a great deal of torture inflicted before their eyes, and they had become quite judges of its effects.

When Dunstable had for the tenth time been thrust to the bottom of the brimming wash deck tub, Shever called for a pair of scissors, and proceeded to hack off the hair from the poor victim's head. Many were the jokes indulged in by the *gentle* barber at the expense of the idiot, as some of the grinning wags around him asked for " locks of his hair to send to their grandmothers," and when the last clip was made they felt quite sorry there was no more left.

Bruised, demented, and bewildered was the shivering specimen of humanity when they removed the gag, and leading him to the fore-rigging told him " to run for his life three times over the mast head."

As he did not reply or offer to move, the boatswain gave him a kick, upon which he said, " Thank goodness for that ! " This raised a laugh among the jolly tars who were standing around him, and one of them, emulating the warrant-officer's exampl also dealt the fool a kick.

" I can't go up that ladder," he pleaded. " I'm not up to that move. Thank goodness for all things ;" and added, in the slang of the beings who had reared him, " my nibs ain't vardi for that."

"Shever, muster the boys, give each a strip of raw hide, and let them flog this fellow aloft," said Crushe.

The active boatswain soon did as he was directed, and the boys were mustered and equipped in a very short space of time.

"Now, my lads, lay on to him as hard as you like," shouted the first lieutenant.

Dunstable sprang into the rigging when he saw the boatswain arming the boys, who were all willing enough to advance, but afraid of their victim's vicious looks. At last one rat of a boy sprang up beside him, and brought his strip of hide stinging across the poor fellow's naked body. In a moment up went his foot, and with a kick under the jaw, which made the boy bite the tip off his tongue, the hunted man stretched the little brute senseless upon the deck, completely stunned by his fall from the rigging.

Upon seeing this the sailors became furious, and urged the boys to attack him in a body.

"Lay into the brute, you warmints," bellowed the boatswain.

"Give it him, my lads!" cried the first lieutenant.

"A shilling for the next who touches him!" roared Cravan.

Dunstable gave one loud idiotic shout, then darted aloft like a squirrel, followed by twenty vindictive little devils thirsting to avenge the blow he gave their chum. Now one would reach him, when sting would go the torturing raw hide, making the idiot curse and howl like a demon. It was glorious sport for the lookers on, almost as good as bear-baiting.

Up, up they go, pursued and pursuers, until they reach the main-royal-stay; but only one boy followed then, the others hung on to the rigging and watched the sport; they were afraid to go on, the man's eyes glared so. Dunstable saw at a glance if he could only get across he would be safe from his persecutors. Away he clambered up the stay, hand over hand and foot over foot, like an experienced sailor.

The men below turned the quids in their cheeks, and observed to each other that "he warn't sich a darned fool arter all, you know, as he could get about aloft like a regler knowin one." But suddenly he stopped. His right leg slid from the stay, and hung helplessly down; soon the left followed, and he dangled aloft, holding on by his long, lean, sinewless arms.

A groan of horror burst from the crew. "He'll fall! O God, he'll fall!!" said Clare, who, roused out by the noise, had come on deck. All eyes were strained towards the poor wretch, who now began to show signs of total exhaustion. With a fearful wail he let go one hand, and swayed, with the weight of his body entirely thrown upon the other; then suddenly he released his grasp, and shot down towards the deck.

Those who could bear to look saw him strike the main-top-gallant-stay, turn over twice in his descent, and fall across the bridge.

Up sprang Clare, and tenderly he lifted the now broken form of the wretched idiot. Crushe, with livid face and trembling lips, asked him if the man was dead. Tom could not reply. He was too indignant to trust himself to speak; but giving the lieutenant a look of scorn, he raised the body in his powerful arms, and reclining the inanimate head upon his shoulder as gently as a woman would have laid her babe's, bore his mangled burden to the surgery.

The little doctor did his utmost to save the man's life,—amputation of one limb was resorted to, but all without avail. Crushe ordered a screen to be placed across the steerage, and every few moments went to know "how the fellow got on."

But the end was not far off. Maimed by accident or design, mutilated by the surgeon's art, weak and weary, the spirit of Dunstable would have passed away without a struggle, but Crushe came down; and when he saw his enemy standing before him with no sign of pity, but rather a contemptuous expression upon his cruel face, the victim raised his head, and with his eyes gleaming with unnatural brightness, gasped out, " *You* did this, you monster ! *you* did this ; tell my mother *he* murdered me !" Then, with a terrible convulsion, the muscles of his body trembled, and the soul of the idiot passed to the other world, where, we are told, " there will be no more sorrow, nor any trouble known, no more misery or injustice, but all will be joy and peace."

There lay the victim with the marks of the cat upon his body, the effects of the sand torture still visible upon him, and with the livid wales raised by the raw-hide thongs growing more distinct each moment. There lay the idiot, foully murdered, and done to death by Crushe and his subordinates ; yet none dared tell of it, or raise their voice in denouncing his murderers.

The doctor told Clare to arrange the body for burial, and the sailor who had himself suffered so much performed the last few offices for the dead. When this was done they carried it up, placed it aft upon the quarter-deck, and spread a flag over it. There it lay until the commander was notified that the ordinary seaman who fell from aloft was ready for burial. Then Puffeigh directed Crushe to "bury the fellow," adding, " he considered it a good riddance;" and that officer, with the blood of his victim on his conscience, stood at the port, and with mock humility read from the prayer book of the Church of England the solemn service "for the burial of the dead, who die at sea." There, with the crew gathered round, the man whose bloody work it was which the flag covered, this sin-steeped wretch, with holy words upon his accursed lips, " committed his brother to the deep, *in the sure and certain hope of a joyful resurrection when the sea shall give up its dead.*"

"Hands, make sail !" A breeze had sprung up, and all that was mortal of Dunstable was soon far astern.

Crushe made the following entry in the log-book of H. M. S. Stinger, where it looked like a very ordinary accident.

" 8.50. A.M., lat. —— long. ——. Departed this life, Charles Dunstable, ordinary seaman belonging to this ship, having died from the effects of injuries received through falling from aloft."

" Departed this life," hounded to death, and forced into another, and we hope a happier, state, was this man and brother. " May he rest in peace."

Some time after this, an old woman dozing over her misery by the side of a wretched fire in a London garret, received a letter from a kind-hearted midshipman belonging to the Stinger; and when a friend read the contents to her she cried and rocked herself, saying, " She had lost her boy, her dear, good, darling Charley."

CHAPTER IX.

CAPTAIN PUFFEIGH was still on the sick list when the ship arrived at Singapore, where, upon coming to anchor, despatches were received directing the Stinger to refit within twenty-four hours, and proceed to Hong-Kong. ,

Crushe bullied and drove the crew from 4 A.M. until 11 P.M., consequently the men deserted at every possible chance, in spite of sentries, master-at-arms, and lynx-eyed midshipmen; and although strict search was made before any craft was allowed to leave the ship's side, very few of the stow-aways were discovered and recaptured in that manner. The lieutenant dared not send a boat's crew on shore, as he knew they would bolt to a man. Even his trusty bullies failed him, and were as anxious to get away as any of the others. Everything seemed what sailors term "jammed up," and the ship appeared to be in the greatest disorder, although in reality she was very rapidly being fitted for sea.

The commander was confined to his cabin, where he amused himself by swearing at Jerry, Boyldwyte, or any stray quartermasters, who were sent down to him with messages.

On deck Crushe indulged in the most fearful language towards the men, who, in their turn, vented the rage they dared not show before their officers upon the boys. As the lads scorned to be outsworn by any sailor breathing, they entirely discarded ordinary words in their conversation, and communicated with each other by oaths of the most powerful and horrible kind, that elegant and improving style of conversation being rather encouraged by the genial first luff, who often declared "that in a gale of wind a sailor who swore was worth two who prayed."

Forward, the deck was strewn with greasy, undu.ating, fizzing, bursting hoses, through which hundreds of gallons of lukewarm water were forced into the ship's tanks from the boats alongside; while amidships a gang of noisy coolies pitched coal upon the deck, or shovelled it down the shoots, to the airs of the day, popular among those coloured minstrels, their tunes being graphically described to the commander by Jerry as "strong convulsions set to music."

The stewards vied with each other in buying all the lame, blind, and aged poultry brought off to the ship by the enterprising bum-boat men. Wild-eyed, ragged, half-starved, goat-like animals were purchased as sheep and brought aboard by the confiding Bolydwyte. When they were cut adrift, these brutes cruised round the quarter-deck, and picked up a meal of swabs and green paint. There had not been much rain fall for some months in Singapore, and probably anything green was welcome to them. Crushe let them roam about unkicked; he did not like to insult the captain's sheep, and as it would be a difficult matter to poison hide and frame-work, the animals appeared rather more lively than otherwise after their feed of oakum and carpenters' stores. Patriarchal cocks, that had for years been "laid up in ordinary," and excluded from all decent shore fowl-society, limped about the ship, and looked knowingly at the guns, as much as to say, "Ah! there has been great improvement made in these articles since we were hatched." The only bird worth looking at was one called by Boyldwyte a goose, but by the assistant-surgeon derisively pronounced a Dodo. Altogether the ornithological collection on board was one calculated to puzzle a naturalist, and drive a poultry fancier out of his mind.

The engineers, who are never outdone by "those midshipmen fellows in the gun-room," came out quite strongly in purchasing live stock. One of the first acquisitions was a pig, which they directed their steward, Angus Mac'Squabble, "to have killed and dressed without delay," so roast pork figured on their bill of fare. During the afternoon this came to the ears of the doctor, who sent for the second engineer, and pointed out to him the risk he ran in partaking of such unclean food. By way of enforcing his argument, he exhibited some highly-coloured illustrations of the delightful creatures found in swine's flesh.

Donald looked at the diagrams—as he termed the pictures—asked the man of science any amount of questions, and then coolly remarked,

" Hech, mon docter ! it's ay verra weel for ye to tell me aboot you, bit as I've eaten an unca guid pund or twa o' the puir beastie, I think I'll gist fa' tult agin, and risk the rest at supper."

Upon hearing this the surgeon gave up further argument, and put away his pictures.

The well-kicked steward, who catered for the midshipmen, was sent on shore early in the morning to " secure the best the market afforded."

Much to the annoyance of the young gentlemen, he did not return until late in the evening, when, staggering into the mess-berth, and throwing a dead turkey-buzzard upon the table, he looked solemnly at the senior midshipman, and said, " Th-there's all the (hic) game I could come a (hic) cross," then wept bitterly, and requested one of the young gemmen 'ud knock his head off, as he was tired of life. Unluckily for the fellow, his only friends in the mess were absent on duty.

The indignant middies held council, and found it imperative on their part to make an example of the fellow, who, after stealing their two hundred dollars, had insulted them by bringing off a stinking turkey-buzzard, instead of a boat load of sea stock; nothing short of a cobbing would meet the requirements of the case. It never, for a moment, occurred to them that had they treated the steward better, he would not have so misbehaved himself.

No doubt the man was not sufficiently appreciative of all their favours, and the many kindnesses they *imagined* he received at their hands. It was also very wrong indeed for him to lose the money and get intoxicated ; but he was a poor weak-minded fellow, and human, although some of the young gentlemen—his masters—often tried to persuade themselves to the contrary.

Torture being rather the popular amusement on board the Stinger, not one of those present imagined the order " to give the Yahoo fits " was a cruel one ; and when the senior midshipman, who gave it, proceeded to gag the steward with a towel, willing hands were put forth to hold " the brute." After binding the bewildered victim to the mess table, the young gentlemen worked away at him, until they got tired of the amusement, and then kicked him adrift with instructions " to fetch aft some grog water," upon which he replied, " he would see them blessed if he did."

Finding the man determined to resist lawful authority, they reported him to Crushe, who directed him to be lashed up in the fore-rigging. Strange to say, after he had been suspended by the wrists for an hour he fainted, so he was cast adrift, and told " he might turn in." He never turned out again, being found dead in his hammock when the young gentlemen wanted their coffee the next morning. The doctor was sent for, and he declared the man had died in a fit some hours before ; so they entered it in the ship's log as "a death caused by intoxication and over exertion." No one ever made inquiry about the parish apprentice, and the matter was soon a thing of the past.

Captain Puffeigh declined to receive visitors, and Crushe was obliged to do the honours of the ship. During the morning one of the principal magistrates called to pay his respects to the commander, and was entertained by the first lieutenant. It was quite amusing to hear Crushe speak of the crew, and the old Anglo-Indian thought he had never met a more humane, kind-hearted officer.

"Is it not strange," he remarked, "that although we give our men good pay, excellent food, and the kindest treatment, yet no sooner do they touch shore than they abuse the confidence reposed in them, get drunk and desert?"

"They ought to be flogged, sir—yes, sir! The lash is the thing. I advocate the lash for such fellows. You're a devilish sight too humane, sir."

"My dear sir, pardon me! not the lash. We can do without that."

"True! Well, you are right; the cause of humanity forbids its use. I honour your sentiments, sir. I was hasty."

Crushe led the old fellow into a promise, "that he would use his utmost endeavour to cause the arrest of every deserter then on shore;" and, true to his word, by night all were seized and sent on board again. When the last man was caught, he shocked the worthy old magistrate by describing the Stinger as a "hell afloat," and declaring "Crushe was a cold-blooded tyrant." One of the officials who heard this statement seemed desirous of inquiring into the matter, but he was overruled by his brother magistrate, who informed him that "the noble young officer was a most gentle, kind man, and he would pledge his honour that the sailor spoke falsely." The deserters were double ironed and placed in an empty shell room, where they spent a most uncomfortable night.

Mrs. Puffeigh had a very dear cousin residing in Singapore, and her husband was intrusted with a small parcel, which she instructed him "to deliver to darling Horace with his own hands." The package was sealed; and although quite capable of such meanness, he was afraid to open it. Several times he determined to drop it overboard, but anticipating certain after consequences, let it remain in his valise, where it served as a kind of mental blister for the amiable old man. As upon arrival in port the doctor pronounced him too unwell to visit the shore, he determined to act the invalid, and decline to see the object of his jealousy, even if he came off to call upon him.

Mr. Oldcrackle was a wealthy merchant, who had not visited England for some years; and his flirtation with Mrs. Puffeigh consisted in an exchange of letters, exceedingly amusing as far as the writers were concerned, and of which the gallant captain of course knew nothing.

When the Stinger left England the lady wrote to her dear coz as follows:

"MY DARLING COUSIN,

"Blue-Beard leaves for your out-of-the-way place to-day. I have given him a small parcel, which contains my portrait. Don't be a dear old donkey over it, as you were over the last. If the seal is broken, tell me. I know B. B. is inquisitive, and will cure him if he has dared to tamper with my private affairs. When are you coming home?

"Your loving little coz,
"HELEN."

"P. S. Take care of B. B., and see he does not get into mischief. He is a very harmless old thing."

Puffeigh was in his bath when Mr. Oldcrackle's brown servant arrived on board with an invitation for the captain to take up his abode at his bungalow, during the Stinger's stay in the harbour. The gallant warrior did not condescend to fully peruse the note, but directing Jerry to tell him "he would send up the parcel that evening," he dropped the letter in the water, and vented his feelings by blessing the writer *sotto voce.*

As Thompson was leaving the cabin for the purpose of carrying out his instructions, he heard the servant's voice near the after-skylight, speaking to the quartermaster of the watch; so, to save a journey on deck, Jerry got upon the table, and putting his head up the hatch, told the flunkey "to give the captain's compliments to his master, and he would call upon him that evening;" then slipping off his perch, disappeared from the astonished gaze of the coloured individual.

"Captain sahib berry funny man," remarked the oriental to the quartermaster.

"You'd find him a sight funnier if you shipped under him," replied the old salt.

When the servant reported the matter to Oldcrackle, he told him, "Captain sahib hab handsome eye, like debil."

About six o'clock in the evening Puffeigh sent Thompson on shore with a note, "declining Mr. Oldcrackle's invitation on account of ill-health, and begging to forward a small parcel from his dear wife."

Knowing his cruise would be a very short one if he went in sailor's attire, the coxswain did not scruple to avail himself of the captain's wardrobe, from which he borrowed a shooting suit and opera hat. These he made into a parcel, and took upon the quarter-deck, telling Crushe "they were the things the captain had ordered him to carry on shore." As it was not prudent to send a ship's boat with the sailor, the lieutenant called a waterman alongside, and directed him to "take the coxswain to the nearest wharf." Jerry touched his forelock, and said, "Any orders, sir?" upon which Crushe laughed; and giving him some money, directed the impudent sailor "to bring him off a dozen fine green pines, and mind not to come without them."

The coxswain stepped into the boat, and as soon as the Stinger was lost in the gloom proceeded to strip, and re-clothe himself in Puffeigh's garments, in which, if we except the opera hat, he strongly resembled a poacher. The boatman did not trouble himself,— it was no business of his,—as the sailor gave him a liberal fare; so after having landed the man, he hauled up his boat for the night, and retired to the bosom of his family.

Jerry was not a stranger in Singapore, having visited the place in a merchant ship; therefore upon landing he at once proceeded to the house of an old acquaintance, who made a living by selling fruit and rum to the sailors on board ships in the harbour, and poisoning them with bad liquor when they called to have a good time on shore. Having ordered some pines and deposited his sailor's clothes with his friend, the coxswain stepped into a sedan, and directed the bearers to take him to Mr. Oldcrackle's. Before starting the generous hotel-keeper handed him a bottle of ale and a cigar, entreating him to "julde julde, and be back soon," as he wanted to have a good long talk with him; i. e. make him drunk and rob him.

After a pleasant ride, during which the sailor smoked his cigar, and imbibed the nauseous mixture given him as ale, the bearers turned into a well-kept compound, upon which Jerry threw the empty bottle into the shrubbery, dropped his cigar, and took out the parcel addressed to Mr. Oldcrackle, and so found himself opposite the bungalow.

Out came a servant, who salāmmed and "desired his excellency the captain sahib would alight."

The somewhat puzzled tar paid his bearers, and followed the servant into a spacious hall, whence he was conducted into a side room, where he found a suit of white linen clothes laid out.

"Will the sahib deign to put on these?" inquired the obsequious flunky.

It now dawned upon the mind of the bewildered sailor that he was being taken for his commander; and as he knew a good dinner awaited him, he accepted the situation. When he had completed his toilet he drank a glass of brandy pawnee, and ordered the servant "to lead the way to the banquet."

Upon entering the dining-room the guests rose, and Oldcrackle came forward and welcomed him in true East Indian fashion. Jerry handed the parcel to the merchant, then turning to the other gentlemen he observed, "Having done that, I beg to take my leave."

"My dear fellow, you're not going off like that. Come, sit down, I've asked these gentlemen specially to meet you; indeed, you must stay."

"'Pon my word I'm almost inclined to."

"Come, Puffeigh, sit down like a sensible fellow," added the host, saying which he led the not unwilling coxswain to the table, and seated him at his right hand; at the same time directing the butler "to fill up the captain sahib's glass with champagne.

Thompson was now formally introduced to the guests; and finding they all took him for a genuine royal naval captain, fell to at the viands, and ate as if he had not tasted food for a week.

"You don't get such a curry as that on board, do you, Puffeigh?" said Oldcrackle, who, like most old East Indians, had very little appetite left, and consequently looked upon a man who could make a good hearty meal as a lucky fellow.

"No," replied his visitor, "our cook ain't up to this; pea soup and duff is more in his line."

This observation of *the captain* set the table in a roar. "Capital!" screamed one, "Haw, haw," laughed another.

They all thought the commander was speaking facetiously of his French cook, and were immensely tickled with his peculiar phraseology.

Oldcrackle saw that the captain was a six-bottled man, and admired the quiet manner in which he tilted off a glass of champagne—no sips. No sooner was the glass filled than up it went to his lips, when in an instant it was emptied and returned to the table. We may add this raised him in the merchant's estimation, but it puzzled him why Helen described Puffeigh as "a harmless old thing;" however, he came to the conclusion that it must be a term of endearment, and thought no further about it.

European residents in those days kept up the old English custom of drinking healths, so in due time the host arose, glass in hand, and begged "to propose the health of his guest and cousin, the worthy naval hero who sat by his side. Gentlemen, I can say that this day I have found a relation, a cousin. This gentleman has hitherto been unknown to me. I propose his health, with three times three, and one,

'For he's a jolly good fellow,
And so say all of us,' &c., &c."

The genial old merchant led off the above ditty, which was roared forth by the guests in chorus, all standing bumper in hand. When the noise had subsided Jerry was called upon to make a speech in reply; so fortifying himself with a glass of burgundy, he rose, first pulling his forelock in true nautical style (which funny action raised a laugh, and delayed his speech for a few minutes), and spoke as follows:—

"Ladies and gentlemen, I beg yer pardin, I wish there was some ladies present,

bless 'em, I love all of 'em (roars of laughter). Gentlemen, you flatter me. I am a
very humble individual (cheers), and did you know all, you would do anything but
drink my health (renewed cheers). Gentlemen, I am proud to meet with such jolly good
fellows (cheers, and cries of 'Bravo, captain'), I would be proud to see you all
aboard the Stinger to-morrow, but we sail at daylight (cries of 'No, no! stay here for
a month'). Gentlemen you don't know how I *should* like to stay here for a month
(cheers). I am a plain sailor (cheers and cries of ' You're a brick, old fellow'"), I came
here little thinking I should have such a blow-out (loud laughter), and I can say I
never was better treated in my life (cheers, and cries of ' give up the sea and settle
here, old boy'). Gentlemen, here's towards you, and I wishes you many happy returns
of the day" (roars of laughter and cheers, amidst which Thompson seated himself, and
motioned the butler to bring him another bottle of wine).

A very merry time followed the delivery of this speech, no one imagining it was
said in sober earnestness. They had often heard worse from captains of the old school;
so they drank the " jolly good fellow's " health again, and swore he was a "tremendous
brick."

After a time the party adjourned to the drawing room, and the merchant took the
opportunity to have a quiet chat with his cousin's husband. Seating themselves in the
verandah, the following conversation took place :

" I like this portrait of your wife immensely."

" Do you ? I don't think it's flattering."

" Have you any family ? You see I am quite ignorant of your affairs." (Sly dog,
he received a letter from his dear cousin nearly every mail.)

" Aw, well, there's no family that I know of."

Oldcrackle lay back in his chair, and fairly roared with laughter. After a time,
however, he again questioned his guest.

" You ought to be very happy with such a girl as Helen. How can you bear to
leave her ? "

" Well, you see, we now and then have a row—she goes to balls and stays out all
night, and then I blow up a bit—but it all comes right again, and I buy her a lot of
diamonds, and that makes it up." (Jerry was a little adrift here, so he replied in what
he considered the correct style in high life.)

" Oh !" thought Oldcrackle, " that's what Helen means by B. B.; well, although he is
not bad looking, he is by far too rough a fellow for a gentle being like her ; " and then
the old merchant thought what a different match the girl would have made if she had
only waited for him.

Thompson now lighted a cigar, and puffed away like a locomotive, to avoid
answering further questions.

At this moment a very pretty half-caste girl glided into the verandah, and taking
her place behind the merchant's chair, commenced to fan him. Alayâ was a great
pet of Oldcrackle, her father having died in his service, and we will do the
merchant the justice to say, he was a kind master, both to the widow and daughter—
the latter having budded into womanhood without any one regarding her otherwise
than as a child.

" Well, Alayâ," said her master, " do you see the captain sahib ? "

The girl nodded and smiled at Jerry.

" Go and fan him, child."

Alayâ walked round, and taking position behind the coxswain's chair—so close that
he felt her balmy breath upon his forehead—proceeded to cool his face with a soft and
gentle motion of her fan, at the same time looking down upon him, from under her

long silken eyelashes, in a manner that would have seduced a much less susceptible individual than our sailor.

"Oh Lor! ain't that lovely!" ejaculated the coxswain, as leaning back he brought his eyes to bear upon those of the lovely girl, who fanned and smiled—smiled and gazed upon him, until Jerry, instead of being cool, was in a high state of fever.

Oldcrackle was all this time gazing upon Mrs. Puffeigh's portrait; and as he slightly turned his back upon *her husband* when he did this, failed to observe the little flirtation going on at the other side of the verandah, although the moon was shining brightly. At last he said, in a dreamy kind of manner,

"Ah! she's a lovely creature."

"Werry," echoed the sailor, pursing his lips, and blowing kisses towards the delighted girl by his side.

"You're very fond—of—her—are—you—not!" mused the merchant, who was half asleep, and almost dreaming of his English cousin—(she did not paint when he knew her).

"Werry." Saying which Jerry, seeing his host was now asleep, placed his arm round the supple waist of the girl, and drawing '_ towards him, gave her a sounding kiss.

Oldcrackle woke with a start, and sat bolt upright in his chair, calling out, "What's that?" Upon turning round towards his guest, he saw the latter with his hand held to his cheek, as if he had just slapped it in order to crush some insect.

"What's that, Puffeigh?"

"A thundering big mooseskeeter just settled on my—" here the sailor slapped his face again, as if he had just killed another tormentor.

Alayâ was sitting behind the coxswain's chair, apparently fast asleep.

The old merchant murmured something about "soon being used—to—those—th—things," then snoozed off again, and snored.

Alayâ woke up, or pretended to do so, and the enchanted sailor soon was supporting her in the former manner. Poor girl, she was far too deeply in love to sit upon a chair, so Jerry kindly placed his arm round her waist to prevent her falling, while she fanned and drove him out of his senses at the same time. At last he whispered to her,

"Do you love me, Alayer?"

The girl nodded several times.

"Kiss me!"

Alayâ did not know it was wrong. "The sahib was lovely, and no one had ever noticed her so before."

"Kiss me!" repeated the enamoured tar.

With a startled face, and quickly gazing round to make sure that no one was looking, the beautiful girl stooped forward, laid her soft lips upon those of the delighted sailor, and gave him a tender loving kiss; then, like a timid fawn, drew back and trembled with fear of discovery.

At this moment her master awoke.

After a yawn and stretch, Oldcrackle turned to his guest, but finding him to all appearance asleep, he ordered Alayâ to wake him.

When that difficult matter was accomplished, for the sailor pretended to be very fast asleep indeed, the merchant asked him "how he had enjoyed his forty winks."

"I thought I was in Mayhomed's Parodice," replied Jerry, winking at the now placid Alayâ; "and I would werry much rather never to have left again."

"You sly dog!" said the other, and added *sotto voce*, "A married man, and talk so."

The sailor laughed, saying, "Ah! I'm a deal slyer than you imagine."

A hearty laugh followed this speech, then, hooking his arm within that of the *eccentric captain*, the delighted Oldcrackle conducted his *relation* into the drawing-room, where they found every one engaged in playing whist.

Thompson was pretty well employed in imbibing soda and brandy until a late hour, and was far from sober, when Oldcrackle, who had also taken a great deal more wine than his usual quantity, challenged him to play a game of whist, to which the sailor solemnly agreed. Alayä was watching them from the verandah. Seeing the girl, her master bade her fetch him a pack of cards. When she brought them into the room, Jerry caught her round the waist, and "declared he would marry her, if they would only schend for a parson." Up sprang the guests, who crowded round the "captain," and enjoyed the scene immensely.

"Yesh," added the sailor, with the greatest gravity, "I'll marry her, she is the best and mosth beautifullish girl I ever met in all my bornish daish."

"Let me go, sahib! let me go!"

"No, you beaufitlish girlsh in the world. I'll keep you heresh for ever, and die with you in my armsh."

After a little persuasion he released the trembling Alayä, and was led to bed by his host, murmuring all the time that "Alayer was the only angel he had ever seen."

"The idea of his spooning over little Alayä!" observed one of the guests.

"He's mad!" said another.

"Not at all, gentlemen, he's like all naval men,—rather susceptible, and Alayä's pretty face has turned his brain; he is a thoroughly good fellow, so let us drink the health of Captain Puffeigh, and that of his officers and crew," observed Oldcrackle, who now returned.

The party then separated, and many were the comments on Captain Puffeigh's extraordinary behaviour.

Where was Alayä?—Crouched in the verandah under the captain sabib's window, and crying quietly for "love of the beautiful one, who kissed her, and made her heart beat so; the handsome sahib who took such notice of poor little Alayä. Now he was sick and might die. Oh, sad! and his slave not near him. Would she could creep between the jalousies, and crouch at the foot of his bed. She could see his eyes now, they were—"

"Alayä!" cried her mother, "where are you? Come, my child, there's no more fanning to do to-night; go to your mat."

So the little half-caste retired to rest, or rather curled herself up on her mat, and wept until morning broke.

Before sunrise Jerry was up and stirring. After a search he secured his clothes, and was quite ready to leave the bungalow, but he still crept about the passages, candle in hand. Did he want to say good-bye to his kind host? No. Was it a soda and brandy he required? No. As he explored the matted corridors, he murmured, "I wish to goodness I could find out if Alayer's about, I would so like to apologize to her for my rudeness."

However, not finding her, he left the house, managing to get away without observation.

Thompson walked down to the hotel, changed his clothes, packed Puffeigh's up with the pines in a basket, placed a bottle of grog under all, and taking a shore boat, made the best of his way on board his ship.

Crushe was walking the quarter-deck, when the coxswain reported himself as having "come aboard."

"Why were you not back last night?" demanded the angry first lieutenant.

"I was huntin' ov your pines, sir; they were werry scarce, and I came off the moment I got 'em."

"That will do, you brute; you have the best of me this time," said Crushe, with a grin.

So Jerry got the better of Puffeigh, Oldcrackle, and Crushe, and not one pang of remorse ever seemed to trouble him with regard to Aláyá. Perhaps we do not know what he felt. She certainly was too good for the fellow they married her to very shortly afterwards, and to this day Aláyá dreams of the "beautiful captain sahib," who made her heart beat so.

The Stinger sailed at 9 A.M., and Oldcrackle never saw his real cousin. When Puffeigh was on his way back to England he only remained at Singapore an hour; and not having much regard for his wife's relation, he did not call upon the hospitable merchant, so the fraud was never discovered.

The letter which Puffeigh gave Thompson was posted by the latter in the galley fire.

CHAPTER X.

When Singaporo was well out of sight Crushe mustered the deserters, kept until that time below in irons. Thirty-five men and one boy answered to their names, and were paraded before him. Among them were many of his pets, who, until their attempt at desertion, had been considered reliable fellows. These he surveyed with unmitigated disgust, as much as to say, "You brutes, after I have loaded you with favours, you turn upon me and desert, like the rest of them." The boy was no other than "the son of Bill Jordun," who, in spite of the guardianship of Old Jemmy, had contrived to reach the shore in an empty water-tank, there to be duly collared and returned to the kind care of the humane lieutenant. Crushe determined to flog the child, as an example to the other boys : consequently, when the deserters were mustered, he singled out the lad, and bullied him in a most unmerciful manner.

"What is that little beast's name?" he demanded of the ship's corporal.

"Bill Jordun, sir," replied the man, touching his cap several times, to show his profound humility.

"Come here, you little hound. How dare you desert? I'll have you flogged over the breech of a gun, you son of a dog! Do you hear me—curse you?" exclaimed the first lieutenant.

"I can hear you, sir."

"Then why don't you answer me, you vermin?"

The boy bit his lips, and swallowed the insult, determined not to irritate his tyrant by replying ; but upon glancing up, and seeing the sneering look of Crushe directed towards him, as if he were dirt beneath his feet, he fearlessly observed,

"I didn't answer, as you didn't give me a chance—'sides, I don't want to be killed, like Dunstable was. I ain't afraid of you, though, although I knows my life ain't worth much in your eyes."

"Stop! you mutinous little blackguard, you shall get your deserts. I wish to Heaven I could give you four dozen. Ship's corporal, take the little beast down below."

The boy, now driven to desperation, replied in a mocking way,

"Yes! take him below, take him down below—that's what the devil will do to you some day—see if he don't."

Shever, upon hearing this unwarrantable abuse of his superior, stepped before the ship's corporal, saying, "Allow me to handle this brute," seized the undaunted infant by the throat, and lifting him off the deck, carried the precocious child below, where Master William used anything but proper language. The boy had often heard the men indulge in profanity when being put in confinement, so he considered it the correct thing to do; and it must have been very horrible, as, upon his return to the quarter-deck, the boatswain reported that "he had to shut his ears, it was so awful."

While the lad was being attended to, Crushe stood beside the capstan, and amused himself by taunting the prisoners, and on the slightest word from them would exclaim, "Silence, you brutes! by Jupiter I'll make some of you hold your tongues with a cat, if you don't shut up your jaw. You imagined you could give me the slip, did you? bless you. I'm glad some of you have tried it on; particularly you, Mr. Byrne.

You're fond of praying, now pray for a miracle, as you'll get four dozen crosses on your back in spite of your faith. You're all right this time, and the devil himself won't save you. I'm only sorry I can't flog the lot of you."

When Crushe had exhausted his spleen upon the deserters as a body, he directed Cravan to have them brought singly before him. Some, like the boy Jordun, were mutinous; these he determined should be flogged: while others held their peace, and escaped with various light punishments, from "one month's pay or grog stopped," to "black list for a week," or "watered grog for an unlimited period."

"In the old times we could have flogged all of the brutes," he observed to Cravan, "but it would not do to try it on now; besides, the old boy would be afraid to sign the warrants."

"You might flog them into mutiny," replied Nosey. "That fellow Byrne muttered something about better strike for their rights like men, than be treated like dogs."

"Did he?" exclaimed Crushe.

"Yes, and two or three of those you have set down for flogging seemed half inclined to be mutinous; besides, did you not hear that little whelp Jordun allude to Dunstable, just as if you murdered him?"

"That was a joke. I murder him, ha, ha!" laughed Crushe.

"Ha, ha!" echoed Cravan, but the merriment on both sides was forced. They remembered how the poor idiot looked when he lay dead in the sick-bay, and the first lieutenant felt the words, "murdered him," stir even his dull conscience.

Captain Puffeigh was brought on deck during the day, and the seven men were duly reported to him. Without the slightest inquiry, upon the word of his first lieutenant, he sentenced two to receive four, and five of them three, dozen lashes upon their bare backs. Small boy Jordun was then paraded, and when he found all chance gone of obtaining justice from the gallant captain, he became very insolent; observing that the skipper would get a thundering good pounding if ever he showed his strawberry nose in Portsea, and that Crushe had better look out for hisself, when *his* father heered *he* had been flaked.

"The depravity of the little fiend! To speak to me in that audacious manner upon my own quarter-deck! He ought to be keelhauled. Don't you think so, Crushe?"

Of course the first lieutenant agreed with his commander.

Keelhauling, gentle reader, was a frightful torture invented in a brutal age, and it is still sighed after by creatures like Puffeigh and Crushe. The punishment consisted in slinging a man in a peculiar manner, by a rope suspended from one yard arm, and running under the ship up to the other yard. Thus the victim was drawn down into the water, under the ship (which sometimes lacerated him in a frightful manner), and then run up to the yard arm on the other side. If he survived this he was lucky, as generally the operation finished the victim. Puffeigh felt sorry that he could not break the insolent boy's spirit by these gentle means, as the child's tender frame was admirably adapted to bear such a punishment.

The commander shook his elegant signature upon the foot of each "warrant for punishment." He was not a learned judge, nor had he "patiently and carefully gone into each case," according to admiralty orders.

Upon the morning after Puffeigh signed the warrants the Stingers, were all turned out at daylight. It was lovely weather, and as the ship steamed up the China sea everything around her looked calm and peaceful, while on board all was terror, discontent, and unhappiness.

William Jordun, boy of the second class, was the first victim: and as small lads are tied over the breech of a gun, and flogged on a corresponding portion of their own anatomy, there was no grating to rig; consequently the preliminaries were of a primitive and unostentatious kind; the only persons to be present being Crushe, the assistant surgeon, and the ship's boys. Master William knew that in a manner the eyes of the fleet were upon him, so he determined to take his punishment like a stoic. The worthy and innocent lads who swarmed round the gun across which he was secured did all in their power to keep up his spirits, and until the dreaded first lieutenant made his appearance a casual observer might have imagined the boys were mustered to assist at some pleasing kind of ceremony.

"Don't you holler, young Bill, and I'll give you a plug of genewine Wirginny," observed one small specimen.

"I've got a tot of grog stowed away for you, chummy, if you gives plenty ov lip," consolingly remarked another.

"The way that ere lad do keep up 'is pluck, agin all odds!" mumbled Old Jemmy, who was surveying the infants much as a dog fancier might a lot of bull pups.

"You shall have that 'ere pair ov trousers wot's too small for me if you jaw all the time, and don't sing out," put in a long specimen, who was on the look-out for the appearance of Crushe and the assistant surgeon up the after-companion. At last he cried, "Here's the sangvenary tyruut; hold yer jaw, all ov yer."

As the boy was lashed to the foremost starboard gun, the lieutenant and doctor had to walk almost the vessel's length; so by the time they reached the group the lads were as quiet as mice, and looking at the prisoner in a virtuously superior manner.

"All the boys here, ship's corporal?"

"Yes, sir."

Upon this Crushe read the warrant, and without more ceremony ordered the boatswain's mate to "do his duty."

When the corporal removed the frock which hitherto had covered the boy's person, the lad blushed, and shut his eyes for a moment, his position being a most ignominious one. Price advanced cat in hand, and was about to administer the first cut; but seeing the boy's fair skin with its faint blue veins, he threw down the cat, and folding his arms, looked at his superiors like one bewildered.

The first lieutenant stared at the boatswain's mate for a moment, then demanded in a severe tone if he had been drinking; adding, if he did not wish to be disrated, he had better go on with the flogging, and mind he did his duty effectually.

Price looked at Crushe, then at the boy, and at length murmured "Can't do it, sir —darn me if I can—I'd rather be flogged myself," saying which he picked up the cat, and threw it overboard.

"Go aft and stand between two guns, you miserable old fool; I'll disrate you for that, you drivelling idiot," bellowed the first lieutenant.

"Boatswain, do your duty."

"Yes, boatswain, do your duty," mimicked the impudent little victim; "do your duty, it's a *pleasure* to you, ain't it?"

Mr. Shever flogged boy Jordun in a highly expert and savage manner, but the lad being wonderfully tough-skinned, he merely succeeded in inducing him to use some very powerful language for such a small child. Not a groan or tear, but with true nautical freedom, did he bless Crushe and the rest of his enemies, asserting as the tails curled round his defenceless body that he should "live to see the lot of 'em swing for murder afore he died, so help his never, he would."

When a man or boy is actually undergoing punishment he may give vent to his feelings in any way he pleases—say his prayers, or worse—generally worse, we are sorry to state; and Master William Jordun, boy of the second class, feeling he was being looked upon as a sort of martyr by his fellows, endured the pain, and slanged his superiors like a grown up sailor. It was a fitting prologue to the performance which followed.

Having received his two dozen lashes, he was cast off considerably worse in body and mind, and sent aft to remain in the sentry's charge until sunset. We know he was a foul-mouthed little monkey, but what made him so? The example of his superiors; and it is not surprising he was bad, considering the beautiful and edifying language he constantly heard on the part of Crushe, Shever, and others.

By the time the foregoing was completed Puffeigh had made his appearance with the officers and engineers upon the quarter-deck, where the grating was already rigged for punishment. The same performance was gone through as upon the occasion of Clare's sentence being carried out, with this exception, the boys mingled with the men, and as the first victim was "seized up," six others, among whom was Byrne, were brought forward "to be improved" until their turns came. Three of them bore their punishment without a word, and were sent below to have their backs dressed by the surgeon. One man cried and roared like a child under chastisement. Another fainted, and was flogged during the time he was insensible (some of the crew observed that *he* took it "like a lamb"), while the other two victims, driven almost out of their senses, cursed and swore in a fearful manner, Byrne vowing he would murder Puffeigh, Crushe, or Shever. "I'll have revenge on one of you devils," he yelled, as the last stroke of the lashes scored his back like so many knives.

"Iron him; see he doesn't do any damage," quavered Puffeigh, when he saw they were casting the man off. "Put him below under a sentry's charge until we arrive at Hong-Kong. I'll try you by court-martial for that threat, you brute."

The man showed fight, breaking from his keepers, and endeavouring to get at Puffeigh, who thereupon beat a retreat to his cabin, saying he was tired. After a desperate struggle the sailor was secured, gagged, double-ironed, and placed below under charge of a sentry, who was instructed to "keep his eye on him, and not to allow any one to speak to him." For three days the prisoner remained perfectly quiet; upon the fourth, thinking the threats he had made were mere empty talk, he was released by order of the commander, Crushe having requested the same might be done, as he wanted the man's services.

It is customary when a ship is in the Chinese sea to keep a number of loaded arms in a rack under the charge of a sentry, as in case of falling in with a pirate they may be required at a moment's notice. Byrne had been freed from confinement, and was standing by the arm rack, waiting until the ship's corporal had replaced his irons below, after which the prisoner was to be taken before the first lieutenant, and officially dismissed to duty. The sentry had gone on deck to report the time, and no one was in the steerage. At this juncture Crushe called down the hatchway directing (as he thought) the ship's corporal to "make haste and bring up the prisoner." At the sound of the hated officer's voice, Byrne darted to the arm rack, seized a loaded musket, rushed up the main hatchway, and seeing an officer standing near, fired. The ball entered the back of his victim, who immediately fell upon the quarter-deck as if shot dead. The assassin threw down his weapon and gave himself up to the sergeant of marines, who was the nearest man to him at the time, exclaiming as he did so, "There! I hope the brute is dead, then he'll never kill any more sailors."

Twenty men sprang forward to raise the body from the deck, all horror-stricken at the dreadful tragedy which had been enacted before them. Few knew who it was that had been shot; and as nearly all had imagined it to be Crushe, when they found that the inanimate body was that of Lieutenant Ford, their excitement knew no bounds. It was with difficulty the men could be kept from lynching the prisoner, although they knew full well that he had killed the good young officer by mistake, instead of shooting one of their tyrants.

When the assassin found who it was he had fired at, he became almost insane, crying out to his guards to shoot him, and endeavouring to beat out his brains upon the deck.

" O God!" he shrieked, " I've killed the best officer in the fleet. I'd have died for him; it cannot be so, you lie, you soger, and do it to frighten me. It was Crushe, the devil, that I killed, not Lieutenant Ford. Shipmate, say it wasn't *him* now, for Heaven's sake."

" Sentry," roared the first lieutenant, "gag that brute !"

The surgeon was called, and by his direction the body was taken below and laid upon a cot in the sick-bay, Tom Clare, the gentlest of nurses, being directed to " attend to the instructions of the surgeon, and remain with the lieutenant until further orders." After a time Ford opened his eyes and recognized those about him. Having made a superficial examination of his wound, the doctor placed him in an easy position, directing Clare not to let him excite himself by talking, and absolutely forbidding Tom to allow any one to see him; then walking aft to the captain's cabin he reported his opinion to Puffeigh, viz.: that Lieutenant Ford was severely wounded, and he did not think it possible he could survive more than a few hours. The captain heard the report without observation, and when the surgeon had retired he sent for Crushe, telling him what the doctor had said. As he was speaking Clare entered the cabin, and hurriedly informed them that Lieutenant Ford wished to see them at once, and the doctor said they'd better come.

Puffeigh turned pale, and muttered something about not being well himself; but finding the first lieutenant did not help him out, he mustered courage enough to face the dying man, taking Crushe with him, in order that the latter might not escape the scene.

Ford had asked how he was hurt, and if he could survive. These questions had been replied to by the doctor, who informed him that he had been accidentally shot by one of the men, and that probably he might not live long. The wounded officer heard this announcement without a shudder, and presently inquired, " Who was it that shot me?" As the surgeon did not reply, he turned his brilliant eyes full upon the face of Clare, who being thus mutely appealed to, observed,

" Byrne, sir, but he didn't know it was you."

" I forgive him, with all my heart," said Ford. " Send for Captain Puffeigh."

Knowing the poor fellow had but a short time to live, the good surgeon sent Tom Clare to the commander, as we have just related.

Upon the captain's entering the sick-bay, Ford motioned Clare to give him some water. Seeing this, the doctor administered a stimulant, as he knew the wounded officer very much desired to make a communication before he died.

" Send that sailor away," whispered Puffeigh.

" He cannot leave his charge," quietly observed the surgeon, who now lifted up his finger, to enjoin silence.

Looking towards the captain, Ford spoke as follows :—" Captain Puffeigh—the poor fellow—who did this—deserves—your pity. I forgive—him—and Crushe—knowing it was you he in—tended—to kill, I shall be happy to die—for YOU—if I can—be assured you will—cease—to tyrannize—over—the crew—Don't flog—any—more. Promise me —to save Byrne's—life."

" I'll do all I can to save him, Ford—but you are not dying—" quavered Puffeigh.

Ford tried to stretch forth his hand, to grasp that of his senior, but his strength failed him, and with a faint smile he exclaimed, "God bless—you—for the prom—" but ,was prevented finishing the sentence by the blood rising in his throat.

Puffeigh was so frightened that he had to be supported by Crushe, as he left the dying officer's presence. When they arrived aft the latter coolly observed,

"I'm sorry for Ford—but it was a very narrow escape for either of us."

"Yes," replied the captain, "it was, no doubt, an act of Providence that we escaped.

The brutal officers actually imagined their Creator had specially interfered to save one of their miserable lives; and they were not the first tyrants who have flattered themselves in that manner.

Lieutenant Ford never rallied sufficiently to give directions as to the disposal of his affairs, but lay calmly and patiently, as if waiting for the messenger of death. Once he murmured "Florence." He evidently was conscious that he was dying, yet death seemed to have no terror for him. The doctor and Clare prayed for the poor fellow, each according to his faith, and the Christian's lips moved in response to theirs. Whatever his belief might have been, he certainly was a good man, and far above the narrow prejudices of sect. He lay there—calm and peaceful—with a rapturous, heavenly expression of countenance, as if, though still lingering by its earthly form, his spirit was fore-tasting the joys of a better world. About noon he breathed his last; and so quietly did the soul pass away, that when the sorrowing midshipmen, who were silently grouped round the entrance to the sick-bay, were informed that the happy face was that of a dead man, they could not believe it. One by one they came in and gazed upon their dead friend, some finding it hardly possible to restrain their grief.

About sunset the body of Lieutenant Ford was committed to the deep—cast overboard into the sea—to be devoured by fishes, or float about until dispersed by the water —far away from friends, and the gentle being who loved him so dearly, and to whom he had been so tenderly attached.

Puffeigh buried the body with all the puny pomp of an officer's funeral at sea. It mattered little to the noble spirit whether a few meaningless ceremonies were performed or omitted; "his soul was gone aloft," and could not be recalled or affected by the commander's "service."

The sailors were all deeply grieved at the sudden death. Ford had always treated them in a kind and proper manner, and his untimely end was probably as sincerely lamented forward as aft. No man felt more sorrow than his assassin. The remembrance of his own sufferings seemed to have been entirely forgotten by him, so absorbed was he in the recollection of the dreadful crime he had committed. Crushe heaped every kind of insult and torture he could devise upon the man, who bore all with the resignation of a martyr.

Upon one occasion the first lieutenant cursed the prisoner to his face, and observed, "Ah! you brute, you thought to murder me, did you?"

Upon hearing this the man quietly replied,

"Forgive me, sir—I am sorry for it."

"Forgive you, you hound! Yes—I'll forgive you when you're swinging from the yard-arm."

Instead of checking Crushe in his shameful tyranny, the death of his brother officer seemed to make him perfectly reckless, he doubtless thinking there was now no appeal or chance of hearing for his victims. He never for a moment appeared to remember that Ford's words about "dying for him" were true, and indeed, one day, when discussing the good officer's death, he remarked to Cravan,

"Possibly I should have done the magnanimous had I been in poor Ford's place. He could afford to say, 'Bless you, shipmates,' as he knew very well that his anchor was tripped."

Nosey did not make any reply to this brutal speech, as the mere recollection of the affair made him shudder.

When the Stinger arrived at Hong-Kong, Byrne was sent on board the flagship, and after a few days had elapsed, a court-martial was called upon his case. A well-known lawyer offered gratuitously to assist the prisoner, but his services were respectfully declined.

Crushe, the ship's corporal, and sergeant of marines, were the principal witnesses against the man ; some petty officers were also examined, but not a word was said that would lead any member of the court to imagine the first lieutenant was anything but a gentle, humane officer.

The man had no defence, nor would he throw himself upon the mercy of the court, all he wanted being to die.

After mature deliberation, the court found the prisoner "Guilty," without the usual recommendation to mercy, and the president passed sentence of death in the ordinary form ; adding that the prisoner was to be hanged from the yard-arm, and that the sentence was to be carried out on board the Stinger.

Byrne received the sentence with a calmness which was almost touching ; and after bowing to the president was handcuffed, and taken back to his cell.

The chaplain visited the doomed man, but the latter declined his services, observing that he did not require government religion, as his own faith was sufficient to carry him through.

One morning at sunrise the Stinger steamed out of Hong-Kong harbour, with several boats towing alongside. These had brought "black-list men " from various ships in the fleet, who were detailed to assist at the execution of Byrne. Forward on the hammock netting, abreast of the fore hatchway, and over a gun port, a grating was rigged platform wise ; to this the fatal noose was secured by a rope yarn, the fall being led across the deck to the starboard side, so that the black-list men could not see the object which they were to run aloft.

When the crew were mustered and duly placed in position, the prisoner was brought up from below, guarded on either side by sentries. As he ascended the fore hatchway his eyes fell upon the grating, but he preserved his coolness, and in fact gave a sigh of relief at beholding it. When he had removed his jumper, the commander gave the order to pinion him. This being done, as far as the arms were concerned, Puffeigh read the warrant for execution, then turning to the man, observed,

"Prisoner, if you wish to say a few words to your shipmates you can do so, but be brief and temperate in your language."

Facing round towards his shipmates, Byrne spoke as follows :—"Messmates and shipmates, I didn't mean to kill Lieutenant Ford, and I willingly die for my crime ; but if any of you ever become free men again, tell the world how sailors are treated. Good-bye; God bless and deliver you from all your slavery."

The commander bit his lips and looked round at the men, who, upon hearing these bold words, uttered a murmur of pity.

"Silence !" he roared. "Boatswain, do your duty."

Shever and his mates had stationed the black-list men at the fall, on the other side of the deck · and upon receiving these instructions he helped the prisoner to mount the platform. When he had taken his stand upon the horizontal grating, the boatswain and his assistants secured his lower limbs. As they were doing this, Byrne evidently prayed, as his lips moved, and every now and then he reverently bowed his head. Then upon a signal from the captain, Shever fitted the cap, and having adjusted the fatal noose, slipped off the grating, and stood beside Puffeigh.

The captain nodded assent. "Hoist away!" piped the boatswain, and the same was repeated by his mates. The gunner's-mate fired the gun which protruded from the port under the platform where the wretched man was standing, and Byrne was run aloft in the smoke. The rope was so adjusted, that upon the body nearly reaching the yard-arm a seizing parted, and the man fell about three feet below the yard, the drop breaking his neck most effectually.

The black-list men hurried over the ship's side into their boats, and the Stinger steamed slowly out of the harbour with the body of the late able seaman swinging from the yard-arm. After steaming for an hour in the direction of Cap-sing-moon Passage, the boatswain was directed to cut the body adrift. Shever went aloft, and out upon the yard-arm like one about to perform a noble action. Upon arriving at the end of the yard he drew forth a knife, and leaning over severed the rope by which Byrne was suspended, upon which the body shot down like a plummet, and disappeared beneath the water. Shever peered down after it, shading his eyes with his hands, to see if it rose again.; but beyond a few bubbles over the spot, there was nothing to be seen, the body possibly being seized by sharks.

"He's gone, and be hanged to him!" said the boatswain. Upon which he looked down upon the up-turned faces of the crew and grinned like a baboon, then reclosed his knife, placed it in his pocket, and descended to the quarter-deck, where he reported the business to Crushe.

"I think we did that werry scientific," observed the brute to his superior.

"Very well indeed, Mr. Shever," sneered the first lieutenant. "When they want a hangman on shore, you'd better volunteer for the appointment."

The boatswain smiled and saluted, as if a great compliment had been paid him. After which he went below—drank freely, and was finally put to bed for sunstroke, brute as he was, the morning's work being too much for his nerves.

Report says that the ghost of Byrne duly haunted the ship, and from time to time appeared to sundry sailors and small boys, whom it frightened out of their wits, but it never seemed to trouble the captain, or any of its former persecutors, possibly thinking it had enough of those worthies' attention when in the flesh, without troubling itself about them when in the spirit. We leave this mythical point to be settled by spiritualists.

CHAPTER XL.

AFTER the body of Byrne had been disposed of, the Stinger returned to Hong-Kong, where the men, one watch at a time, were permitted to visit the shore. Many of them deserted, and succeeded in making good their escape in American ships, which left the harbour about that time; others joined piratical Chinese vessels, and became notorious for their cruelty towards their captives; while the less cautious sailors, getting intoxicated and overstaying their leave of absence, were re-captured by the ship's corporal and sergeant of marines, who were paid the usual blood money for their activity in securing the deserters. When the ship was thoroughly refitted, and the vacancies in her crew had been filled by drafts from other vessels, Puffeigh was directed to proceed to sea in search of pirates; the admiral imagining that, if he sent the Stingers away for a time upon active service, their commander would be enabled to get them into something like discipline, they having been represented to him as "a lot of worthless wretches, who could only be kept in order by the cat-o'-nine tails."

During their cruise Crushe succeeded in bringing several of the new men to the gratings, and his general language and conduct towards the crew were as bad as ever.

After having searched the coast for over six months, during which time they captured and destroyed a great number of junks, lorchas, and other piratical craft, the Stinger returned to Hong-Kong, where her officers and crew received their letters and newspapers, which had accumulated at the Post-Office during their absence, the delivery to the crew taking place as follows. The ship's corporal and Sergeant Spine having obtained the sack of mails, proceeded forward with it, and upon reaching the forecastle shot the contents into a dry wash deck tub; then the boatswain piped, "Hands, lay forward for your letters." Every one was on the alert, and a dozen men who could read clustered round the tub, and assisted in the pleasing task of distributing the epistles.

"Bill Bowker!"

"Gone ashore. I'm his chum—here, chuck it over."

"Jerry Thompson!—one, two, three letters."

"Heave 'em here," cried the wag, who had brought up a bucket in which to receive his correspondence.

"Charles Smith!"

"Vich Chawles is it?" demanded a stumpy individual; is it I or Conkey Smith?"

"Tommy Sims!"

"Runned away," observed one of the boys.

"Charles Dunstable—oh! he's dead."

"Harry Tomlin!"

"Bolted at Singapore."

"Tom Clare! three letters for you, old man."

"Jerry Thompson Jerry Thompson! here you are, a regular bunch of 'em. All the girls in Portsmouth must av bin awriting you, Jerry."

"Werry possible," coolly retorted the coxswain. "It's more than they'd do to you, old fetch-and-carry."

"Mister Robert Brown! Here Bobby, here's a letter from one of them ere lords as you is related to."

"Chuck it over ere, and hold yer thundering jaw," growled the gentleman alluded to.

When the tub was cleared of its contents, a sale of letters commenced, i. e. those who had none purchased one or two at second hand from their more fortunate shipmates.

"Now, then," shouted a freckled-face Pat, "here's a chance for yez, my boys,—a letthur from me Cousin Eiley—full av love and tinderness. Who sez a pint ov grog for this? wid two songs, one called 'Teddy Regan,' and the other 'Nora O'Shane,' put into the bargain. The letthur is worth all the grog, as it's chockfull of family matters. Come, me boys! who sez a pint?" Upon this a big, stupid-looking topman called out in a half-ashamed manner,—"Heave it over here, Tim, I'll give ye a pint for it next time I'm cook." Having received it, the man walked below to his mess, where he indulged in the luxury of spelling over the letter, which we will give, with his comments upon the same.

"*Limerick* (I wish I was there).

"MY DARLIN TIM (that's affectionate, anyhow),

"Ye will be sorry to learn that your aunt O'Brien is dead, an' has bin waked and berried, rest her sowld." (She's a good religious girl, anyhow.) "Peter McMahon swears he'll kill ye the fust time he sets eyes on ye, as yer brother Michael split the skull of his father's uncle during the wake." (Never mind, Tim; I'll help you.) "Tim achushla machree, send us yer half pay, for the love of Mary—we're nigh starved at times, an' it's hard work for a poor girl to keep straight, and she so poor and so many temptations round her." (Poor girl, I'll send her my half pay if he don't. Tim ain't half thoughtful for her.) "Mary Connor is married, and her husband gone to sea with a black eye she gave him" (I suppose he deserved it, anyhow); "an' Kathleen Shea wants to know if ye mean to keep yer word with her." (If he don't I will.)

"Yer mother sends her love, and with the same from yer loving

"EILEY ROONEY."

(Bless her dear heart, how life-like she do write; that's what I call a nateral sort of letter.)

At the first quiet opportunity, the sailor questioned Tim as to what his Cousin Eily was like, and the answer he obtained was a quencher to his passion. "She's an ould devil, as keeps a fruit stall, an' is as ugly as the skipper, an' that's saying no little, me boy. But if ye wants to fall in love wid an illigant slip ov a colleen, I'll intrejuce yez to me Cousin Nora for a trifle ov grog." However, once bit twice shy, and the now enlightened sailor concluded to leave Tim's relations alone.

Thompson received about twenty-five letters in all, including one in the German language from Miss Pferdscreptern, which having opened, turned over, and held in every conceivable position, he reluctantly sold to a foretopman, who, not being able to read, did not care whether it was in German or Hebrew. After picking out Mary Ann's epistles, Jerry sold the balance of his correspondence unopened, and realized thereby a very handsome profit.

Clare had three short notes from Polly, that is, they were written for her by a friend, as she was unable to write even her own signature, although she contrived to spell out the letters Tom sent her, he always writing in a very rouud hand for her accommodation. Clare found that his wife had made him a father, and that the mother and child were doing well.

"God bless the dear creatur and her babby," he murmured, and a big tear stole down his cheek and dropped upon the paper.

As the correspondence was written by a stranger, he did not expect there would be many tender passages, but he found the letters cold and formal, and for the moment cursed his fate, and imagined how warmly she would greet him with her own lips could he but see her then. However, he knew she was naturally shy; and comforting himself with the reflection that they would meet when his time was up, he put the letters in his tobacco box, and went in search of Jerry Thompson, to whom he imparted the news.

"Well, I'm werry glad to think it's a boy, but wouldn't you have liked a gal better, Tom ? "

"I like either a gal or a boy ; it's all the same to me."

"Well ! you're a father and I ain't, but if I was in your shoes I'd prefer a gal. I always likes the gals afore any other sex. By-the-by, I have heered from my Mary Ann."

"Have you ? What does she say ? "

"Well, first of all she says her missis av bin werry dicky and likely to croak, and the sawboneses sent them off to Nice for the air, and she's as hearty as a brick, and a learnin' French like one o'clock. But I hope she won't learn it on the same principle as I did German."

Clare who was very little interested in his friend's recital, inquired rather vaguely, "Have you ever learned German ?"

"Yes—well—I—excuse me ; there's the old man a hollerin' for me. Good-bye, Tom." Saying which the coxswain got up and walked briskly aft, as if in obedience to the captain's summons.

The ship had been in harbour about a week and everything was adrift, as is usually the case during refitting, when a signal was made from the flag-ship for "the Stinger to proceed to sea." A number of the men had just mustered upon the quarter-deck previous to going on shore, and were of course dismissed to duty again, and the signal made for all boats to come off at once. Knowing the ship was short-handed, some of the crew being absent on leave, the admiral sent about forty picked seamen and twenty marines on board, and in a few hours everything was ready for sea, upon which they slipped anchor, and made the best of their way through the Cap-sing-moon Passage.

Crushe adopted quite a conciliatory manner when speaking to the supernumeraries, knowing it would not do to bully them as he did his own men, consequently the former thought "the Stingers were a dissatisfied lot, who, without a cause, gave their first lieutenant a bad name."

By daylight they arrived off the bay to which they had been guided by Hoo-kee, their pilot, who, clad in a cast-off suit of Puffeigh's, walked the bridge in a dignified manner ; never leaving his elevated position until the first shot was fired, upon which he darted below, and hid himself in a sand-tank until the engagement was over.

Hoo-kee told Puffeigh that they were off the entrance of a bay which contained a regular fleet of piratical junks, commanded by one Sah-wang ; and he strongly urged him to send away his boats and attack the junks under cover of the fog, it being impossible to take the ship in during the time it continued. Upon this Lieutenant Wilton, who had been appointed to the vacancy caused by Ford's death, informed the commander that he " knew every inch of the bay, having surveyed it about a year ago." After a short consultation, and being urged strongly by the master, who was also an old China ranger, Puffeigh reluctantly consented, and with the leads going in both chains, the Stinger slowly steamed into the bay, in spite of the fog, which was, to use a nautical expression, as thick as pea-soup.

The master went out upon the jibboom and watched for the slightest lift in the fog, while the captain and Lieutenant Wilton piloted the ship from the bridge.

"Starboard!" cried Wilton. "Starboard!" bawled Puffeigh. "Junk ahead! port your helm!" roared the master from forward.

Round went the wheel, and the Stinger shot past a huge junk, which loomed through the fog like a line-of-battle ship.

"Steady! Let go the anchor!" commanded the master, who thereupon came aft and reported to the captain that during a break in the fog he had seen several junks ahead, and it was advisable to heave short, and prepare for warm work, as soon as it cleared.

Puffeigh fussed about like an old woman, first directing the guns to be loaded with shot, then countermanding the order, and giving instructions to load with shell; and finally, by the advice of the master, who almost took charge of the ship, he ordered them to load with grape and canister. The gunner and his mates prayed for him.

Crushe worried round and blustered like the Pistol that he was, now and then ordering some youngster out of what the lad considered a snug place, swearing he'd have no skulking cowards in his ship, and all the time wishing himself somewhere else.

The man who talks big before an engagement is generally very quiet during the fight, and it proved so in this instance. Puffeigh was not afraid; but being thoroughly incompetent to take his ship into action, had to rely upon the master and Lieutenant Wilton.

The ship had been cleared for action before they arrived off the bay, so there was very little to do after they had anchored, but to man the capstan, ready to weigh, the moment they could descry the pirates.

Wilton requested permission to go ahead of the ship and explore the bay, but thinking the risk too great, the commander would not allow him to do so. The men were standing round their guns, which were all fully manned—here and there along the deck being stationed powder-monkeys — i. e. boys detailed to pass the leathern cases containing charges of gunpowder, who, seated on their cartridge boxes, looked into the fog as knowingly as the oldest salts in the ship. Some of the men munched biscuit, which was surreptitiously obtained from below by the more daring boys, who risked punishment to curry favor with the seamen; and all of them imbibed pretty freely of the usual fighting drink—oatmeal and water—tubs of that Scottish beverage being placed in different parts of the upper deck.

Crushe, Puffeigh, and Mr. Beauman, the master, were consulting upon the bridge, when suddenly the fog lifted, upon which the skipper became very much excited, and directed the port bow-gun to be fired, "to wake 'em up, you know."

"For Heaven's sake, don't do that!" urged the master; " we will wake them up in a moment; they mustn't see us just yet."

Upon this the captain held his peace, and left the manœuvring to be done by abler persons, contenting himself by looking very imposing, and whenever he could catch a sentence bellowing it through his speaking-trumpet to the officer for whom it was intended. The men laughed at him behind his back, as all of them could see he was utterly adrift.

Away steamed the Stinger straight for the nearest craft, which proved to be a lorcha, and by no means a despicable enemy. She was evidently well manned and armed, and quite prepared for the man-of-war. The rest of the pirates were further up the bay, some of them being but partly visible, as the fog still lingered there; but they were all now awake, and firing crackers to their gods, or beating gongs in a very energetic and ferocious manner.

The big lorcha suddenly swung round, and sent a hail of shot across the Stinger's decks. No one was hurt by this discharge, the crew all being down behind their guns, which formed, as it were, so many breastworks for them; but the ship was twice hulled, once badly on the port bow near the water line. The Stinger quickly put her helm a-port, as the lorcha was again endeavouring to swing into position, so as to give her another broadside. They were now within a cable's length of the pirate; but, in spite of her rapid firing, they steamed right ahead. Wilton and Mr. Beauman were on the bridge with the captain, who, when he saw they intended to run into the lorcha, and carry her by boarding, bristled up, and seizing his speaking-trumpet bellowed forth,

"Hands, repel boarders on both bows!"

Up sprang the men, who obedient to orders rushed forward and swarmed upon the forecastle. Crash came another broadside from the pirate, killing two men and wounding several others. One moment more, and the steam-ship ran into the lorcha. Smash went the bulwarks of the latter, and with a hearty cheer the sailors swarmed over the Stinger's bows, upon seeing which many of the pirates leapt overboard. Thompson was delighted, and had several combats with his enemies, who were rapidly disarmed and kicked over-board by the good-natured fellow. As he was one of the first men below, he had the honour of killing the pirate-captain, Seh-wang. On entering the stateroom, Jerry found himself confronted by that huge Chinaman who was fencing at him with two swords, uttering most unearthly sounds as he did so. The sailor quietly cut down his guard, and then told him to get out of the port, upon which Seh-wang fumbled in his dress for a moment, then drawing forth a revolver, shut both eyes and pulled the trigger. Snick went the cap, but no other report followed. Upon this Jerry ran him through the body, and having looted him, i. e., taken everything valuable, he coolly secured his plunder and went on deck, reaching it just in time to jump on board the Stinger, which was now becoming a mark for the pirates at the upper end of the bay. When he got to the quarter-deck he informed Puffeigh that he had killed the Chinese captain, but as the lorcha was fired by the Stingers, the fact of his killing Seh-wang was never proved, although the Chinese declared he perished with the ship, and Thompson lost special mention for bravery; but he consoled himself with his loot, and considered the account balanced. Had the fact of his having searched the body been known, Puffeigh would have compelled him to disgorge his plunder, his maxim being that all such articles belonged to himself.

The Stinger now made the best of her way up the bay; as she did so, keeping up a galling fire from her bow guns. Having arrived nearly within short range of the pirates' fire, Puffeigh ordered the anchor to be let go, and when the ship swung to the tide, she being broadside on, poured a telling discharge into the junks, two or three of which were shortly afterwards discovered to be on fire. The pirates replied in a most determined manner, and a severe engagement ensued, during which the ship was badly hulled and several men killed or wounded. Old Price, who was acting as captain of the starboard bow gun, was cut in two by a chain shot. Boy Jordan, who seemed to think the engagment was a sort of theatrical spectacle, and who ran about as unconcernedly as possible, received a ball in his left arm — upon which he went below to the doctor, and after observing that he thought he was wounded, the plucky child fell upon the dead body of a man stretched out upon the floor, and fainted away from loss of blood.

Clare quietly did his duty, but the lash had taken all enthusiasm out of him; towards the end of the action he was hit on the forehead, but he merely bound his neck-handkerchief round the wound, and kept at his gun.

The Chinese fired all sorts of missiles—bar, chain, and round shot—musket balls, and copper cash—some going far beyond the Stinger, and others falling a long way short. Finding there was little chance of beating off the man-of-war, the pirates set fire to their ships and abandoned them. Upon seeing this Puffeigh ordered his men to cease firing; and having cleared the decks and weighed anchor, the Stinger steamed towards the town, passing, as she did so, the line of piratical vessels, many of which were burning most furiously.

Old Jemmy was standing upon the carriage of his gun, looking over the side, and passing comments upon the junks as the ship steamed slowly passed them, when a gun on board one of them was discharged by the heat, and the ball striking the old man, stretched him senseless upon the deck. Several men sprang forward to assist him, and he was carried below and handed over to the surgeon.

The Stingers counted thirty-five craft in all; and as these were moored in a line so as to mask the town, they were not aware, until they rounded the last junk, of the little amusement which was going on between the townspeople and the pirates who had taken to the water. It seems that the former, finding matters were going against the free-booters, had turned out *en masse*, and prevented their landing, and when the man-of-war hove in sight, round the stern of the last lorcha, they were engaged in the lively business of knocking the pirates over the heads with bamboos, clubs, or stones. Upon seeing their British allies, they boldly put off in their sampans, and slaughtered their former tyrants most perseveringly.

"Where's the pilot? Where's Hoo-kee?" demanded Puffeigh.

After a search, the too-brave Chinaman was found, and being interrogated by the skipper, sagely informed him that, "Peacee man lib here catchee pilong and gib he fum-fum," this information being a not very lucid explanation of the state of affairs going on alongside the ship, which any child could understand, without its being thus oracularly described by the Chinaman.

Taking the advice of his officers, Puffeigh left the pirates to be dealt with by the townspeople, and the Stingers were piped to breakfast. All were quite ready for the food which they brought on deck and devoured as they viewed the slaughter of the pirates, the same being a novel zest for their meal.

Puffeigh took this opportunity to reconnoitre the bay, and found it was surrounded by high hills, with its entrance masked by rocks, which rendered it a most desirable resort for pirates, as without previous intimation any ship might pass up and down the coast a hundred times and not suspect the existence of an inlet in that place. He now perceived the burnt hull of an English merchant-ship lying near the town; and as he had been sent to avenge the outrage of this very seizure, he determined, when his men were refreshed, to land and endeavour to ascertain the fate of the crew of the burnt vessel.

"Boat alongside, sir," sang out the sentry on the bridge.

"What is she?"

"Chinese, sir."

"Send Hoo-kee here."

Upon this the pilot walked to the gangway and saluted the Celestials, who climbed over the side, speaking of course in his own vernacular.

"Hi! you dogs. I'm pilot here. If you don't cumshaw me (i. e. fee me), I'll get these red-haired devils to burn your town about your ears."

"Most illustrious sir!" exclaimed the foremost moon-face, "we are very poor, but" (puffing through want of breath) "we will pay you two hundred dollars to assist us, if you'll come on shore and fetch it."

"What does the fellow say?" demanded Puffeigh.

"He say, some peecee pilong come catchee he long tim, and he no savee how many peecee Eingleesh man him kill."

"Bring them aft, here."

The self-appointed deputation of towns-folks walked aft, and falling upon their knees, kow-tow'd (i. e. knocked their foreheads upon the deck), and then awaited the great Fanqui's pleasure.

"Tell them to get up."

"Get up, you fools; this old rice-bag doesn't know what kow-tow is."

"We'd rather not, my lord. Tell the great man we can't *lie easily* when we look at his terrible hairy face."

"What do they say, Hoo-kee?"

"Why, him say you too muchee lansome, and he fraid speekee you sposc him lookee you in him face."

"Hum!" The flattery tickled the vain old fellow, who thereupon allowed the deputation to remain upon their knees, and by the assistance of the pilot learnt, that Seh-wang left one night, and that on the following morning they saw a foreign-built vessel anchored in the bay. Some of the pirates who landed to visit their wives told them that they had killed all the Fanquis but one woman, whom they had landed and removed from the town to a joss-house, which they pointed out upon one of the neighbouring hills, where it was presumed she would now be found.

Upon hearing this, it was determined to land the sailors and marines, and march to the joss-house, which the towns-people stated was about seventy le (ten miles) from the town.

"Mr. Shever, pipe man and arm boats."

In a few moments the ship's boats were in the water and the crews in their places, the pinnace with its brass howitzer, and first and second cutters with their rocket apparatus, being, on account of their armament, the last boats ready. Much to his chagrin, Mr. Beauman, was left behind in charge of the ship, the whole of the executive officers being detailed for shore duty. About twelve o'clock Puffeigh stepped into his gig, and the flotilla proceeded towards the shore, the master having instructions if he saw a white flag flying in the gig, to shell the town, ten men and boys being left on board to carry out this duty.

Upon reaching the shore a number of the townsfolks came down, and welcomed the party, whereupon Puffeigh assumed a grand air, and told the "elders" that they need not be alarmed, as he would not hurt them, this being translated to them by Hoo-kee, as follows:—

"You crouching dogs, this vermilion-faced devil says if you don't hand over the dollars upon our return from the joss-house, he'll blow you into the water."

"Tell them I want two guides, and that I will reward them if they are faithful."

"Do you hear? You common things! The vermilion-visaged devil says he wants two guides, who are to go with us at once."

Having selected a couple of active looking volunteers, the party commenced their journey. First marched the sailors under command of Lieutenant Wilton; these men drew the brass howitzer and its limber-boxes, it being fitted for use as a field piece. Next came a sedan containing Puffeigh, borne by six Chinese, twelve others being secured to act as relays. Bringing up the rear were the marines under control of

Crushe, these men carrying the rocket apparatus. Jerry Thompson walked by the side of the sedan, having charge of the bearers, and acting as a sort of aide-de-camp to the captain.

The fighting party marched through the streets to the tune of "Old Dan Tucker," played upon a violin, by one of the blue-jackets; and a more jolly set of fellows could not be imagined. All their troubles forgotten, all animosity buried, everything absorbed in one idea—the rescue of a poor girl from slavery.

Leaving the shore party to make the best of their way to the joss-house, we will return to the Stinger.

Master Jordun, who had been attended to and placed in a cot, finding the place pretty quiet after the departure of the fighting party, got up and cruised round the sick bay. He had made a critical survey of nearly all its occupants, and thought it time to return to his cot, fearing the surgeon would come back and give him a scolding, when his attention was suddenly arrested by hearing a husky voice repeat his name.

"Young Bill! I say! Come here."

"Who's that ere a flyin' my number?"

"Me—yer old chum, Jemmy," was the faint response.

"Where are ye?" demanded the boy, who could not see any resemblance to his friend in the mummy-like figure from which the sound appeared to proceed.

"Here I am, and it's all up with me, my boy—I'm going fast. Although that infernal sawbones sees I'm all right, Jemmy ain't long for this world."

"Humbug! You're all right. Why, I'm wounded and a walkin' about."

At this moment the surgeon entered, and asked the boy why he was out of his cot.

"Old Jemmy called me, sir."

"Is that the doctor!" quavered the old sailor.

"What do you want, my man? You must keep quiet."

Upon this the old fellow, calling the surgeon to him, desired he would bear witness that he left "his clothes, pay, and prize money to that ere kid Bill Jordun."

"I'll see that it is done; but if you remain quiet, you will recover."

Old Jemmy kept quite still until the surgeon left again, upon which he called to the boy and told him to step out of the sick-bay, and go to his ditty box, in which he would find a bottle of grog, and to bring it to him at once, never mind who said no.

The young scamp, desirous of pleasing the man who had made him his heir, did as he was directed; and having secured the bottle, took it to his friend, who begged him to put it to his lips—"gentle, my boy." The lad did as he was desired, and having held it there until he thought the old fellow had imbibed his share, he removed it and took a pull at it himself.

"Give us another nip," piteously pleaded the mummy.

"It ain't good for you, old 'un—you knows it isn't," replied the boy; who, however, replaced the bottle to his friend's lips, and allowed him to empty its contents.

"I'm blowed! if he ain't a sucked it dry!" ejaculated the lad. "I say, Jemmy, how do you feel now?"

But old Jemmy replied not, so the boy covered him up and left him.

About five hours after this the sick-bay man, thinking the old man was very quiet, proceeded to uncover his face, and found he was dead; upon which he reported to the surgeon that, "Old Jemmy were dead, and that he smelt werry strong of rum." Boy Jordun became delirious during the night, and as he also was perfumed in the same manner, the doctor concluded that some numskull had given them a glass of grog, and blamed his man for not keeping a good look-out.

Some time after when the boy was informed of the death of his friend, he snivelled, and declared " he was werry sorry, as the old bloke was allus a thundering good old kove to him."

Finding everything was pretty quiet, the master boarded all the junks which were not much injured by fire, and hoisted the British flag upon them as prizes. By the time this was done it became necessary to return to the ship; and having set the watch, and made the rounds, Mr. Beauman retired to rest, thoroughly done up. Nothing occurred to render it imperative that he should be called during the night, and the Stingers not on duty slumbered in their hammocks; while those who were compelled to remain upon deck kept their eyes open, and thought how calm and peaceful the bay appeared, with the stars shining down upon the water, beneath which were sunk eleven hundred pirates, who twenty-four hours before had been alive, and quite unconscious of their approaching fate. A few of the more superstitious among the watchers declared that every now and then some of the murdered men would rise to the surface, groan and sink again. Probably it was the noise of fish they heard, but to the day of their deaths they believed that " Bloody Bay " (as they termed it) swarmed with spirits that night. One man was so affected by his fears, that he left his post, and going below was led into the ward-room, where he came across a bottle of brandy, a portion of which he found himself compelled to swallow. No doubt he was under the baneful influence of the spooks when he did this, as when he was found helplessly reclining upon the fore hatchway, he gravely declared that it was seeing so many ghosts that took away his senses. As the man had been twice flogged, the humane master forgave him, and determined not to report the circumstance to the captain, when the latter returned; which act of clemency so touched the delinquent, that he made a vow not to take another drop of grog during the time he belonged to the ship. And to his honour be it said, he faithfully kept his word.

More than twenty-four hours had passed, and he had seen no sign of the landing-party. Beauman got the ship in order, repaired the rigging, and obtained some fruit and vegetables from the shore, but when the sun went down the second night the master was still left in suspense, and, to tell the truth, became quite uneasy, never leaving the deck a moment during the night. When morning broke a sampan came off with a message from the head man of the town, from which Beauman, who could speak a little Chinese, made out that the Stingers had found the pirates at home, but had been beaten off with great loss, and were fleeing towards the mountains.

He knew that the landing party was but small, and if they had fallen into an ambuscade all of them might be murdered; but knowing how unblushingly the Chinese can pervert the truth, he made up his mind to await further developments. Sending the messenger back with a polite intimation, that if the expedition did not return within eight-and-forty hours he would fire upon the town, he devoted his energies to instructing the boys how to act in case the party were lost, and in training his guns upon prominent buildings, the ship being moored broadside on to the place. During the day they buried the dead, and eight bodies were conveyed to a small island near the entrance of the bay, and decently interred.

When night set in Beauman became restless, and began to think there was some truth in the story brought off from the shore. " Sixty hours away from the ship, and no sign of them yet. Poor fellows! they have been captured and put to death."

CHAPTER XII.

WE will now return to Puffeigh and his party, whom we left upon the march towards the joss-house.

Along canal banks, over paddy fields, across bridges, by villages, whose inhabitants would run out, hoot and spit at the foreign devils, and vapour about what they would do were they only able; past private residences surrounded by every accessory known to a luxurious people; skirting walled towns and small cities, they wended their way without stop or rest. Now and then their course lay through orchards, or fields skirted with lychee trees, but no one was allowed to break off a branch, although the commander knew that a few bunches of the fruit would have been a boon to his men. The sedan bearers trotted on with Puffeigh; and as the latter considered that his men ought to walk as well as the Chinese did, it never once entered his mind to order a halt until night surprised them as they were entering a village.

" What is this place called ? " demanded the skipper.

" Hong-soo."

" March to the joss-house ! "

" Pilot says he don't think they rate one, sir," observed Jerry. " It's a werry one-horse sort of a place."

However, in a short time they unearthed the " elders " of the village, who, after striking a smart bargain with Hoo-kee, proceeded to show the way to the joss-house, which was found upon examination to be clean and tolerably large. Having opened the massive outer doors, the " elders " pointed out a number of sheds built against the wall of the court-yard. These they offered for the accommodation of the men, who were soon in possession, and had their supper under weigh in quick time. After directing the howitzer to be placed in position with its muzzle pointing towards the entrance, and the guard being set, Puffeigh followed the obsequious " elders " into the joss-house, and as there were no side chapels, he was obliged to take up his abode before the idol. The villagers furnished the party with any quantity of candles, and in a short space of time the temple was thoroughly illuminated, and presented a very animated appearance. The " elders " now withdrew, promising to return with some chow-chow, which they informed Puffeigh was being prepared for his supper. The great doors of the joss-house were thrown back, and the captain and officers looked out upon the court-yard, and watched the men as the latter prepared their meal.

A number of the women of the village had established a market in the centre of the enclosure, and were driving quite a trade in fried eggs, sweet potatoes and little pork pies, while here and there were men carrying huge buckets containing boiled rice, which they sold to the sailors for anything they could get, taking money or goods according to circumstances. Thompson was in attendance upon the officers; and having found a jar of water, which he tested by forcing one of the bearers to swallow a quart, he proceeded to serve the brandy pawnee.

" That's a luxury," observed Crushe. " Thompson, you are one of the few men of the fleet who is not a fool; upon my word, you're not."

6

" Nobody but you ever thought I were, sir," retorted the coxswain, and with this observation Jerry retired behind the idol, and took a quiet drink.

At this moment a gong was heard, and in marched the " elders," heading a procession of food-bearers. Having deposited their burdens, the coolies withdrew, upon which the " elders " spread the feast out upon the floor of the temple, and invited the officers to partake of the repast.

Puffeigh felt very bewildered at this unlooked-for hospitality, but the fact was, upon their entering the place, Hoo-kee had struck a bargain with the " elders," that, upon consideration of his being paid fifty dollars and free chow-chow for the officers, he would prevent the Fanquis from sacking and destroying their village. Hence all this civility ; the " elders " being delighted to find their visitors did not wish to cook and eat any of their infants, that being, according to their traditions, the usual food of the " red-haired, foreign, out-side barbarians."

Puffeigh looked at the food, and then asked Hoo-kee if it were all right ?

" Belle good peace chow-chow, nomba one, fust chop," replied the pilot, who seized a bowl of rice, and a pair of chop-sticks, and proceeded to illustrate the truth of his assertion.

Thompson hovered round the officers, and gave his opinion of the dishes, recommending some, and warning them against others, as his fancy suggested.

"That looks terribly like a boiled dog," he remarked to Crushe, who was turning over a stewed fowl. "It's either that or a cat ; don't you eat none of that ere, sir."

The lieutenant left that dish ; and seizing another near it, boldly commenced to eat, shutting his eyes to any peculiarity of aspect or taste which he met with during his meal. Puffeigh enjoyed his greatly, but was very much disconcerted by Jerry's remark as he cleared away the last bowl.

" Did you like the last raghot, sir ?"

" Well, it wasn't bad ; but why do you ask ?"

" Oh ! it's nothing, sir, only a fancy o' mine."

" What !—wa—what was it ?" he fiercely demanded.

" Oh, a mere trifle, sir ; only a hinfant's ears left in the dish, that's all, sir ; they're fond o' ears, I believe."

" Where's the dish ? give it here, you fellow !"

Thompson brought forward the bowl and exhibited two substances which certainly resembled infants' ears, but were in reality those of a young deer, the head of which had been served up with a delicious white sauce. Puffeigh, however, did not know this ; and although he pooh pooh'd the affair, and told Jerry that he was a thick-headed fool for his pains, was nevertheless internally uncomfortable, so that a meal perfect in quality and cookery gave him anything but pleasant sensations.

When the officers had finished their repast, Thompson retreated to the back of the idol, where he feasted with the pilot. Everything might have been compounded of dog or cat, for all he cared, as upon completing his meal he observed to his companion, " Well, Hookey, this is the first blow out as I've had o' your grub ; and, taking it as a whole, it's werry good, but werry rum-looking sort of stuffin ;" then filling a glass with brandy, the coxswain winked at the Celestial, and observing, " Here's teowards you, Walker," he drank, after which, stretching himself upon the floor, he dropped off into a profound slumber.

Hoo-kee walked out of the temple, and paid a visit to the " elders," who proposed a friendly game of cards ; and the festive youths drank samshoo and gambled until the morning broke. Hoo-kee had met his match ; and upon counting up his losses found, not only that he had lost the fifty dollars he had squeezed out of the head men over night, but had been relieved of a large sum besides; but he left the party fully impressed with the idea that, had he been allowed to play one more game, his luck would have turned.

When he reached the joss-house he found the commander ready to start; and, with fiddle going, the Stingers filed out of the court-yard on their way towards the pirates' head-quarters. The townspeople had either told an untruth, or had not known the distance, for the party must have marched thirty miles before they sighted the place to which they were bound, although it was plainly visible from the deck of the Stinger. They had been marching up-hill, and probably the road was circuitous, so it was fully noon when, upon their turning a bend, the building suddenly burst upon view. The vanguard halted until Puffeigh came up. Seeing the place was to all appearance deserted, he directed Crushe to take a party and reconnoitre, while he ordered the rest of the men to halt, and stand at ease.

The lieutenant advanced cautiously, thinking the pirates were trying to draw them into an ambuscade; but after carefully surveying the outer fortification, which he found completely abandoned, entered the gateway. Before him was a wooden edifice, probably a joss-house, as described by the townspeople, and in front of it several cheerful-looking wooden gods, or demons, who served as a sort of scare-crow guard to the temple. There was no litter or signs of men having been there for some time, but on entering, Crushe noticed some exploded crackers upon the floor, and a smell of recently burnt joss-stick lingered suspiciously about the place.

Having examined the altar, torn down the dress of the idol, and kicked over the vases used in worshipping, Crushe walked out of the temple, and proceeded to examine the outbuildings, which were lean-to sheds built against the circular wall surrounding the place. Judge his astonishment upon seeing these places filled with Tartar ponies, about six of these animals being stalled in each compartment. But where were the men?

After an unsuccessful search, Crushe had to give it up; and leading out one of the most likely-looking ponies, returned to the commander. Puffeigh examined the beast —looked sagely at his teeth and patted it—then observed that it was no use for any one to cause a delay, and gave the order to advance and take possession of the place, upon which the party got in motion; and having entered the enclosure, a boat's ensign was hoisted on the wall, and the officers and men camped within its shelter, until Puffeigh should determine what to do next.

The interior of the joss-house was exceedingly dark; and as the outer court was cool and well shaded with trees, the captain decided not to take up his quarters in the temple. Sentries were set, and the men lounged about the place, and amused themselves in the best manner they could. About four o'clock Puffeigh determined to hold a consultation; and, in order that it might be private, withdrew into the joss-house, taking with him all his officers, and his coxswain, who carried the liquor case. Having squatted himself upon the floor, the latter proceeded to unpack the brandy, when his attention was suddenly arrested by a slight noise in the roof, and at that moment a man fell headlong from aloft, and dropped on Cravan, whom he stretched senseless upon the floor. In an instant a shower of spears and shot came hurtling down from aloft, and the terrified officers bolted to the door; Jerry, who had collared the China-man, dragging his prisoner out, Cravan being rescued by Lieutenant Wilton. The sailors and marines were soon on the alert, and it was with difficulty that Puffeigh prevented them entering the joss-house to avenge the assault. With the assistance of Hoo-kee, the commander learnt that, finding their retreat cut off, the pirates had taken to the roof, and over two hundred of them were now clustered there, the prisoner who gave this information informing the pilot that he had been crowded off his rafter by the pressure of his companions.

Having given orders to remove the ponies a safe distance down the road, Puffeigh offered the prisoner his life upon condition that he would lead him to the place where the English lady was confined. The man, who declared he had been compelled to join the outlaws by force, joyfully agreed to do this, and informed them that the pirates clustered on the roof of the temple were the men who had murdered the officers and crew of the burnt ship. Upon hearing this, Puffeigh directed the pilot to order them to surrender, but they replied by throwing a spear at the man, which narrowly missed his head. Finding it was useless to parley with them, the captain ordered the men to collect all the straw and bamboo cane they could find, and pile it up in front of the temple doors. Having made a great heap, he instructed them to set it on fire, when up rose a thin cloud of smoke, and a flame flickered for a moment, then burst into a blaze, the smoke and flame presently roaring into the open door, as if it had been the mouth of a chimney. The pirates set up a yell of defiance, and swarmed upon the roof, from which the marines picked them off with their rifles; and within half an hour of the match being applied, in place of the joss-house with its rafters swarming with human beings, only a few smouldering embers remained inside the circular walls. Having literally smoked out the vermin, Puffeigh ordered his men to mount the ponies; and piloted by the prisoner, who was bound and placed between two marines, the party made the best of their way to the pirates' cave.

When night fell they camped down, and the sailors moored the ponies to their bodies, i. e. fastened the halters round their waists while they slept; and the men would sometimes wake with the disagreeable sensation of finding their steed endeavouring to nibble off their whiskers or hair. With the morning's dawn the party got once more in motion, and, in spite of the night's drawbacks, they seemed a thoroughly jolly set of fellows. Thompson rode his animal in a variety of ways, much to the astonishment of all present; and his eccentricities kept the whole party in a roar of laughter.

About 2 P.M. they entered a pass, in which, they were informed, they would find the cave containing the lady. The defile was weird and gloomy; and had the pirates been in possession, they could have defended it against an army of soldiers. The men rode in twos, and not a word was spoken. After proceeding about three-quarters of a mile, the vanguard halted, and Puffeigh was shown a hole in the side of the ravine, which the prisoner declared was the cave. Upon this the party dismounted, and leaving their horses in charge of a picket, advanced to the cave, climbing a steep road to do so, the difficulties of which increased at every step.

The cave proved to be a deep one, and scattered about its entrance were all manner of articles, plundered from the burnt ship, the most prominent being a piano—how they managed to hoist it up there was a puzzle to the invaders. Thompson procured a torch, and when the captain directed his officers to make a thorough search for the captive girl, Jerry, who was always first, hunted out every hole and corner. As he advanced he suddenly heard a woman's voice, so he called out, "Cheer up, miss! we're here! You're saved!"

With a scream of joy, a young girl dressed in Chinese costume tore away a heavy curtain which was suspended from the roof of the cave, and rushing into his arms, fainted; upon which Jerry followed the first impulse of his heart, and kissed her.

"Here! she! is! Hoorah!!!"

In a few moments the officers were by his side, and carrying out the inanimate form, placed it upon the ground near the entrance of the cave. Thompson did his best to bring her to, and behaved in such a frantically delighted manner, that the men thought he had gone out of his mind.

"Pretty creature, she's a coming to; Lord love your face, how sad you does look!" cried the excited sailor.

After a time the poor girl managed to realize she was rescued, and to thank her deliverers; she told them that the pirates had not offered her any insult, and their women had treated her very kindly; but at the mention of the ship from which she was taken, she became so much affected, that they forbore to question her.

Having secured the young lady, the Stingers retraced their steps, and when night came on they camped. The poor girl would not take rest, but sat by Thompson, who she persisted in declaring was her deliverer. Jerry was exceedingly kind and attentive; in fact, he watched her as a brother would a sister. The situation was most romantic: the lady had been in great distress, and he the first to find her. "I'd rather ha' done this than have a hundred pounds given me," he said to Lieutenant Wilton, and undoubtedly he spoke the truth.

At daylight the party remounted, the lady being accommodated with the coxswain's steed, he having found a sumpter-horse laden with the captain's plunder, upon the top of which he perched himself, so as to keep the young girl in view. The fiddler headed the procession, and lightened the march by playing patriotic airs. The men felt free and happy, chatting and laughing like schoolboys. However, they did not remain long in that blissful state, for on nearing a village Crushe (who had allowed them to enjoy themselves only on account of the captain's not expressing a wish otherwise), upon Puffeigh observing they were too noisy, at once brought them to a sense of their position by ordering them to "stop their row, unless they wanted to taste the cat." A number of the vanguard were smoking; and when the lieutenant bawled out his order, those of the men who had not before indulged in the weed, then lit their pipes. Observing this, Crushe rode forward and commanded them to stop smoking. One of the marines, who had displayed great bravery during the attack on the pirates, upon hearing this order, threw his pipe away, certainly without intending any disrespect to his officer; seeing which the bully swore at him, heedless whether the words were heard by the young lady or not; and after abusing the soldier for some moments, ordered him to the rear, and placed him under arrest. The man laughed in his face, and told him that as he was sure of a flogging anyhow, he preferred staying where he was. Crushe vented his rage in a further flow of abuse, but determined to let the matter drop until they arrived on board the ship, besides not caring to say more before the supernumeraries.

Towards dusk they sighted another village, and upon nearing it found the "braves" drawn up to oppose them, who soon made known their intentions by discharging a shower of gingall-balls which rattled over the Stingers' heads, but did not hurt any of them. Upon this Puffeigh threw this party into disorder in his endeavour to bring forward the marines and pass the young lady to the rear; giving his orders in such a confused manner, that in a few moments there was a general stampede, and it was with great difficulty the officers succeeded in recalling the marines, who were racing away towards the pirates' cave, having lost all control over their ponies. However, at length they were overtaken and brought back, meanwhile the "braves" had remained quite quiet, evidently thinking they had driven their invaders away.

The howitzer was placed in position; and having sent the horses to the rear, Puffeigh directed the gunners to shell the village. Bang went the piece, and the shell twinkled in the air like a star, and then burst over the place. Upon this a perfect hail of gingall-balls was discharged by the "braves," who then threw down their weapons and fled inside the walls. Crushe fell wounded in the back, and three of the men were discovered to be hit, but their injuries were all in the front part of their bodies.

Finding that the villagers had retreated, the commander, deeming it imprudent to follow them or to attempt reprisal, gave the order to remount, and proceeded on his way. Crushe was soon able to sit upright, but declared he was in great pain, while the wounded men, being but slightly injured, had to get along the best way they could.

About 9 o'clock P.M. they entered the town of Ping-chao-ting, off which the Stinger was moored, and soon after that Mr. Beauman welcomed them on board, as though they had escaped from slavery.

The captain's cabin was allotted to the young lady, who upon entering it fell upon her knees, and fervently thanked God for her wonderful deliverance from captivity. During the evening she informed Puffeigh that after the pirates had murdered all the people belonging to the ship but herself, they had plundered and set it on fire. Knowing it would be useless to search further, the captain determinded to embark the horses on board the most seaworthy of the junks, and to proceed to sea the next day at noon.

At daybreak the bay presented quite an animated appearance, the horses being taken off to the junks by the townspeople, who appeared very desirous of doing everything in their power to get rid of the "Foreign devils" as soon as possible. Hoo-kee obtained his dollars and left the Ping-chao-tingers fully impressed with the importance of his influence with the Fanquis ; and prize crews being put on board the junks, the cables of the latter were cut, and the Stinger having taken them in tow, steamed out of the bay with five junks and two lorchas astern. When fairly outside these were cast adrift, and, setting sail, made the best of their way to Hong-Kong, the man-of-war keeping steam up, and occasionally rendering them assistance as required.

Upon arrival on board, Crushe sought the assistant-surgeon, who, having examined his wound, pronounced it to be a bayonet thrust through the muscles of the back— painful, but not dangerous. It being impossible to find out how this was done, the first lieutenant did not make any stir in the matter, but determined to flog the "infernal marine," who had, he felt sure, made an attack upon him during the confusion. However, upon sending for the sergeant, he learnt that he had not been seen since they arrived in Ping-chao-ting. The man remained behind, and proved so useful to the townspeople, that they appointed him superintendent of fortifications ; and after a few months under his fostering care became the most celebrated pirates upon the seaboard, and nearly sunk H. M. Brig Booby, which was sent to wipe them out. The marine flourished for about two years, until one day, undertaking to thrash the Taontai for some fancied insult, he was seized and thrown into prison, where he lingered and died.

The young lady was carried on shore and handed over to the gentle care of the Sœurs de Charité. Shortly after her arrival at the convent she was taken seriously ill, and for some weeks her life was despaired of ; however, the good sisters nursed her so skilfully, that with the blessing of God she recovered, and lived to become a happy wife and mother.

It seems she had, with her father, been a passenger in the ill-fated ship, and we cannot do better than give her own words in describing the tragedy.

"My name is Ada Moore. The ship was called the Lima, bound from London to Australia, by way of Hong-Kong. My dear papa owned the vessel, and he intended to establish a business in Adelaide, Australia, and to send the Lima backwards and forwards for tea. Our captain's name was Froom, he was a distant relation of ours.

We had a beautiful passage out, and every one was in good spirits. About six ø clock on the fatal evening we made the land, and Captain Froom determined to anchor; he having overrun his reckoning, I believe, but I don't know. One thing I am certain of, he said he was not quite sure what place we were near. I was in the cabin with my dear papa—he reclining upon the settee and I playing the evening hymn, when I heard a scuffle upon deck and stopped playing. Upon this Mr. Raynor, our boatswain, entered the cabin all bloody, and falling down at my father's feet groaned and died. My dear papa called out to the captain who was on deck, but not getting a reply, he started up and was ascending the companion when a Chinese rushed past him, dealing as he did so, a blow which cut his face and made him bleed. Then he turned on poor papa, and stabbed and chopped him. At this dreadful sight I fainted, and when I recovered found myself tied hand and foot and laid across the grating abaft, upon the poop. I saw them throw something overboard, I think it was a body, upon which I again fainted. They brought me to by throwing water over me; and although they were very frightful in their appearance, they did not offer to molest me in any way. I found they were towing the ship into harbour. Upon our arrival off the town they took me on shore, and I was placed on horseback, and conveyed to the joss-house which has since been destroyed by Captain Puffeigh. They kept me there for four days, and Chinese clothes were given me, with orders to take off my own. This I had to do; and although I begged them to allow me to keep my clothes, they would not permit me to do so. I was removed to the cave, and an old woman placed in charge of me. From her I understood I was to wait until Seh-wang returned, and I dreaded the name which seemed full of terrible import. None of the pirates were living in the cave, but they constantly arrived with plunder from the Lima. I saw my piano brought up among other things. I was praying for death, when I heard the joyful words, 'Cheer up, miss!' and I rushed out from behind the curtain, and beheld Mr. Thompson, the sailor, who, with the others, I shall pray for until the day of my death. I remember the journey down—how they fought for me, and I cannot express my appreciation of the gentle attentions shown me by Mr. Thompson, who was most thoughtful for me, and who never ceased his guard over me, until I was safe on board the Stinger."

The captured ponies were sold in Hong-Kong, and the amount they brought received by Puffeigh, who, as the Stingers heard no more of the matter, it may be presumed *forgot* to account for it. The junks, &c., &c., were declared lawful prizes, and handed over to the highest bidder, the amount realized being sent to England as prize money, which was not paid to the surviving Stingers for some years.

A subscription was set on foot to present Thompson with a testimonial, but the captain threw cold water upon the movement, and it was abandoned. Jerry was quite lionized; and whenever he set foot on shore, would be noticed by all the residents, and in a short time became a popular man with the Chinese ladies'-maids, who felt a great interest in the "blue jacket who had rescued the lady single-handed against about two thousand pirates," the story resolving into that ere it reached the ears of those young women.

On several occasions Thompson was called into the merchants' houses, and questioned by the ladies as to the young lady's recapture; and upon the recital of the particulars, he would be feasted and wined to his heart's content.

Jerry never owned to having kissed the young lady; *that* he kept to himself, his version being, "Yes, mum (your good health), I saw the young lady, who looked like a sufferin' angel, as she lifted up the curtain (Thankee, mum, I'll take jist half a glass more), and with that she gave a scream, and fainted right away in my arms (I don't mind if I do have another slice of that cake), and I hollered out, Hurrah! here she is. Did she thank me ever? Yes! she put out her hand and sea (Here's teowards you agin, mum, and may you have health and happiness) 'God bless you, Thompson, for all your care on me.' And the tears stood in her beautiful eyes, and she trembled, and gave me a ring, which I wear next my heart."

Sometimes the lady would inquire if Jerry had left a sweetheart behind him, upon which he would remark "that he must go, as his time were up." The recollection of Mary Ann would cross his mind, and render him uncomfortable for a moment. However, that sensation did not last long.

CHAPTER XIII.

ABOUT three weeks after the occurrences described in the foregoing chapter the Stinger was ordered to Japan, to join the squadron cruising off that coast in search of the Russian fleet, which was supposed to have wintered in one of the northern ports of the island.

Puffeigh was very anxious to fall in with a prize, his principal reason for taking command of the Stinger being to save house expenses, and make as much prize money as possible. In order, therefore, still further to retrench his expenditure, he discharged his steward before leaving Hong-Kong, and, of all persons in the world, took the boy Jordun as his attendant; assigning as a reason that the boy being unfitted for heavy work, it was better to make a steward of him than to send him home, where he would be a burden to his friends. Not only was this excuse untrue, but the captain actually saved money by having the boy as his servant; and that exclusive of the salary he would have paid a proper steward. William Jordun was rated captain's steward, and his rations claimed by that officer, who was paid for them, the boy being fed upon the scraps and leavings of his master's meals.

Of course, under these circumstances, none of the officers were ever invited to dine in his cabin; and it was amusing to hear the excuses he invented in order to explain his not having a competent servant.

"It was very unfortunate my not being able to obtain that French steward, was it not?" he observed to one of his officers. "I made up my mind to ship the fellow when the admiral bagged him."

"He lost a good situation, and no doubt he has since regretted it," replied the officer with respectful sarcasm.

Master William had never much fear of Puffeigh, but when he became his servant the little he had quickly vanished, and he talked to his captain in the most confidential and cheeky manner, as the following conversation will sufficiently show:

"What did you do with those chops left by me at dinner yesterday?"

"Chops?"

"Yes, two large fat chops; surely you did not eat them for your dinner?"

"I never seed you leave no chops, sir."

"You did not see two chops left yesterday?"

"No, sir, there was no chops left that I seed; you must ha' eat 'em and forgot it."

"Well, you little thief, you stole them. I'll flog you if you don't confess."

"I a thief, sir! Well, how you can say that, I don't know. Why, I might as well say that you stole 'em."

"Silence! What did you have for your dinner yesterday?"

"Let me see. I had two chops—some taters—"

"Hang you, you little thief! Why did you deny having stolen them?"

"I denigh avin a hooked them, sir. Oh! where does you expect to go to?"

"I'll flog you. Go to the pantry and think over that. As soon as we're in port and I can get a steward, I'll flog you."

"Well, I never. You flog me for eatin' my dinner. I'm allowed as much as I can sat by the government, and you takes and grabs my rashions, and gets paid for 'em, and I eate yer leavins,—them yesterday were two chops,—now how you're going to flog me for that, I can't see."

"Silence!"

The boy Jordun pulled his forelock, and left the captain's presence.

The ship had been cruising about in the Gulf of Tartary for over four months, and fresh provisions were getting low, when one morning they sighted a French man-of-war, Le Terrible, and Puffeigh received a present of three sheep from her commander. Most captains under such circumstances would have divided them with their officers, but he was too mean, and kept them all to himself; the weather being cold the meat did not spoil when killed.

Master Jordun lived like an alderman during the time two of the sheep lasted, and, in spite of the watchful care of his master, managed to give away sundry fat morsels to his friends; but when the third animal was slaughtered, Puffeigh watched its being jointed, and directed the pieces to be hung up in his gig, which was secured to the stern davits, and furthermore ordered a sentry to be placed over the same, day and night.

The hungry midshipmen and still more hungry crew watched the joints, the number of which became less every day, until at last there was only one remaining, this being a leg, which through exposure and hanging had become as tender as venison. Puffeigh had expressed his determination to have it for his dinner the next day, Sunday, and during his evening walk sent twice for his cook, and gave him fresh instructions as to the manner of dressing the delicacy.

Eight o'clock P. M., and the sentry who took up his position over the mutton was cautioned to keep his eyes open. At twelve the man was relieved, and a marine named Foley went upon guard, and at four o'clock the corporal reported him as intoxicated to the officer of the watch, upon which they discovered that the mutton had vanished.

When this was made known to the commander he became greatly enraged, and swore he would flog the sentry and all the watch if the thief were not discovered. After church was over, Puffeigh mustered the men, and having abused them as "thieves and burglars," proceeded to order several of the watch to be placed in irons, upon which a midshipman named Holt addressed him as follows:—

"The men are innocent, sir. I saw the mutton go."

"Where, sir? why did you not speak before?"

"I have been below all this morning, and did not know what was going on, sir?"

"What do you know of the theft?"

"I saw the meat at eleven o'clock, and shortly after twelve it blew a strong breeze, and the mutton was blown away, as when the wind lulled it was not there."

Now Mr. Holt was the nephew of one of the Lords of the Admiralty, and his uncle's heir, so Puffeigh chose to accept his version, and even dismissed the marine with a light punishment. The fact was, the middies had given the sentry a strong dose of grog, and then appropriated the joint, which was cooked in the engine-room by a friendly stoker.

A few evenings after, they sighted several ships, and as two of them looked like Russian men-of-war, the Stinger got up steam, and was soon in full chase after them. The sun was sinking upon the horizon, and the ships plainly visible, when suddenly one of them vanished from their sight. Puffeigh and his officers were puzzled,—there was one of the vessels, but the other had disappeared.

"It's the flying Dutchman," observed an old quartermaster.

"Beat to quarters and clear for action," shouted the captain.

The engineers drove the Stinger at the top of her speed, but night soon hid the pursued ship; and after running far past the place, the commander determined to lay to until daylight.

About four bells in the middle watch a man on the look-out reported "ship right ahead," and a large vessel sailed past them, looming in the fog very much like a frigate. Puffeigh was turned out, and, hurrying on deck, gave directions to bout ship and beat to quarters. In a few minutes the ship's course was altered, and the men at their guns ready to pour a broadside into the enemy. There was a thick mist falling, and every thing on deck was wet and sloppy; yet, in spite of that, the men were stripped to their waists, and as eager for the fray as a lot of tigers. Puffeigh was on the bridge, speaking-trumpet in hand, and gave orders to fire if the ship did not reply to his hail the third time.

"Ship ahoy! What ship's that?"

No reply.

"Ship ahoy! What ship is that?"

Again no response.

"Ship ahoy! Of what nation are you?"

Before any reply could be heard one of the captains of a forward gun pulled his trigger line, and immediately the others discharged their guns. A howl of execration broke from the enemy, upon which the Stingers let drive another volley.

"Cease firing! let us wait for reply," roared the commander.

Now loud upon the breeze came the words, "Dod rot ye! What do you mean by firing into us in that fashion?"

"Are you an enemy?" blurted Puffeigh through his speaking-trumpet.

"If I had a few barkers I'd darn soon show you who I was, you cussed fool. I'm Amos Pelton, of the Minnehaha, of Martha's Vineyard, Massachusetts, United States of America."

"This is Her Britannic Majesty's ship Stinger. Are you damaged?"

At this moment the man at the wheel put his helm aport, and the ships collided. After striking the whaler just abaft the foremast, the Stinger swung round, and dropped alongside, causing the boats of both vessels to double up like hat-boxes,—yards locked, iron gear got entangled, rigging carried away, and general confusion prevailed, and for a short time the vessels hugged, ground, and rasped each other, like savage leviathans. Upon order being restored, the crews vied with each other in their efforts to free their respective ships; and when at last their exertions were successful, each quickly cleared away the wreck, and proceeded to ascertain the amount of damage it had sustained, and to repair the same to the best of their ability.

When morning broke the Stinger discovered the American vessel under easy sail upon her port bow; and after breakfast the captain was seen to leave his ship in his gig. Puffeigh received him upon his quarter-deck, and politely inquired what he wanted?

"Wall, capt'n, I guess John Bull 'ull have to pay for last night's amusement. Eleven shot holes in my ship's side, a fore-topmast carried away, and a vallyble dog killed, air to be paid for, capt'n."

"Why did you not answer my hail, sir? I hailed your ship three times."

"Wall now, Capt'n, we never heard you, an' my horn was below, an' I didn't get it up for a minute. I was jes a going to hail you, when bang goes your guns, and I hollered out to you to know what on airth you was about."

"Her Britannic Majesty's ship, captain—"

"All right, capt'n don't waste your words on me, we'll not fight over this little affair. I'll just fix matters, and run down to Shanghay, and git your consul to foot my bill."

Having settled the matter so far, Captain Amos Pelton, who, as if in rivalry of the man-of-war captain, sported a suit of some sort of naval uniform, next asked Puffeigh "if he had seen any Rooshians," upon which the latter informed him "that he had seen two the evening before, but both had escaped."

"Ken I have a word with you in private, capt'n?" mysteriously observed the Yankee.

"Yes, sir; come below."

Having descended into the captain's cabin, Captain Pelton imbibed some of Puffeigh's brandy, then drawing his chair towards him asked in a whisper, "ef he wanted to find out the Rooshian ship which he had lost sight of last night?"

"I do; and would guarantee you a handsome reward if you give me any information."

"Wall now, capt'n, your runnin' in to me ain't jes the most friendly kind of act, but I'll leave that for our consuls, and if you don't mind acting squarely, I'll give you the ren-dez-vous of the Rooshian. Le' me see, she's called the Volganoski. I ken give you her next rendezvous ef so be you remunerate me."

Puffeigh looked at the captain for a moment; but as he appeared as serious as a judge, he thought he would trust him, so he demanded what sort of remuneration he required.

"Wall, capt'n, this air brandy is good; say two dozen of this, a dozen of sherry wine, a dozen of whiskey, a barl of cabin biscuit, some fine sugar, some sardines, some canned meats, and about a coil of inch and a half manilla rope, an' I'll give you the rendezvous."

"That's too much. You want all my private stores, and their value comes out of my pocket."

"That's jis what I ask them for. I don't want none of your infernal government contract stores. I'm a reasonable man, and not a darn'd fool, and I prefer tew have the best. Say, capt'n, I'm off! You won't take my offer? Good day!"

"Here! I'll do it, but what security have I that you will not deceive me?"

"*De*-ceive *you* capt'n? why, dew I look like it?"

After some delay the articles were placed in the skipper's boat, upon which he returned to Puffeigh's cabin and wrote the following:—

"Rendezvous of the Russian ship Volganoski.

"On the 12th May this ship will be found at anchor off the Island of Sado in the Japanese Sea."

"Thar, capt'n ef you jis go there right away, you will capture her sure pop, and I wish you joy of your bargain."

"Well, sign it, Captain Pelton."

"No, airee; ef I did that, it might fall into the hands of the Rooshians, and I don't care tew risk it;" saying this, the cute skipper left the cabin, descended into his gig, and in a few moments was alongside his own craft; then hoisting in his plunder and boat, he set sail, and made off in the opposite direction to which the Stinger was heading.

Puffeigh did not impart the information he had received to any of his officers, but kept on his way to the rendezvous, off which he arrived five days afterwards, but found no signs of the Russian ship. Upon returning to Hong-Kong some months after this, the following letter was handed him, and upon comparing the handwriting, he concluded it was from Captain Amos Pelton.

"*Shanghae,*

"To Captain Puffeigh of the British Ship Stinger,

"You will be delighted to hear that the ship which disappeared so suddenly from your sight one evening in the Gulf of Tartary was the Volganoski, and she had on board the Russian admiral, *with the treasure of the fleet.* She furled sails just before sunset, and became invisible to you, and when it was dark altered her course and passed you, *leaving me to fool you, which I did with the Rendezvous.* Your brandy was good, and I should very much like to sell you another Rendezvous for some more."

When the worthy commander read this, he foamed at the mouth, and wished he could have the whaling captain under his command for one day. Probably had his amiable desire been gratified, Amos Pelton would have been again too many guns for him.

After remaining at the rendezvous long enough to find that he had been hoodwinked by his informant, Puffeigh proceeded to the Gulf of Tartary, where he vented his spite upon his crew, whom he drilled almost out of their senses; for, as usual in such cases, what was amusement to the officers was torture to the men.

In the course of a few days he fell in with H.M.S. Choker, who reported the presence of the Russian fleet in one of the bays at the head of the Gulf of Tartary, and despatched the Stinger to convey the news to the admiral at Chickodadi. Captain Puffeigh made all possible haste, and arrived in port just as the admiral was leaving for the north, and was by him directed to remain in harbour until relieved by a smaller ship. The Stingers did not much enjoy their stay in this port, as immediately upon arrival a cordon of boats was placed round the vessel, and all communication with the shore strictly interdicted by the Japanese authorities.

Two months were passed in this dull port, and the Stingers began to imagine themselves forgotten, when one morning H.M.S. Squeezer steamed into the harbour, and delivered mails and despatches, by which Captain Puffeigh found himself directed to proceed at once to the Gulf of Pechele, information having been received that one of the Russian ships, which had escaped from the Gulf of Tartary, was cruising off the mouth of the Pei-Ho. No time was lost in getting away from Chickodadi; and two hours after the reception of orders the Stinger was well on her way towards the coast of China.

We must do the Japanese the credit of stating, that they did not court the visits of the British ships, and only acted according to time-honoured custom, in refusing to have anything to do with "outside barbarians." As the Stinger was getting up anchor the harbour-master came off with a present of a boat-load of fresh provisions, which Captain Puffeigh courteously accepted, and coolly appropriated to his own use.

In the mean while Clare, who had been unwell for some time, at last reluctantly went to the doctor, and that functionary, upon making a strict examination of his case, discovered that he was suffering from disease of the heart, no doubt brought on by the shock his system had sustained when being flogged.

One evening Tom was sitting by the fore-hatchway in conversation with Thompson, when he suddenly asked him "if he believed in ghosts?" Jerry, who imagined his shipmate was joking, at first laughed at the question, as he did not believe in any such appearances, and seldom scrupled to ridicule those who affirmed they did; but the serious manner of his companion soon attracted his attention in a way which prevented his taking it lightly.

"You laugh! Well, Jerry, believe it or not, I saw Polly a few minutes ago, and she smiled on me and then vanished. This is the sixteenth day of August; I won't forget this day."

"You're out of order, old man; it's the physic you're takin' has made you light-headed."

"No, I ain't light-headed; I know what I'm about; I say I saw Polly, and *she's dead*," saying which his head dropped, and he remained some time as if buried in deep thought.

"Come, come, old man, rouse a bit, Polly's all right; you've got the blues, and are out of sorts; you'll be all right in a day or two."

However, when Clare became better he did not lose the impression that his wife was dead, and although he went about his work as before, a great weight was at his heart. Thompson would approach the subject, and try to ascertain if his shipmate were still under the hallucination, but Tom evaded his questions, and almost resented his friend's officiousness.

Puffeigh continued his plan of retrenchment, and the boy Jordun was half-starved, being often indebted for a full meal to the officer's steward. Upon one occasion the commander actually directed half a fowl to be cooked for his dinner, and the remainder hung until the next day. Jordun severed the bird, and took half of it on deck in order to suspend it from the stay with the rest of the provisions, but presently returned to his master, saying, "he didn't dare hang it, as the men chaffed him so."

"Chaffed you! Who dared do that?"

"Why," blubbered the boy, "the whole bileing on 'em forward was a-larfin and cuttin' jokes at the arf of a fowl—askin' if we killed arf at a time, and I was afraid to hang it arter what they said. I can't bear to go agin pop'lar opinion like that, it's too trying."

"Popular opinion, you little ass! Who put that rubbish into your head?"

"You did, sir."

"I did?"

"Yes, sir! Don't you remember, when Captain Interest said you wouldn't be posted until you got back to England, you said, 'Oh, won't I?' ses you, 'the people at home will hear about my rescuing the young girl from the pirates, and there's no going agin pop'lar opinion.'"

At that moment a boot went flying after Master Jordun, such attacks being very common on the part of his master when he found himself worsted in argument with the lad.

CHAPTER XIV.

HAVING reconnoitered the Gulf of Pechele from Tang-chu to Lan-ho, the Stinger proceeded into the entrance of the Gulf of Leao-tong, when, finding water running short, they landed at a place called Ngan-chow, where they found a fresh water creek and plenty of game. As the country seemed void of population in that part, Puffeigh determined to invite a couple of officers and go shooting; so about 6 o'clock upon the morning after they anchored, the captain, Lieutenant Wilton, Mr. Beauman, and Jerry landed, and proceeded in search of sport.

The party spent a very pleasant time, during which they shot a few ducks and several species of snipe, and about 8 o'clock they halted for breakfast, Jerry, who was literally laden with articles of food and culinary requisites, soon getting a fire under way, and having a small frying-pan in operation. After a little delay the cloth was spread, and the officers fell-to at a savoury meal, consisting of choice portions of wild duck fried in butter, which they devoured as fast as their cook could prepare them.

"I must rate you my chef, Thompson," observed Puffeigh; "your talent's lost forward."

"I don't care about bein' anything but what I am, sir. I can't cook like this regler, if it's anything in the cooking line you want me for, sir. I can only do this now and then, as I generally spiles all the grub of my mess when I'm cook, sir."

"Never mind, hand me some more duck, and we will be contented with your cooking for us on such occasions as these, my man."

At that moment Mr. Beauman shaded his eyes with his hands and looked towards the hills, upon which Puffeigh handed him his field glass; and when the master had surveyed the object of his suspicion, demanded what he was looking at.

"I can see a body of Tartar Bannermen riding this way," replied the master, "and we had better return to our boat, as they are ugly customers."

"Finish your breakfast,—there's time; they are miles away."

However, the meal was nearly over, so at the earnest solicitation of the master they left the place and proceeded towards the boat, which was distant about three miles. Having crossed the sand ridge thrown up by the sea, they walked along the cool beach, and, as they deemed the Tartars still a good way off, did not hurry. After a pleasant walk, they arrived off the place where the gig was anchored, and upon the captain's making the signal, the crew got up anchor, and pulled in towards the beach. They were within about two hundred yards of the shore when an exclamation on the part of Mr. Beauman caused the captain's party to look round, and to their astonishment they observed two Tartars riding along the sand ridge, not fifty yards off, and whiz came an arrow which narrowly missed Puffeigh Before they could recover from their surprise the Tartars were upon them and engaged in combat with Beauman and Thompson, Puffeigh and Wilton managing to escape and reach the boat in safety. The Tartar method of capture was at once novel and annoying, as it consisted in seizing the victims by the clothes, and then attempting to ride off with them. Beauman recovered his presence of mind sufficiently to draw his revolver and shoot his captor's horse; then having got over the shock of the fall, he shot his assailant through the heart, released himself, and retreated towards the boat, not aware that Thompson was still in the enemies' hands.

Jerry felt himself lifted by the collar of his serge shirt; and as it was slack, every now and then he received a bump, the ground being somewhat broken into mounds; but thinking it useless to be carried off like a captive turkey, he managed by turning a little to fix his teeth in the Tartar's leg. On that his captor let him go with a curse, and as his horse dashed off frightened by the clatter of Jerry's cooking utensils, it took him some time to rein him in. But no sooner was Jerry on his pins than he made a dash towards the boat. When Puffeigh saw this he ordered his men to back to within a hundred yards of the shore, and called Thompson "to swim for it;" but at that moment the main body of the Bannermen rode over the sand ridge, and Jerry bawling to the officers to leave him to his fate, and not risk their own lives, coolly awaited their arrival. They were soon down upon him, and having seized him they discharged their arrows at the retreating boat and then rode over the sand hill out of sight. Had Puffeigh and his party endeavoured to rescue him the whole of them would have been captured, and we will do the captain the credit of stating that he expressed very great concern about Jerry's untimely fate.

Upon arrival on board Puffeigh found the water-party had returned, so knowing it would be useless to endeavour to recover a man who was probably murdered by that time, he made sail and returned to Chickodadi, where he received his dispatches, and found he was ordered to proceed to Hong-Kong. Great was the regret of all the Stingers to hear of Jerry's untimely end, and it was long before they got over his loss; in fact, he never was forgotten, and his witty stories, popular songs, and amusing sayings, often were quoted, and the Stingers would tell new shipmates "what a jolly good fellow he was," and how sorry they were when the "thundering Tartars carried him off."

A few days after leaving Chickodadi they overhauled H.M.S. Blister, and were ordered to remain by her, as it was feared she would not reach Hong-Kong without assistance, she having about twenty-four hours before collided with and sunk a transport.

Now be it known that Puffeigh had taken a great dislike to Sergeant Spine of the Royal Marines, so one Sunday morning, after abusing that well-drilled and intensely rigid individual, he wound up his tirade by directing Corporal Kerr of the Royal Marine Artillery to remove the three good-conduct stripes which decorated his arm. The sergeant was a thin bamboo-shaped fellow, long in body and small in head, his tight leathern stock giving him a chronic stiff-neck, and making his countenance when at rest strongly resemble that of a half-choked kitten. He was always drilling some one; and so inveterate was this habit with him, that when not operating upon others he drilled himself. Spine had a certain number of motions in which to perform every action of his life. He would rise, or rather turn out of his hammock in six, dress in eighteen, eat his food with eleven, and say his prayers with three, and it was amusing to hear him give himself the word of command, which he would do in an undertone, even when in the presence of his superior officers. The commander considered the sergeant wanting in proper respect towards him; so when Crushe reported the man as "an illicit dealer in sardines, pickles, blacking, and other luxuries," not knowing how to class the offence, or otherwise punish the non-commissioned officer, he hit upon the idea of cutting off the sergeant's good-conduct stripes, thereby degrading him in the eyes of the Royal Marines and Artillerymen, who were serving under his command, and affording a rich treat to the sailors, who are always delighted to witness any punishment inflicted upon their enemies—the sergeant of marines of ship's corporal.

A warrant had been made out and duly signed by Puffeigh, and when Divine Service was concluded, the marines and sailors were mustered upon the quarter-deck, and the commander read the warrant which stated, "That whereas, Sergeant John Spine, Royal Marine Light Infantry, had upon sundry and divers occasions sold illicitly, disposed of, or induced others—to wit, the seamen and boys belonging to H.M.S. Stinger —to purchase sundry articles, to wit, sardines, pickles, and blacking at more than four times their value, and the said sergeant having pleaded guilty to the offence, as a punishment his good-conduct stripes were taken from him."

When the warrant was read Spine drew himself up (one), saluted (two), stood at attention (three), and then addressed his commander.

" Captain Puffeigh, twenty years, as boy and man, have I served my country, and I have always endeavoured to do my duty. You have directed my good-conduct stripes" (here he spoke with emotion) " to be cut off, and I am ranked with felons—yes, Captain Puffeigh, with felons."

"Don't talk rubbish, sergeant !"

" I am a non-commissioned officer in the Royal Marine Light Infantry, and know full well what discipline means, sir, but I respectfully protest against this punishment, and demand to be tried by court-martial."

" Is that all, sergeant ? " sneered Crushe.

" I wasn't addressing you, Lieutenant Crushe. Sir, Captain Puffeigh, will you have me tried by court-martial or not ? Sir, will you do me that act of justice ? "

" No, sergeant."

" You won't, sir ? "

" No, sergeant, and be hanged to you, you precious old peddler! Considering the way you have robbed the men, I let you off very cheaply ; I ought to disrate you to corporal."

" Good Heavens, sir ! you don't mean to say you'd think of doing such a thing ? "

" Just as soon as look at you ; there, go below."

Sergeant Spine descended the ladder like one in a dream, walked to his store cupboard, took out several packages of blacking, tins of sardines, and bottles of pickles, giving himself the word of command for each action, then walking to the coaling port, which was opened to ventilate the lower deck, he cried, " one," and threw the blacking overboard ; "two," sent the sardines after it ; " three," and pitched the bottles of pickles clear of the side : returning to his cupboard he changed his badgeless coat for an old one upon which the beloved stripes still remained, doing this in five motions ; then pulling forth an old silk handkerchief, spread it upon the floor, in two evolutions, and kneeling rigidly upon it, shut his eyes and drilled himself into prayer. After remaining a few moments in an attitude of devotion he rose, grasped his rifle, loaded it, with the usual number of motions, directing his own actions, which attracted the attention of boy Jordan, who was lounging near upon one of the officers' chests, when he espied the lad, who, eyeing him suspiciously, coolly said, " I say, Stripey, you ain't agoing to shoot yourself, are you ? "

" No, my boy," replied the excited soldier, who now altered his plan of suicide.

" Then what are ye a loadin' yer musket for ? "

Spine crossed over to where the boy was sitting, grasped him by the arm, and fiercely exclaimed, " Boy, bear witness that Captain Puffeigh, Royal Navy, has driven me to this !" then marched to the coaling port, and saying " one," " two," deliberately dived overboard.

7

William Jordun laughed, as if the soldier had done some very amusing feat, then went upon the quarter-deck and informed the captain that "the sergeant had drowned himself overboard."

"Bless me—you don't say so?"

"Yes, sir. He sed to me, 'Bill Jordun, bear witness that Captain Puffeigh told me to do this,' and then he went and posted hisself in the coal-port, like a letter in a office-box."

"Man overboard!" shouted the sentry upon the bridge, and upon running aft the captain saw the sergeant struggling in the water about three hundred yards astern of the ship.

"Make a signal to the Blister to pick up man overboard."

"Ay, ay, sir," replied the signal-man, and in a few moments the signal was fluttering to the breeze from the mizzen-mast of the Stinger.

All hands ran aft and saw the Blister lower a boat, which picked up the sergeant and took him on board.

"Affirmative flag over church pendant," signalled they, to show the man was recovered.

"Thank you" (by the same process), replied the Stinger.

Sergeant Spine never rejoined his own ship, as upon being taken on board the Blister, he fell upon his knees and piteously requested her commander "not to send him back to hell;" so upon arrival in Hong-Kong he was despatched to the hospital-ship, where he was declared to be insane, and sent home. He was received in Portsmouth barracks as a martyr, and his stripes restored to him upon parade, but he never got quite right again mentally, and was soon afterwards pensioned off, when he retired to his native town, and went into business as a dealer in pickles and other luxuries, being enabled to start a shop with the money he had wrung out of the men and boys on board the Stinger. He still does everything according to regulation, and his only sorrow is that he cannot induce his wife to submit to his eccentricity in this line. "I won't lay the breakfast by revolutions to please him, blest if I will!" observed Mrs. Spine, and her friends highly approve of this show of spirit.

Much to the disgust of his crew, Puffeigh kept by the Blister until they entered Hong-Kong harbour. His men imagined that every hour's delay shortened their stay in port, so they grumbled and growled after the manner of men-of-war's-men, and wished the disabled ship in Davy Jones's locker, forgetting all the time that duty, not his own pleasure, kept their captain by the disabled craft. They wrongfully accused him that time, although it mattered little to him what they said or did, provided he did not hear them openly express their opinions.

The mails were received and distributed in the manner before described, and Thompson's letters returned to the post-office with the words, "Dead. Killed by Chinese Tartars," written across them, as every one believed that Jerry was no more an inhabitant of the earth. Mary Ann received hers, and grieved most sincerely for the loss of one she loved better than any other being in the world. Miss Pferdscreptern, who also had a letter returned to her, after looking at the fatal words for about an hour, heaved a deep sigh and ejaculated, "Hombogs he tusant go for to gits todt, Scherry is not ein narr," then reclined in her chair, and woman-like indulged in a cry,—observing to her neighbours, "Ach, he vos ein goot veller, und I skall never gets ein oder mann likes him, ach Gott!" The poor girl mourned the loss of her lover for above a year, when one day the skipper of a coasting schooner solemnly proposed to her, and she soon afterwards became Mrs. Captain Schwartz.

How Thompson's other loves received the news of his decease we know not, but doubtless the report was a severe shock to several ladies besides those mentioned. In Hong-Kong the general belief was that under any circumstances Jerry was not dead, the Chinese ladies'-maids scouting the idea of a man who had killed so many pirates being wiped out by a few mangy bannermen; however, they put on white dresses as a sign of mourning for him, and when they met for gossip would speak with regret of "the brave fighting sailor who ate so many pirates."

Clare received a number of letters from his wife, in which she gave glowing accounts of the progress made by their little one, whom she had named after her beloved husband. Tom was delighted to receive these proofs of her affection, but he argued, "these letters are all dated June. *I saw her spirit on the 16th of August.* When I get a letter dated any time after that, I shall think, as poor Jerry did, that it was my imagination, but until then my heart is sore heavy."

The Stinger was refitted with great despatch, and her men were allowed unlimited liberty to go on shore. From a bully, Puffeigh suddenly toned down into a fatherly commander professing the utmost solicitude for the health, comfort, and moral welfare of his crew. Hours of work were shortened, the black-list done away with, no one punished when reported by the first lieutenant, and a degree of license reached which should never be tolerated on board any ship. From rigid and overstrained discipline they relaxed into the greatest disorder, such being the usual action of persons like Puffeigh, who carry everything to extremes. Crushe endeavoured to change this state of things, and twice reported men for gross insolence; but upon hearing the evidence, the captain dismissed the sailors, and shortly afterwards rated them petty officers. The first lieutenant chafed under the restraint, as he knew now his power was gone, the men would take advantage of the commander's weakness, and treat him with indifference.

One day, after having been openly insulted by the captain-of-the-fore-top, Crushe sought a private interview with Puffeigh, and plainly told him if he did not alter his behaviour towards him, that he would resign the service, or do something which would cause the matter to be investigated.

"So you think I am too indulgent to the brutes, do you, Crushe?"

"Yes, sir, and that at my expense. I do not know why I am thus treated."

"Now listen to me! We have—that is, you and I—been handling our crew *rather sharply*, not that I for one moment argue that they ought to be better treated, but we have kept them down with the lash, and, between ourselves, killed a few in so doing. Now, my dear Crushe, one of us must suffer if some blackguard among the crew tells the story; and I begin to see trouble if those infernally low newspaper fellows get hold of such a man. Now, it's not likely to go beyond the ship if you bear this for a few days more. I'll give the hounds liberty—make them think I'm a good fellow, hang them! and you must put up with it. If I get into hot water with the rabble at home, you are certain to follow, and I shall plead sickness, and throw all the blame on you; and you know no court-martial would convict me. I'll make the crew act in a manner which will belie any statements made by one or two dissatisfied beasts among them, who fancy they have a right to be treated like men; then if they come forward to give us trouble, we can bring overwhelming proof that our men were the most happy, jolly, devil-me-care fellows in the navy."

"And I am to be your scapegoat, Captain Puffeigh?"

"My dear Crushe, the next mail will bring news of our promotion, you to commander, and I to post-captain; then you may laugh at your detractors."

"But why not obtain these results without humiliating me? I am insulted by the

brutes who formerly trembled when they saw me ; now they laugh at my threats, and
appeal to you, who dismiss them, and encourage their insubordination."

"My dear Crushe, as I said before, I must leave this ship with a good name, as far
as the men are concerned ; and as one or two of your acts ended in the death of the
fellows you took in hand, I think you had better not oppose me, or we might both be
called to account by the newspaper people."

The first lieutenant, like all cowards, shrunk from inquiry into conduct which he
could not defend ; and was therefore obliged to put up with it, and make the best of
the matter. It was gall and wormwood to him, yet only fair that he who had played
the part of bully should be humiliated in the eyes of those over whom he had
tyrannized.

A few days after the foregoing conversation the captain announced his intention of
giving a ball, and, true to his mean instincts, requested the co-operation of his officers.
Now, as anything that afforded them an opportunity of meeting fair women was
eagerly seized upon by these gentlemen, it was soon arranged that the commander
should be released from all pecuniary expenditure in the matter, and the expenses
borne by the commissioned officers and midshipmen, according to rank. Puffeigh
approved of the idea, and gave the use of his cabin and gig, in fact. of everything
allowed him by the service, but he did not offer to contribute wine or any article which
would have to be paid for out of his own purse. He went on shore, invited every one
he knew, and talked loudly about the preparations that were being made on board to
entertain *his* guests, but he omitted to inform his acquaintances that his officers had a
hand in the matter ; fortunately for the service there were few like him.

The Stingers worked with a will and soon turned the quarter-deck into a ball-room.
A double awning was spread and screens laced along its sides, then stores of loot from
the pirates' cave were brought forward, and the roof draped with red, white, and blue
calico. Active sailors brought off palm branches and decorated the main and mizzen
masts, until they looked like trees. The band of the regiment stationed on shore was
spared for the occasion by the colonel, and the orchestra provided for them hung with
scarlet cloth edged with gold lace. Officers and crew worked together, and the men
vied with each other in their efforts to please the officers who directed the affair. The
only ones not actively engaged in the work were Crushe and Cravan, who endeavoured,
in spite of the confusion, to carry on the ordinary routine; but as no one attended to
them, finally concluded to give it up, and amuse themselves by passing sneering
remarks upon what they were pleased to term the "attempts at decoration."

At last the eventful night came ; and although leave of absence was freely offered
to all the crew, not a man but Clare availed himself of it, and he took the opportunity
to visit another ship, on board of which was a man who had just come from his wife's
native place. About eight o'clock the guests arrived and were received at the gangway by a number of officers and escorted aft to the reception-tent which was placed
upon the quarter-deck abaft the mizzen mast. The middies were in high glee ; and,
wonderful to relate, appeared as united as a band of patriots; old feuds were buried
and forgotten by the delighted lads, who under the benign influence of beauty became
as mild as lambs. This happy state of things lasted until the dancing commenced,
after which whenever a middy succeeded in engaging the hand of any much-prized
lady for a dance. he had immediately upon its conclusion to descend into the gun-room
and engage in combat with his rivals: there was no delaying until the morrow.—
their nautical blood was up, and have it out they must. It was nothing uncommon
upon a young lady inquiring for her late partner to be told by the victor that Mr. So-
and-So had gone on duty, which meant that the young gentleman named was below,

holding the handle of the Downton-pump to one of his eyes, or trying to arrest the bleeding of his nasal organ by the application of a cold ramrod to his spine. Of course this was an exceptional case, the middies belonging to the Stinger having been, through the meanness of their captain, for a long time deprived of an opportunity of entertaining ladies on board, and were consequently somewhat excited by so unusual an influx of youth and beauty.

The naval and military heroes carried off all the belles as partners, and those rash civilians who had ventured on board found themselves obliged to dance with the "roses of a former summer," who were therefore not upon that occasion left "blooming alone." About eleven o'clock supper was announced, and the guests were escorted to the lower deck, which they found decorated, and laid out as a spacious supper-room. The number invited had been somewhat increased at the last moment by the arrival of a large party of merchants and their families from Canton; this and a run upon the champagne caused the master who catered for the refreshment department to seek the commander and tell him that the champagne had given out; thereupon Puffeigh, who was seated between two lovely girls, called for his steward, and handing him the key of his wine-room, told him to give out some of his wine, adding, "I give this as my share, Beauman." The master told his steward to get what champagne he required from the boy Jordun, and there the matter ended as far as he was concerned.

Master William was delighted. "What! the old un give me charge of the key!" he exclaimed. "Come along, steward, we'll hand out the shampegnee." The steward deputed by Beauman did not descend to the store-room with Jordun, but pressed a sailor-waiter into his service, who having passed up two baskets for the use of the guests, quietly demanded two more.

"What for?" asked the proud holder of the key.

"Why, for ourselves, my keovy; don't we want a drink?"

The boy did as requested, then locked the store and returned the key to Puffeigh, who quietly inquired, "how many dozen did they take?"

"Four, sir;" and added, "Please, sir, I'm ill, may I turn in? I can't see for boil."

As the captain had no particular use for his steward, he gave him permission to retire, upon which William went forward and assisted in the absorption of the champagne. Happy sailor's! imbibing wine stolen from their late enemy; and still happier Puffeigh, surrounded by youth and beauty, totally unconscious that his choice "Grand vin du Czar" was being poured down the throats of his sailors forward. Some few of the men held aloof, and would not join the revellers, as they feared the punishment which might follow; but the others profited by their squeamishness, and the stolen draught was not less sweet on account of the risk of after consequences. Master Jordun drank very little of the wine,—he didn't care about that,—his object was to punish the captain's stores, but he watched every wire cut and secured the corks and empty bottles. These he contrived to take aft and place with the others; and in the excitement of the next day, Puffeigh forgot to examine into the matter, so the theft was not discovered.

Supper was over, and the dancing recommenced, when a rocket fired from a steamer entering the harbour announced to the guests that the P. and O. S. S. Aya had arrived with the mails. A boat was sent on board the flag-ship, and in about an hour the officer returned bearing dispatches from the Admiralty and Puffeigh announced to his guests that he was promoted to be post captain. This news was received with acclamation, and when he informed them that Lieutenant Crushe was promoted also, and that they were both to leave the next day by the down coast steamer, the gentlemen cheered, and the ladies crowded round the dear captain and charming commander. More champagne was obtained, but upon this occasion a midshipman was intrusted with the key of the captain's private store. The health of "Captain Puffeigh, God bless him!" and "Commander Crushe, God bless him!" was drunk by the company, who imagined both officers to be gentlemen in every sense of the word, as indeed they were so far as the guests could discern; but those who pay friendly visits to a man-of-war cannot be judges of what the working of the service is like, although such casual observers may imagine they know all about the matter.

The excitement forward was very great, and an extra allowance of grog was served out to the men in order, as Puffeigh observed, that they might join in the general festivity. "Give them a good drink apiece,—I order it; let all of them, boys and all, have a good glass of grog."

"Generous dear!" murmured a young lady near him. "How good he is; thinks of his men first of all."

"Give the men the remains of the supper—pipe hands to supper. There's lots for them; they will pick the bones for us."

"Dear fellow!" exclaimed an old maid, ogling him through her eye-glass; upon which Puffeigh shuddered and turned towards one of the pretty girls near him.

"What generosity! he's a prince of a fellow!" gobbled a fat tea-taster, who had shouted himself hoarse in his attempt to render proper respect to his dear friend Puffeigh. "By Jove! old boy, you're a brick. Gad you are, you know."

The captain heard all these observations with the greatest composure. The rum was the property of the government, and did not cost him a penny, and the remains of the supper were not his. Ergo, he could well afford to be generous. The crew fell upon the remnants of the feast, and soon made a clearance of the same.

It was nearly daybreak before the ball was over, and the guests bade their entertainers a cordial farewell, and made the best of their way on shore.

The "Hong-Kong Gong" thus commented upon the affair:—

"The Ball given last night on board H. M. S. Stinger went off with great éclat. We there heard announced the agreeable intelligence that Commander Puffeigh and Lieutenant Crushe go home by return steamer,—the former posted, the latter promoted to commander. Deservedly high as is the character borne by her Majesty's naval officers, it is seldom that even in their ranks we find a commander so thoroughly worthy of all the encomiums paid to his class, and it is with unaffected sincerity and feelings of deep appreciation that we speak of Captain Puffeigh as the true type of a British naval officer. A lion before his country's foes, he shines in peace as the accomplished and highly-educated gentleman,—a man whose qualities endear him to his friends, the soul of the festive gathering, and adored as a father by his men, who worship his heroism. To resume, we say that as a man and an officer, he sheds fresh lustre on the service he adorns, and of which our country is so justly proud. All that we have above said is applicable to Commander Crushe, and we associate them in our warmest wishes for their unfailing prosperity."

By dint of pumping salt water over and into the most obstinate cases, those of the crew who had indulged too freely were at length sobered enough to get their breakfast. Puffeigh was all fuss and worry getting ready to leave the ship, and Crushe certainly did not wish to lose the chance of going by the next steamer. About 2 P. M. the new commander, Captain Paul Woodward, arrived, and with him his first lieutenant, Lovell Russell. The new captain read his commission, looked at the men, some of whom presented rather a sleepy appearance, and then proceeded to arrange the transfer with Puffeigh. Crushe pointed out his good men to Lieutenant Russell, who glanced at them and remarked, "Although in point of fact they may be men whose acquaintance would be an infinite acquisition, yet their first appearance is calculated to convey anything but an agreeable impression."

When the official business was transacted between the commanders Puffeigh observed, "Now about private stores."

"Let our stewards arrange that,"

"I haven't one, Woodward. Ah!—that is—aw!—I am without one now. Only a boy."

"Well, let him give up your stores, Puffeigh ; we can't be bored with those things, you know."

At last it was agreed to take the stock as it stood upon Puffeigh's books, so the unsuspecting Woodward paid not only for good stores and whole bottles of wine, but also for the damaged goods and broken bottles with which the storeroom was well furnished. Woodward was no mean spirit, but a generous, noble fellow, who believed all the world as good and honourable as himself, so he gave the griping old captain a draft upon his agent for the full value of his private stores, and then called for wine with which to entertain his officers and visitors.

Master Jordun was in despair, and wanted to know "if he were going to be kidded hout ov a situvation in that ere manner?" Upon this Puffeigh sent to the surgeon, who out of pity for the lad invalided him home in the same ship as his master. William looked anything but an invalid; but knowing that his wound troubled him at times, and that his life was not destined to be a long one if he remained in China, the kindly doctor stretched a point, and assisted by another equally good fellow, packed him off.

At length the homeward bound P. and O. Steamer came into harbour, and the crew was mustered to say farewell to their late commander. Puffeigh, who had imbibed pretty freely, was in full uniform ; and when the men went aft he uncovered his head, and, with tears in his eyes, thus addressed them :—

"My lads (here a tear trickled down his left cheek), I am leaving you for ever—most likely for ever—but I am—I am (another tear, this time upon his right cheek) sorry I am going. I took charge of you when you were a pretty rough lot (sobbing), but I leave you a fine, happy set of fellows (more sobs). God bless you, my lads. We've been through danger together (more tears), and I've led you to victory. Now we are to part. It is the will of our Queen (bowing reverently). She approves of your actions, my actions, and the actions of Lieutenant Crushe (more tears). All I can say is that we must part. We shall probably never meet again on earth (with great emotion), but we may meet in heaven. My lads, you know what it is to obey. I've been a father to you. I have not spared the rod; but look at you, how happy you have been (more tears). Obey others, for my sake, and in you prayers remember the old captain who tried his best to make your service under him a—hap—py one—God—bless you (more emotion and undulation of waistcoat). Good-bye, my gallant lads."

Saying which the old hypocrite shook hands with the biggest scoundrels among the crew, and descended to his boat. As he left the ship the sailors manned the rigging, by order of their new commander.

"Now, my lads, three cheers for your old captain.'

Puffeigh was standing up in his gig, ready to receive the honour,—head uncovered, and eyes sparkling with success,—but not a sound came from the crew ; true, the boatswain and officers commenced, but they broke down upon finding the men were silent.

"Come, my lads—Hip-hip," urged the generous Woodward.

At this moment a tremendous groan burst from the men : this they repeated twice, then scrambled down from aloft, and went aft upon the quarter-deck, where stood their new commander, quite horror-stricken, at their proceedings.

" My lads, this is shameful conduct ! "

" Captain Woodward," observed a smart topman, "Captain Puffeigh flogged and treated us like dogs ; we can't cheer him."

" Boatswain, pipe man the rigging, and give three cheers," firmly directed the commander, as if he had not heard the speech.

This decisive conduct brought the crew to their senses. Up they sprang into the rigging, and soon three cheers rang out upon the breeze.

Puffeigh, who was now some distance from the Stinger, stopped his boat ; then, rising, bowed towards the ship, and cursed the crew as mutinous hounds, of whom he was well quit. After that he resumed his seat, and soon reached the P. and O. Steamer, where he was received like any ordinary passenger.

Crushe heard how Puffeigh was treated, and knowing the crew hated him even more than they did their late commander, deemed it advisable to leave in a very quiet manner, so he hurried over the side without saying good-bye to any one ; and as few of the officers cared, even for appearance' sake, to shake hands with him, it was a matter of congratulation among them when they found he was gone.

Boy Jordun received all the honours, being sent in the pinnace with the baggage. All the crew and marines shook hands with him, and he was literally laden with presents. Just as he left the gangway a quarter-master came to him to say the captain wanted him. William went aft and saluted Woodward, who thereupon gave him a little advice and a five-shilling-piece for the assistance he had given his steward in taking an inventory of the furniture, &c., purchased by him of the late captain. Jordun looked at the money and then at the captain, and with a bow observed, " I saved yer from being done on the gear, sir, but you will find a hawful lot of duffers among the bottles."

Woodward, who did not exactly understand the purport of the boy's speech, upon this patted him upon the shoulder, told him to be a good boy, and dismissed him. When the pinnace left the ship's side a ringing cheer burst from the crew, three times three and one over being roared forth with all the force of their powerful lungs.

" Good-bye, young Bill "—" Good-bye, chummy "—" Good luck to ye."

William Jordun stood up in the boat, gave three cheers by way of reply, and—then blubbered.

" Mind you don't forget the parcel ! " shouted a voice loud and clear above the babel on board.

" You may take your halfadavit I won't," murmured the boy as he drew his cuff across his eyes, and composed his mind to go on board the steamer.

The Lota had the blue peter flying, and was nearly ready to slip from her moorings when the pinnace went alongside, and Jordun soon found himself rid of his charge as far as baggage was concerned. After a search he found Puffeigh's cabin, where he delivered sundry small articles.

The P. and O. steamer was splendidly found, excellently manned, and well commanded. Wonderful to tell, they did not flog their crew or treat them like animals ; yet, notwithstanding this, they managed to keep them in a very complete state of discipline, so good that it puzzled Puffeigh. However, as he despised anything that savoured of the merchant service, he held his tongue and accepted the hospitality of the commander, as homage to his superior rank, whereupon Captain Turner, who never toadied a man in his life, quietly cut him, and confined his civility to wishing him good morning when going his rounds.

As they left the harbour, dinner was announced; and Captain Turner being engaged on deck, Puffeigh assumed his place at the head of the table, a very inquisitive lady, who was placed in his charge by her husband, being seated upon his right; the boy Jordun standing by, having been directed to wait upon her, as a sort of extra attendant. Dinner was nearly over, and Puffeigh well warmed with sherry, when a steward pointed to a long parcel which was laid upon the glass-rack overhead, and asked the captain if he knew it was there.

" What is it ? "

" Don't know, sir," said the head steward. " It was brought on board for you just as the ship turned ahead."

" Hand it down."

The parcel was reached from the rack and placed upon the table, and the lady read the address, which ran as follows :—

" The Honourable CAPTAIN PUFFEIGH,
                    Late Commander of
                                H. M. S. *Stinger*.

"Fruit, with care."

" What can it be ? " said the lady.

" Who sent it ? " queried Crushe, who was seated on the captain's left.

" Who received it ?" demanded Puffeigh.

" I did sir," replied the head steward ; " it was brought by a sampan-man."

" Let the steward open it," observed Crushe.

" He will change it for some horrid ship's fruit if he does," whispered the suspicious Puffeigh. " Jordun, open the parcel, and let us see what it contains."

The captain's loud voice and arrogant manner had caused many of the passengers to leave their seats, and Jordun's proceedings were closely watched by all present. Upon removing the brown paper cover a box was exposed, and the lid of this being lifted, master William drew forth a cat-of-nine-tails, the thongs of which had been painted vermilion to simulate blood-stains. The boy gaped at it with horror depicted upon his face, then suddenly dropped the weapon, when from it fell a paper which one of the by-standers officiously picked up, and read aloud as follows:—

"To Captain Puffeigh and Commander Crushe, in rememcrance of their cruel treatment towards their men. The lash for the commander, the handle for the captain."

Puffeigh gasped with rage, then turned towards Crushe, but found his place vacant, upon which he beat a retreat to his cabin and sent for boy Jordun, but master William returned a message to say that " he was an invalid, and not able to wait upon him any more " The passengers got hold of the lad, who gave them full information as to the cruelties practised on board the Stinger, and some of them wrote long letters, which they swore they would send to the *Times*. It is probable that the indignant civilians forgot to forward their epistles, as none of them were published. Puffeigh and Crushe were cut by all their fellow passengers, but they consoled themselves with thinking how immeasurably superior they were to such fellows as merchants and China traders, and were quite contented with each other's society.

Upon arrival at Southampton, Puffeigh found his wife, and was soon on his way to his home. Crushe went to his aunt for a month, then proceeded to see his wife, who loved him in spite of his cruelty and neglect. He had not been there many weeks before he received orders to proceed to the Pacific, where he was hated by nearly all under his command.

William Jordun steered straight for his father's inn, and arrived at it one day just as the family were sitting down to dinner. He walked in, put down his bundle, called for a pint of beer, and drank "all their jolly good healths," before any one made out who he was. However, his mother recognized his voice, and flying towards him, hugged him to her bosom, crying, "My own kinchin Billy—my dear little kid."

Mr. Jordun, who had seated himself before a huge lump of boiled beef, upon hearing this started up, and with a very large oath snatched the boy from his mother's embrace, and hugged him no less frantically.

"What, my bo' Bill—my littleest kid come home agin—Lord bless you, my boy. I'm so glad to see you."

When the heads of the family had done with him, William was condescending enough to allow the women-folks and customers to welcome him. After they had finished the lad took a seat between his father and mother, and fell-to at the food, between the mouthfuls relating his adventures. His parents were deeply interested in his recital, and when he concluded his meal, a pipe was filled by his mother and handed to him, and he shared his father's gin and water as he proceeded with his story. When he informed them that he had been left all Old Jemmy's prize money and pay, which would amount together with his own to about thirty pounds, his father observed that it must be put in the Savings Bank for him.

"I knows a better game nor that, dad."

"What is it, bo'?"

"Vy, lay it out in a skittul alley, and put over the gangway, Bill Jordun and Son."

Upon hearing this observation the man laid down his pipe, shook hands solemnly with his son, and declared, "that it was a bargain."

That is why the sign of the Blue Posts at Portsea came to run as follows:—

WILLIAM JORDUN AND SON (WM.),

LICENSED TO SELL

BEER

TO BE DRUNK ON THE PREMISES.

N.B. A good dry skittle alley.

And here we take our leave of master William Jordun, being unable to give our readers any further information concerning that undaunted youth.

CHAPTER XV.

WHEN Thompson saw the main body of the bannermen riding over the sand ridge he knew it was useless to resist, so he quietly awaited his fate. After surrounding him, one of their number grasped the sailor by the collar and attempted to lift him off the ground, upon which Jerry clambered up and seated himself behind his captor. Having secured the dead body of their companion, the party set spurs to their horses, and were soon out of the captain's sight. Puffeigh knew it would be useless to fire at them, as such a proceeding would only make matters worse for the prisoner. When they had proceeded about a mile they threw the dead body into a field, then dismounting and placing Thompson in the centre of the group, squatted round him, lighted their pipes, and held a council of war.

"This barbarian looks like a western devil to me," observed their leader. "I am uncertain whether to kill him now, or to take him to the military governor."

"If we slay him at once we shall be sure of his body," put in a squint-eyed bannerman. "These western devils are all necromancers,—here this moment, when—pouf—you look, and they have vanished. I vote we kill him by degrees. We need not return until sunset,—then dismember him, leave his body as an offering to the Kiang-shi, who walk at night, and take his head to the governor."

"That's like you, Kwo, always jumping at ideas. Why, do you think we are little fools to indulge in torturing this devil? What will our rulers say if they do not witness his death struggles?"

"Bah! you know everything, Ting. But listen! Here is a foreign devil, calm, unmoved, and as resigned to his fate as one of the most favoured nation. If we take him in, the people will say, 'Where is the tiger?' and lo, you will show this lamb, when they will jeer at us, and insult our bravery. 'What,' they will cry, 'thirty braves, and only this mouse captured!' See! if we carry in his head, a large reward will be paid us, and we can lie as much as we like as to the manner of his capture. My plan is all benefit." Saying which Kwo rose; and, in order to show his contempt for Jerry, slapped the latter across the face, crying, "Ha, dog! ha, coward!" and was at once knocked over by the sailor, who remarked, "Come, stow that little game," and then resumed his squatting position.

As Kwo was by no means a favourite in his corps, they only laughed at his mishap, and did not attempt to punish their prisoner for his audacity.

These bannermen are not regular troops, but a sort of volunteer corps, who are ordered out for drill four times a year. They are drawn from the shopkeeper class of citizens, and this service entitles them to many privileges. When called upon during a war, they are employed in defending their native towns. Upon some occasions they have fought bravely, and in many parts of China monuments are erected to commemorate the prowess of gallant bannermen. However, as a rule they are very timorous soldiers, and not much depended upon by the military governors. Some of the northern bannermen are mounted upon Tartar ponies, while in the southern provinces they are foot soldiers. Their weapons consist of bows and arrows, spears, knives, and tridents. Firearms are of course known to them, but a wise and benevolent government has prudently ordained that "only in exceptional cases shall they be armed with such dangerous engines."

The party who had captured Thompson had, upon the preceding day, been to a grand review of the bannermen of the Eleven districts, and as most of their number had friends in the city near which the review took place, it was determined that they should not return to their native town until daylight the next morning. They had bidden their hospitable entertainers farewell at sunrise, and being brave with wine when they sighted Puffeigh and his companions, and thinking they were a party of southern merchants who travel about those parts with Chinese trinkets, the bannermen laid their heads together, and determined to attack and rob them, it being a custom of the volunteers, when upon what they called active service, to behave like the regular troops of his Highness and Mightiness the Father and Mother of the Empire, who were never known to leave a sapeck in the pouch of any unfortunate wayfarer they chanced to fall in with during a march. Great was their astonishment upon finding they had fallen across some Western devils; and when they succeeded in capturing one of the party they felt as brave as lions, and quite as eager to see blood.

After much discussion, the leader of the party, a tailor by profession, named Choo-Too, the combined words forming also a nickname which might be translated "pig-stomached," commanded silence, and thus addressed his fellows,—" My honourable persons, will you with reverence hear the words of this little one ? I, Choo, had this morning a dream, in which I saw Kwan-ti, the god of war, sitting on a cloud which smelt of gunpowder. Abject, I grovelled in the dust, as I (in my own mind) never before believed in Kwan-ti. Then crackers exploded and gingalls discharged all around him, after which he spake as follows:—' Choo, arise, and get thee to the sea-shore, you and all your company, there ye will meet with fortune, and capture a devil, fear him not, he will be harmless, but watch well that he escape not, or woe be to ye all.' "

At this moment his speech was interrupted by the prisoner requesting "one of the *old ladies* to hand him a chaw of baccy."

Choo frowned upon the undaunted one, and thus continued:—"This little one then swooned, and so remained until found by you, my honourable friends."

"Wonderful ! wonderful !" exclaimed the other bannermen, but added aside to each other, " Why, we imagined Choo-Too was drunk."

"Now, my honourable friends, I think it better we secure this malignant western devil, and take him to our native town. None of the regular troops, with all their bravery, have ever been able to catch sight of one of these creatures, much less capture it alive, so we will gain honour and perhaps a reward, if we take him to the military governor, or even give him up to our own mayor, who will probably pay us for such a curiosity."

"But why not torture him a little now ? " observed a weasel-faced dealer in bean-curd.

" No, no !" cried the majority. " Let us take him to Sse-tsein ; he will then be properly tortured, and we shall be able to show our valour before our honourable parents."

Thompson tapped the last speaker upon the shoulder, and quietly observed, " Well done, old man ; I don't know your lingo, but if you're going to skin me alive give us a chaw of baccy ; " saying this he pointed to the tobacco-pouch suspended from the soldier's girdle, and which the Tartar handed him, whereupon the sailor took a pinch, and gravely placed it in his mouth, then closed the bag, and returned it to him, winking as he did so in such a sly manner, that the whole party roared with laughter.

" He eats tobacco ! he eats tobacco ! " they cried.

Before they re-mounted Choo made another speech, in which he instructed his men what to say concerning the capture of the sailor.

"My honourable friends must all speak thus, even if put to torture. We were returning from Hong-loo, when suddenly a body of at least five hundred western devils opposed us, and commenced an attack upon our party. We, with swelling breasts dilated with over-bravery, eyes flashing like the hands and feet of Luopo. with headlong prowess spurring our steeds to the death, in hopes to salute heaven in doing such bravery, we, a handful, rushed upon our foes, and killed them all but about a dozen, who fled in a small boat. Suy-peh (old Suy), whose hands have become palsied by age and breeches making, first seized the demon we have captured, but it took the whole of us to secure him. Mo-tim was killed—we left his body upon the field, after having carried it out of the reach of the retreating barbarians; and as he was killed in action, the owner of the land will be able to bury him at his own expense, without inquiry, which will be a saving, as otherwise a dead body would be a bad present for him."

"Stop!" cried Suy-peh, "your words are golden, yet vain ones. Do you think, my illustrious friends, that Chung-sung, our learned mayor, will believe such shallow lies? He will ask, 'Where is the blood upon your garments? where your wounds? where the dead bodies or even heads of those western devils you have slain?' Tell the truth, and you will gain all credit, and be considered great warriors enough, without each of us endeavouring to get by memory the bombastic speech of Choo-Too. I think he might have invented something better, and, for my part, I don't believe a word about his vision. I'm too old to be cheated in that manner."

"Suy-peh, you're a breeches-mending old fool!"

"Choo, you are well named Choo-Too. I spit at you."

Probably a fight would have ensued, but the friends of the parties separated them, and having taken Jerry up behind him, Choo scowled at Suy-peh (who made a face at him by way of retort), and then gave the order to march.

Thompson stuck to the tailor, who was not a good horseman; but the sailor hung on to the animal as well, and in this manner got along very nicely, until they arrived at the suburbs of the town, where the party dismounted and partook of hot rice spirit. This increased their valour to such a degree, that they treated their prisoner to sundry kicks and cuffs, to show their friends how they had tamed the foreign devil. Upon remounting they placed him on a miserable scarecrow of a horse, borrowed from the landlord of the inn, and proceeded towards the town gates, stopping every few yards to tell their story, and enable the women and children to pelt the prisoner with mud, filth, or stones, or spit upon him, as their playful fancy dictated.

Poor Jerry experienced some very rough treatment, but never for a moment lost his pluck. When a heavier stone than usual was thrown at him, he would turn round and cry, "Come, missis, stash it;" but otherwise he took the proceedings as part of the rites upon such occasions, and when a pretty girl abused him, would reply in a most admiring strain. As they neared the gates they fell in with a party of women headed by the wife of the bannerman who had been killed by the master. The woman was supported by her sons, who did not seem to be much concerned about their father's fate, as they laughed and chatted with the crowd; this was strange, as the Chinese always profess to venerate their parents in the highest degree.

After Choo had spoken his piece, to which the widow listened with the deepest attention, she advanced to the prisoner, and raising her voice to a shrill falsetto, thus addressed him, "Oh!!! you lwan lwan (mean-looking) fuh-hwy (reptile), wo yaou ne teih naow kae (I want your skull)." Then she proceeded with increased volubility to abuse his father, who she declared was hangman to the devil, and his mother, who she swore was anything but a lady ; his sisters and all his female and male relations were likewise abused, the excited widow winding up with the following, which she poured forth in the patois of her district, without once stopping to take breath. "Ha! white-livered bear-faced red-nosed blue-lipped silk-haired bull-eyed pig-skin'd blood-drinking hairy-headed man-eating woman-featured foreign devil—Ha! Haw!! Hah!!!"

"Thankee, mum, ha! ha!—I ses too, I hopes you're well."

Upon this the widowed one ran towards him, seized him by the right leg and threw him off his horse, then turned and fled. Thompson was not long upon the ground, but in the confusion he got separated from the bannermen, who had to fight their way towards him, as the crowd wished to lynch the prisoner. At last, however, he was rescued from their clutches and carried in triumph through the outer gate into the guard-house, where the regular troops took charge of his case ; and making prisoners of the whole party, carried them to the ya-mun of the military commander, a Tartar by the name of Kcong. An immense crowd followed the procession ; and when they arrived, the great gates were opened, as it would have been impossible to admit the party through the ordinary entrance. When they were all inside the court-yard the guards shut the gates, and refused admission to the curious. The prisoner was now secured by formidable-looking chains made of rod iron, each link being about a foot in length. They looked very strong, but Jerry coolly surveyed them and inquired of the executioner "if them were his best darbys." As the man of blood could not under-stand him, he contented himself by scowling at the western devil, who laughed at him and declared "he was the rummiest old keove he had met with since he landed."

The bannermen were seated upon the flag-stones, smoking their pipes and drinking hot spirit, which they purchased of the executioner. Thompson motioned them to give him a drink, upon which the official held out his hand for the sapecks. Jerry seized it, and gave him a good hearty grip, which made the grim one dance and swear, much to the amusement of the volunteers. However, the fellow thought it best to take it good-humouredly, and bringing him a cup of the spirit, bade him drink. After a time it was announced that the bannermen might go to their homes, as the mandarin did not intend investigating the matter that night, he being too far gone in opium. So having given in their names to the scribe, the valiant band departed. Thompson nodded to them, and observed "that he was very sorry to lose their cheerful society," and then followed the executioner, who, seizing his chains, pointed to a low doorway, and motioned him to go before.

They passed across immense court-yards and by large buildings, many of which were in the last stage of decay, and at length emerged into the open air. Jerry looked about him, and found they were in a beautiful garden, surrounded on all sides by high walls. After walking for some moments they came to a low building partly sunk in the ground, which Thompson correctly imagined to be a magazine. Having skirted this the executioner stopped, unlocked a door, and motioning the prisoner to enter, proceeded to fasten him by his chains to a staple driven in the wall. This done, he drew forth a cord, and placing the sailor's hands behind his back, lashed his wrist-irons together and left him. When the sound of his jailer's footsteps died away, Jerry quietly slipped off the iron rings, and lighting a match looked round his cell, which he found was the guard house of the magazine. Seeing a lamp near, he reached it, and having lighted it proceeded to rid himself of his other irons. He stopped several times to ascertain if any one were about, but finding all quiet, resumed his occupation, and in a short time freed himself of his encumbrances ; then took the lamp, and made a careful examination of his prison. It was merely the outer court of the magazine, and before him he found the door leading into the same, the only fastening of which was a bolt. It appeared to him that the keeper of the place usually occupied the outer chamber, as he found a leathern chest secured by a curious ark-shaped brass padlock, and a complete suit of Tartar's clothes.

Knowing how small his chances of escape were if he did not attempt to get away before he was tortured, he determined to fire the magazine, even if he had to go with it. The chest he coolly cut open, and found in it one silk holiday suit, one artificial queue, two common suits, one cotton helmet—an article much worn in the northern provinces—(it is like a cap with an all-round curtain attached), one holiday cap, and about 600 cash or sapecks—small brass coins pierced with a square hole, and strung upon twine for convenience of carrying. In a few moments he divested himself of his sailor's attire, and was dressed in one of the ordinary suits of clothes, his curly hair being concealed under the cotton helmet; then making the other garments into a bundle —retaining only the little bag containing the waist-ribbon given him by Mary Ann, his ring, the gift of Miss Moore, and a tin box of lucifer matches—he secured the money to his girdle, took up the lamp, and cautiously entered the magazine. Before him he saw several hundred packages of joss-stick, but no powder—the place was large, and partly empty. As he advanced, the rats would dart out of his way, and run squeaking into their burrows among the joss stick. He was about to give up his search, when he spied a door, and having drawn the bolt, found himself in a vast chamber, which had no doubt at some time contained an immense store of ammunition.

"Here's a place to perform Ally Barber! Here's jars enow for forty hundred thieves!" he cried, as, carefully setting down his lamp, he lifted the lid of one of the jars and found it was empty. Taking up his light he cautiously advanced until he saw before him a large heap of powder, which had evidently been emptied for some special reason, as it was carefully enclosed with boarding so that none of it touched the floor. Having placed his lamp in a safe position, he proceeded to pull down the end board, and to make a train towards the door. This was the work of a few seconds; and when he had run it across the joss stick compartment, he headed it by heaping up a small pile of powder in his cell. The door of his prison proving too strong, he tried the window, through which he found he could, with a little exertion, manage to squeeze himself. Upon this he threw out his bundle, placed two long pieces of well-lighted joss stick with their unburnt ends in the powder piled upon the floor of his cell; then worked himself through the window or air hole, and made the best of his way across the garden: calculating that the joss stick would burn about a quarter of an hour, and by that time he would be out of danger.

He walked along for some time until he stumbled over something, which proved to be a man, round whose neck was fastened a cangue, or collar of wood. The poor wretch groaned when he felt the shock; and as the sailor soon found out what was the matter, he proceeded to undo the fastenings. The man at first resisted, fearing he would be punished, but finding the "silent one," as he dubbed Thompson, was really a friend, he let him go on. Having released him, Jerry gave him the other plain suit of clothes; and when he was dressed in it, the pair made their way towards the wall. Suddenly they saw a flash, upon which the sailor threw himself upon the ground. Up shot a light, bang went a report, and the Imperial magazine of Sse-tsen was blown into atoms. So terrific was the shock, that the ya-mun was totally destroyed, the mandarin and a great number of his household killed, and the walls levelled to the ground. Hundreds of prisoners were released, and these ran about crying to their gods to help them. The mandarin's women hobbled about and wrung their hands, and the place looked like an ants' nest when it is disturbed by the kick of a passer by.

Thompson's companion cried, and called upon Buddha ; but finding himself unhurt, ceased his supplications, and motioning his companion to follow him, led the way out of the place.   As they passed over the heaps of ruins, they noticed many of the prisoners making good their escape, but no one seemed to know by what means the magazine had been fired, and Jerry did not understand what they were talking about, and had he done so, would not have enlightened them.   After threading their way through dense crowds of people and walking for some time in comparatively deserted streets, Mo, that being the name of the Chinaman released by Thompson, suddenly motioned his benefactor to stop, then walked forward and left him.

" He ain't agoin' to give me the slip now we're safe," muttered the sailor ; however, in a few moments the man returned and signalled him to follow, when he found the reason for the caution exercised by Mo.   They had to pass through one of the gates of the outer wall, and as at night the guards sometimes stop those who seek egress, the clever Mo had gone forward to ascertain how matters stood, and to his joy found the place deserted, upon which they passed through without trouble, Jerry taking the opportunity of acquiring a dirk, which was hung upon a nail near the doorway.   Mo walked on until they arrived at a canal, when he began to peer cautiously at the various boats.   Having proceeded some distance along the bank, he at last made out the craft he required, when he placed his fingers in his mouth and blew a shrill signal.   In a few moments it was answered, and a woman launching a small sampan, sculled towards the spot where they were standing.

" Mo ! is that you, my lord ? "

" Yes ; make haste, Jow !   I have one with me.   I have broken from prison,—Come ! "

The men entered the crank sampan and were quickly conveyed on board a cargo boat ; and as there was a little breeze, Mo and his wife pulled up the anchor, hoisted sail, got out their oars, and were soon on their way down the canal.   Great was their astonishment when, upon going below, they discovered their friend was one of the great western devils, but, as Mo observed, " He is a good devil, since he has rescued me from that infernal prison, let us therefore chin-chin him (be friendly,) and we shall be fortunate, —besides, he will assist us without payment."

Jow saw no reason why they should not ship this man provided he kept quiet, and did not betray them.   It seems that upon their arrival at Sse-tsein a few days previous to the one upon which the sailor was captured, Mo had landed with his only man to receive the cash for some salt which they had smuggled on shore upon a previous visit. The person to whom they had sold it, instead of paying them as he promised, had informed the military mandarin, whereupon the latter seized Mo and his man, and threw them into prison.   As neither of them would give the name and number of their boat, or say to what place they belonged, the mandarin directed them to be beaten, and condemned the principal, Mo, to wear the cangue until such time as he should confess his crime, when probably his boat would be seized, his wife sold, and himself strangled.

Mrs. Mo, or rather Jow, was very pretty, and she knew it ; so did her husband, who had great difficulty in obtaining a *crew* who did not want to make love to her.   Now, he thought he had found the very man, so, devil or no devil, he made up his mind to ship Jerry as second mate and crew combined.   He told his wife what he had determined, and as Jow saw that the devil was not quite as ugly as he had been painted to her, she reluctantly gave her consent, the truth being she had determined never to speak well of the crew in future.

Mo shaved Thompson's head, face, and eyebrows, then attached the artificial queue they had brought from the ya-mun, and sent him on deck for his wife's inspection.

"What do you think of him?"

"Ugly beast! frightful! he makes me tremble!" cried Jow in an affected voice, while secretly she thought she had never seen such a handsome crew in her life.

Mo treated him very kindly and passed him off as a dumb man from Kwantung, and Jerry began to like the life immensely. Jow was, as her name suggested, a soft fascinating woman, and whenever her husband was away would, when addressing the crew, relax her severe expression of countenance, and before he had been shipped a week, they were desperately in love with each other. He was so handsome, so daring, so kind, and so a hundred other things, while poor Mo, who was an excellent fellow as Chinese husbands go, was (behind his back) so stupid, so cowardly, so ugly, so in-every-way-mean. Women are clever in finding excuses even for their little peccadilloes, and Jow was as smart as the rest of her charming sex. Being a Chinese woman, this little weakness must be forgiven her, remembering she was almost sold to one, who, like all his countrymen, consider women to be mere animals created to minister to the wants of men; therefore, when she found a being who treated her kindly, waited on her, showed he considered her his equal, ay and in many things his superior, she sinned according to our ideas, but really unconsciously avenged the wrongs of her sex; and Mr. Mo being the victim, let those be sorry for him who have no better opinion of women than he had.

The Big Dog, that being the name of the boat, discharged her cargo at Yungping, took in a load of skins for the southern market, and proceeded towards the Pei-ho. All went on pleasantly, and Mo began to teach his crew Chinese, and when that gentleman was absent, Jow continued the lesson, so in the course of a few weeks the sailor became quite proficient; but when upon duty Jerry was scolded and frowned upon by the lady in such a splendid style, that Mo would brag to his fellow captains that he had a woman who was as women go priceless. "She is young, she is beautiful, can cook, sing, and make clothes. Her words are all for me; she is my wife, my slave, my little puppy; at my frown she quakes, at my command she flies. She is mine in thought, and I do not beat her, because I have no friends to be edified with the punishment. When I leave her she takes her seat by the rudder, and watches for my return; she is to me as the earth is to the potter,—I mould her to suit my taste; she remains as I form her ideas, if women can have any but what we gods give them."

Thus, in his sublime egotism, would Mr. Mo descant upon the excellent qualities of Jow; while all the time Jerry was paying the most gallant attention to that lady. True, it was a harmless flirtation, as he had not learnt enough of the Chinese language to enable him to propose an elopement, but he was getting on very rapidly, and in six weeks, by the time they arrived at Lin-tsin, the crew made up his mind, come what might, he would run away with the fair Jow, boat and all. Mo discharged his cargo, loaded his boat with merchandise, on account of a house in Ngan-tong, and upon the first "lucky day" the Big Dog proceeded down the Imperial Canal, and in due time arrived at her destination, where Mo received instructions to go on to a place called Hong-hien, on the borders of the lake Hong-tse.

It was one of Mo's fixed principles "never to do to-day what can be put off until to-morrow," so when he heard he was to go on to another port, he determined not to start until he had enjoyed a run on shore. Having provided himself with a bag of cash, he, after bidding his wife sit up for him until he chose to return, proceeded to a noted gambling-house, where he played cards until morning, then picking up his weary frame, walked down to the wharf, when, lo! he found his Big Dog was gone.

Mo sat down upon a pile, and uttered the following lamentation, which soon drew about him a crowd of loafers who seemed much amused with his outburst.

"Alas—unfortunate I. Last night I left my boat as I thought safe. Now, in my absence, cruel, relentless thieves have seized upon her, taken my boat, and have probably killed that excellent animal, Jow. Poor beast, how she will miss my voice."

Here Mr. Mo was interrupted by a dirty-looking boatman, who demanded, "how much will you give me if I tell you where your craft is?"

"I'll give you five hundred cash if you will take me to her," excitedly exclaimed Mo.

"Well," replied the fellow, "hand over the sapecks, and I will put you on board in a few hours. Your boat is at Mung-shang, she couldn't well get further than that, as the wind changed about an hour ago, and it will probably blow so for two or three days longer."

Mo paid the money at once, and pretending not to hear the chaff of the crowd, entered his friend's boat, and proceeded in search of his Big Dog.

Upon the departure of his captain for the gambling-house Jerry, assisted by Mrs. Jow, got the boat under weigh, and ran down to Mung-shang, where after much labour, they contrived to anchor the craft. It was quite daylight when they arrived off the town, and as they anchored among a number of other canal boats, which had arrived from Ngan-tong that morning, they thought themselves pretty secure.

Having got off safely with the fair Jow, Jerry proceeded to what he called "make an honest woman of her," and after endeavouring to explain to her that a union like hers was no marriage, he "asked" himself three times in English, as follows:—

"I publish the banns of marriage, between Jerry Thompson, bachelor, and Missis Jow—ahem!—Chinese female. If any of you fellers (looking across at some people who were taking their breakfast upon the deck of a canal boat anchored a short distance from the Big Dog) knows any just cause why we shouldn't be jined in the bonds of matrimony, just sing out."

As the "fellers" addressed did not take the slighest notice of his appeal, the sailor took Jow by the hand, pressed a ring upon her finger, and a kiss upon her lips, and, as she appeared to acquiesce in the proceedings, declared they were properly wedded, and the articles signed.

This remarkably concise ceremony being concluded, the happy pair began their honeymoon, Jerry by descending to the cabin, where he poured out a cup of Mo's choicest samshoo, in which to drink success to the wedding, while Mrs. J. (Jow or Jerry according to taste, the initial serving for both) proceeded to prepare breakfast for her new lord. Alas! that such a simple act as the latter should prove so fatal to all their dreams of future happiness, and give an affair with so comic a début a tragic finale.

After having lighted the galley fire, Mrs. J. proceeded to the boat's side to draw a bucket of water, but the rope being too short, the first operation was unsuccessful.

"How provoking—the bucket didn't get nearly low enough," soliloquized the fair creature. "It will never do to call Chè-rè, O-mi-tu-fuh! (O great Buddha) what shall I do?"

Uttering this short "prayer under adverse circumstances," Mrs. J. stood on tip-toe, shook the rope, lowered it until she felt the bucket touch the water, reached over, saying, "Hech! he-ch! the bucket won't—fill—he-ch!" when she suddenly lost her balance, and, with a cry of fear, plunged headlong overboard. Poor Mrs. J.! in her descent she must have struck her head against the boat's side, as, upon rising to the surface again, she made no effort to swim, but quietly sank to rise no more.

This catastrophe was calmly witnessed by a number of sampan-men and the "fellers" on an adjoining canal boat, to whom Jerry had appealed when publishing his banns; but not one of them made the slightest attempt to save her, believing "that the River God had got her," and it would be calling his vengeance down upon their own heads if they tried to rescue her from his grasp. They sat and watched the affair much as they would have done the death of a kitten, and when it was all over, coolly remarked to each other, "that she didn't kick much when the God grasped her."

Jerry, busy below with the samshoo, did not hear the splash; and when he again returned to the deck was informed by a sampan-man, who was waiting for a fare alongside a neighbouring boat, that his woman had given herself to the River God. Other spectators of the tragedy added their testimony to the boatman's, and Jerry found that without doubt Mrs J. was gone.

After diving in the water, and searching under the boat, in hopes the poor creature might have "lodged" there, but finding that she was indeed carried off by the River God, Jerry reluctantly gave up his search, and returned to the Big Dog, which was by this time swarming with sampan-men, who, taking advantage of the owner's trouble, were plundering the craft in a most business-like manner.

Jerry was overcome with grief and despair, but even under these circumstances did not choose to be robbed; so after thrashing the thieves out of the boat, he prepared to leave her. Mo's dog, a most savage brute, was chained up forward, and when the sailor had provisioned the sampan belonging to the craft, and secured the cash he had taken from the magazine at Sse-tsein, he released the beast, and quitted the boat, which by this time had become odious to him.

Mr. Mo arrived at Mung-shan soon after Jerry's departure, and was duly informed of his bereavement, upon hearing which he sat down and uttered—not a prayer for the departed—but some very naughty words.

After sailing a short distance in the sampan, Jerry landed at a little fishing village on the other side of the lake; and having found a young fellow who was desirous of seeing something of the world, he shipped him as his crew, and the pair worked their way back to Ngan-tong, and thence down the Imperial Canal, during which trip Thompson became very proficient in the Chinese language. At Kuachú his crew abandoned him, and he proceeded alone until he reached Lake Tai-hú, where, selling his boat, he landed and tramped his way toward the green tea district. The world seemed a weary place for Jerry; and although he saw many pretty girls working in the fields, he did not care to enter into conversation with them. Everything appeared to go wrong with him since Mrs. J. died, and he wanted a severe shock to rouse him from his lethargic state.

One morning he entered the town of Whey-chú, in the heart of the green tea district, and as he spoke rather peculiar Chinese, the guard arrested him as a Canton rebel. After having floored several of the soldiers, he was overpowered, and thrown into prison, and found he ran an excellent chance of being beheaded, as the public prosecutor declared him to be a rebel spy. There was no opportunity of escaping, as at Sse-tsein; and, to add to his trouble, he was taken sick with fever. After being incarcerated in a horrid hole for more than three weeks, he was examined, when he declared "that he was no rebel, but an Inkili Hung-mow-jin," or foreign red-headed man. This announcement was received with derision; but, upon consultation with his assistants, the mandarin, before whom he was taken, determined to send him to Hang-chow, where a commissioner was sitting to decide upon the fate of all rebels who were captured in the province of Che-Keang. As he argued, "If this is a western barbarian, although he isn't vermilion-headed, I ought not to put him to death, the emperor having instructed me to forward all such to Canton, or the nearest port where those Fanquis congregate. Now, as that would involve a large expense, which, in these times of rebellion, we cannot very well afford, I will send him to Hang-chow, where the Imperial commissioner will determine whether he is a rebel or not."

One day as Jerry was dreaming his time away in his cell an executioner entered, and, bidding him follow, led the way into the Court of Mercy, where he was forced upon his knees, and ordered to bow to the mandarin who presided. The father and mother of the city addressed a long speech to his prisoner, and then dismissed him with a gesture of contempt, upon which he was dragged off, as he imagined, to execution, they leading him into a room, and striking off his irons.

"I'm glad it'll soon be all over," he observed in English. I'm tired of this dog's life."

The executioner called in two Tartar soldiers, who seized the prisoner, and fastened a rope round his neck, each of them taking an end; the door was then opened, and he found himself once more in the sun-light. His guards led him with every show of caution until they got clear of the city, then they coiled the rope round his neck, and jogged along in a very friendly manner.

"Ha!" he exclaimed, as he cast his eyes back towards the town. "Good-bye, you infernal pest-hole. Jerry is himself again, and if all goes well will be upon his own hook in twenty-four hours, at the furthest."

CHAPTER XVI.

THE day following that upon which Puffeigh left his ship Captain Woodward mustered his crew and made them the following speech :—"My men, I yesterday read my commission and took charge of this ship as your commander. I did not care to address you then; but as I always like to start fairly with my crew, I take this opportunity to do so. I find you are lax in your duty, and that there is a common use of profane language among you which I wish stopped. I may as well tell you that I am in every way averse to flogging. I consider you are men, and that the lash is degrading and brutal. I am determined you shall have your rights, but you must always endeavour to be worthy of them. I wish you to understand that you start fairly with me. I do not know any of your former good or bad behaviour. What a man is to-day is my guide; and those who have been astray have now an opportunity of taking their place, without reproach, with those men who have behaved well. You who are petty officers will, I know, for the sake of your manhood, cease to use those foolish, meaningless oaths and childishly absurd expressions,—cease from this hour, not to please me alone, but out of respect for yourselves. Remember, you have to set an example to your shipmates, and I shall disrate any petty officer who continues to make a fool of himself in that manner. And you able and ordinary seamen, remember you are men, and do not, when addressing each other, use expressions that you would not address to me. Boys, think how much better you are when you speak decently, and how low and degrading you appear in every one's eyes when you forget to do so, and bring yourselves to a level with the vilest outcasts. I don't expect you will leave off all of a sudden. Don't commence by making yourselves ridiculous in attempting the use of fine words, for that would be childish, but try your best to drop so foolish a habit as that of swearing, and when rid of it, never take to it again. Let all remember you have your rights as men, and that no one is justified in abusing you or treating you otherwise than as reasonable beings. Serve your country, and endeavour to do it well, and you will be treated fairly and justly. I don't want the cat-of-nine-tails to assist me in keeping order in the ship. You shall have six months to break yourselves of your foolish habit of swearing, and after that time I shall punish all who indulge in it. All I want is promptness and attention to duty on your part, and for you to take pride in yourselves and your beautiful ship. I don't wish to curry favour with you,—you will find I am strict in all my ideas, but I think a good deal of a sailor who is honest and true, and who knows if he does his duty he has nothing to fear. Be respectful to your officers, and try to elevate yourselves, remembering there's a clear stage and no favour."

This speech was received by the crew with a murmur of applause. Clare, or rather those like him, but more fortunate in having hitherto escaped the lash, rejoiced, as they saw a bright prospect before them, and a chance of getting justice, and all felt delighted when they found their new captain was one of the few officers who did not believe in flogging his men. When they were dismissed after his speech, they sat about the forecastle in groups, and chatted over what he had said

"It's all very well for him to blarney us over like that, but see if he don't have some on us to the gratings afore the six months are up. He ain't agoin' to kid me in that way," observed one of Crushe's pets.

" Who asks you to be kidded, as you calls it ? " replied a petty officer who had over-heard the foregoing speech. " I tell you what it is, if I hears any swearing in my mess from you, or any other idiot, out you goes; so stow it. I don't think the captain expects we're going to pull long faces, or sing psalms all day; but I for one mean to drop such language, anyhow, and I'd advise you to do so too."

The boys, who were naturally more impressionable than their seniors, did their best to avoid using bad expressions, and it was most amusing to hear the way they would interrupt themselves when having an altercation with each other. Of course there were some who kept on for a time, but, finding the majority of their shipmates regarded their language as mere idle vapouring, they gradually left it off. The great secret of Captain Woodward's success was, that he never himself used an improper expression when addressing his men, or in fact at any other time; he was truly a manly fellow, and before he had been in command six months, any of the Stingers would have gone through fire and water to show their appreciation of his kindness. Those men whom he found unfitted for the positions to which they had been promoted by Crushe he quietly disrated and exchanged into other ships, thus sparing them disgrace before their old shipmates. He went upon the principle that his men were entitled to as much consideration as his officers, never forgetting, however, the respect due to the latter, but rather increasing their individual authority in the eyes of the crew.

Captain Woodward was of middle height, with strongly-knit frame and massive head surrounded by thick curly hair. His eyes were large and piercing, and few men could stand their searching glance. Honest, frank, and affable, he endeavoured to raise to his own level all those with whom he came in contact, but it was delightful to see him put down a bully. No matter how savage the fellow was, he left his presence tamed. The boys would watch his movements and anticipate his orders, quite proud to be able to serve him; and the men found that if they behaved themselves properly, their complaints, when they had any, were attended to; but woe betide the growler or tale-bearer who dared take up the captain's time.

One morning, about three bells, the ship being at that time cruising along the coast, in search of any pirate craft which might be "seeking whom it might devour," the captain was chatting with the first lieutenant, when the latter directed the boat-swain's mate of the watch to go below and lash up his hammock, in order to give him an opportunity of getting his nautical bed on deck at the same time as the rest of the crew. The man, whose name was Blain, and who was commonly known by the sobriquet of Mary or Polly Blain, had not been below many moments before the sensitive ears of the commander were shocked by a string of the most horrid imprecations, evidently proceeding from the mouth of the before-mentioned Blain. Lieutenant Russell was about to order the man upon deck, when the commander desired him to let him be for a moment, and then a rough voice was heard in reply to that of the boatswain's mate. Words ran high, and were soon followed by blows, but after they had fought a couple of rounds, the sergeant of marines, who was turned out by the noise, parted them, and ordered both the combatants upon deck.

Mr. Blain was the first to make his appearance up the hatchway, and as he held his nose with one hand, and balanced a hammock upon his shoulder with the other while he came along the deck, he presented such a ludicrous appearance that Captain Wood-ward could scarce refrain from smiling. Having deposited his bed in the netting, he walked aft upon the quarter-deck, and stood at attention, but still kept his hand to his nose.

"Why do you apply your hand to the most prominent member of your countenance?" demanded the polite first lieutenant.

"I'm fraidee my nosh will fall offsh," snuffled the man.

Shortly after this his opponent was marched aft, holding his jaws with both hands, like a person suffering from neuralgia. The sergeant of marines, who was a very smart and effective officer, made them stand as nearly at attention as circumstances permitted, and then reported them to the first lieutenant, who, after a casual glance, remarked, "that never, during the entire course of a varied and somewhat peripatetic career, had it been his destiny to find brought before him individuals so totally deprived of the slightest vestiges of intelligence;" and having thus delivered himself, reported the offenders to his superior officer.

As Captain Paul Woodward imagined neither of the men would like to acknowledge having used the very shocking expressions he had overheard them indulge in during the heat of their argument, he was desirous of hearing the case himself, instead of the preliminary inquiries being made by the first lieutenant, and he anticipated some amusement from the proceeding; as old sailors will invent the most astounding stories in order to explain away their faults. Assuming a severe expression of countenance, the commander advanced to where the men stood; upon which Blain pulled his forelock with one hand, and held his nose with the other, while his opponent cautiously removed his right hand from his jaw, saluted, and then clapped it back in its place, as if fearing to leave it for one moment unsupported.

"What are these men's names?"

"Thomas Blain, boatswain's mate, and James Spry, quarter-master, reported for fighting upon the lower deck," observed the sergeant with a military salute.

"State your charge, sergeant."

With another flourish, and drawing himself up to his full height, until he looked like a human tower, the soldier stared straight before him, and thus delivered himself:—"At five minutes to three bells I was aroused by the noise of quarrelling and swearing, and turning over in my hammock, beheld Thomas Blain, boatswain's mate of the watch on deck, bumping James Spry, quarter-master, who was turned in, in his hammock. James Spry looked over his hammock, and observed to Thomas Blain in anything but elegant or refined language, that he was not a gentleman, and he had never thought much of him, or any member of his family. Upon this Thomas Blain called James Spry all the vulgar titles in his biography, and then James Spry jumped out of his hammock, and struck Thomas Blain, upon which a fight ensued; and I got up, put on my uniform, and took them in custody. At that time Thomas Blain had James Spry upon his back, and was endeavouring to bump his jaws against the shot in the rack, upon which James Spry seized a vinegar breaker, and struck Thomas Blain across the nose, nearly extricating it from his visage."

"Is that all, sergeant?"

The soldier saluted by way of confirmation.

Turning to Blain, the commander asked him what he had to say in defence of this charge. Holding his nose with one hand, and with the other pointed towards his enemy, he snuffled out as follows:

"Your honour, I'm as innicent as a babe unborn as to them insinuwations of the sergeant's; however he ken go to say I swore I keant think. I was ordered to go below by the fust lieutenant to lash up my 'ammick, and I vos a passin' by that of Chuckle's, as ve allways call Jemmy Spry, ven he looks oves the edge ov his 'ammick, and ses he to me, he ses, 'You miserabull old ay-nay-tommy,' ses he just in that aggrewating tone; 'you old feg-end, you somethink old sneak,' ses he, 'what are you a skulkin' below in your watch on deck for?' Ses I, '*If* you please,' werry civil, yer honour, 'Chuckles, old man, *don't* use sich langwage to a old shipmate, and swearing, too, ven you knows as how the capting don't hold with no sich,' ses I. Vith that he ups and jumps out of his 'ammick; and after having used verds vich my mouth couldn't be polluted to go for to repeat, he calls me a old chiser, and said he'd be somethinked if he would'nt give me toko for yam, and ups and hits me."

"Did you not abuse him in return, my man?"

"Me, sir? me allow sich language to come from my lips? vy, I'd die first. I ses to him, gently and mildly, like I'm speaking now, 'Chuckles,' ses I, 'I'm grieved to the heart to hear a first class petty officer agoing on in that ere pellucid manner.'"

"Then you deny having used improper language?"

"I'll take my oath I never said D. once, sir. Well, your honour, he being no hand with his fists, I soon got him down, upon vich he seized the winnegar breaker, and after using some most horrible language, vich made my teeth stand on edge, he hove it across my mug, and cut my nose nearly off."

"Very good, my man. Now let me hear your version, quarter-master."

Mr. Spry spoke somewhat indistinctly, as he persisted in supporting his jaws with both hands, but Captain Woodward made out the following:—"Yer honour, I was a laying in my hammock a sleepin' like a infant, when all of a sudden I felt a wiolent pain jest here" (here the speaker let go his right jaw, and having indicated the small of his back as the spot where he felt the pain, he took a fresh grip of his chin, and proceeded with his story). "Well, yer honour, the collusion woke me up, and I peeped over the edge of my hammock, where I saw Polly Blain a standin' on a attitude of defiance and a grinnin' at me like a Cheshire cat. Ses I, 'Wot's that for?' Ses he, 'You in-fer-nal old *dot*,' ses he, 'come out if you are a man.' Upon which I politely said, 'If you please, Thomas Blain, don't be so wery aggrewatin', or I shall be forced to inform the first lieu-tenant;' upon which he up and said, 'The first lieutenant be jiggered, and he didn't care a *dot* for him,' etceterur. Upon which I closed my ears, not being given to bad lan-guage myself."

"Do you mean to say you did not swear, as he asserts?"

"Sir,—Captain Woodward I'd scorn to tell a lie; and since that ere beautiful speech of yourn I've made a wow never to swear again. No, sir, I'm reformed—I *used* to swear a little when the last captain was in the ship, but I'm a altered man now, sir. Well, sir, I argyfied with him, civil and peaceful, for a few moments, and then he struck me and threw me down, and jammed my jaws agin the shot-rack, knocking out over fifty teeth, vich he forced me to swaller, as he wouldn't give me time to gasp. Just as he lifted me for the tenth time to heave me upon the shot-rack, my right hand finger somehow slid inside the handle of the winnegar-breaker, and afore I could prevent him, Thomas Blain run his nose clean up agin the breaker and nearly cut it off; upon which he became furious, and would not listen to reason, so I was obliged to repeat the blow in self-defence, as he swore he'd murder me if he could only get at me."

"Is that all?"

"Yes, your honour,—that's all."

Woodward surveyed the men for some moments, then addressed them as follows:— "My men, I am sorry to see you in this plight, and still more, to hear you spin such yarns. I overheard your quarrel, and was disgusted with your obscenity. You, Blain, used language unbecoming a petty officer, and for that I disrate you to be an able seaman. You, Spry, who are old enough to know better, I also disrate; and as I do not consider either of you fit to associate with the decent men of my crew, I direct you shall leave your messes, and be messed together until such time as you are able to agree, and have left off using profane language. Sergeant, send for the ship's steward."

In a few moments Mr. Polson came up from his bread-room, winking and blinking like an owl in the light.

"Steward, to what messes do these men belong?"

"Let me see, sir. Spry belongs to number two mess, and Blain belongs to number seven."

"Very good. How many messes are there?"

"Twelve seamen's, and four Rile marines' messes, sir."

"Can you make a seventeenth mess?"

"Yes, sir. That is if they mess before the armourer's bench on the supernumerary mess table."

"Very well, steward, enter number seventeen mess in your books, and put down in it these two men's names. Mind, no one else is to join them."

The commander then turned to the sergeant and directed him "to see that the two able seamen took their mess traps and gear into their new mess, and ordered him on no account to allow either of them to take a meal at any but that table," and dismissed the mutilated ones to the comforts of each other's society.

At that moment the pipe went for the cooks of messes to lay aft for their flour and plums.

Spry and Blain were somewhat non-plussed, as each had sworn never to speak to the other when not on duty. They, however, walked forward, when a bright thought occurred to the former, and he motioned his new messmate to toss for the cookship. Blain gravely drew a penny from a small bag in which he kept his money, and twirling the coin in the air, held it hidden between his flattened palms before the face of his opponent. Spry being unable to cry head or tail, looked solemnly and pointed to his own head, upon which Blain removed his uppermost hand disclosed the coin, which was head up. Blain thereupon took a tin dish and drew the rations, after which they sat down to breakfast, back to back. As their meal consisted of cocoa and dry biscuit, there was no need for either to request the other "to pass the sauce," and as far as the actual requirements of the case were concerned they got on very well upon the silent system. After breakfast Spry went on deck, leaving his messmate to make the duff and otherwise prepare their dinner. At twelve o'clock both men sat down and devoured their meal in silence; and when the pipe went for grog, the cook of the mess proceeded on deck to draw their allowance, which having tilted into a basin, he, being without a measure, grimly pushed over to his companion. Now, when two sailors face each other over a bowl of grog they are very apt to forget all differences; and the maimed ones, after pushing the basin backwards and forwards between them, as neither would so far lower himself in the other's eyes as to drink first, at last ventured to exchange glances. There was the grog—strong, dark, and tempting, so they took first a look at that and then at each other, then their hands slowly crept across the table, and there was another friendly contest who should be most polite in silently insisting upon the other taking the first sip. At length they spoke simultaneously.

"Spry, old ship, I'm a fool."

"Blain, old man, I'm a duffer."

And then they drank alternately to each other's health, and swore perpetual friendship.

" You see, Jemmy, old man—"

" Call me Chuckles, Polly, it sounds friend*ly*er like."

" Vell, Chuckles, old man, you don't know how sorry I vos to assault you as I did. However, we're both the better for it."

How Mr. Blain drew this induction we cannot understand, but from that hour they became fast friends and left off swearing. If either of them were very much tried, as was sometimes the case, it would be noticed that his mouth would move in a *peculiar* manner, which might have been taken for wordless or pantomimic "cussing," but when interrogated upon this point, the old fellows would solemnly deny that their lips had moved to form anything but silent prayers. Some months after they were re-rated petty officers, and it was amusing to see how fearfully shocked they would try to appear whenever they heard any one use strong language ; and to such a degree of godliness did old Spry arrive, that upon one occasion he reported a shipmate for calling him an "old damper," and it was with great difficulty that the first lieutenant brought him to understand that it was a term of derision, not an oath.

" It sounded werry much like a D to me, sir."

"My worthy man, I regret to be compelled to observe that if the gross ignorance under which you labour renders you incompetent to seize the signification of the expression *damper*, and causes you to contemplate it as a profane expression, you must continue to retain your erroneous impression, as the most elaborate explanation and analysis of the term would be lost in the cimmerian gloom which overspreads your benighted intelligence."

Spry bowed reverently, and turned away quite overcome by the lieutenant's speech, as he observed to his chum Blain, "Not werry well able to make out if the lieutenant were not a cussing of him in Chinee," as Russell was one of the few officers who could speak that language.

Although the Stingers were a reformed crew in many respects, yet they were not a dull one, as their captain and officers encouraged them in getting up amusements of every kind. They felt they were men, and did their best to show their appreciation of their commander's kindness. Of course there were many rough characters among them, but they were kept within bounds by the better class of men. Clare was more reconciled to his fate than ever he had been, but the lash had done its work with him, and no one would have recognized the handsome Tom Clare of former times, in the quiet, gloomy-looking sailor who moved among his fellows like an automaton. One day Captain Woodward sent for the man and offered him a rate, but Tom respectfully declined the honour.

" Why not ? take it, my good man."

" It's too late, sir ; too late."

" Come, come, my friend, don't look back upon the past. I hear you have been in trouble. You must forget your punishment, as you have done your weakness. You have overcome one, now conquer the other."

" Overcome what, sir ? "

" Well, Lieutenant Crushe informed me that you had been brought to the gratings through drink."

" Now, God forgive him for that shocking falsehood. No, sir, I was once strong, hearty, and always as anxious to do my duty as I am now. I was unfortunate enough to offend Lieutenant Crushe when I served under him in the Porpoise. Well, sir, to make a long story short, when I joined the ship I found him in command, and he stopped my leave, and threatened to flog me. Heaven knows, I tried hard enough to please him, but it weren't no use. He worried and hounded me until I deserted."

"That was very, very wrong on your part, my man."

"*I* know it, sir; but I had just been married to as good a girl as ever a man was blessed with, when I found myself ordered to this ship, and when here, a prisoner by his orders. So arter I had in vain appealed to Captain Puffeigh, and had tried every way to get leave, I deserted, and were arrested the same day by a corporal, who grossly insulted my wife, for which I struck him. I were brought on board and reported to Mr. Cravan, who was the officer of the watch, and he, too, called my poor girl foul names, and I struck him. I know that was wrong, but I could not help it. No *man* would ha' stood by and heard her whom he loved spoken of as he did of my wife. Then they all swore agin me at the court-martial, and I was tried, condemned, and received fifty lashes, while my wife was a fainting in a boat alongside. I wern't allowed to see her, and now I believe she is dead!"

"Come, my friend, you must not despair. I will do my best for you, and you will yet lift up your head if you try."

"Thank ye, sir, you're werry good; but your great kindness can't take the disgrace away from me, or the scars off my back, and, worse 'an all, can't bring my wife back to life."

"How do you know she's dead? Have you positive information?"

"Yes, sir; on the 16th of August I seed her spirit, and she smiled mournful like upon me, and then faded away."

"Your visions are but part of your present state of ill-health, my man, and next mail will probably bring you news from her. Meanwhile, as we shall be in Hong-Kong to-morrow, I'll rate you my coxswain, and give you plenty to employ your mind, and divert you from your morbid ideas."

Tom thanked the commander, and walked forward to prepare his clothes for his new duties, while Woodward sent for the surgeon, and told him of Clare's illusion.

"Its a sad story, Captain Woodward, but unfortunately true. Crushe did as he says, and also exercised great cruelty to others; but we cannot bring odium upon the service by exposing him."

"What do you consider is the matter with this man Clare?"

"Heart disease, brought on through the severe flogging he received. He is a highly sensitive man, and the disgrace and separation from his wife—who is, by-the-by, a very superior woman—are slowly killing him. You have done a very humane act in making him your coxswain, and the change of life may be the means of arresting his malady."

Woodward and the doctor walked out about the quarter-deck arm-in-arm, and chatted upon various subjects until lunch-time, when they went below, and the commander pressed the surgeon to join him. During the time Puffeigh was in command great coolness had existed between the captain and senior surgeon, as the former would often direct the latter to put men off the sick-list, when he did not consider they ought to be under treatment. As the surgeon knew full well that the men in question required rest and medical attention, he always vehemently protested against such arbitrary measures, and had many altercations with Puffeigh upon that subject. The doctor argued: "If a man is sick on shore he is sent to the hospital, and no civil power ever thinks of compelling the surgeons to turn the man out and send him to work; therefore, as a professional man, I will never, to please any captain, put a man off the sick-list who ought to be under medical treatment. I know I am under the command of the captain, but I do not consider that his position entitles him to direct a qualified surgeon how to treat his patients. I am not desirous of opposing the lawful authority of the commander; but I do not, will not, and never shall acknowledge his right to dictate to me in matters relating to my own department, or influence my professional opinion."

The Stinger arrived at Hong-Kong the next day, and Clare was despatched to the Post-office for the mails. Tom anxiously eyed the bags as he hastened on board with them, hoping for the best, yet fearing there would be a letter for him, containing the sad news of his wife's death; but to his joy, he received several letters, and one dated "16th August," from which he learnt that his wife was alive, yet did not give him any particulars as to her state of health. However, they were full of long accounts about his boy; and in one of them was a portrait painted by the good young lady who had been engaged to Lieutenant Ford. Tom improved from that day, and ventured to tell the captain that his words had come true. Woodward was delighted to see the melancholy face become animated and knowing one of his class had oppressed the man, he felt doubly pleased to be the means of giving the poor fellow hope in the future.

Mr. Shever considered himself an ill-used individual, and would bore the carpenter and gunner with long-winded accounts of his former greatness. Of course he was very circumspect in his behaviour, knowing he would be turned out of the ship if the captain knew of his previous conduct towards the men. Finding it would not do to swear, he became very pious, and under the ministry of Silas Bowler, a converted Royal Marine, was, as the latter gentleman expressed it, "gathered to the flock." It was truly a wonderful alteration, and one calculated to give his shipmates disgust for the particular faith to which the boatswain was a convert. Like most illiterate persons, he took to the musical portion of his belief, and would sit and sing hymns for hours together, much to the disgust of the midshipmen, whose mess-room adjoined his cabin; and it was not an uncommon occurrence to have the warrant-officer and Silas Bowler howling a portion of hymn No. 31, Utah edition, which ran thus :—

> "Oh! how delightful 'tis to see
> A sinner turned to saint,"

while the irreverent middies would drown the hymn of praise by singing,

> "Oh! how disgusting 'tis to see
> Our boatswain turning saint."

Whereupon Shever would cease his howl, and pour forth a jargon of hard words and impious phrases, during the delivery of which the mischievous wags in the gun-room would groan and ejaculate after the manner of the particular saints of whom Mr. Bowler was a shining light. The boatswain imagined by these means to attract the attention of his commander or first lieutenant, but he was undeceived when the former told him "that he did not wish his ship turned into a conventicle," and the latter reprimanded him as follows :—

"I would be most loath to incur the accusation of insensibility to the sublime chords of sacred melody, but must formally state, as my candid opinion, that the howls which issue from your cabin strike my auricular nerves in a manner diametrically opposed to the suggestion of aught celestial, and produce an effect the reverse of enchanting. With regard to your supplications to heaven, I would strongly suggest the propriety of their being made in a less audible manner, as it is beyond the bounds of possibility for me to surrender myself to the soothing influence of somnolence during the performance of your orations."

Upon receiving this rebuke, Mr. Shever proceeded to his cabin, where he found private Silas Bowler, seated upon his easy chair, quietly enjoying a nap. Without a word of explanation, he seized that pious marine, hauled him into the steerage, shook him until he awoke, then with a well-directed kick sent him flying forward, where that meek individual fell upon his knees and prayed, "that the devil might be cast out of that good man, the boatswain." Having vented his rage upon the soldier, Shever took out a bottle, filled a glass with rum, and drank the health of Captain Crushe, "and may all such duffers *as some people* perish," and from that day shunned the spirit of faith according to private Silas Bowler, and clave only to that more potent spirit yclept rum.

CHAPTER XVII.

Upon finding himself comparatively free, Thompson's spirits rose, and he chatted with his guards in a most affable manner. After giving him to understand that if he made any attempt to escape they would strangle him, he was allowed to untie his rope-collar and carry it wound about his body, under his clothes. At night they stopped at the residence of a military mandarin, who billeted them upon the keeper of a tavern, their order running as follows:—

"You Teen, keeper of the house of entertainment for travellers called 'The abode of ten thousand satisfied desires,' are directed to afford lodging and food to two imperial soldiers named Yung and Pang, and their prisoner Kwo-chau-ho-che, given on the ninth day of the tenth moon, &c., &c. Respect this.

"(Signed) HAN,

"Second assistant governor."

Pang, who was a sort of corporal, read the chop or order, then observed with the greatest complacency, "that the fleas of Teen's establishment were larger and more fierce than any others in that part of China," upon which Yung retorted that "they must be large and powerful, to be able to bore through such a tough skin as Pang's," and with many other merry observations the soldiers beguiled the journey until they arrived at "The abode of ten thousand satisfied desires," which turned out to be a dirty little inn, situated outside the walls, near the execution ground. Yung purchased a small portion of opium, and procuring a pipe from Teen, was soon in a state where all prisoners are free. Pang, who pretended to be very much disgusted, thereupon enjoined his prisoner to keep an eye upon his comrade, and retired to an up-stairs room, where he indulged in a debauch of warm rice-spirit. Jerry mingled with the guests, and soon found the place was a notorious lodging-house for thieves and low characters.

As the soldiers were both fast asleep, Teen had them conveyed to a dirty cell in an outbuilding ; and knowing Jerry was their prisoner, directed him to be accommodated with a mat in the same apartment. About ten o'clock a woman brought them a bowl of rice, and a pot of tea, upon which the prisoner supped, and by eleven o'clock all the night-lights of the establishment were extinguished, except the one in the cell occupied by the soldiers and their prisoner. Finding they were both too far gone to resist, the sailor first secured their wrists and ankles, then laying them side by side, lashed them together, in the same manner as he would have done a hammock. After gagging them, he opened the door and walked into the inn. The dogs, aroused by his entry, began to growl and bark, upon which a watchman arose, and having rubbed his eyes proceeded to open a door, imagining he had heard some one knocking for admittance : seeing this the sailor quietly slipped through, and found himself in the street.

After walking for some time he began to feel weary, but knowing that if he did not get clear of the place by daylight some one might identify him, or notice his un-shaven head, he kept right on, every now and then finding himself dozing as he walked.

At daybreak he found he was ascending a range of hills, upon the slopes of which he observed large tea-plantations. Groups of girls crossed his path upon their way to gather tea, and some of them passed jocular remarks, or invited him to join them and assist in their labour. About seven o'clock he met a travelling barber who, for a few sapecks, shaved, trimmed, and shampooed him, that operation taking place by the road-side, and only attracting the notice of two or three children who were on their way to school.

When Jerry had secured his guards, he had searched their persons, and removed the purse he found upon Corporal Pang; justifying this act upon the grounds that when he was arrested in Whey-chú, these same soldiers had plundered him of all his money, therefore he was merely regaining his own. Having paid the barber, he proceeded into the country, stopping every now and then to refresh himself. By night he had travelled a good distance; so imagining himself safe, he entered a tea-house, and having supped, turned in with about forty other travellers, and enjoyed their society in company with a host of agile tormentors. The room was a spacious one, and at the upper end a fat-lamp was kept alight all night. Jerry could not sleep, not being iron-clad like his companions, so he sat up and took a survey of the place. It was amusing to watch the features of the sleepers, who, unmindful of the ticklers, were snoring in a great variety of keys. At times, however, when their tormentors pulled rather too savagely, a solemn oath would issue from the sleepers' lips; and upon one occasion a savage-looking Tartar, roused by the bite of some patriarchal and artful Pulex, kicked the person who was sleeping by his side. The gentleman thus assaulted was reclining with his face towards his assailant, and as he received the kick in his waist, he was completely doubled up by the blow. After remaining quiet for a few moments, the fellow opened his eyes, and being a peaceful Chinaman, upon finding the person who kicked him was a Tartar, quietly turned over, as much as to say, "Now batter away if you will," but he declined to remonstrate with the person who kicked him. Not that he acted in this inoffensive manner from want of feeling, or usually "when his brother smote him upon the left cheek, offered him his right." Had it been a Chinaman weaker than himself who thus assaulted him, he would have very soon retaliated, but the Tartar's savage face and burly form rendered him as quiet as a lamb.

Thompson was highly amused with the performance; so, picking up a straw, he proceeded to tickle the Tartar. For a long time the man bore it, probably the irritation not amounting to much; however, at last, upon the sailor thrusting the straw up his nose, he lifted his foot and again kicked the Chinaman, who thereupon assaulted the celestial next to him, and he in return favoured his companion. A tremendous row ensued, upon which the landlord and his assistants rushed into the room, and laid about them with bamboos, until order was restored.

Long before daybreak they all cleared out, and the sailor, having partaken of a light breakfast of rice and tea, made for the hills. After going a short distance, he fell in with a party of tea-gatherers, who invited him to join them. As he had no definite plan for the future, he accepted their offer, and, receiving a basket, was soon toiling up the hill-side. The business was one which required the labourers to be at work by sunrise, as the kind of tea they were gathering is not picked when the sun gets too far up. A light fog hung about the hills, and the faces of most of the women were enveloped in wrappers, but as the day broke they took off these cloths, and revealed some very pretty countenances.

Upon their arrival at the plantation to which the party were bound, the leader appointed the pickers and carriers: the former were expert young girls, who had been trained to the business from childhood, while the latter consisted of the "dull-heads," or men ; and as the sailor was supposed to be a poor Cantonese, who could know nothing about picking tea, he was directed to hold the basket for a sprightly girl named A-tae.

Now, it is usual for the girl who picks the finer kinds of tea to be dressed in much better clothes than her basket-holder, and as A-tae was a beauty, and tolerably well off, she was smartly attired ; true, her garments were not very costly, but they were new and jauntily worn. Her dress consisted of two pieces, the usual loose blue trousers and wide-sleeved jacket, her hair being braided in queues which descended to her waist, while her head was protected from the sun by an immensely wide bamboo hat.

When the overseer directed the sailor to bear her basket she had not cast eyes upon the latter, having been listening to the silly story of a companion, so, thinking it was the usual "dull-head," she waved him to follow her, and turned into one of the rows ; then dexterously grasping a handful of leaves, she cried, " Come here ! " and upon his placing the sieve-like basket under her hands, showered the leaves into it with marvellous rapidity. Having exhausted one bush, she was moving towards another, when, catching sight of her attendant, she uttered a little scream, and coquettishly turned away her head. Seeing her agitation, the enamoured basket-holder inquired if she were unwell.

" No ! I'm—Come here, you fright ! "

The girl worked like lightning, ordering her holder about in a most imperious manner. At last curiosity overcame her, and she demanded the name of her slave.

" I have no name."

" No ! How shall I call you, then ? "

" Call me Sa " (ugly of the sort).

" Oh no ! oh no ; that would be cruel."

" Call me Cha-tee " (a mean fellow).

" No, no, for you are not mean."

" What will you name me, then ? " said Jerry, looking as though he could devour her. " What you call me shall be my name."

A-tae trembled, as she cast a timorous glance towards her basket-bearer, and replied, " I call you Sho " (beautiful eyes), saying which she laughed, and added, " but surely you will not take that name ? "

" I'll call myself anything you choose to name me."

" Then I give you this,—Yung-Yung " (good-humoured face).

" And what may I call you ? "

" Me ! Don't you know ? " said the pretty girl, looking at Yung-Yung in a manner which made his heart bump again.

" What ! not know my name ? "

" I do not. I am a wanderer and a stranger here."

" Poor fellow. Have you no friends ? "

" None here. Will you be my friend ? "

" You don't know my name, yet ask me to be your friend. Speak lower, and look down while you talk, or the overseer will send some one else with me to-morrow."

" *What* is your name ? "

" A-tae."

After casting his eyes about in order to ascertain if any of the pickers were watching, he bent over the girl, who was very deeply engaged in removing some fine shoots from the lower part of a plant, and when she rose, as her cheek came quite close to his, he kissed it gently, and said,

"A-tae, I love you."

The girl gave a nervous little laugh, then asked him what he meant.

"I want to marry you."

"Where do you come from, Yung-Yung-Sho, that you speak thus? Would I could be given to one like you; but I shall be, like other girls, sent off to slave for some man of my own class, or sold to a mandarin." (It will be perceived that A-tae was, although a Chinese, an advocate for woman's rights). "Oh, Yung-Yung-Sho do you think Buddha knows how badly they treat us poor girls?"

"Can't you run away with me?" observed the now thoroughly "gone" sailor; "slip off in the night, and go away to a country where the women are thought as much of as the men."

"That's where Buddha is, Yung-Yung-Sho. _There_ we shall be men. I know all about that, and have my Tieh papers at home. I'm not as stupid as most girls. You are a benevolent man thus to listen to the nonsense of little me. But why do those Yuen-chae (police runners) point this way? Are you wanted? If so, flee. That way, that way; up among the rocks, and hide in the caves."

Jerry had little time to say farewell, as he noticed the two soldiers, accompanied by police runners, making towards him; so, after bestowing a fervent kiss upon the lips of the astonished A-tae, he sprang over the tea plants and sped away like the wind. The poor girl sunk upon the ground, cried, and wrung her hands like one demented. Her companions gathered round, and finding she was in trouble, prevailed upon her to go home. Meanwhile the soldiers and their party chased the agile sailor, running until they got out of breath; and when they last spied him he was darting into a wood, which was set apart for the use of Buddhist priests, and where they felt sure of bagging him during the course of the day.

A-tae walked home like one in a dream, and was questioned by her mother, who anxiously inquired if she had "seen a spirit," she looked so scared and pale. She had seen one, the recollection of whom would never again be absent from her mind. She was in love, had been spoken to by a being, one of the opposite sex, who neither commanded nor treated her like an inferior animal. Was it a dream? Was he not one of those genii who, assuming the appearance of gods, use their fatal beauty to destroy all whom they fall in with? What could he be?

Poor little girl! She was sorely tried; so taking a few sticks of incense, she burnt them before the picture of the Kitchen god, in order if possible to get _him_ on her side. But she didn't tell her mother about Yung-Yung-Sho.

Towards the evening she became very ill; and by night her anxious parents sent for a doctor, who, after writing a prescription, submitted it to them.

"How much will it cost?" demanded the father.

"Two hundred cash," gravely replied the man of physic.

"Can't you do it a little cheaper? we are poor people."

"I don't think I can. Let me see. I can leave out the dried rats' tails—they are costly—and the alligator's blood may be omitted. Well, say one hundred cash."

The mother was a clever woman, and didn't believe in the doctor's nostrum's, so she demanded how much the gentlemen wanted for the prescription.

"Fifty cash."

"Pay him and let him go, my lord," she observed to her husband, who thereupon handed over the cash, and the doctor departed. When he was out of sight the old woman nodded shrewdly towards her husband, as much as to infer, "trust me for

9

being smart," then having prostrated herself before the picture of the Kitchen god, gravely burnt the prescription, and pouring some warm tea upon the ashes, carried the drink to her daughter, and compelled her to swallow it, saying soothingly, " You'll be all right to-morrow."

" Oh, my heart, my heart ," moaned the poor little girl.

" Oh, it is not your heart, A-tae, it's your brain that has become oiled by the sun. You'll be all right now, as it will congeal again ; " and having delivered herself of this very Chinese opinion, the old lady withdrew, leaving the poor child to combat a disease as old as the hills, and for which there has never been but one cure since the world began. Nothing but the possession of the loved one will satisfy the poor souls, who, like A-tae, suffer from this awful affliction. No doctor can cure them,—possibly the priest may,- but not the man of medicine.

When the girl's mother saw her husband the latter did not ask how fared his darling A-tae. She was but a girl, and her death would not cause him to shed a tear, but the mother made up her mind to one thing, as she informed her help. " If that girl gets a little better, I'll take her to Nan-woo," a very sanctified Buddhist bonze, who lived in a hole in a rock situated in the Buddhist grove, distant about eight li from her house. But A-tae became worse, so they bled her. This took away what little strength she had left, and the gossips said she would soon salute heaven. Upon the afternoon of the fifth day some of the women round her bed were speaking about the hunt after the stranger who had been working with A-tae upon the day she was taken sick, and after observing that " he must have bewitched the child," they mentioned something which had a wonderful effect upon the girl, and which caused her to rally from that moment.

Jerry, having distanced his pursuers, determined to search for the caves of which A-tae had spoken. There was little difficulty about the matter, as the rocks were full of them ; so having found one which he thought would suit, he quietly stretched himself upon the floor and went to sleep. As there was nothing to encourage the presence of the pulex family, he slumbered without annoyance. After dreaming of A-tae, and imagining they were about to united at the altar, with Mr. Shever acting as best man, and Miss Pierdsereptern as bridesmaid, Mary Ann being present in charge of a small family of Chinese children, one of whom strongly resembled Captain Puffeigh, the bewildered sailor woke, and upon rubbing his eyes, discovered that he was being watched by one of the police runners, who, when he saw him open his eyes, gave a loud alarm. Jerry got up, stretched his limbs, and then, walking to the entrance, took a critical survey of his position. The cave was dug out of the limestone rock and was approached by two paths, while in front was a steep decline down which it was impossible to escape. Gazing to the left he saw Corporal Pang, supported by a police runner armed with a short sword, while approaching upon his right was private Yung, similarly assisted. Thompson whistled.

Pang suddenly stopped, and called upon him to surrender.

Yung bawled to him to give up at once, or he'd kill him when he got hold of him.

The undaunted sailor only whistled all the louder. Seeing he was quietly awaiting their arrival, as if determined to give himself up, the soldiers clambered up the hill until Yung who was nearest him, stopped to breathe, upon which Thompson rushed at him, bowled him over like a ninepin, floored his attendant with a blow in the chest and then darted down the pathway and disappeared from sight; and Pang arrived at the top of the hill to find his companion in arms *hors de combat.* Yung being picked up by his comrade, and having acquainted him with the particulars of the assault, they again set off in search of the troublesome western devil. It was a smart chase, as the runners knew every inch of the ground; and after having sighted him several times, but to lose him again the next moment, one of them saw him disappear up a sort of ravine, from which they were certain he could not escape.

"It is the retreat of Nan-woo, a very holy bonze, and he is as safe in that hole as a rat is in a bottle," observed one of the police.

"He is a wizard, and will fly out if all other means fail him. Oh, I know we shan't catch him," grumbled Yung.

"How can we fail, your excellency?" replied one of the attendants. "That path leads to a high rock, in which is a small hole, where Nan-woo entered fifty years ago. On each side of the path is a precipitous rock, which no man can climb; therefore, your foreign devil, upon finding the path leads to *nowhere*, will retrace his steps. Let us, therefore, crouch down upon either side of the rocks at the entrance, place a cord across the pathway, await his return, and when he arrives we will lift the line, and trip him up."

"Capital, capital!" cried the soldiers. Thereupon the party divided, and crouching down behind the gigantic boulders which lay beside the entrance to the gulch, string in hand awaited the return of the sailor. They calculated he would possibly have a little chat with the bonze, then, finding there was no other outlet, would fall into their hands, and be captured without difficulty. Every now and then some noise, probably caused by rabbits, would make them start and clutch their line, but after waiting a considerable time, hunger reminded them that they had started upon the expedition without taking breakfast, and they determined to proceed up the ravine, and boldly bring the "eccentric one" to bay

Having explored nearly the entire length of the place, they turned a bend in the pathway, and found themselves before the retreat of Nan-woo; but where was the sailor.

"I expect he is in there along with the bonze," whispered Yung.

"Bosh! How could he get in there? Why, it is five feet from the ground, and the hole is too small."

"Ask the hermit if he has seen a man?" put in one of the runners.

Upon this Pang, who did not believe in Buddhism, and consequently had little respect for its bonzes, advanced to the opening, and rapping his sword handle against the screen, demanded if the old gentleman inside had seen a fellow trying to climb up the rocks which surrounded his cell.

Fumbling at the slab of limestone which formed the screen before the entrance or pigeon-hole of his cell, repeating as he did so the words " o-mi-tu-fuh, o-mi-tu-fuh," the old bonze at last succeeded in pushing the panel into a hole, cut out for its reception in the side of the rock, and then asked the soldier what he wanted, upon which the latter repeated his question.

The old bonze looked at his interrogator for some moments; at length appearing to understand him, replied, "My son, since first I entered this abode, these eyes have never beheld a man attempt to scale those rocks—o-mi-tu-fuh, o-mi-tu fuh."

"Come along, Pang; he's cracked. Let us seek the fellow in some other place; or, better still, we will return, or join the first party of rebels we come across, as it will never do for us to go back to our native town, and say we have lost him."

After a strict search they gave the matter up, and dismissing the police runners, proceeded to the nearest rebel town, where they were received with open arms by Ma-chow-wang, who commanded the insurgents in that district.

When the sailor entered the ravine, he imagined it had another outlet, but upon discovering the small oven-like opening in the rock at the end (the same being open at the time), he, taking it for the entrance to a burial vault, after running to give himself impetus, sprang up, clutched the ledge with his hands, then forcing in his head and shoulders, wriggled through, and dropped upon the floor.

Nan-woo was slumbering, but in his sleep repeating the words "o-mi-tu-fuh;." upon which Jerry shook him, then prostrated himself, and, to the best of his ability, repeated the same words to the astonished bonze, who looked at him with horror, and quaveringly demanded who he was.

"O-mi-tu-fuh; o-mi-tu-fuh!" ejaculated the prostrate sailor.   However, at length he got up, and, in his best Chinese, prayed the bonze would save his life, and hide him from his enemies.

Nan-woo was a merciful old fellow; and as he had long desired an assistant, or disciple, agreed to shelter the fugitive.   Having instructed him to hold his tongue, the old bonze took his position behind the screen, and awaited the arrival of the soldiers; how he got rid of them has been described.

When night came the old fellow lit a lamp, and Thompson had an opportunity of seeing what his quarters were like.   The cell was an irregular apartment, cut out of the solid limestone rock.   There was no furniture, but an old mat, while a water jar, and an earthen chatty, containing a few handsful of dry rice, were the only kitchen articles the bonze possessed.

Jerry surveyed the latter for a few moments, then asked if that was what he lived on? upon which the old man nodded, and taking a handful of rice, threw a few grains into his mouth, then drank a sup of water.

"Well," exclaimed the sailor in his native language, "here's a go.   I've been and signed articles to a toad in a hole, and got to live in a box office, on dry rice and water."

Their frugal meal having been partaken of, the old fellow chin-chinned his disciple, and with the assurance that no man would dare come up the gully at night (as he had declared it was haunted), the old gentleman dropped down upon his knees, and o-mi-tu-fuh'd at such a rate, that Jerry set it to music, and joined in a sort of chorus.

"I wonder what the deuce it means?   I used to hear poor Jow a saying of it.   O-mi-tu-fuh (stretching himself, and yawning); don't I wish I had a tooth full of grog."

When the sailor awoke the next morning he found the old bonze still at it,— "o-mi-tu-fuh, o-mi-tu-fuh!" and he kept it up all day, repeating the words in a mechanical sort of manner, which at times greatly irritated his companion.

About ten o'clock a woman came, and asked what she should do to obtain luck.

"Bring a dish of boiled rice and some tea, and place them in the road before my cell, as an offering to the evil spirits.   Do this daily for a week."

When she had departed another arrived, and the sailor amused himself, and improved his knowledge of the language by listening to their wants.   At last one came whose story caused the man to be all ears.   It was A-tae's mother, who thus detailed her daughter's symptoms.

"She has devils in her brain, who speak for her, and I fear she will die."

Nan-woo, who had great faith in a youthful constitution, gave the afflicted mother two slips of bamboo, upon one of which was written, "Decline present benefit, and receive greater reward in futuro," while the other ran as follows: "Ten thousand devils are not as tormenting as a bad heart."

A-tae's mamma read these, and accepted them as the words of an oracle, of course torturing their meaning to suit her daughter's case.

"When A-tae gets well, what shall she do?"

"Bring me every morning, for one month, a basket of fruit and some young tea, · then I will assure her perfect health."

Jerry gave a sigh of relief. "I'll see her again somehow," he thought.

It was a few days after this that the gossips were chatting around A-tae's mat, and the following is what they said: "Oh, Mrs. So-and-so, have you heard the news? You remember how two soldiers hunted the man who frightened this poor child so? Well, they chased him to Nan-woo's hermitage, and the bonze told them as soon as the thing saw him it burst into a flame and vanished."

"Did you ever?" cried one gossip.

"Bless us!" said another.

And little A-tae winked behind their backs.

"Oh, splendid Yung-Yung-Sho, I shall see you again, my lord, my emperor, my deity. I shall live if I can only look upon you now and then. We will be like the Neih, who enjoy sublime love by merely glancing at each other. O dazzling Sho! You shall be my god, and I will burn incense to you day and night. My whole frame thrills with exquisite delight when I hear your voice. My eyes light up like lamps at night when I view you, Sho. · Oh, my absorbing god, never look coldly upon A-tae. You will always speak gently to me, will you not? Always be so kind and tender to your little A-tae, who loves you from your queue to your shoes." Thus apostrophized the happy girl, and it was no wonder old Nan-woo's charms worked, for Cupid was directing them; and as musk overpowers every other odour, so, beside love, all pleasures in this life are utterly dwarfed and lost. 'Twas love nearly caused the death of A-tae, and the same potent spell restored her to life and hope.

"Now, whether you like it or not, you shall visit Nan-woo next week," observed the girl's mother.

"I'll try," dutifully replied A-tae. "I'll go, mother, even if it kills me. I'd rather die than displease my parents." Cunning little A-tae!

CHAPTER XVIII.

"Having received information that a notorious pirate, named Yaou-chung (short-tailed ruffian) is operating upon the coast between Chusan and Amoy, you are hereby ordered to proceed from Chinhae (where it is expected you will receive this dispatch), and carefully examine the coasts, particularly about Hae-tan Island. In the event of your capturing the pirate, you are directed to deliver him to the Taontai of Amoy, who will dispose of him as he sees fit, the pirate having a short time since seized a passenger junk, on board of which were fourteen mandarins belonging to that place, whom he enclosed in an iron cage and burnt alive. As we wish to show our power in these seas, it is desirable that you totally exterminate the band, and level their settlement to the ground."

"A very nice little job, is it not, Russell?" observed Woodward, who had just received the above dispatch from the admiral at Hong-Kong.

"As you most logically observe, sir, the occupation does most fully merit the title you so aptly apply to it, of a nice little job, and it will be as well to attempt the matter without procrastination."

"There, there, my dear Russell, why not say we've got to do it, and will do it well?"

"That, sir, would, no doubt, be a concise manner of expressing it, but I prefer to adorn my language with more classical and florid expressions."

Upon hearing this reply, the good-tempered captain nodded to his eccentric lieutenant, and directed the ship to be got ready for sea. In a short time the anchors were up, and the Stinger steaming towards Hae-tan, every one being upon the *qui vive*, and anxious to fall in with the notorious pirate. As Woodward anticipated some warm work when he met the freebooter, he ordered all useless top-hamper to be stowed below, the top-gallant yards and masts struck, and rigging snaked, intending to use steam alone in his trip down the coast.

After a careful examination of the coast, and hearing some horrible tales of the cruelties perpetrated by Yaou-chung, Woodward arrived off Hae-tan at dusk one evening; and having slowly steamed across to the main land, anchored until daylight the next morning. About five bells in the middle watch, some junks passed, when he quietly turned out his men, not a sound being allowed or light shown, and the crew learnt that the piratical fleet was sailing in, and that by daybreak an action was inevitable.

It was impossible to distinguish the junks with the naked eye, but with his night glass, Mr Beauman made out nine large vessels, on board of which the Chinese, unaware of the presence of an enemy, were firing crackers and beating gongs in a most unguarded manner. When they were out of hearing, Captain Woodward got up anchor, and hugging the land, crept after them, and at daybreak saw the last of the fleet put up its helm and run into port. In a few moments the Stinger was tearing away at full speed for the place, the men watching their captain, who, assisted by the master, manœuvred the ship splendidly; and although the odds were eight to one, no one doubted his ability to do all he might undertake. Every one seemed impressed with a consciousness of responsibility, and appeared fully determined to do his duty; and when the ship swept round the point, and they found themselves in the entrance of a large bay, which was studded all over with junks, although they felt inclined to cheer, they held their peace, knowing, by the eyes of their commander, that they must repress their enthusiasm.

Woodward stood upon the bridge, glass in hand, and gave his orders as calmly as he would have done had he been entering Hong-Kong harbour. At last he suddenly rang upon the engine-room bell the signal to "stop her," but before they could do this the ship struck upon a mud bank, and at that moment the pirates sighted her, and altering their course, turned back and opened fire. It was a trying time: the vessel swinging across the passage, and forming as it were a target for their guns. After a while the junks suddenly ceased firing, and bout ship, when, having sailed some distance up the bay, they formed in two lines, and again bore down towards the Stinger, the execution of this manœuvre occupying about three-quarters of an hour.

Having in vain tried to steam off, and after running his crew backward and forward upon the upper deck, Woodward ordered the foremost guns to be transported aft, and then repeating his tactics, found the ship once more floated, whereupon the guns were returned to their proper positions, and they awaited the arrival of the pirates, who were about a mile distant. Upon her starboard bow were five large junks, the foremost of which was doubtless the flagship, it being beautifully painted and gilded, while on the port bow were four smaller craft letting off crackers, and making a great din with their gongs. When their guns arrived within range they commenced firing their bow chasers, Woodward surveying them through his glass as coolly as though they were performing their evolutions for his amusement. The shot flew over the Stinger, and now and then one would strike her hull, but there stood the captain quiet and undaunted, while his men, taking example from him, were as still as statues. Suddenly a heavy shot struck the funnel, near which he was standing, and cut a piece clean out of it, when he quietly lifted the handle of the engine-room bell, and rang out, "Go ahead, full speed," then waved his orders to the first lieutenant and master, stationed along the deck, who transmitted them to the men at the wheel.

In a short time they reached the junks, but still no signal was given to fire, although the pirates were blazing away furiously, and some stray shots struck the hull and rigging. The men, who were all crouched down behind their guns, wondered when they were to commence, and now and then would peer over the pieces and watch the unmoved commander. At last, just as they got abreast of the foremost junks, between which he had steered, the words "Commence firing" rang out from Woodward's lips, and at the same instant he signalled "Stop her" to the engineers.

The men sprang up with a cheer of defiance, and poured a discharge of grape and canister into the junks on either side, (flash) bang (flash—flash—flash) bang—bang—bang—(flash) bang; and the excited sailors loaded and fired with tremendous energy. In a very short time a thick pall of smoke completely enveloped the ship, and with great difficulty the captain managed to keep her in position between the line of junks—she in the mean time drifting slowly ahead. After the first few discharges the men lost their hearing through the stunning reports, and would vainly bawl at each other, while their bodies were grimed with the smoke of the powder, every one of them being stripped to the waist. The powder-monkeys were as active as their namesakes, feeling their way in the thick smoke, so as to avoid being knocked down by the rammers or sponges, and cautiously treading clear of the tackle laid along the decks. It was wonderful how clever the youngsters were, and with what accuracy they would return to their own guns, although it was impossible to see them. The flashes, which at first dazzled their eyes, now merely made them blink for a moment, while their dulled ears only heard a faint boom, and after a time did not notice even that.

Woodward sprang up aloft, and saw the ship was heading right, and that the first two junks which they had passed were on fire. Upon his return to the deck he met the master, who bawled something in his ear; but as he could not understand what he said,* he motioned him to go aloft, and keep a look-out.

Although the Stinger steamed quite slowly between the lines of junks, she had not lost a man; and the pirates being unable to depress their guns sufficiently to hit the ship very often, had actually been firing into each other. When Woodward found that the shots were striking the ship in an oblique direction he rang the signal, "Go ahead, full speed," and in a short time was clear of the junks, which, however, kept firing away at each other for some thirty minutes.

After they discovered their mistake he came to anchor, and putting on a spring, raked them fore and aft with grape and canister. In a short time the two lines of junks closed upon each other; and as they were nearly all on fire, the pirates abandoned them, and took to the water. Much to Woodward's chagrin, he observed that the big junk, which he supposed was commanded by Yaou-chung in person, had managed to put out her fire, and was escaping through the passage to the sea; however, as it was impossible to pass the burning vessels, he steamed up the bay, and landed at a town about five miles from the entrance.

The Taontai came down to receive him, and Woodward found that the pirates had that morning entered the place to collect tribute when they were overtaken and destroyed by the Stinger; and so grateful were the townspeople, or rather their governor, that he offered the ransom money to the captain, who of course declined the gift. Woodward did not want to risk his ship too near the burning junks, and he showed his prudence, for about 9 A.M. two of them blew up, and shortly afterwards the others followed; and as the explosions seemed to blow out every vestige of flame, they floated about the bay mere shapeless hulks, and became a prey to the swarms of thieves, who went out of the city in boats to pick up wood or any loot which they might be lucky enough to come across.

Seeing the mouth of the bay clear, the captain bade, the civil Taontai adieu, and steamed out to sea in search of Yaou-chung's junk. Upon clearing the headland at the mouth of the harbour they beheld the pirate with all sail set standing out to sea, but as soon as he saw them he trimmed his sails, and ran behind Haetan. Now, Woodward knew there was no shelter for the pirate upon the weather side of the island, so he altered his course, and steamed along to leeward, expecting to catch the junk as it rounded the opposite point; but Yaou-chung was too smart for him, as he had anchored, it being a calm day, just round the point behind which Woodward saw him disappear.

Having waited for two hours, the captain proceeded round the further point, and, to his annoyance, saw the pirate standing out to sea, with his sails so closely hauled, that he seemed to be going in the wind's eye. Now, every nautical writer has described a stern chase, and doubtless the old adage "A stern chase is a long chase" has been sufficiently hackneyed, but it was a very long one upon this occasion, as it must be remembered the Stinger was only an auxiliary screw, and it was quite dusk before they overhauled the plucky Chinaman.

* Mr. Beauman informed the captain that he need not fear the pirates throwing fire-pots upon his decks, as none of them had the usual basket (from which they throw those missiles) at their mast-heads.

Woodward was at his post, and had given instructions to the master to lay the ship alongside the junk; and taking command forward of the starboard watch of boarders himself, instructed Lieutenant Russell to head those of the port watch, who were ordered to board the pirate abaft, directing the men to crouch behind the nettings until they struck the junk. Forward, the captain of the forecastle was securing the end of a chain, to which was fastened a grappling-iron, and abaft, the captain of the afterguard was similarly employed. The Stinger showed no light, and made no sound, save that caused by the regular beat of her screw. Suddenly the junk put about, and tried to rake the ship, but Woodward was too good a sailor to allow his enemy to catch him asleep, and the pirate threw his shot away upon the water.

After various manœuvres, too tedious to describe here, the gallant captain at last got his ship in exactly the position he wanted her, and putting on full steam, ran her crash into the bows of the junk. Up sprang the captain of the forecastle, and the grappling-iron was firmly secured in the side hamper of the pirate, upon which Woodward shouting to his men, " Come on, my lads !" leapt sword in hand on board the junk, landing his party upon the forecastle, from which they drove the pirates with great slaughter. The Stinger was then laid alongside, and with a loud hurrah, Lieutenant Russell, led his men over the hammock-netting abaft, obtaining in a few moments possession of the poop. The pirates, driven to the body of the junk, fought like demons, and twice repulsed the Stingers, once nearly recovering possession of the poop, which was, however, gallantly held by the first lieutenant.

When Yaou-chung found he was cornered, he conceived the bold idea of trying to board the Stinger ; so, giving instructions to his men, he, in spite of the shower of pistol-balls and musketry which was poured upon him from the poop and forecastle, succeeded in boarding the ship, before the master, who was in command, became aware of his manœuvre. Beauman was attending to the after grapnel, when he saw the pirates pour over the nettings just by the main hatchway. Without a moment's hesitation he darted below, ran forward upon the lower deck, sprang up the fore hatchway, and scrambling on board the junk, told the captain of the pirate's move.

" All aboard !" shouted Woodward. Then directing two of the men to cast off the grapnel, he abandoned the junk, and drove the pirates aft upon the quarter-deck of the Stinger; the men who had cast off the grapnel on board the junk, running aft and telling the first lieutenant the news. Russell thereupon placed his men so as to cut the pirates down as they were driven off the ship's decks abaft. As all this was done upon a starlight night, the Stingers could just make out friends from foes, although at times the pirates and crew got a little mixed, and even assaulted their own shipmates.

Yaou-chung led his men like a tiger, and certainly fought well ; but just as he reached the wheel a light shot up on board the junk, and Woodward saw him motioning his men to press forward and attack the sailors again. With a loud cheer the Stingers threw themselves upon the foe, and their captain, wielding a cutlass which he had taken from one of his men, cut Yaou-chung down with a swinging blow. When the pirates saw their leader fall, they surrendered, and within a quarter of an hour seventy-three of them were secured and put in irons, together with Yaou-chung, the cut given by the commander having more stunned than otherwise injured him, his skull being thick enough to stand a chop from a cutlass.

When all was quiet, they carefully examined the prize, which was found to be filled with valuable plunder; then they threw the dead overboard, and taking her in tow, proceeded towards Amoy, where they arrived within eight-and-forty hours after the capture of the junk.

The notorious Yaou-chung and his associates were duly handed over to the Taontai, after which the Stinger refitted and stopped up the shot-holes in her sides. She had been hulled eighteen times, but upon mustering her crew after the action, only thirteen casualties were reported, not one of which proved fatal. One man lost a limb, and another three of his fingers, but otherwise the wounds were slight. Of course it was by the merest good fortune they escaped as they did, for had the ship, when between the junks, been but for a moment in such a position that their shot could have taken effect, no doubt her decks would have been swept.

It was a bold action, and the merchants of Amoy, to show their appreciation of Woodward's gallantry, offered him a service of plate, which he courteously, yet firmly, declined, alleging that his officers and men had quite as much to do with destroying the pirates as himself. He, however, did not object to their presenting his crew with a gratuity, which amounted to over three thousand dollars; and as he knew how slow the prize courts were, he told his men to clear out all they wanted from the junk, after which he despatched her to Hong-Kong, where she was condemned and sold. Not a bale of silk or ball of opium would he keep for himself, being too proud to share in the plunder; and beyond a few flags, taken from the various pirate junks he had destroyed, he returned home no richer than he came, his principles being totally unlike those of his predecessor, who upon one occasion, after taking a junk, coolly appropriated a number of balls of opium, which for security he stowed in the lockers of his state room, the said opium being described by him as "his perquisites."

After remaining in port a few days, a grand banquet was given by the Taontai, to which the captain, officers, and crew were invited; and as he was instructed to be upon friendly terms with the Chinese authorities, Woodward accepted the invitation, little dreaming of the surprise which the Celestials had in store for them.

About three P. M. the Stingers left their ship, and landed at a place designated by the Taontai, where, having found a guard of honour drawn up to receive them, they proceeded at once to the governor's residence in the following order:—First marched the executioner's assistants, who cleared the way with whips; then a bannerman, bearing the Taontai's flag and a gong, which he beat every few seconds. Following him was a body of bannermen, who preceded a sedan, in which was seated the crafty Tartar governor, who took advantage of the captain's ignorance of the rites, and appropriated to himself the place of honour. Immediately after the governor's chair, came the Stinger's band, playing "Oh, dear, what can the matter be?" then the sedan, containing Captain Woodward, followed by several others, occupied by the officers and engineers.

By some mistake the chief engineer, Mr. Sniff, had taken the chair which was intended for the captain; and as the procession wended its way, the people applauded vociferously. This elated him to such a degree that he bowed repeatedly, first to the right and then to the left, which being a novel proceeding for an official, caused the mob to shout with laughter. We may here remark that the bobbing of the mandarin in the style of the tea-store images is a fiction, got up by the artists in those statuettes, and that a Celestial dignitary would as soon think of standing upon his head as of bowing to the populace when proceeding on official business. Under those circumstances a mandarin is about as motionless as a wax figure, and it may be imagined that the Amoyans, who turned out to see the procession, were immensely tickled by the antics of Mr. Sniff, whom they termed the "nodding, red-headed barbarian of the west." The royal marines came after the sedans, and the blue jackets followed them, a detachment of Tartars forming the rear-guard.

After marching to the Taontai's palace and partaking of some refreshment, the captain was informed that as there was no convenient hall in the city, a building had been prepared outside the gates, where it was hoped that the brave western men would condescend to partake of the humble fare provided for them. Hereupon the procession again formed, and marched through the city to a clear space beyond the walls, where they found an immense bamboo edifice erected. Upon one side of this was an enclosed space, which the Stingers imagined was fenced in to form a promenade ground for them during the intervals of the feast; but upon entering the building, they found there were no windows or doors upon that side of the edifice. The whole place was draped with banners and hung with "living-flower-mats," i. e. mats of split bamboo, upon which flowers were sewn in patterns; these decorations might by a casual observer have been taken for beautiful carpets, so evenly were the blossoms arranged upon them. At the extreme end was a raised cross table for the Taóntai and guests of rank, while along the length of the building two tables, laden with sweetmeats and fruits were spread for the accommodation of the crew. The officials were entertained with an infinite variety of courses, all more or less delicious, and none of them badly cooked or repulsive to their taste, while knives and forks were provided, and champagne and bitter beer poured out without stint. Much to the satisfaction of their hospitable entertainer, his guests did every justice to the meal.

Upon the entry of the men the whole place was lighted with candles, and a Chinese band struck up a tune, which it screwed out, with more or less rapidity, during the time the banquet lasted. No doubt the Celestials thought it very melodious, and at times the attendants upon the sailors would nod to the noise, as we do to our music, but the effect upon the visitors was, to say the least of it, excruciating.

When the sailors had taken their seats a number of attendants entered with huge kettles of warm wine, which they poured into little cups that were placed by the right hand of each guest. Now, as a sailor's capacity for liquor of any kind is well known, it may easily be imagined that they looked rather blue upon finding such small measures allotted them; but by dint of repeatedly filling during the course of the banquet, they managed to get enough, although not one became intoxicated. When the attendants imagined the sailors had deluged themselves sufficiently with wine, they proceeded to remove the remnants of the sweets; seeing this, the jolly tars, who imagined dinner was over, motioned them to leave the dishes, which they entirely emptied of their contents. Upon this the waiters cleared the tables by beat of gong. In a short time a file of men entered, and placed all sorts of food before the astonished foreigners; and as the provisions were supplied by fifty hotel-keepers who were obliged, under threat of severe punishment, to furnish a certain number of dishes, some of them were palatable, and others the reverse; however, the men were all satisfied, and attacked the viands with the full determination of trying everything which came within their reach and would shout to a shipmate at another table, or pass favourite dishes from one to another in a most amusing fashion.

"I say, number ten mess!—hi!—you at the other table come over here; we've got some biled bore-constructor, and its stunning."

"Charley, how are you gettin' on?" observed a hardy-looking topman to a marine who was seated opposite him.

"I'm all right. I've eat a whole roast duck, and am trying some fried boot-heels, which ain't bad. Will ye have some?"

When the dishes were removed a procession of servants entered, bearing four pigs, roasted whole; these were deposited upon the tables, and soon nothing but the bones remained. When these had been disposed of, the attendants placed bowls of thin soup before each sailor, after having partaken of which many of them felt anything but well.

When the feast commenced, a heavy curtain was drawn across that portion of the edifice where the officers sat. As the Taontai knew the sailors would finish their dinners long before the officials, he directed the attendants upon the men to let them eat their food, and then supply them with unlimited warm wine and tobacco, with which they managed to pass the time until eight o'clock, when the gong announced the Taontai and his guests had completed their meal.

A crowd of attendants now proceeded to unhook the centre of the curtain, covering the wall upon that side of the edifice facing the enclosure, and upon its removal a guard was placed across the gap, the dinner tables cleared away, and seats placed for the guests,—the Taontai and his officials upon the left, and Captain Woodward and his officers upon the right. Footlights were then placed upon the ground in front of the guards, who, now that the party were seated, retired, and left them gazing upon a square enclosure, and they had full opportunity of listening to the enlivening agony of the Chinese band, which redoubled its noise and worked away as if desirous of carrying on until something gave way.

At a signal from the Taontai the doors of the banquet-hall were thrown open, and the Amoyans poured in until they became so closely pressed, that you might have walked upon their heads without fear. Captain Woodward imagined they were going to entertain them with a theatrical performance, so he smiled at his host, and puffed at his cigar, little dreaming he was about to witness a horible tragedy, which none but a Chinese would have imagined acceptable to a foreigner. At length when a gong had been struck nine times, the Taontai arose and thus addressed his guests :—

" Most illustrious, brave, and honourable men of the western seas, I have this day endeavoured, out of my poverty of means, to show you how much I think of you and all your nation. I thank you for the brave act which resulted in the capture of Yaouchung, and I invite you to see the clemency of his Majesty the Emperor whom we all revere, extended to the defiled dog and his blood-stained accomplices. I salute you respectfully."

When this speech was ended Lieutenant Russell observed to Woodward, " The conviction has just dawned upon my mind that they are about to consign the pirates to Hades, by the hands of the public executioner, and the present company are to witness the performance."

" Nonsense ! " replied the commander. " They surely do not intend carrying out the sentence here."

" Let me entreat you not to suffer a misconception to lead your judgment astray, as even my limited acquaintance with the Chinese language enables me to affirm that the pirates are shortly to be submitted to the pangs of torture in our presence."

" I'm sorry, as we cannot back out, and must, as it were, countenance the butchery by our presence. The sly Taontai has arranged this matter very cleverly ; do you not think so, Russell ? " said the captain.

Further conversation was cut short by the appearance of the chief executioner, a most revolting-looking wretch, who advanced into the arena ; then, kneeling upon the sawdust with which the ground was covered, bowed his forehead (or kow-tow'd) nine times, after which his assistants, who were, like him, clad in black tunics and conical-shaped wire hats, came forward and went through the same performance.

Having paid their respects, the black band brought out several movable screens, which they placed before the opening, upon which the music recommenced. After a short interval the gong again sounded, and some persons behind took the screens and carried them out of sight, when the spectators beheld about sixty men, clad only in blue trousers, kneeling with their hands resting upon the sawdust, it being noticed that all of them were deprived of their queues. At the back of the arena was a mat-covered pile, over which an assistant executioner, armed with a ladle was throwing some liquid.

At a signal from the Taontai, a scribe read the names of the sixty prostrate men, and when that was completed called to four executioners, who stepped forward, paid their respects to their master and his guests, then taking up their positions, each at the head of fifteen recumbent criminals, raised their short swords and awaited the final order. Their weapons were very keen-edged, thick-backed affairs, slightly curved, and loaded with quicksilver, in order to give force to the blows. The chief executioner received the orders and directed his assistants, he taking the left-hand row, over the last man of which he was now standing, with his eyes fixed upon the Taontai.

So rapidly had all this been accomplished that the Stingers could hardly comprehend the meaning of their action; but when the Governor elevated the claw-like nail of his right thumb, and the four executioners simultaneously swept the heads off four of the recumbent figures, they all understood it was a real execution, and not a theatrical representation that was being enacted before their eyes. As the movements of the executioners were regulated by those of the chief, it will be sufficient to describe his action.

When he gave the swinging blow with his sword which swept off his first victim's head, he dexterously skipped across the neck of the body, and planting himself behind his second victim, repeated the cut, upon which off flew another head, he continuing his blows until he had decapitated four of the kneeling ones, when he changed his sword for a keener weapon and recommenced his labour. In a few moments fifteen heads were lying upon the sawdust near the trunks of their former bodies. It was wonderful to see how easily he sliced them off, and with what rapidity the whole of them were executed.

When all was finished the executioners picked up the heads, and carelessly placed them upon their trunks; then advancing to the front, knelt, kow-tow'd, and retired. In a few moments a number of men entered, and dragged off the bodies and heads, after which fresh sawdust was sprinkled, and the arena raked clean, in the same manner as the supers prepare the ring of a circus for a new entertainment.

Captain Woodward, who was thoroughly sick at the sight, but had kept his seat out of courtesy towards the Taontai, now arose, and begged he would allow him to retire with his officers and crew, adding that such a method of execution was quite foreign to the ideas of all "the men of the west;" but the Taontai only pointed to the swarming mass of Chinese behind them, and declared it would be impossible for them to leave until the executions were over, adding, "You will be pleased with the next performance, which you will probably never have another opportunity of witnessing."

Finding escape was impossible, the captain partly turned his back upon the arena, and the gong sounded for the next piece of barbarism.

A large body of the wire-hatted, black-dressed executioners now advanced and kow-tow'd, four of their number bearing long poles, to the end of which were tied lighted torches. After their prostrations were completed, two of them walked to the back of the arena, and pulled at the lines which held the covering of the pile. A yell of execration broke from the Chinese spectators as, upon the mats falling down, they beheld a heap of wood, on which were placed two cages, one a large affair twenty-five feet long, by about four high, in which were chained thirteen of the officers of the pirate craft; while, in a smaller cage, above the other, was secured the notorious pirate who had given the Stingers so much trouble. When the sailors recognized this villain they gave vent to a murmur, which certainly did not indicate pity.

A mandarin now advanced, and thus addressed the spectators :—" List, ye people of Fo-keen district. Hardly a moon ago this Yaou-chung seized an imperial junk, and after killing the crew, whom he tortured in a barbarous manner, deliberately enclosed thirteen of our honourable colleagues within an iron cage, and burnt them to death. To-day Yaou-chung (you descendant of a dishonoured dog) and thirteen of his head men receive the clemency of our father and mother, the Emperor, the common men of his crew having been despatched with the sword.   Beware ! and follow not the example they have set, or you will be treated likewise."

Neither Yaou-chung nor his officers paid the slightest attention to the speech, but seemingly chaffed the executioner, who was basting them with some liquid.   At length the latter retired and the mandarin gave the signal, when the torchmen applied their brands, and in an instant the pile was alight.   The thirteen men were soon writhing and screaming, as their bodies were wetted with spirit which the executioners had thrown upon them, but for some time Yaou-chung remained as quiet as a statue, although the torture must have been fearful; however, after the wood began to burn up he gradually showed signs of suffocation, and must have been insensible long before the flames reached his body.

When all was over the crowd dispersed, and Captain Woodward marched his men back to the wharf and embarked them in boats in which they were conveyed on board the ship.   Of course there was no help for it, and it was all right according to the Chinese way of reckoning, but the gallant officer determined, that when next asked to a Chinese banquet, he would, before accepting the civility, ascertain if it were " a dinner to be followed by an execution," or only a friendly " chin-chin."

CHAPTER XIX.

Little A-tae improved wonderfully in health, and within five days after her mother's visit to Nan-woo announced that she was ready to set out for the sacred grove. Her parent did not content herself with sending only some fruit and tea, but added sweetmeats and sundry delicacies, including a little rock salt, which she packed in a neat bamboo basket, and gave her daughter, with many minute instructions as to her deportment.

It was a lovely autumnal day; and as the girl bent her steps towards the hill she mechanically sang a very old Chinese ditty called "The life of a leaf," while her thoughts, wandering more fleetly on, were already with her beloved Yung-Yung-Sho. Strange to say, after the first few stanzas she altered the words in a manner, which would have puzzled any Celestial who overheard her. The original song ran as follows:—

> "Of the young bud, covered with down,
> Soft as the breath of a zephyr,
> Unfolding to the sun, a leaf appears,
> Tender as the cheek of an infant.
> At first thin, delicate, transparent,
> Developing quickly, veined like the hand of a maiden
> From first to last always beautiful.
> After reclining in the light of the golden sun,
> And coquetting with the silver moon,
> For many days,
> The early (eager, forward) frost kisses it gently,
> Gemming it with beauty.
> It blushes at the embrace;
> Emboldened, the touch is repeated,
> When lo, the ruddy colour flies, and
> The leaf, pale and trembling,
> Drops upon the bosom of the earth."

That is what she should have sung, but she altered it in this manner, for after uttering the words,

> "From first to last always beautiful,"

pouring her heart out in melody, she sang,

> "Oh! charming Yung-Yung-Sho,
> By day my sun, by night my moon,
> Always thus to remain.
> I cannot forget the gentle embrace
> You gave me in the tea field.
> My face burns with happiness,
> But you will never repeat it?
> Oh! will you?
> Soon again I shall behold the bright light of your eyes!
> Ah me! then pale and trembling
> Shall I sink upon the earth,
> And die of very happiness."

As she sang this her eyes sparkled, and a smile illuminated her face. Was she not going to meet her true love, her own Yung-Yung-Sho? Under those circumstances even a plain girl would have looked charming, and little A-tae appeared happy as a bird and bright as a diamond.

The girl proceeded at a brisk rate until she came to the entrance of the ravine, upon which she stopped and tormented herself with surmises. "He has fled. He *was* killed, for my mother did not mention him. I am devoured with affliction; I must go back," she thought, but after a while summoned courage, and walking up the pathway, found herself before the hole in the wall.

"Ahem!" said a voice, which she knew did not belong to Nan-woo.

A-tae blushed, cast down her eyes, and lifting the tribute basket placed it gently upon the ledge, but was too much agitated to speak.

"Ahem!" repeated the person inside.

"Sho," timidly whispered the girl, still looking at the ground; and ere she could raise her eyes the stone screen was pushed back, and Jerry, thrusting forth his arms, seized her, and lifting her up, imprinted a burning kiss upon her lips.

"O Sho, don't."

"You beauty, how I have longed to see you!" whispered the happy fellow. Of course his Chinese was not perfect by a long way, but he managed to make her understand, and what he could not utter with his tongue he expressed with his eyes, his only drawback being his inability to kiss her often, as the operation was not only awkward, but absolutely dangerous. After a delicious half-hour, during which he told her that she was the most beautiful woman in the world at least twenty times, she asked for Nan-woo.

"Oh, he's asleep.'

"Wake him. Good-bye. I'll come again to-morrow, my lord," said she, kissing her hand in imitation of her lover; then, assuming a demure expression of countenance, awaited the awakening of the bonze.

After shaking the old gentleman until he began to fear he would dislocate his neck, the sailor succeeded in getting Nau-woo to open one eye, and to slowly utter "O-mi-tu-fuh," upon which the deputy bonze repeated the irritation until he got through a good many "O-mi-tu-fuh's;" then he informed him that *a person* wanted him, and added in his own language, "If I ketch you a winkin' at her I'll stop your rice, so mind." Not that the bonze was likely to be guilty of such a breach of discipline but the sailor was so love-stricken, that he would have quarrelled with A-tae's shadow from very jealousy.

After receiving the offering, Nan-woo glanced at the girl and observed, "Bring another to-morrow; go, you are better;" then squatting upon his mat recommenced his "O-mi—" refrain, assisted in the performance by his deputy, who growled out a deep bass, whistled, or sang a falsetto accompaniment, as the whim took him. Not that it mattered to the bonze what he did, provided he kept within the cell, as after Jerry had been with him a week, except when spoken to, he took no more notice of his disciple than he would of a tame kitten.

One of the police runners was related to A-tae's family; and being a cool, calculating scamp, who did not believe in the supernatural, could not make out how it was that Jerry had left the ravine. Knowing he would receive a large reward if he captured him, he communicated his suspicions to A-tae's brother, a rowdy named Hew-chsou, upon which they determined to keep an eye upon the Buddhist grove, particularly about the ravine; and as winter had set in, they searched diligently for footprints in the snow.

The girl returned every day, and upon some occasions had the inexpressible happiness of speaking to her lover, when one morning, to her astonishment, she found Jerry out of the cell, and waiting for her at the entrance of the ravine.

"Oh, my lord! O Sho! Hie thee back. If they see you we are lost."

"Nonsense. I've been cooped up long enough, and mean to have a cruise. I can't stand it any longer; besides, Nan-woo's asleep—he spends half his time so now; I think he won't live long. But what makes you look so pale?"

"My lord Sho, for ten days, in fact, since the snow first fell, I have been watched by two men,—one is my brother Hew-chaou, and the other the police runner who hunted you. Oh, do not expose yourself to these wolves. My brother is a bad man, and would sell your head for a sapeck, and the runner is a tiger."

"I don't fear them, A-tae, but I'm getting lonely and am half-starved. Will you leave this place and go with me?"

"I can't," she sobbed.

"Why not?"

"We should not get ten li before they would track us. Then what would become of you, my lord Sho?"

They had walked up the ravine and were now just outside the cell, when suddenly the head of the old bonze protruded from the hole, his eyes wide open with astonishment and terror,

"O-mi— come in you fool! O-mi-tu-fuh, you blind idiot, come in!" saying which he threw his arms about, and behaved in such a ridiculously frantic manner, that out of compassion Jerry kissed A-tae, and wriggled through the hole into the cell.

Nan-woo was a very proper old man, and the sailor's proceedings quite scandalized him, but after a few hours he relapsed into his vegetable state, and things went on as before. One night in the depth of winter the deputy was awakened by the moans of the old fellow, and hastened to his assistance, but after having made him some tea he retired again to his mat, imagining the malady allayed by the warm drink. However, when day broke he found his senior would soon repeat his last "O-mi," as he was going fast. Thinking the case required religious consolation, he did his best under the circumstances, and as, with all his faults, Thompson was not without some sort of religion, he managed to remember a prayer or two, which he repeated to the dying bonze, winding up by way of a hymn with

How doth the little busy bee,"[*]

repeated slowly. Nan-woo looked at him with a stony expression of countenance, and about eleven A.M., after a faint struggle, with a half-uttered "O-mi-t—" upon his lips, the old bonze breathed his last, "saluting heaven" from the arms of his sorrowing companion.

"Here's a fix. On a lee shore, skipper gone, and nothing but breakers all round. Well, poor old buffer, you saved my life and put up with me, and now you're gone, I'll bury you decently;" saying which he pushed the body through the hole, and having taken it out of the ravine succeeded in burying it in a snow-drift, where the mortal remains were found in the spring, and interred by a brother bonze.

After the death of Nan-woo the sailor set to work and pulled down the rocks which had been piled up in front of the cell fifty years before, when the old bonze entered it, the occupation tending to keep his blood in circulation, and preventing him from thinking of his loneliness. He knew none of the old women who frequented the place in fine weather would be likely to visit him then, and it was not until his companion had

* Very inappropriate at the death-bed of a Buddhist bonze.

been dead a week that A-tae again made her appearance. Before the snowy weather set in the girl had managed to bring him several articles of warm clothing, and a number of bundles of rice-straw, which he formed into a bed, so his situation was not quite so forlorn as might have been imagined, his great trouble being a fear of starvation; and when A-tae came pattering up the path he gave a cheer, and rushing out caught her in his embrace.

"Please, Sho!—my lord—don't!"

"I'm so glad to see you; you can't tell how lonely I have been. The old man is dead, and, but for you, I would have left and risked capture."

"Hist! Did you hear a noise?"

"Nonsense! It is your imagination."

"I fear my brother has followed me. He is very suspicious, and wanted my mother to prevent my coming, but I said I must, or I should never have any luck. Hist!—I hear it again; 'tis some one moving. Let us hide."

"Who would hurt *you*?"

"My brother would kill me if he found me with you. I know his passionate nature."

"Stay here until night falls, and then we will dress in the old bonze's clothes, and leave the place.. In his winter hoods no one will be able to know who we are, and once at Hang-Chow, there are a thousand chances to reach the sea, where I can ship in a junk, and take you as my wife."

After much persuasion the girl agreed to remain with him, observing that death would be preferable to such misery as they had endured for the last few days.

The words had hardly passed her lips before her brother suddenly sprang from behind a rock, and, drawing a short sword, plunged it into her body.

With a cry like that of a wounded tiger, the sailor jumped at Hew-chaou, and seizing the sword, delivered cut after cut until the rowdy was covered with wounds. After a desperate struggle, during which both fought like demons, the Chinaman, in endeavouring to pick up a stone, received a blow upon the nape of the neck, which stretched him dead. Seeing this Thompson gently lifted up the body of A-tae, and carrying it into the cell, endeavoured to bring her back to life. When she became conscious he asked her where she was wounded, upon which she motioned to her side, and again closed her eyes, as if in great pain.

"Poor little thing—my curse on the brute who did it. How could any one with a heart do such a cruel deed?" he observed in his own language. Then added in Chinese, "Fear not, A-tae, you will soon be well."

The girl opened her eyes upon hearing his voice, and thrilling faintly, begged him not to sorrow for her, she was so happy resting in his arms.

Thompson gazed upon the loving face, but in spite of vain endeavours to restrain his emotion, his lips quivered, and big tears coursed down his cheeks.

"Don't weep, Yung-Yung-Sho."

"God—help—me. I deserve to lose you, as a punishment for my sins."

"Speak my own language."

"A-tae, my heart is broken, and would I were in your place. I have not loved you as I should. I am not worthy of such love as yours, you pure lily."

Upon hearing this the poor girl lifted her head, laid her cheek upon his, and kissing him gently, said, "Yung-Yung-Sho, I'm—so—happy!" then dropped upon his shoulder, and giving him a look of ineffable love, closed her eyes, and in a short time all her earthly troubles were over.

¹ When he found that she was dead he clasped her to his heart, and lavished the most endearing epithets upon her—"Open your eyes once more! O darling A-tae! Look at me again! Your heart still beats." But the light of the beautiful eyes was dimmed for ever, and the loving little heart would never beat for him again. All day he held her in his arms, and when evening came he lit a lamp—which had been her present—and watched her body through the long winter night. At times, fancying she smiled at him, he would bend over her and listen—but to hear the beating of his own heart,—then he would gently kiss her lips, and resume his lonely watch.

There, in the presence of a woman who had shown by her every action how tenderly and dearly she had loved him, the sailor looked back upon his past life, and contrasted the conduct of the girl before him with that of his former loves. "None of them were half as good as she," he thought, and he vowed henceforth to shun the society of the opposite sex.

At daybreak he took her once more in his arms, and buried her in the snow near the entrance of the ravine, taking care to arch stones over her in such a manner that no wild animal could get at the body. The snow was falling fast when he did this, and in a short time the tumulus was completely hidden with a veil of spotless purity; then he returned to the hermitage, and having dressed in the winter suit of the bonze, left the ravine. As he passed the place where his lost love lay so silent, he knelt reverently and prayed that she might be in a happier state, where she would never have a sorrow; then, with a heavy heart, he wandered forth, going he cared not whither.

After walking for about five hours, he came to a small village, where he met with a party of actors about to start for Hang-chow; as he wished to disguise himself, he slipped into a room and pulled off his bonze's dress, under which he still wore his old one; then sought out the manager of the company, and having informed him that he was a first-rate "fool," was offered by the impressario a salary of a hundred and fifty sapecks per month, with board and lodging. As salary was no object, he at once closed with the offer.

His employer gave him a cat-skin robe, directing him to put it on and go into the public room, where he could give them a specimen of his powers. After rigging himself in the costume he suddenly darted into the large hall, which was then full of company, and falling upon his hands and knees, aped the manner and melody of a tom-cat to such perfection that, upon his return to the manager, the latter "chin-chinned" him, and made up his mind that when they arrived at Hang-chow he would bring out his new actor as a star of the first magnitude. As they performed at all the principal towns upon the road, and were sometimes delayed by heavy falls of snow, the company did not arrive at their journey's end as soon as they anticipated, but the delay gave Jerry an opportunity of perfecting himself in his part, and when he kow-tow'd to the audience in the "Theatre of the Gods" at Hang-chow he received a perfect ovation.

He now desired to earn enough money to take him to Ning-po, as he had overheard a boatman say that there was an English ship-of-war wintering there, and, in justice to him, it must be said that, although surrounded by pretty girls who would willingly have become Mrs. Lew (that being his theatrical name), he never even smiled upon one of them; indeed, it was months before he spoke to a woman, and the once susceptible sailor was now as distant as he had formerly been free with the fair sex.

After delighting large audiences in the "City of fair women," the manager announced his intention of proceeding to Ning-po. When he asked Jerry to accompany him, the sailor at once agreed. As the party was now a large one, having received several additions to their number, they determined to go by sea; so Ch'un making a bargain with a captain, they proceeded to the port and embarked on board the Roaring Tiger, a large junk used in the fish-trade. When they got to sea, Thompson showed the actors that he was a good sailor; and, although feeling thoroughly miserable himself, he kept them in a continual state of merriment by his absurd antics. They succeeded in reaching Chin-hae without having encountered a gale; and, as the ship had been directed to anchor there, until examined by the custom-house officials, the passengers proceeded up the river in boats, the manager engaging one to convey his troupe. Upon nearing Ning-po Jerry saw, towering above the masts of the junks at anchor below the city, the lofty spars of a man-of-war, which, upon a nearer approach, proved to be the Stinger.

"There she is! there she is! there she is!" he cried in his native language. Upon which his companions shook their heads, and observed to each other that the *fool* was going crazy.

When their boat passed the man-of-war he could contain himself no longer, but shouted to Tom Clare, who was arranging the yoke in the captain's gig, then waiting for the commander at the gangway.

"Tom! Tom Clare!" he bawled, "here! look here!"

As Clare, upon looking up, only saw a Chinese passenger-boat, he merely glanced at it, then resumed his occupation, imagining he had been called by some one on board, little dreaming it was his old friend Thompson come to life again. His non-recognition by Clare seemed to alter all his plans; and instead of burning to return to his ship and old associates, he suddenly determined to remain as he was. "Why should I go aboard that hooker where all have forgotten me, to be flogged like a dog, when I can always earn a living here? No, I'll not make myself known agin. They soon forgets one, anyhow." He did not consider that they all believed him dead, and that his Chinese costume and shaven head completely disguised him.

Having landed, the manager escorted them to a small inn, where they settled down for the night, and the next day he directed Jerry and his leading tragedian to put on their best costumes, as he wished them to give a specimen of their ability before a very rich man, who often entertained his neighbours with dramatic performances; so about noon, having enveloped his body in the skin-dress, fastened on his cat-faced mask, and adjusted the strings of his tail, the sailor proceeded with his companions to call upon Mr. Ah-mu-chow.

Their journey through the streets was a good advertisement for the company, as the manager would stop at every few paces, and announce the number of his troupe, and the beauty of their dresses. After a long walk they arrived at the residence of the great man, who, they were told, was still in bed. Upon being shown into the vestibule Jerry created a roar of laughter by crawling about with a bundle in his mouth, in the same manner as a cat conveys her kitten, and it was with difficulty that his master succeeded in preventing him from entering the adjoining chamber where the great one was taking his "pick-me-up," preparatory to his undergoing the fatigues of giving audience to the toadies, who were waiting his appearance in the "chamber of conversation." At last a gong sounded, when, with measured strides, and contempt expressed in every line of his face, the mighty Ah-mu-chow entered the apartment, upon which the obsequious ones fell upon their knees and kow-tow'd, as if they were driving nails in the floor with their heads; Jerry, who did not relish such grovelling, standing in a perfectly rigid attitude, with his tail as straight as a bamboo.

Without glancing at the prostrate forms, the haughty Ah-mu walked to the end of the vestibule, where, assisted by his servants, he seated himself on a stool, and posed according to the method prescribed in the "Book of Rites," after which he announced to his secretary that "the dogs might speak," whereupon the manager advanced upon his knees and handed in his petition, which ran as follows :—

"An humble petition to his Lordship, his Mightiness, his stupendous and awful Greatness, whom the gods call Ah-mu-chow.

"I Ch'un-foo, before you, being but dirt, scum, dross, and rubbish, humbly (timidly) raise my eyes, and beg you will deign to cast a glance (sideways) upon my appeal.

"Hearing you (out of your boundless wealth) often patronize such scum as us actors, I venture to beg you will allow me to introduce, for your honourable amusement, two members of my corps—Lew, of the cat-like form, and Tsew, who can repeat dramas by the hour."

[Trembling, and with bowed head.

After hearing the foregoing read by his secretary, the haughty Ah-mu (a wealthy ship's comprador, who had made money during the war) condescended to look at the actors, whereupon the cat advanced, and performed some absurd antics, which drew from him a smile of approval. Having gone through his principal feats, although the manager asserted they were poor when compared to what he could do upon the stage, Lew retired, upon which the sombre Tsew stepped forward, and thus spoke :—

"Before the great dragon had encircled with his mighty coil the imperfect matter from which sprang—"

"There! there—go to—I don't understand YOU," said the haughty one, with a frown. "I'd rather see 'Lew-of-the-cat-like-form' than hear your sombre and long-winded orations. There—stop."

Upon being thus rebuffed, the great tragedian looked daggers at the shoddyite, whom he regarded as very small potatoes, although at first he had been civil to him from motives of policy; and folding his arms, strutted out of the apartment.

"You, Ch'un-foo, listen. I like the performance of your cat, who is very amusing, but at present I do not intend giving a theatrical treat to my numerous friends in this part of the city; however, if you will perform on board a Fanqui ship which is now lying off this port, I will give you a thousand cash, and provide you with boats and refreshment for the night. You may get ready to do this on the second day of the next moon, when a grand sing-song is to be given to the head man of the Western barbarians, who permanently resides in our beautiful city.

Upon hearing this, Ch'un-foo, finding the great one meant business, at once dropped his supplicating air, and, after much squabbling about terms, agreed to perform before the Fanquis upon the appointed night for the sum of three thousand cash; then, having kow-tow'd in a business-like manner, left the presence, without for a moment taking notice of the black looks cast upon him by the assembled toadies, who were much enraged to find such a large sum squandered upon a low actor. When he reached the inn he found Tsew packing his baggage, swearing he would leave a city where the burlesque antics of a clown were preferred to the legitimate drama. In vain Ch'un-foo argued it was only one man's opinion, and that thousands of the Ningpooians were dying with anxiety to hear him; nothing availed, go he would, and, to the manager's indignation, set-out for Hang-chow, without waiting for an offer or cumshaw (a present) which might have been proffered him, had the impetuous tragedian not been so precipitate. It will thus be seen that even in China the legitimate drama is sometimes thrust to the wall, and for a time compelled to give place to burlesque.

After performing to crowded houses, and creating quite a sensation in the city, the company announced they would close their theatre for one night, having been commanded by a wealthy person to enlighten the Western barbarians with their unique exhibition, and upon the second day of the tenth moon they rehearsed a new piece, and arranged the programme for the night.

About eight o'clock the party presented themselves on board the Stinger, and with the rest Jerry was conducted abaft, and desired to remain upon the monkey-poop until they were required. The port side of the quarter-deck had been turned into a fine theatre, while forward seats were arranged, tier upon tier, each swarming with sailors and marines, all eager to witness the theatrical performance, which had just commenced when the Chinese arrived on board.

The sailor chatted with his companions, shutting his ears to tunes which, at any other time, would have quickened his pulses and made him merry, for the feeling of resentment at being forgotten by Clare was so strong within him, that he steeled himself to meet his shipmates, and imagined, in the bitterness of his heart, that he could now look upon them with indifference.

Lieutenant Russell, who was foremost in all that could make his men happy, was chatting with the comprador Ah-mu, who had begged that officer would allow him to introduce a band of actors for the amusement of his good patrons, the Stingers; and no one would have recognized the " haughty one " in the sneaking, fawning, bum-boat man, who watched every action of the lieutenant as a dog does his master.

" Would any of your men like a glass of grog ? " observed Russell to the manager, in Chinese. Thompson was about to reply for his leader, but, remembering he was forgotten, held his tongue; however, in a few moments the captain's steward came aft, and gave each of the troupe a glass of rum, upon drinking which Jerry began to relent ; but before he had time to think, the bell rang for them to make their bow upon the stage.

Upon following the lad who called them, the sailor and his party found themselves upon a well-built stage, before which a green curtain was suspended, and it was with difficulty he repressed his desire to speak to the men stationed with blue fire at the wings, who turned out to be two of his old messmates, but the bell went again ; so following the example of the others, he threw himself upon his knees, and when the curtain rose, the audience discovered a row of Chinese kow-towing behind the foot-lights. Upon seeing this the crew gave three hearty cheers, and prepared to witness wonders.

At a signal from Ch'un-foo, who knelt a few paces behind the party, the actors arose, and then Jerry saw before him many well-known faces, but they all looked at him in a distant manner, and there was no kind greeting or any expression but expectation upon the faces of those present. As he glanced round the assembly he missed Captain Puffeigh and Crushe, as well as some few others, while he wondered how long Captain Woodward nad been in command. He had ample opportunity of scrutinizing his old shipmates' faces, as the manager opened the exercises by delivering a long oration in Chinese, during which he lauded Lew-the-cat to the skies. The sailor was very much amused at noticing the great Ah-mu standing respectfully behind the first lieutenant's chair, he being allowed at the performance upon sufferance, as he had provided the Celestial actors, Russell knowing that the comprador would soon squeeze enough profit out of the ship to defray all his outlay upon that head.

Finding Ch'un-foo's oration was rather a long one, the first lieutenant directed his band to play, by way of putting a stop to his loquacity, upon which they struck up " Auld Lang Syne," but ere they had fairly started the manager ceased speaking, and Jerry advanced, and was about to address them preparatory to commencing his performance, when, thinking he was going to favour them with a speech in the same style as the manager, Russell nodded to the band to "go ahead." As the tune fell upon his ear, a change came over his heart, and the " Cat," after vainly endeavouring to control his feelings, burst into tears, seeing which the first lieutenant stopped the tune, being unwilling to mortify a man, who he imagined was only going through his usual performance, and, like many other professional gentlemen, could not brook being thwarted; for otherwise tears from a Chinaman would have been quite incomprehensible.

A dead pause succeeded, during which the sailor, to the astonishment of the audience and horror of his manager, coolly tore off his disguise, and stood before the assembly in the common wide trousers and jacket of the country, then putting his hand to his forehead, fumbled for a lock of hair, but shook his head when he recollected it was shaven, and after a great effort cried out,

" *Don't you know me, shipmates ?* "

Of course there was a tremendous excitement among the audience, but none of them recognized him, for they all believed *him* dead months ago. They, however, cheered the Chinaman who spoke English, and then waited for him to go on.

With the tears trickling down his painted cheeks, he stepped off the stage, and pointing to Tom Clare, who was in attendance upon the captain, cried, "Tom Clare, don't *you* know me? I'm Jerry Thompson!" and in an instant thrust his way through the crowd, and seizing his old friend, hugged him as a woman would her child.

The uproar which followed was deafening. Some shouted, while others laughed in a delirious sort of way; but at length when every one of the officers and crew had shaken him by the hand at least ten times, and all knew that the dead Jerry had come to life again, he requested the captain would order the boatswain to "pipe belay;" then stepping upon the stage and kow-towing in the orthodox Chinese style he proceeded to give his delighted audience a short account of his wonderful adventures, after which he took his seat between two of his old friends, until the performance was concluded.

The next day Thompson was formally re-entered upon the books of the Stinger, and as the captain did not rate two coxswains, he appointed Jerry captain of the forecastle, and within a week after his return, he fell into his old ways, and was as much at home on board the man-of-war as ever.

When he confided his story to Clare, who was greatly moved by his recital of A-tae's death, the latter asked him if he intended writing to Mary Ann. For a few moments he seemed buried in thought, but after a while he informed his friend that, under the circumstances, he thought he would wait until he got over the loss of A-tae before he renewed his correspondence with his former love, adding, "She'll keep until I gets home, and I don't feel like writing just now."

Evidently Jerry looked upon Mary Ann's love as a connoisseur does wine,—imagining it would improve as it grew older. A-tae had spoilt him for ordinary affection, and he could not so soon forget the "pale lily" lying beneath the snow, near the entrance of a ravine far away in the Che-keang district.

CHAPTER XX.

THOMPSON could scarcely credit his senses when he heard that flogging had been abolished on board the Stinger.

"What!" he observed to the boatswain, "are we free, then?"

"I'm surprised at you, Thompson; as if you was not free afore!"

"Well, Mr. Shever, you don't mean to tell me that you really believes that a man thinks hisself free, when at any moment he may find the cat-o'-nine-tails flying across his back, do you?"

"You don't look at it in a proper light, Jerry. A commander on one of her Majesty's ships-of-war has got to be a big man, or no one thinks anything of him. Now, all the while he has power to flake hie men they fears him, and he can cow the biggest roughs among them; but take it away, and see what a lame-entable prelude would follow."

"Gammon! You ain't a-going to persuade me to that, sir. Why, look at us now. Don't all of the fellers like the captain and first lieutenant? and they doesn't hold with flogging. Formerly the cussing on board was strong enough to curl an iron rod, and now we gets on very nicely, and lots of our men are learning to read and write in Lieutenant Russell's evening school. It takes more than articles of war to keep blue jackets in order, and I knows I shouldn't like to be flaked, and don't believe you would, sir."

"Nonsense, Thompson! I'm surprised you can't look at this in its proper light! Ain't all a captain does right? Why, they knows more than any one else; and if any one offends them, ain't it proper for 'em to take it out of their backs? I say so! The men is inferiors, and the officers is born to rule over them, therefore if dissatisfied demagogues and age-itators choose to think they is as good as their officers, let 'em do it; but as your friend, let me advise you to steer clear of all such fools."

"I don't believe one man is born a bit better than another, sir; and as to your idea that God made some men to rule others, it's all my eye. I think that the captain in his sittyvation is just as much bound to do what is right as we who are under him, and I know the cat-o-nine-tails ain't any use in keeping discipline, and that it's played the deuce with many a good feller."

"Chut, chut. Why, I know lots of really good men who would leave the service when their time expired, if flogging were abolished."

"Then all I can say, Mr. Shever, is, that you knows a lot of fools; and if any of them was to up and say such a lie in my company, I'll tell them just what I do you. I've heered a slave in the Brazils say as how he wouldn't be free if they gev him the chance, and that slavery was a thundering good thing for everybody wot hadn't got no money."

"Well, he was right. It is a fine thing for poor people. What are all the poor people at home but slaves? only they ain't called so. He was a sensible man, and spoke the truth."

"Hold hard, sir! Hear me out. Well, I kept my eye on that feller, and thought what a precious mean thing a man was when he gave up all ideas of trying to assert his rights, but the slave would every day have some chat about how comfortable it was to think he would be provided for in his old age by his indulgent master, until we got a little sick of it, particular as his old man hoisted him up one morning, and gave him a lot of lashes with a cowhide."

"Well, I suppose he deserved it?"

"Hold hard! let me finish my yarn, sir. He was flaked upon the wharf, and all of us chaps— we was in a merchant ship where the skipper daren't flog us—looked on and swore we'd pound his master if we only caught him alone. Well, would you believe it? when he was cast off, the feller actually walked to his master, knelt down, and, afore everybody, begged he would forgive him for having given him so much trouble."

"He was a sensible man."

"Werry sensible. We sailed that night; and just as I was castin' off the gangway plank down rushes the slave, and as he spoke English very well, he hails me. 'What do you want?' sez I. But afore I had hardly got the words out of my mouth he jumps aboard, and saying, 'Hide me, I've killed my master,' dived below and hid hisself."

"Do you call that sensible behaviour?"

"Rather, Mr. Shever. I held my tongue, and when we was out to sea hunted him out, and giv him some grub, when he told me that as he couldn't put up with the lash no longer, he had killed his owner, and chanced escaping in our ship, and that all his fine talk about liking to be flogged was only done to blind his master."

"Do you think that a small affair like a flogging justified him in killing his superior?"

"I don't know anything about superiors in that way, sir, but I knows one thing, that if any man was to flake me for his own amusement, I'd not hesitate to do as he did, as I don't think I belong to the dog speecee, if you does, Mr. Shever."

With a look meant to express contempt blended with pity for one so utterly lost to reason, Mr. Shever stopped further discussion by replying, "Silence, you ungrateful young man! Never speak to me again unless on duty. I wash my hands of you and all as holds such revolutionary opinions. I'm sorry Captain Puffeigh is not in command;" saying which he turned away with an oath, and went below.

Jerry eyed his form as it vanished down the hatchway, and then remarked to the men who had gathered round him during the conversation, "Sorry the old skipper ain't in the ship. Ugh! you blood-thirsty brute! Sorry you can't cut us up with the lash, as you did under bully Crushe. Cut my acquaintance! I cuts yours, as I'd scorn to be upon speaking terms with a warrant-officer as holds such opinions as you does. I wish your wife could hear you talk like that; she'd put you to rights, I know."

Thompson heard the news of the attack upon Canton; and, with the rest of his shipmates burned to be present at the bombardment of that city. The sailors seemed to think that they would prefer to be where they could give hard knocks, and it produced no little amount of growling when mail after mail arrived, and still no orders to move. At length, however, when the spring had well advanced, a P. and O. steamer calling at Chin-hae, sent up dispatches directing Captain Paul Woodward to start for Hong-Kong with all possible dispatch; whereupon he proceeded to get ready for sea, and within twenty-four hours they dropped down to Chin-hae, and getting up steam, left for the south. The steamer carrying the dispatches had also brought their mailbags, and Clare had several letters from his wife, parts of which he read to his friend; while, strange to say, the latter received one from his mother, of whom he had not heard for years; and as it will serve to show how forgetful some sailors are of those for whom they really entertain great affection, we give her letter.

" Nonnington, Kent.
" 2 January.——

" MY DEAR BOY,

        "I am rejoiced to hear you're alive and well,* and you will be pleased to know I am, considering my age, quite hearty. I suppose you don't think I'm alive, or would have written to me. Now I hope, if these few lines reach you, to receive a letter in return from my youngest born, who I love, although I have not seen or heard from him for eleven years. You will be wondering how I came to hear of you. Well, to make a long story short I were a sitting by the fire one snowy night about a month ago, when some one knocked at the door and begged shelter for pity's sake, as he were near frozen. Your Cousin Ellen, who lives with me—I live now in 'Trotman's Charity.' You know the row of almshouses. Very comfortable they are, too, and good of the founder, who has been dead two hundred years. Well, Ellen, who writes this for me, went to the door and saw a man covered with snow, and nearly starved from cold. I asked him to come in and draw up to the fire, seeing he were a sailor; and after he got a little thawed, he told me his name was Harry Tomlin, and that he'd run away from a man-of-war at the Cape of Good Hope, then entered a ship bound for Australia, where he landed without a shilling; and he gave us a long account of his adventures, how he'd made some money, and had arrived in England a few days ago, and were bound to Eythorne that night, but had been overtaken by the snow, and nearly frozen to death. Me and Ellen heard his story with tears in our eyes; and when he had finished I asked him if ever he had been in a merchant ship, as I had a dear boy who were a sailor, and who were, I feared no more. Upon which he says, ' But why not in a man-of-war, marm ?' 'Because,' I said, ' my Jerry were too good-tempered as a lad to spill people's blood, and I know he wouldn't enter a man-of-war; Heaven forbid,' said I. ' Jerry, marm,' he said. ' Why, you never mean to say Jerry Thompson, do you ?' Upon hearing of which I fainted away, and were some time before I could hear all about your being so good and clever; and, in fact, you ought to be a captain but for the regulations not allowing. He left the next day after giving me your direction, and I have sent this letter to the place he said. Now, my dear boy, write me as soon as you can, and believe I love you as much as ever. With love, in which Ellen joins, I am your affectionate mother,

                                        "FANNY THOMPSON."

        "P. S. The old lady gets about wonderfully, and with your aunt, Mary Golder, is living in the alms-house where Miss Hoodruff used to live. They both talk a great deal about you, and it will be a dutiful act for you to write to her now and then. Probably you have forgotten me, as I was but a child when you left, but I remember you gave me a kiss when you bade me good-bye.

                                " Your loving cousin,

                                        " ELLEN."

        Thompson read the foregoing very carefully, and before they arrived in port wrote a long letter in reply, which he sent home by the first mail, and never afterwards missed an opportunity of letting his mother know about his welfare.
        Upon their arrival in Hong-Kong, where a large fleet was assembled, Captain Woodward received orders to proceed to the Bocca Tigris Forts in the Canton river; and without an hour's delay, after getting in provisions, water, and ammunition, they steamed out of the harbour, and in a short time anchored off the Wantung Forts,

                        * She knew nothing of his reported death.

where they landed their marines and as many blue-jackets as they could spare, to form a garrison.

One morning, as the bugle was going for parade, a steamer hove in sight, and in a short time Captain Woodward received instructions to embark on board his boats with his spare seamen and the whole of his marines, who were each to carry at least sixty rounds of ammunition, and when the gun-boats came up, to go on board them, and proceed to the attack of the Imperial junks then assembled in Chow-chan Creek. When the boats were manned and armed, the commander directed them to pull out towards the flotilla, which had not been long in making its appearance. As the gun-boats came up, it was noticed that each was towing a long string of boats, cutters, pinnaces, and gigs, and upon seeing the Stingers, one of them stopped to receive them on board; then, having made fast her boats, gave a shrill whistle, and started after her companions, Beauman, who was left in charge, dipping the ensign by way of salute as they passed the ship.

The gun-boats steamed away at full speed up the Canton river—now between high banks, which completely shut them in, and prevented their seeing anything of the surrounding country; now in places where the stream wound through a flat district, entirely given up to rice cultivation; while their appearance, instead of intimidating the Chinese who worked in the fields, seemed to give them a great deal of amusement, as in some places the labourers would gather upon the banks and shout derisively to the Fanquis, who were going up to be eaten by the Imperial tigers at Chow-chan. Here and there on either side of the banks they passed the ruins of forts destroyed by the ships the year before, but no attempt was made to molest them until they arrived within about three miles of the barrier, where a drunken bannerman stood upon the bank with a "brave's" matchlock, and after shouting and gesticulating, brought the whole flotilla to a standstill.

"What do you want?" hailed the interpreter.

"Go back, you red-headed, unshaven barbarians, you pink-eyed, man-eating fiends—go back! go back!"

"What does he say?" demanded the commander of H.M.S. Squelcher, which was the leading boat.

"He says we're to go back."

"Tell him to—Go on ahead, full speed," testily replied the latter, as he noticed through his glass that the bannerman was intoxicated.

"Signal flying from the Jolter. What have you stopped for?

"Reply, All right, and go on ahead."

Seeing the audacious red-haired demons did not comply with his modest order, the bannerman levelled his matchlock and managed to plump a ball aboard the Squelcher, upon which her commander directed a sentry to fire. The marine coolly raised his rifle—took a careful sight—then crack went the piece, and the daring bannerman, placing his hands upon his waistband, as though suddenly seized with cholera, doubled himself up and rolled down into the river, where he was drowned like a kitten.

After passing through the barriers, which were formed of thick piles driven across the river, the flotilla came to anchor a little below the entrance of Chow-chan creek, and just astern of H.M. ships Blowfly and Porpoise; on board of which the men who could not find accommodation in the gun-boats passed the night.

About an hour before the first streaks of light dawned in the sky the men were turned out, the boats manned, and made fast to the gun-boats. The latter got up anchor, and steamed slowly towards the enemy. A thick mist hung about the fleet

of junks anchored up the creek, and it was not until the gun-boats opened fire with
their heavy rockets that the Chinese seemed fully awake, although they had been
beating gongs and letting off crackers all night; however, when they found the
rockets flying about them, they returned the compliment to the best of their ability,
and a small fort situated upon an eminence to the left opened a deadly fire, but it
was at once assaulted and carried by the officer who commanded the expedition.
This done, the guns of the fort were directed upon the junks ranged upon two
sides of a delta formed by the junction of Chow-chan with another creek, then the gun-
boats crossed the front of the low island, and, under a murderous fire, proceeded up the
right channel.

Boats were sunk,—oars cut off short at the loom,—and men killed and thrown overboard during the terrible moments they were exposed to a perfect hail of shot from the
war junks; but in spite of the shower of missiles, which included copper nails, cash,
and links of chain, the gun-boats steadily advanced, and threw shot, shell, and rockets
into the enemy with great precision; and although several of them got aground, they
managed to get off again, and renewed the fight with greater vigour than before.

Some most gallant acts were performed, and one captain led on his men sword in
hand until his boat was sinking under him, when he stepped from it into one that was
passing, and, in spite of the deadly storm of missiles which flew around him, coolly tore
a strip of blue serge off a sailor's garment, and hoisting the scrap upon a boat-hook,
cried, "The blue never surrenders," then again cheered the sailors on to the attack.
He had with him in his gig a fine Newfoundland dog, but as the coxswain who attended it, was killed and went down with the boat, the animal would not leave the
spot, but was picked up some time afterwards. After a desperate combat, during
which a great many men were killed or wounded, one of the junks blew up, and it
was soon observed that the rest were endeavouring to move off towards Chow-chan.

The gun-boats finding the range of the junks, which were fast getting aground
through the falling of the tide, now kept up a deadly fire with their heavy bow guns;
and, after a desperate resistance, the Chow-chan fleet, commanded by one of the most
able scholars of the country, was reduced to a mere wreck. Some junks escaped and
reached Canton, where Yeh immediately imprisoned their officers for not having
thrashed the "red-headed barbarians," but the greater part of the fleet, burnt down to
their magazines, then blew up and scattered their timbers all over the creek. The
ship's boats approached the burning vessels, and even passed them, in spite of the war
rockets piled inside the junks, which would ignite, and tearing through the sides, go
flying over the boats, in some cases dropping into them and killing the sailors.

As the Chinese admiral expected a pretty severe engagement, he had ordered that men
who had never before been in action were to be chained to their guns, and this command
was pretty generally adopted by the captains. When the junks exploded the poor wretches
were elevated in batches; and their yells, when they caught fire, were plainly heard by
the sailors, who, however, did not seem to be much affected thereby.

Not contented with merely destroying the Chinese fleet, the fire-eating captain who
had lost his gig, upon falling in with a few of his own boats, actually pursued some
flying junks as far as Chow-chan city, and, mounting a boat's gun upon the wall, coolly
declared he took possession of that place. After having terrified a number of the Chow-
channers nearly out of their senses and causing the Taontai to almost die with fright,
he recalled his men, and returned to the flotilla, which by that time had mustered
preparatory to returning.

As they passed down the creek they picked up the dead bodies of those who had
been killed and thrown overboard during the action, and having conveyed them along-

side H. M. S. Blow-fly, the crew of that ship, after dark, buried them in the mud of the river.

When the flotilla arrived alongside the ships they discharged most of their men to them, and anchored until the next morning, the Stingers being drafted to the Porpoise. They had been all day without taking a regular meal, and were consequently very hungry; but, to their astonishment and disgust, after having smelt the savoury perfume of the soup, which was boiling in her coppers, they with the crew were piped aft to hear the "Thanksgiving after a victory" read by a well-fed clergyman, who had (very properly) "viewed the battle from afar."

There, with the enticing vapour of rich soup steaming from the galley, and rendering them more hungry than before, the grimy, tired, thirsty tars were tortured with a form which might just as well have been gone through after their bodies were refreshed; but the Reverend Mr. Service considered his feelings ought to be consulted before a lot of common sailors, so he had the first innings; and as he prayed the wicked tars did just the reverse, and when the service was over, they were out of temper, the soup burnt, and a general feeling of discontent experienced by all, except the Reverend gentleman, who beat the assistant-surgeon twice running at chess; and, upon retiring to rest, dreamed he was appointed Bishop of Chow-chan, with a large endowment, and permission to live in Paris, or go anywhere but to his See.

Upon their return to the Stinger, her crew learned they were to proceed to Hong-Kong and refit; so within a week of the battle of Chow-chan the whole of them had enjoyed a run on shore in the settlement, and, getting short of money, were quite ready for sea again.

During the vessel's stay in port on this occasion a most interesting event occurred, at which all the Stingers were invited to assist. This was the marriage of Miss Moore, whom they had rescued from the pirates, with a wealthy merchant of Hong-Kong, named Mackay; and on the day of the ceremony the crew, having been granted a holiday, marched to the church, and formed a double line from the door of the sacred edifice.

As the bride, leaning on the arm of Captain Woodward, passed through this guard of honour, the grateful girl stopped and inquired for Thompson.

This ordinarily self-possessed individual, on stepping forward, was so confused, that he blushed like a maiden.

"How are you, my good friend?" said the warm-hearted girl. "I should indeed have been sorry if you had not been here to-day."

"I'm pretty well, miss," replied the sailor, bewildered by the charming sight, and perhaps slightly uneasy in his mind relative to the kiss he had been bold enough to take from one so lovely, under circumstances previously related, "and it's real glad I feel to see you looking so well and so beautiful."

"He must go into the church with us, Captain Woodward," pleaded the young lady.

"Anything in the world to make your happiness complete," smilingly rejoined that gallant officer.

By some means Thompson was placed in a pew near a Chinese lady's-maid, who during the ceremony made big eyes at him, and otherwise endeavoured to attract his attention; but he was proof against her allurements: so, finding her glances thrown away upon him, she turned her battery against the heart of a susceptible midshipman, who thereupon fell in love with her, and, before many days were over, seriously offered to wed her, a proposition which she wisely rejected. When the ceremony was completed, and the former Miss Moore saluted as Mrs. Mackay, her husband looked about, and asked where the sailor was to whom he owed so much. Upon which the master pointed out Thompson, who was looking at the group with a very admiring air.

"Thompson, let me thank you for your great care of the dear girl who is now my wife. Come, she wishes to speak for herself."

During this speech the bride had been saluted by nearly all the officers, and there was no mistaking the meaning of the happy bridegroom when he led the sailor forward and presented him to his wife. Had he been the Thompson of old no doubt he would have availed himself of the occasion; but instead of that he bowed, and wishing her every happiness that the world could afford, amid the smiles of the officers, quietly pulled the stubby hair upon his forehead, and left the church.

"I could no more ha' kissed that beautiful woman afore all them there officers than I could have flied," he observed to one of his chums. Possibly he was a little quelled by the presence of his commander, but the fact was he thought of A-tae, and the memory prevented him taking advantage of a woman's gratitude for the very slight service he considered he had rendered.

While the wedding breakfast was in progress, the sailors and their friends were entertained in the grand marquee, erected for their special accommodation; and in the evening Jerry and others performed for their amusement, the affair terminating with a grand hornpipe by the company, who declared they would like to rescue a young lady every day, if the exploit would be followed by such a real good feed as Mr. Mackay gave them. They enjoyed themselves like men, and a few of them danced until they were obliged to retire to the outside of the marquee and sleep off the effects of the exercise; but as a body they behaved in a manner which was a compliment to their officers, and a credit to themselves.

Mrs. Mackay was always a firm friend to the sailors belonging to the men-of-war, and many were the baskets of fruit she sent to the sick on board H. M. S. Dead-and-alive; while, through her intercession, several poor fellows escaped the lash, as she would, when men misbehaved themselves on shore, get her husband to plead in their behalf; and was so much thought of by the sailors, that when she appeared in the streets they would cease their talk, take their pipes out of their mouths, and salute her with the utmost respect.

Thompson was often invited to her house, but would never stay more than a few moments; however, one day she entrapped him into conversation, whereupon he told her about A-tae. After hearing his story to the end, she wiped her eyes, which had been suffused during his recital of the tragic fate of the poor girl, and bade him never forget such a love, but at the same time not to shut his heart against the sex, as she doubted not there was a good girl waiting for him somewhere; and if he would take courage, no doubt when he reached home he would meet with her. To which kind speech Jerry replied with a touch of his old drollery.

"That's true enough, miss" (he always persisted in calling her so, in spite of her gently correcting him), "but the worst of it is, it ain't only *one* as is a waiting for me,— that's what I'm thinking of. It's hard, ain't it? to be afraid of former promises."

It will thus be seen that there was still some hope for the love-stricken sailor, who after that interview somewhat recovered from his apathy, and before they left Hong-Kong had almost made up his mind to write to Mary Ann. However, upon hearing they were ordered to Japan, he changed his determination, and decided to wait until they returned.

What was Mary Ann about all the time? Waiting patiently for him, he imagined. Let us take a peep at her.

Upon receiving the news of her lover's death the poor girl went into mourning, and grieved as much as though he had been her husband; but being good-looking, the young men of her acquaintance did not give her much peace, so she quitted the service of Mrs. Puffeigh, and went to live with her sister, Mrs. Shever, who had opened a small dress-making establishment in Portsmouth. Here she endeavoured to forget her sorrows; but at times her sister, who was uncommonly fond of digging up buried memories, would refer to the departed sailor, upon which they would both have a good cry, and then fall to work upon the dresses in hand with greater energy than ever. However, after some months had elapsed, the young man described in Jerry's letter as the "carpenter who was after no goode," would come in and chat with the lone women, and even bring papers of candy, and other love offerings, which he cunningly presented to Mrs. Shever, who regularly handed them over to Mary Ann, as soon as her lover had departed. This diagonal sort of courtship was kept for a long time without his coming to the point, until one afternoon the sighing swain appeared with an order for the theatre, and Mary Ann being absent, the boatswain's wife shut the door, and fiercely demanded what he wanted to be always lolloping about their premises for, upon which, being cornered, the bashful youth blurted out,

"Your sister, of course."

"What do you want with her? Mind, I'll have no trifling."

"Who's agoing to trifle? do I look like a trifler?" demanded the brawny youth with an injured air.

"Well, you'd better not, that's all! But what do you mean by your candy, and your theatre orders? Speak out!"

"I means all right; that's what I means. I never walked with a gal before in my life, and I likes Polly too much to come here and not mean anything."

"But what do you want to walk with her for?" screamed the excited matron who began to fear her sister would return before she had wormed the confession out of the bashful young carpenter.

"Why I wants to marry she, but she be so mighty shy, that I haven't had a chance," bellowed the youth in his own patois; "there! now I feels better, havin' told you."

Upon this Mrs. Shever mollified her manner, and having agreed to his proposal to visit the theatre, she dismissed him with the remark that if he didn't declare his intentions that evening she'd wait for him, as he left the dockyard the next day.

About half-past six Mary Ann and her sister were dressed and awaiting his arrival, when a knock was heard at the front door, and presently in marched the enamoured youth, bearing in each hand an enormous bouquet made up of cabbage roses, and other sweet-smelling but somewhat gaudy flowers. As he advanced he caught Mrs. Shever's eye, and recollecting her threat, plumped down upon one knee, dropped his offerings, and blurted out,

"Mary Ann, wilt have me for your feller?"

The boatswain's wife prudently left the room.

"Come, lass, thee might as well say yea. I'm moighty fond of thee."

"Really, Mr. Jenkins, you have taken me so by surprise, I— Don't squeeze my hand so,—you're hurting me."

"Come, my dear lass, put me out of moi misery. Say no, and I'll blow out moi brains; say yes, and I'll gie thee a hearty kiss."

Just then Mary Ann heard a light tapping at the window, so she observed in a very low voice, "I should—be very sorry—to—to—think you—would injure yourself out of regard for me—so I" (here the tapping became very distinct) "will say yes to save you from—"

"Bless thy heart, my dear gal. I'll treat thee like a queen," cried the elated carpenter, giving the blushing girl a hug, which almost took her breath away, at which opportune moment her sister returned.

"Good gracious! why, what are you about, Mr. Jenkins?"

"Only adoin' what *you* told me," replied the lover.

"Me told you, Mr. Jenkins?"

"There, there, name the day, and let's get it over," said the youth. But Mary Ann was not to be carried by storm in that way; so she put off replying to the question until they returned from the theatre, where unluckily they saw "Romeo and Juliet" acted; and the girl would persist in crying during the performance, as it reminded her so strongly of the never-to-be-forgotten night. However, after partaking of a light supper consisting of a beefsteak-pudding and baked potatoes, upon Mrs. Shever artfully reminding the lover that Polly had not replied to his request, and begging it might be done at once, that she could drink their health and happiness with her first sup of porter, the poor girl consented; and upon the day Mrs. Mackay advised Thompson "to think of the good girl waiting for him somewhere at home," Mary Ann found herself, "until death did her part," joined to the young carpenter who was after no good, and became Mrs. Joseph Jenkins, thus demonstrating the folly of Jerry's illusion, "that Mary Ann would keep."

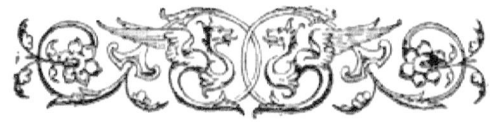

CHAPTER XXI.

CAPTAIN WOODWARD'S kindness towards him and the good news he received from his wife, effected a wonderful alteration in Clare's appearance, and the little doctor congratulated him on his returning health.

"I'm better, thankee, sir—wonderfully better—but at times my heart beats so that I can hardly breathe. I think it's better, though, since I've been coxswain."

"You see how foolish you were to worry yourself about what has proved to be an idle fear, as all your surmises have turned out to be incorrect"

"I'm well enough now, doctor. Don't you think so?"

"Yes, you are well; but you must take care of yourself, and not get excited."

"I mean, don't you think I'm in my senses?"

"Certainly I do, Clare."

"Well, doctor, I saw my wife's spirit on the 16th of last August—this month is July. I've heard from her, and know she is alive as far as I can tell at this moment. I consider the 16th of August to be her day, and if she visits me agin, I'm sure she will die before I see her."

"I shall have to put you upon the sick list if you talk like that. Why, you are as superstitious as ever."

Tom smiled sadly, but assured the doctor that it was not superstition, but faith on his part, adding, "in my country a fetch sometimes comes every year for fifty years, but the person it represents always dies on that day."

The doctor looked at his patient for a few moments, and told him that he would engage to cure the worst cases of fetch that Tom might bring to him; and as his own was a pretty decided one, he should put him under treatment for it at once, although he was not to be considered upon the sick list.

The doctor's plan was effectual, for in a short time the seaman renounced his delusion, and became quite convinced that it had proceeded from disordered digestion: and before they left for Japan he penned the following letter to his wife, from which it will be seen that his orthography had improved under Lieutenant Russell's instructions.

"H. M. S. Stinger,
"Hong-Kong, 23 July,——

"MY DEAR WIFE,

"Your two last letters were written by a strange hand, please tell me who it is. I was greatly delighted to hear from you, and to know you are well and hearty, and the baby well—he must cheer you a good deal. I have had all manner of fullish thoughts about you, thinking you was dead, but the doctor, who is a perfect samaryatan, has given me a lot of stuff, which has taken away all my visions. Now, I have a wish. I want you to write me upon getting this, and say that on the 16th of August you were well and hearty, and it will give me great joy, as I had a foolish idea on that point. I have also a wish to know how you look. Can't you send me a sun picture? I'd give anything for a sun picture of you. Lieutenant Russell takes them, and has

11

promised me one for you. I am very comfortable in this ship, the captain is a perfect gentleman. If all was like him the service would be perfect heaven for sailors. I was truly sorry to hear of the death of your old missis. I hope she is now with him in heaven who was so good on earth. Almost his last words was 'Florence,' and he died a thinking of her. Our first lieutenant is like poor Lieutenant Ford in many things, but he is more grander in his words; he is wonderful clever, and it's a pleasure to hear him lecture. He teaches us to read and write, and is more like a father than anything else. He is the best-dispositioned officer I ev⁁⁁ saw, and would make a first-class captain. Our captain is noble in everything, A ., and as brave as a lion. I am his coxswain now for good. In my last letter I told you all about Jerry Thompson; he is now a petty officer, and as good a fellow as ever, although he is a little touched in his head about a Chinee girl, named Hay-toy, that was killed for his sake. I think he was very fond of her. He is a reg'lar chum of mine, and we messes together. Mr. Cravan has left the ship promoted; he was nobody after our old tyrant and that wretch Crushe had left, as he daren't show his feelings afore our present captain; he went off without a sign of a cheer from any of us, and nobody missed him. We are going to Jaypan, and I hope afterwards, when we have took Canton, to send you word we are coming home. I think with what we have now, and my prize money and pay, we shall be able to live very comfortable. When you goes into Deal call at Mr. Masposlis, and say his son is in our ship, and is a very nice young man; he is our captain's servant, and we now and then has a chat about his father. I must now conclude, with love to father and mother, and a hundred kisses for dear little Tom, and my undying love for you, dear Polly.

"I am your affectionate husband,

"THOMAS CLARE."

"Address Hong-Kong or elsewhere, as usual."

Before the memorable day upon which he was carried off by the Tartars Thompson had given a parcel, containing a crape shawl and several articles of loot, into the boatswain's care, with instructions to deliver the same to Mary Ann if any accident occurred to him; so when Jerry's clothes and other effects were sold before the mast, the things were kept back by the boatswain. Upon Thompson falling out with Mr. Shever the latter sent him the parcel, the existence of which was forgotten by the sailor; and as Jerry, like most of his class, never kept anything long, he made up his mind to send it home to Mrs. Clare, by the first man invalided.

"She'll find it a helligant thing for weddings or the circus," he observed to his friend.

"She don't go to none, leastways, she never says anything about it; besides, keep it yourself, or send it to Mary Ann."

"What for? I'm going to try if Mary Ann has forgotten me, like you all did." (Jerry always felt a little tender upon that point). "You're my chum. Missis C. is a lady I think a deal about. Young Tom is my nevvy, although a unlawful one, and puttin' that altogether, I'm determined to send her the shawl, or to chuck it overheard."

The next man invalided proved to be Private Silas Bowler, Royal Marine Light Infantry, who, after receiving a liberal present, took charge of the shawl; and having successfully evaded the lynx-eyed custom-house officials, upon his arrival at Portsmouth proceeded to deliver it, not according to his agreement, but to his own wife, who wore it at Utah chapel, and quoted the gift to her brothers and sisters in faith, as a proof of good Silas's generosity. The worthy marine ultimately emigrated to Salt

Lkae, where he became a deacon, and, for aught we know to the contrary, one of Brigham Young's most efficient assistants. . It is probable that by this time the crape shawl has changed owners several times.

The Stinger proceeded towards Japan, and in due time came to anchor in the harbour of Chickodadi, where the hospitable inhabitants received them with open arms, the officers and men taking a cruise on shore, finding entertainment in all the free exhibitions then running in the place, including the public bath-rooms, where young and old, bachelors and spinsters, men and women, maids, wives, children and widows, together disported themselves in a most primitive manner, much to the astonishment of the gaping blue-jackets, who swarmed round those institutions and made the most amusing remarks.

"Well, I *am* blowed!" observed an old quarter-master. "If these here Jappanknees ain't a rum set of fellers. Them ere bath houses beats me; and my opinion is, they are either as hinnocent as babbies or a jolly deal ahead of us in cheek. Vy, I ain't been as near blushin' as I was to-day since I was a little kid."

No doubt the old fellow's delicate nerves were immensely shocked by the custom of the country, he being one of those weather-beaten patriarchs whom no one but a very-far-in-landsman would imagine possessed of any greater sensibility than a milestone.

After having spent a very pleasant time in Chickodadi, the Stinger proceeded to Hiko-saki, where they fell in with H.M.S. Blowfly, the commander of which being Woodward's senior, exercised them at all the evolutions known in the service, from shifting topsails to changing cooks of messes by signal, until Woodward began to wish his worthy senior elsewhere. However, the cholera breaking out in the ships, they were cor elled to put to sea, where they lost one pest, but had a terrible struggle against another.

It was a sore trial for them; and men who had laughed at and risked death in a hundred forms were taken ill, and carried off before their shipmates knew they were down. Some, who had for many years been in the habit of drinking any ardent spirit which came within their reach, now, through fear of the terrible disease, suddenly renounced liquor, and swore, if spared, to lead sober lives in future, but they were cut off as quickly as the drunkards. For seventeen days the ship was like a hospital, and ere the epidemic had run its course the bodies of thirty-five men and boys, including the assistant surgeon and third engineer, were consigned to the deep. There was no escape, and many men, who might have recovered on shore, upon seeing their shipmates die around them gave up all hope for themselves, and succumbed to the disease through fear.

The little doctor did wonders, working day and night, until he was completely knocked up; then Captain Woodward took his place to the best of his ability, and set a noble example to all in the ship. Although he keenly felt the loss of every one of his officers and crew, he preserved a calm demeanour; and had not his every action shown how fully he understood and sympathized with the sufferers, he might have been regarded as indifferent to the awful ravages that death was making around him. Tom Clare and Thompson were his right-hand men, and bravely they performed their work, taking watch and watch in the sick bay, and attending the sick and dying with unremitting zeal. Clare, calm and collected, moved about like a good spirit, and many a poor fellow gave his last charge to him, knowing that, if Tom survived, his wishes would be respected,—while Thompson, chaffing the would-be sick out of their whims, was indefatigable in his attentions to those who were ill, and was the life and soul of the convalescents; for, in spite of their sad condition, Jerry's spirits rose while others' sank, and he would often, by some droll remark, be of more service in helping their recovery than all the medical comforts freely issued to them.

It must not be imagined that during such a time there is no joking and fun on board, as after the first shock those who are well, or recovering, often indulge in a display of merriment that to an observer might savour of levity, but which is merely assumed to prevent their dwelling upon the melancholy scenes taking place around them. Sailors are very mercurial fellows, and Jack has often told yarns and sung songs in the fore part of the ship while his messmates were writhing in their last agony in the sick bay abaft.

Thompson felt the loss of his shipmates very keenly ; and, as he afterwards expressed it, never had harder work than when he pretended to be merry upon that occasion, and, no doubt, he did much towards keeping many of the men who were well from thinking of their awful position.

Having run northward until the disease began to decrease, Captain Woodward determined to visit one of the uninhabited islands off the coast of Tartary, and one evening came to anchor in a little bay where he determined to land his men and put them under canvas, knowing he could do so there with safety.

Some misunderstanding having occurred upon letting go the anchor, the commander sent forward to inform the boatswain that he wished to speak to him when the yards were squared, but the quartermaster who bore the message returned with the information that the boatswain had just been seized, and was gone down below. As soon as circumstances permitted, Woodward left the deck and proceeded to the warrant-officer's cabin, where he found Mr. Shever coiled up and evidently suffering great agony. Having administered the usual remedy, he left him in charge of Thompson and Clare, who were chafing his limbs with warm turpentine, that being one of the methods then prescribed in such cases. Shever endured great torture until midnight, when, just as the sentry struck eight bells, he suddenly started up, seized his beloved pipe, which he insisted should not be taken from his neck, placed it to his lips, blew a loud blast, and, shrieking, "Hands, witness punishment," writhed in pain for a few moments, then became rigid and expired.

Thompson brushed away a tear as he gazed upon the distorted countenance of his former friend, then covered the still form with a sheet, observing as he did so, " Ah, poor Mr. Shever, you'd a good heart afore that devil Crushe got hold of you," when he became aware that Clare was in the cabin ; and turning round, saw the latter with his face pale and scared, moving his lips, as if praying for the man who had during life been his enemy ; noticing which Jerry exclaimed, " Tom, you are a good feller to pray for him wot swore agin you and injured you. I couldn't do it."

Clare looked at his friend for a moment, then replied in a voice broken with emotion, " I'm only a mortal man, Jerry, and him wot is under that has been my enemy ; but I can't stand by his body and say I'm glad to see him a-lying there. I forgive him all he has done to me, and hope he will be forgiven by *Him* who knows more about his heart than we does. Poor woman ! I heartily pity his wife."

" So do I, Tom. I always have done that. But what makes you so white and haggard, Tom ? "

Clare sunk into a chair, and covering his face with his hands, sobbed like a child.

" Tom, Tom, don't give way. You, of all others, who is braver than any of us, you ain't afraid now, are you ? "

Clare took his hands away, and mastering his emotion, assisted his friend to prepare the body for interment ; but before the few offices were performed he was obliged to retire, evidently totally unmanned from some cause which he could not sufficiently master his feelings to explain. However, after a time he became more calm, when he sought for Thompson and told him the reason of his agitation.

"Jerry, don't laugh at me, or think lightly of what I tell you."

"Did ever I laugh at a real sorrer in all my born days? Did ever you see me make fun of trouble in others, Tom?"

Clare shook his head.

"Then, old mate, tell me your trouble, and if it's in my power I'll help you through with my best advice."

"I've just seen poor Polly. She's dead, Jerry; she ain't alive. It's the 16th of August, and she's been dead a year. O merciful God, I think I shall go mad!"

"Come, my poor old chap, you're upset with this sad work, you mustn't worrit. Why, gracious goodness, ain't she a-writ to you a dozen times, a-tellin' you about the babby, little Tom? and ain't I sent her a crape shawl by that feller Bowler? and ain't we soon a-goin home to see her, hey, old chap?"

"*Jerry, there she is again,*" said the unfortunate fellow, pointing to the doorway, "There she is. *I'm coming Polly! I'm—*"

Thompson seized his friend and secured him from jumping overboard, as he might probably have done, and for three days watched by his bedside, Clare being down with a raging fever; but he got through, and was out of danger before the crew re-embarked.

Jerry did not go on shore with the others, but devoted himself entirely to his friend and it was no doubt partly owing to his untiring care that Clare recovered. He, however, never reverted to the hallucination, which appeared to have passed away, although he often spoke to his nurse about his wife and child.

Mr. Shever was, with others, buried upon the lonely island; and before the Stinger left, the ship's painter prepared a tablet bearing the following inscription, which was nailed against a tree growing near the graves.

Near here lies the body of
Mr. Henry Shever,
Late Boatswain in H.M. Navy,
Aged 38 years,
who died of cholera off this island on
16th August, 185—,
while serving on board
H.M.S. Stinger,
24 guns.
Commander, Paul Woodward, R.N.

Three fathoms to the left of his grave lie the
bodies of the following, late crew of H. M. S. Stinger.
James Shaw, A. B., aged 32 years.
Thomas Simpson, A. B., aged 27 years,
Henry Rowe, A. B., aged 29 years.
Samuel Tyron, O. S., aged 20 years.
James Dove, Boy of 1st Class, aged 17 years.
All these seamen died of the fatal effects of cholera
while camped on shore near the beach below, much
regretted by their surviving shipmates, who
erected this monument.

WM. BROWN,   PAINTER.

When they had been under canvas a few weeks the cholera disappeared, and Captain Woodward quitted the island, and ran down to Shanghae, where he received orders to proceed at once to Hong-Kong, which he reached after a quick passage, and there found, thanks to his immense popularity, no difficulty in filling up the vacancies in his crew.

Clare, who had by this time recovered, was offered the post of boatswain, but declined, saying he could not fill the rate. The commander then strongly recommended Thompson for the appointment, whereupon the admiral directed him to be made acting warrant-officer until he was confirmed by the admiralty, and within a month after Mr. Shever's death Jerry, who was thoroughly competent, piped, and bellowed orders as naturally as though he had always owned the silver call and chain.

Mrs. Shever was duly notified of her husband's decease, and received the balance of his pay, and a pension from the government, and we must say, that considering the nature of her bereavement, she bore up remarkably well. "He were a good man for many things," she observed, "but a woman might as well be a widder as to have her husband at sea all the time," so after wearing very deep mourning for six months, the boatswain's relict moderated her grief and crape at the same time, and came out in such killing costume, that three ardent admirers offered her their hands and hearts within as many weeks of the change. Strange to say, she refused them, and informed the world about her that it would have to be a remarkably bright fellow who would be taken into Mr. Shever's place in her heart. She held undoubted sway as belle of Crumpton Street, until one unlucky day, the widow of a "retired dustman" took lodgings in the opposite house, and, as Mrs. Shever expressed it, laid herself out to angle for her lovers. Much to the disgust of the late boatswain's widow, the new arrival managed to captivate a young hairdresser, who finding the dustman's widow had more money than his first flame, not only cut the acquaintance of the latter, but irritated her by sitting at her rival's parlour window and playing upon a concertina such airs as "All's Well," "The Girl I left behind me," and several others strongly suggestive of her forlorn state.

It was very aggravating to her when she saw this, and heard what she denominated his "setarical" tunes, but the boatswain's widow was revenged. The perfidious ones billed and cooed for a few months, then got married, went to live in a fashionable street, lost money, fell out, she scolded, he beat her and took to drink, she drove the concern, he eloped with the young girl who sold cosmetics in the front shop, she bolted with the foreman hairdresser by the back door—and—the concern was sold out, and turned into a dressmaking establishment, over the door of which was this name in letters of gold:

MRS. SHEVER,
Dressmaker.
Ladies own materials made up.

It was a better situation than her former one, and the business prospered in it; but, poor thing, she was lonely, and was on the point of despairing, when one morning she heard the wonderful news of Jerry's return to his ship, and from that moment was an altered woman. Mary Ann was duly informed of the state of affairs, and congratulated her sister upon the same.

"He was always fond of you, you know, 'Melia."

"Me? Mr. Thompson fond of me? Oh lor, Mary Ann, how silly you do talk. Why, I don't know if I would accept him if he was to offer this moment."

"Oh nonsense, 'Melia. He ain't here. You knows that, or you'd not go on in that way."

"What way?"

"Saying you don't love him."

"Gracious, Mary Ann, can't I speak of a gentleman of my acquaintance without you being jealous of me, and flying at me like that?" Here Mrs. Shever burst into tears. "You know you've a sneaking regard for him, and don't want to see him marry me."

"However you can say that of me, Mrs. Shever, I can't think. I'm the lawful wife of Mr. Joseph Jenkins, and I don't cast no sheep's eyes at old lovers, who don't think much of one, as they let them as loved them marry, and never wrote nobody until it was too late," cried the girl, also shedding tears, whether of regret or of anger we know not.

Now, the boatswain's widow was a good-hearted woman, and loved her sister very much; so upon seeing her weep she embraced her, and declared that she was a brute to make any one cry who had been so good to her as her own sister Mary Ann. After which they cried in concert, and then became more loving than ever.

"Then you mean to marry Mr. Thompson, 'Melia?"

Mrs. Shever blushed, looked confused, hesitated, stammered and laughed, but at last confessed to her sister that it wouldn't be her fault if she did not hook Mr. Thompson as soon as he landed.

"But you'll have to wait ever so long, dear. The ship ain't ordered home yet."

"Wait! Who wouldn't wait for such a man as that? Why, I'd wait for ten years."

"You'd be grey before then, 'Melia dear, wouldn't you?" exclaimed Mary Ann with a touch of mischief; "and perhaps Mr. Thompson wouldn't have you. Besides, maybe he has fallen in with one of them black gals in Chinee, and won't come back at all. I don't want to dishearten you, but you mustn't be too sure."

"Fiddle. He ain't married no Chinee gal,—he's a deal too smart for that; and if I'm grey when he comes back, I'll dye."

"Hadn't you better write him and say you're well?"

"Oh dear me, no. Why, no lady ever makes the first advances. Gracious me! what would people think if they heered I had wrote to a gentleman who were not my intended?"

"Well," observed her sister as she tied her bonnet strings preparatory to leaving the house, "'Melia dear, I wish you every success, but my opinion is that Jerry Thompson has been and splashed his affections somewhere else, and you'd better not wait for him. I didn't, and I'm thankful for it.

"And so am I, dear—heartily!" added Mrs. Shever as the buxom form of Mary Ann vanished through the doorway. "Very heartily indeed, I may say, as my chances would have been mighty small had you not been disposed of."

CHAPTER XXII.

THE ship remained at Hong-Kong for a few weeks, during which time Mr. Thompson, the acting boatswain, had plenty of opportunity to go on shore; but with his promotion all that beautiful simplicity of impudence, for which he was, when a seaman, distinguished, vanished, and although he knew full well the Mackays expected him to call upon them, it was not until he received the following invite that he summoned enough courage to face his good friends.

" Chy-loon Villa.

" DEAR MR. THOMPSON,

" We have expected you would call upon us ever since your ship has been in harbour. As we know you would prefer not meeting strangers, we beg you will dine with us alone on Friday at 8 o'clock.

" Ever your sincere friend,
" WALTER MACKAY."

To which Jerry replied,

" H. M. S. Stinger.

" MY DEAR FRIENDS,

" I am very much obliged to you, and will be there punctual.

" Your obedient friend,
" J. THOMPSON.

" P. S.   I hope none of the officers will drop in."

Having dispatched the foregoing, the acting boatswain sought the advice of a friendly midshipman as to costume and deportment, and upon the appointed evening proceeded to make the call, about which he felt very nervous. When he arrived at the place he was met by Mr. Mackay, who was waiting in the verandah to welcome him. Jerry seated himself in a rocking-chair, but looked so uncomfortable, that his friend inquired if he were unwell. Upon which Thompson got up, and beckoning his host into a small reception-room, gravely asked him if he thought he would do.

" My dear fellow, what do you mean ? "

" Well, am I all square ?   Rigging all right ? "

Mr. Mackay could scarcely preserve the gravity of his countenance, but after a short pause he replied,

" Why, you look very nice indeed, Thompson.   What makes you ask me such a question ? "

" Why," said the acting boatswain in a whisper, and getting more mysterious than ever, " he said I warn't all square, and I don't want to pay Miss Moore such a ill compliment as to come to dine with you and not be all right, you know."

" Oh, you're splendid.   Why, you look as handsome as a post-captain."

Thus assured, Jerry became more easy in his manner, but he was terribly put out when, upon Mrs. Mackay making her appearance, he found her accompanied by a dark-eyed girl, who was just as affable towards him as his hostess; and when the dinner-gong sounded he actually started, thinking he would have to escort the young lady into the dining-room; but to his relief Mrs. Mackay held out her arm, which the sailor took, and thus reversing the order of things, walked solemnly from the apartment.

The dinner passed off without any mishap, as Thompson had seen enough life to keep him all right at table, while his natural gallantry and devotion to the fair sex caused him to show all proper attention to the dark-eyed young lady seated by his side. When the ladies had withdrawn, his kind host lit a cigar, having in vain tried to induce his guest to do the same, and after a little chat asked him what he thought of the young lady.

"She's a real fine lady, but I'm afraid of her."

"Nonsense, Thompson. Why?"

"Well, she's got a sort of a half-laughing sort of way, as much as to say she thinks I'm a poor sort of a imitation of a reg'ler warrant-officer, and she sees through it."

"Chut, chut; let us join the ladies."

Jerry entered the drawing-room upon tip-toe, as the dark-eyed one was playing the piano, and having taken his seat on the chair furthest from the instrument, fixed his eyes upon her, and watched the motion of her fingers in a curiously anxious manner. When she had finished she turned to him and exclaimed, "Can you sing, Mr. Thompson?"

"Me, miss?"

"Surely you can. Don't you know one song?"

"No, miss. Not what you'd call songs."

"Not a sea-song?"

"Well, I know 'The Gal I left behind me,' and 'Hearts of Oak,' and 'Tom Bowline,' and—"

"Oh, do sing 'Tom Bowline,' Mr. Thompson."

After much persuasion Jerry got over his bashfulness; then, in a full mellow voice, sang that fine old sea-song, and ere the last verse was completed he heard the ladies sobbing as if their hearts would break. When he had finished, the younger lady wiped her eyes, and looked at him with the greatest admiration. He was no longer the bashful-awkward sailor, but a man of genuine tenderness of heart, and she began fully to understand how it was that her friends thought so highly of him. As he sang his voice seemed filled with pity for some lost shipmate, and it would have been an unsympathetic ear upon which such a song fell without calling forth some pitying response; and the young lady, though not intending to do so, looked at the acting boatswain in such a manner, that a much less susceptible person would have easily understood her meaning.

Jerry began to feel uncomfortable. I wish she wouldn't stare at me so, he thought. I'll ask her to sing.

"Please, miss, as it's my call, may I be so bold as to ask you to sing?"

"What song would you like, Mr. Thompson? I am almost ashamed to sing after you."

"Anything, miss; they are all pretty."

Not without a touch of mischief in her voice, the dark-eyed one sang "Love not." Now, had she wished to captivate the sailor she could not have chosen a more inappropriate song. When she commenced Thompson was all attention, but at the words

"Love flings a halo round the fair one's head,"

the poor fellow got up, and walked into the verandah, where he sobbed like a child. A-tae, the truest love in the world, the heart which once so fondly beat for him, now stilled in death—the beautiful lips which, when parted with a smile for him, seemed like an angel's ; the stars which shone down upon him then, were shining upon her silent grave, and he should never see her again. All this flashed across his mind, and, sailor as he was, he wept. However, after a few moments he recovered, and crept quietly into the room, his friends pretending not to have noticed his absence. Mrs. Mackay sang several songs, and played some animated airs upon the piano, which, with a little brandy pawnee, somewhat enlivened the sailor. About eleven o'clock the dark-eyed one went home, and his hostess wishing to have a little conversation with him, begged he would not hurry his departure, as they did not generally retire until a late hour.

The young lady gone, Thompson threw off his bashfulness, and was once more the merry fellow of old, but he cautiously avoided expressing any opinion about the dark-eyed visitor.

" Do you know who she is, Mr. Thompson ? "

" No, miss."

" She is our new governess of the native girls' school ; and, I think, would make you an excellent wife."

" Me, miss ? Me marry ? No, no. I'll keep single. I ain't a marrying man."

" But she was very much interested with your song, and I noticed you were with hers. Take care, Mr. Thompson ; take care."

" Bless your heart, miss, you don't know human nature as I do. Why, if every young woman that I have sung that song to, and who has cried over it, had been sentimentyle over me, I should have been prosecuted for breach of promise years ago. It's only for a moment—they feels sorry for poor Tom Bowline. He's gone aloft, they thinks, and his widder is a-crying about him—probable his half-pay note stopped, and no pension, and her little children going into the werkus. But it's soon all over, and then they are ready for another song of a similar sentimentyle specee, at which they cries, just as they would smile at a comic song, bless their little hearts all on 'em, miss."

" Thompson, you only talk like that to deceive me as to the real state of your feelings. You don't mean what you say,"

" Indeed, miss, but I does. I've a lonely widowed mother at home, and I intend devoting the remainder of a rather precarious existence to her. I am going to die a bachelor, and I think it's just as well for any one in my situation."

Mrs. Mackay laughed, and when she bade him good-bye, said, " We hear the Stinger is going home as soon as Canton is taken. You will let us know when your happy event takes place, will you not, and send us a description of the bride ? "

Jerry shook his head and replied in a mournful sort of way, " Miss, if ever you hears of such a melancholy episode, you may rest assured that I am somebody's victim, not a convict by my own free will."

A few days after the foregoing occurrence, the Stinger was despatched to the Canton River, where Captain Woodward was directed to take possession of a small fortified island called Yin-sin, situated about ten miles below the Barriers ; and, to hold himself in readiness to receive, pay for, and take care of all live stock which could be collected by a party of contractors, who had volunteered to obtain any quantity of cattle the government required, provided the authorities would assist them, and place a war-ship off Yin-sin Fort, to which they could retreat when pursued by the Imperial row boats. As the contractors could not speak a word of English, Hoo-kee, the old pilot, was sent on board to act as interpreter.

Having cleared out and whitewashed the fort, the ship's company were employed in building sheds upon a level piece of ground near the lower end of the island, and in a few days they put up accommodations for over five hundred head of cattle, besides a house for the Chinese contractors; then having thrown up an embankment round the island, which they further protected by palisades driven near the water's edge, Woodward directed Lieutenant Russell to take command of the fort, assisted by the acting boatswain, a gunner's mate, and a garrison of thirty-five seaman.

In a few nights the contractors began to receive bullocks from all parts of the river, and the supply seemed unlimited; but after several lots had been despatched to Hong-Kong, the number brought decreased, and at length only one or two would be forthcoming, and these were very ordinary beasts indeed. Upon the pilot being questioned, he informed them that "Comprador no can catchee peecee Boolaky, him all lib topside river," or, in other words, the supply was exhausted about Yin-sin Fort, and they would have to go further up the river. Woodward did not like to leave the cattle to the sole guard of the garrison, so he concluded to wait for a few days, when he could obtain a gun-boat to assist the contractors, preferring that course to risking the safety of his men.

It was well that he did so, for one night as he was quietly anchored ahead of the island, the man upon the look-out on the port side of the forecastle suddenly announced that a big craft was dropping down upon them, and before they could get up anchor two immense junks filled with brushwood, pitch, oil, and other combustibles, were cleverly floated across the Stinger's bows, and in an instant the fore part of the ship was enveloped in flame. Woodward knowing the probability of such an attack, had an anchor fastened to the jib-boom in such a manner that in case a fire-ship got across his bows, it might be dropped on board the burning craft, then slipping his own bower to the chain of which this suspended anchor was attached, he would be able to drop quite clear of the fire-ship, which being left anchored to his late moorings, would burn itself out, while he was hove off at a short distance.

This was all very nice in theory, but the fire-junks were floated down so silently, that no one saw them until they were almost fast to the bows. When the officer of the watch ordered the suspended anchor to be cut adrift, it was found to be foul and would not start, and Woodward getting on deck, saw at a glance that the ship would be lost if no one could manage to cut the obstruction to their only means of safety. However, he did not show what he felt, but gave his orders in a cool and deliberate manner.

"Pay out the cable, and stand by to slip the anchor."

"Aye, aye, sir," replied the boatswain's mate of the watch.

The fire-junks hung for a few moments upon his bows, but being slack water, did not drop upon her; and the Stinger having steam up, "went astern" slowly, leaving the Chinese engines of destruction moored by the lines by which they had been towed down upon the man-of-war. As the ship receded from their fiery contact the flames ran along her bowsprit and caught the bulwarks, but a well-directed stream of water from her pumps soon extinguished that, and the further burning of the bowsprit and projecting spars was prevented.

The Chinese who were managing the attack seeing the Stinger move from her anchorage slacked their tow-lines, and Woodward saw the junks were coming down upon him again.

"Who'll volunteer to cut away that spare anchor when the junks are again under the bows?"

" I will, sir," cried Tom Clare, who, dressed in a blanket frock and trousers, looked more like an Esquimaux than a sailor. " The fire won't hurt this rig."

" Up you get, then ; the fire won't touch you if you're smart, as the wind has fallen, and is drawing aft. The tricing line has fouled just abaft the foretopmast stay. Don't cut until I give the order."

Luckily the stays were made of corrugated iron wire, and Clare knew if he could feel those he was safe, even though the smoke blinded him. He was determined to save the ship ; and, axe in hand, mounted the head grating, and running out upon the bowsprit, calmly waited for the fire-junks to drop down near enough for the anchor to plump aboard them. As he stood there, with the red gleam of the burning junks showing every line in his face, he looked the handsome Tom Clare of former days ; and knowing how perilous his position was, many of the crew wished almost any other man of their number there instead of him.

" They're coming, Clare. Stand by, and let them get close enough. I'll give you orders when to cut."

" Aye, aye, sir," quietly replied Tom.

Down dropped the burning craft towards the ship, every now and then sending a volume of smoke into the sky, as some store of combustible exploded on board them, flaming like furnace tops, with their entire length an unbroken mass of roaring, singing fire. Tom felt the glare upon his face, and found a difficulty in breathing. Nearer and nearer they approached, until the flying jib-boom was again on fire, and he began to experience the sensation of burning whiskers and singed eyebrows and face. But as no order came, he waited.

" Cut away ! "

Steadying himself upon the bowsprit, which was now enveloped in flame, the gallant fellow gave one smart cut. The obstruction was severed, and the anchor dropped crashing on board the starboard fire-junk. In an instant the chain cable was slipped on board, and the Stinger tore astern at full speed. When they got clear of the burning masses Woodward enquired for Clare, but no one had noticed him come in, and the commander feared he had fallen a victim to his bravery.

" Clare ! Where's Clare ? "

" Clare ! Clare ! " bawled half-a-dozen voices, but no response came. It was a moment of great anxiety, for the Chinese, finding their junks anchored, were endeavouring to drop down another burning craft ; and although the captain would willingly have risked his own life in an endeavour to pick up Clare, he felt the safety of the ship was of more consequence, and was compelled to move down the river until he was below the fort and quite secure from further attempts with fire-junks.

The crew soon managed to extinguish the fire forward, and within ten minutes of Clare's gallant act a number of men were standing upon the spot where he performed it. Loud and hearty were their commendations, and all regretted his sad fate.

" He's drowned. Can't ye see ? When he cut the lashing of that anchor the bowsprit was burning under him, and the tar on the stays was alight. The smoke choked him, and he fell overboard."

" Poor Tom ! and he a gettin' on so nicely. Well, it are hard."

When the fire-junks began to burn down, a number of guns laid in rows in their holds, went off, and sent their shot scattering across the paddy fields. Seeing this, Lieutenant Russell opened fire with the guns of Yin-sin Fort, and after several rounds, sunk one of the ships and blew up another. The third, now no longer obstructed, floated with the tide up the river, and exploding, set fire to some Chinese row-boats which were hovering near.

Lieutenant Russell, knowing the Chinese might take advantage of the confusion, and endeavour to carry off the live stock, had ordered his men to rouse the contractors, and direct them to get the bullocks inside the walls, while he watched the progress of the attack, and kept off a fleet of row-boats, which were evidently bent on following up the fire-ships. The cattle being securely got in, the compradors were rigged in sailor's attire, and all hands got ready to resist any attack which might be made upon their position, the lieutenant knowing it would be useless to depend upon assistance from the ship.

Just as the latter got clear of the fire-junks, and while the attention of the garrison was drawn to their shipmates' peril, a party of "braves" succeeded in making a landing upon a small jetty or pier, which had been run out from the lower end of the island, and in a short time the cattle sheds and compradors' huts were wrapped in flames. Finding the live stock out of their reach, they advanced boldly towards the fort, and threw over the ramparts lighted balls composed of flax steeped in resin.

Wonderful to relate, instead of intimidating the imprisoned Fanquis, the braves found their flaming missiles come flying back upon them; and to add to their discomforture, a party, headed by the acting boatswain, sallied forth from a small gate, the existence of which was unknown to them, whereupon they threw down their arms, and made for the water, but were caught in the gap between the outside slope of the embankment and the palisades. The sailors showed no quarter, and made short work of the braves, who crouched down and allowed themselves to be killed in a calmly Oriental manner.

Having cleared the island of their enemies, the party were about to return, when one of them declared he heard some one in the water, and proceeded to fire his pistol in the direction from which the sound proceeded, when, to their astonishment, they heard a voice faintly cry, "Stop."

"It's one of our fellers," observed a boy.

"Nonsense! How can that be?"

"Hold hard! It's me, C—lare."

Thompson was shading his eyes, and looking towards the water, when he heard this; but in a moment after forced his way through the palisades, and waded towards Clare, crying.

"Just another stroke, Tom, old man, and you're safe; there's bottom all along here."

Hearing Jerry's voice, Clare dropped his feet, and found he could touch the mud, upon which he waded towards his friend, who advanced to meet him with outstretched hands.

"Tom, old chap, however did you come here?"

Clare grasped the acting boatswain by the arm, then fell heavily forward, as if fainting.

"You fellers, come here! He's gone off like a dead un!"

The mystified sailors waded into the water, and bore the inanimate form towards the bank, when, a light being produced, it was found that Clare was in a sort of fit.

At that moment the cutter arrived from the ship, and Tom was placed in it, and conveyed on board. Captain Woodward hastened to the gangway, and himself received the suffering sailor, who was in a very precarious state; and as it was considered desirable to keep him quiet, he was placed in the acting boatswain's cabin, and immediately taken charge of by the kind doctor.

When the latter had attended to Clare, he went aft to the captain's cabin, and reported the coxswain to be suffering from great prostration, resulting from excitement and sudden immersion in the water, adding, "it may be weeks before he is fit to go to duty again."

The next morning Thompson went on board and saw his friend, who looked as if he would not be long with them; but in a few days a marked improvement took place, and Clare was able to get up.

When Tom was well enough to walk up to the quarter-deck, Captain Woodward mustered his crew, and publicly thanked him for his gallant conduct. "I have written to the admiral, and given him a full account of your noble deed, and I hope in a few days to tell you what he thinks of your bravery."

Upon hearing these kind words Tom shuddered. He knew that he deserved them, but the assembly of men reminded him so strongly of the occasion upon which he was flogged, that instead of expressing satisfaction, he felt depressed; his only pleasure was in thinking how it would please his wife when she heard of it; and, to his great joy, shortly after the men were dismissed, a mail arrived from England bringing him several letters from her, one of which was, singularly enough, dated the 16th of August, and ended with the words, "We are all in good health, thank goodness," upon reading which Tom informed his friend that now he had such evidence he would not believe that she was dead, and from that day never spoke of the illusion to any one.

One day, when he found his patient in a suitable state, the doctor questioned him as to his feelings when he was standing upon the bowsprit, with the fire blazing up under him, to which he replied, "Well, doctor, when I heered the captain say he wanted a volunteer, I somehow got hold of an axe and ran out, never thinking or caring for the fire. I felt like I used to afore I were flogged,—bold, plucky like. It seemed an age afore I heard his voice a ordering me to cut, and the smoke came up so thick and stifling that I could scarcely breathe. All at once the flame caught my whiskers and singed my dress! but, thank God, the wind drew aft, and beyond the smoke I didn't feel no hurt, but I thought the captain never would call out. Suddenly I hears his voice, loud and clear as a bell, crying, 'Cut away!' So I ups axe, and away went the anchor, which I knew by the end of the line being gone. Just as I turned to go inboard the screw began to revolve, and as the ship left the junks the smoke drew aft again, and I got half choked and fell overboard. Lucky it were slack water and I a good swimmer; so kicking off my heavy flannel trousers and pulling off my frock, I struck out for the island, where I were picked up by Mr. Jerry Thompson."

Finding the supply of live stock becoming beautifully less every day, Woodward wrote to the admiral and obtained a gun-boat, guarded by which the compradors collected a great quantity of bullocks, in fact, rather overstocked the island, and as they charged a good price for the cattle, they waxed rich and insolent. Hoo-kee was constantly with them; and according to his account, there never were such honest compradors in that line before. However, one morning a little affair occurred which not only damaged the pilot's veracity but convicted that diplomatic individual of collusion with them to cheat the Fanqui authorities. As the ship's company were scrubbing decks, the signal-man observed to the officer of the watch, that there were a lot of Chinese fellows on the banks waving a white flag, which intelligence was at once communicated to the commander, who sent Hoo-kee to ascertain what they wanted, when, upon nearing the bank, the pilot thus addressed them :—

"You precious half-starved, mean-looking miserables, what are you kow-towing there for?"

"We want to see the Fanqui chief," chorussed the villagers.

"Do you? Well, he don't want to see you."

"But we *will* see him, we *will* see him, you man of the two faces! You no Chinese, no Fanqui, eater-of-women's-hearts."

"Who stole our bullocks?" screamed the women among the crowd.

"You shut up, or it will be worse for you, my pretty hens," retorted the ungallant pilot.

"Who stole our ducks?" yelled the children.

"Come," said the officer in charge of the boat, "what do they want? What's all the jabber about?"

"Him say him wantchee mi go way."

"Shove off! oars!"

"Stop, smallee peecee," cried a villager in very decent pigeon English. "Him com catchee mi duck, me wantchee speekee claptlain man."

"Jump in, then, you fellows who want to go aboard," cried the officer: and in a few seconds the gentleman who spoke English and four venerable elders of the village were seated in the boat, and on their way towards the dreaded Fanqui ship, "with their hearts in their mouths," and fear or astonishment exhibited in every line of their faces; none of them being sure if the head Foreign Western Devil would treat them kindly, or have them cooked for the delectation of his red and blue devils, who were reported to be fond of baked Celestials.

Hoo-kee subsided into a sulky state, and did not condescend to cajole or abuse the elders, and it was very evident to the officer that an exposure of some kind or another was in store for that valiant individual. Upon arrival on board, the Pigeon-English-man walked aft, and with the venerable elders performed a solemn kow-tow, and when they had sufficiently consolidated their ideas by knocking their heads upon the quarter-deck, the leader craved permission to speak, which being granted he went ahead as follows:—

"Big peecee claptlain, all peecee man cum catchee boolakki no payee mi one tam cash."

"Do you mean to say that the compradors have not paid you for the bullocks you have sent off to us?"

"Mi no sendee off. Him cum catchee teefee. Him long tim no hab catchee, now alla gonne. Him all same teefee peecee gallee."

"Hoo-kee, come here!"

The pilot advanced with fear and trembling, declaring that the speaker was "a nomba one first-class liar," and "would sell his own long-tim faader for one peecee dolls," but when he had finished the sentence he found a marine at each elbow, with their drawn bayonets pointed at his breast; seeing which he held his tongue, and prepared himself for the worst.

"Send for the contractors, and bring their money bags with them."

As the Chinese supplicants for justice felt rather nervous, they again kow-tow'd, by way of fortifying themselves for what was to follow, imagining that the Fanqui captain would at least behead the contractors, and torture the pilot; further supposing he would seize the cash belonging to the scoundrels, and appropriate it to his own uses, that being the way many of their own rulers would dispense justice under such circumstances. All they wanted, or at least expected to get was revenge—blood for bullocks was their idea.

Upon the contractors making their appearance, they were compelled to disgorge their dollars, whereupon the captain sent for the acting boatswain and told him to rig a block upon which to behead the party, and in a short time the butcher's log was conveyed aft, and placed in position, Thompson sprinkling sawdust round the place, and sharpening the cleaver in a most artistic and dramatic manner.

After a patient investigation, the commander, finding it necessary to make a severe example of the head comprador, directed him to be placed in the gangway, and having given him "time to say his prayers," which the fellow refused with scorn, the marines levelled their rifles and shot him, his body falling overboard and sinking immediately. Then the rest of his band were placed behind a screen, and one by one brought out, and told to place their heads upon the block, and it was strange to see with what composure they shut their eyes and awaited the fatal cut. At a signal from the captain the cleaver descended and cut off their—queues; then, they were led to a port, and bundled overboard, to sink or swim as best able.

When all were disposed of, the captain turned to the pilot and ordered him to confess or share the fate of the others, upon which Hoo-kee fell upon his knees and made a clean breast of it. Not only had the compradors, under threat of bringing the Fanquis down upon the villagers, obtained cattle and other live stock, but actually the scoundrels, sheltered by the ship's guns, had seized and carried away a large number of girls, whom they had sold to Hong-Kong dealers.

The English-speaking villager and his friends were asked of how much they had been plundered, when, finding they had a chance of being repaid, one of the old gentlemen put on a pair of horn spectacles, and taking out a square of paper and a wet pencil, ran off a bill which would have done credit to the ingenuity of a French hotel-keeper.

"Two thousand dollars for women, and one thousand dollars for cattle stolen," observed the spectacled one in Chinese, tendering the bill to the commander.

"How much does he say pilot? Mind you speak the truth."

"Him speekee to tousauce peecee dolla catchee gallee, one tousance catchee hool-akki."

"Paymaster, give them three thousand dollars, and take their receipt."

"Fo—!" cried the most venerable of the elders when the money was handed over, and found to be correct. "What a pack of fools they are, and how weak we were not to ask more;" then, having humbly kow-tow'd, they took up their money-bags and hurried over the side, fearing if they lingered that the Fanquis might change their minds and "squeeze them," as their own officials would have done under like circumstances.

Hoo-kee was sent to Hong-Kong, and kicked out of H.M. Service, after which he hired a bum-boat, and swindled the sailors belonging to the fleet.

A few days after the execution of the head comprador and dismissal of his band, a gun-boat arrived from Hong-Kong, bearing orders for the ship to proceed to Canton.

Visions of loot, crape shawls, old china, wooden gods, bars of silver, curios, and chests of tea, flitted through the minds of the Stingers, who imagined how rich they would be when they got at the treasures in Yeh's palace, while that astute Tartar prepared to repel their assaults; and when the plundering of his ya-mun was hinted at by a nervous mandarin, first drove the craven from his presence, and then, knowingly winking his pig-like eyes, exclaimed, "Plunder *my* palace, indeed! Take *my* city? Never!"

CHAPTER XXIII.

THE Stinger steamed up the river, and in due time arrived off the city of Canton, where Woodward was directed to anchor, and await instructions from the commander-in-chief, the day of attack being kept a profound secret. Yeh obstinately refused to listen to the numerous deputations sent him by influential corporations belonging to the city, who knew full well what would be the result of the combined attacks of the English and French forces.

In vain did old Ho-qua himself seek an interview, and with tears in his eyes beg that the great Tartar would listen to reason and make terms with the fierce invaders, even offering Yeh a good round sum of money if he would allow him to negotiate with the outside barbarians; but the well-advertised tea-dealer, like the rest of the remonstrants, was ignominiously driven out of the governor's presence. Yeh looked upon the whole affair from a Chinese point of view, and could not understand why he, the governor of Kwan-tung—a Tartar of great literary ability—should so far humiliate himself as to sue for peace, because, forsooth, a few red-haired barbarians were thundering at the gates. Let them thunder,—the walls were thick enough : and, as his omens were all propitious, he imagined himself secure ; but took the wise precaution of sending his household and private treasure away out of reach of ill-disposed persons belonging to the city.

Finding him inexorable, the principal merchants fled to their country residences, leaving their stores in charge of faithful servants ; but the bulk of the population, influenced by the governor's bombastic proclamations, went on with their work as coolly as ever, and ridiculed all idea of the combined forces being able to take Canton.

The allies, finding that the Chinese population did not heed the warnings posted and distributed by an armed party among the houses near the water's edge, determined to send a trusty agent actually into the city; but the plan was somewhat a difficult one, as none of the renegades would undertake such a hazardous task. It now seemed impossible to save them, and it was feared that thousands of innocent people would fall victims to Yeh's ignorance and indifference to bloodshed, when some one happening to think of Thompson, Captain Woodward received instructions to sound him upon the matter.

"Do you think you could manage the business without detection, Mr. Thompson ? "

" Bless you, sir, I can post several thousand bills in a couple of nights."

" How will you go about it? Mind, we should be very sorry indeed for you to lose your life."

"Leave it to me, sir. Of course there's risk in it, but it ain't no worse than I've run before for mere fun. Provided no soul but us knows about it I'll do it, and be back in a few days, as right as a trivet."

" Very well, Mr. Thompson ; you ought to know how far you can go."

"Yes, sir, I means to go right in and come out again ; and please goodness if I've any luck, I'll stick a programme right before old Yeh's front door."

The acting boatswain left the ship about dusk, and shortly afterwards returned with a suit of scavenger's clothes and a hat, both very dirty, two filthy pails, and a bamboo bearing-pole, also a Chinese pass, which, being translated, ran as follows:—

"Chuy, Bearer of garbage from the city of Kwan-tung to boats on the river, by

12

this enters and departs from The Gate of Eternal Purity and Joy between the hours of sunset and sunrise."

> " Respect this.
>
> " (Signed) CHIH-FA,
>
> " HO-PO-SO " (Director of Boats),
>
> " KWANG-CHOW-FOO " (City district of Canton).

The ship's barber—a marine named Reece—was called into Thompson's cabin, and in a short time the acting warrant-officer once more appeared in his old character of Lew ; then having besmeared his person with some clay brought on board for the purpose, the upper deck was cleared, and, under cover of the night, Jerry landed and wandered about until he came across other scavengers, with whom he proceeded to " The Gate of Eternal Purity and Joy," that being the sweet name of the dirtiest gate in the city, through which all the rubbish was carried in tubs and pails, underground sewerage being one of the modern improvements unknown to the Celestials.

Upon arrival at the gate, which was guarded by a considerable number of Tartar soldiers, each man was stopped and searched, and Thompson feared they would find the six thousand small proclamations which he had secreted under his jacket, but at that moment the guard was relieved, and as the man deputed to search him felt weary, he merely gave him a kick, and in a few moments Jerry found himself inside the outer wall. Like all other large cities, Canton had its day and its night population ; the latter being composed of night watchmen, who struck the hour on bamboos, scavengers, and the people who supplied them with refreshments, or assisted them in their vocation.

Having proceeded some distance, he came across a blind woman selling a kind of thin paste made of boiled rice, used as food by the night watchmen ; of this Jerry purchased about a dozen pints, and dumped it into one of his pails, after which the crone sung herself into a doze. Knowing the old woman would not be able to inform against him, he put down his pails and relieved himself of one of the twelve packages which were bound round his body. These were printed upon thin Chinese paper, six inches long by three wide, and were so light that but for fear of discovery he might have carried double the number. He took care not to detach more than one parcel at a time, and even that he kept out of sight, by hiding it in the band of his dress. The proclamation ran as follows :—

> " To the Inhabitants of Kwan-tung.
>
> " Your city is in danger of destruction by the guns of the Western men. Heed not the voice of your rulers, but flee all of you who are not fighting men. Let these who are in Yeh's service stay and defend the walls, but you innocent people leave the city, which will shortly be destroyed by fire.
>
> " Respect this notice, which is sent out of pity for the aged, women, and children."

Thompson, knowing it would not do to placard the spot near where he purchased his paste, shaped his course for the inner or Tartar city, and by good luck passed the guard there as safely as the last, he being taken for one of the numerous scavengers who perambulate the place at all hours of the night, in pursuit of their repulsive calling. Once inside, he commenced the business upon which he came, and ere the day dawned had posted about half of the notices, taking particular care to stick them upon the walls before the entrance of large buildings; and when the city awoke he had the satisfaction of seeing hundreds of the poorer classes congregating about the bills, upon which they passed remarks not very complimentary to their ruler.

When the shopkeepers began to unpack their wares Thompson retired to the ruins of a government building, which had been destroyed by "barbarian's" shell the preceding year, and, having found a nice out-of-the-way hole, thrust in his buckets and bearer, then got in himself, and in a few moments fell sound asleep, and dreamt he was anywhere else but inside the Tartar portion of the city of Canton. When he awoke he found it was getting dusk; so, after shaking himself, he fished out his stock-in-trade, placed the pole upon his shoulder, slung his buckets, and trotted out into the streets, crying, " Ah-ho—Ah-ho—Ah-ho," in the most approved scavenger style. His greatest difficulty was to avoid being engaged by some person who had rubbish to get rid of, but by dint of pretending to be deaf, he succeeded in getting away from all such inconvenient patrons.

Jerry found no trouble in obtaining food, which he ate as he stood with the buckets slung from his bearing-pole, after the manner of other carriers, but even at such times he was busy in slyly pasting the notices upon the garments of those with whom he came in contact.

That night he completely " did " the Tartar quarter, getting safely outside the inner wall before daybreak, when he again sought the friendly shelter of some ruins, and spent the day as before. At dusk he once more sallied forth, and wandered all over the city, posting an immense number of placards, and sometimes narrowly escaping arrest by the Tartar sentries, who were beginning to be very vigilant, but his unsavoury aspect threw them off their guard.

Having affixed his last paper but one, he determined to retrace his steps, but ere he reached "the Gate of Eternal Purity" he was stopped, and ordered to follow some Tartar soldiers. Knowing resistance to be useless, and finding that they arrested every scavenger they came across, he followed his captors with a cheerful air, when, to his horror, he found they were conducting him to Yeh's ya-mun, his knowledge of th Canton dialect enabling him to understand their conversation.

When they had secured about two hundred of the "fragrant fraternity," the imperial soldiers ceased their arrests, and bidding the captors not to think of escaping, drove them towards the governor's palace, and when inside directed them to deliver their buckets to a guard, who gave each in exchange a billet of wood marked with a number, by which they could recover their property. They were directed, however, to retain their bearing-sticks.

After a short delay, during which the guard served out to them warm tea and rice spirit without stint, they were marched into the interior of the palace, where sat the angry Yeh surveying a huge pile of silver bars, which he wished carried out of the city. They were part of the imperial treasure, but the governor, who thought it as well to secure himself in case of emergency, determined to remove some portion of it, as, notwithstanding his bombast, he looked out for his own future, and for that purpose deputed two trusty mandarins to convey the silver to a country residence in the White

Cloud mountains, where they had orders to bury it, until the disturbances were over.

Thompson was greatly relieved on finding how matters stood; and that instead of being, as he feared, immediately hurried off to execution, he would simply be detained for no very long period, as the Tartar soldiers had pressed more scavengers than were necessary to convey the treasure.

Yeh was in a great rage, swearing at his officers like a madman. By some means a number of spurious bars had been brought out and mixed with the pile, upon seeing which the governor flew at his assistants, and used Chinese oaths which would have turned a Dutchman pale with envy.

When the scavengers found they were in the presence of the great man who had sent so many thousands to their last account they fell upon their knees, upon which he roared at them to stand up, saying, " I am only the governor's aide-de-camp," but the full face and cunning eye were too familiar, and all of them knew that they were before the dreaded Yeh-ming-chin himself. The governor was in a terrible passion ; and when the keeper of the treasures made his appearance he rushed towards him, and in the usual Celestial fashion slapped his face.

" Take that, you thieving dog. You dare attempt to pass off such rubbish upon me."

" My Lord Yeh, it is a mistake."

But Yeh would not hear a word of explanation, so the victim rubbed his face, and looked round at the scavengers, who gaped at him with stolid faces, expressive of neither pity nor amusement, being fully aware of the danger of manifesting either. As the governor darted about he sometimes thrust the scavengers to the wall ; and so near did he go to Thompson on one occasion, that the latter contrived to slip his remaining proclamation into an open tobacco pouch which was swinging from the great man's girdle, shortly after which feat he and the rabble who were not wanted received orders to clear off.

Having picked out his buckets, and received a red paper, granting him exemption from all enforced labour for the next twenty-four hours, he bent his steps towards the gate, taking care to obtain a load of rubbish on his way. But what a contrast to the night on which he entered the city ! then the place was comparatively deserted, save by brother scavengers who would go limping by towards one of the gates softly crying, " Ah-ho ! Ah-ho ! " but upon this night, where formerly sat the solitary vendor of boiled rice, from whom he purchased his supply of paste, the ground was covered with refreshment-stands, and thousands of Cantonese were pouring out of the city in consequence of having read the notices he had so liberally posted. Jerry heard on all sides how thankful the people were to the foreign devils.

" They don't fight us, these western barbarians, they only so - to punish Yeh ! "

" Bah ! They have nothing to do with it. This proclamation is the work of the Tai-ping-che-houi (Peace society). Those western devils never do any good. They are accursed of the genii, and only live to commit evil acts."

" How like a fool you talk ! Why, I worked for those same Fanquis, and they paid me like men. Imagine me getting twelve hundred cash a day from them for carpenter's work. Indeed, they are an honourable people."

" You ought to be reported to the inspector of crimes for such a speech. You side with the enemies of your country."

Ere he reached " the Gate of Eternal Purity and Joy " Thompson was compelled, by the pressure of the crowd, to stop before a mandarin's residence, where the night before he had posted several of his warnings alongside the ordinary city official documents; and he was very much amused to hear the people read the various notices, offering rewards for the capture of live Fanquis, or the production of their heads.

"To brave men.

"All heads of the dastardly dogs, called Fanquis, brought to me, Ho-pin, who keeps the Pawnbroker's Hall, near ' The Gate of Benevolent Intent,' will be paid for in silver.   Ten taels per head for common men, and twenty taels for superiors of the yellow badge.   I deal in all sorts of charms against death by bullets or fire.   Cash paid for all heads ten days after delivery.   Note given for the same on receipt.   I am a reliable man.

"HO PIN MOKH."

"Hear! Hear! Hear!

"Listen, all ye who burn with desire to avenge the insult offered to our beautiful city.   All of you unite with me to purchase the (fresh) heads of Fanquis brought by our brave soldiers.   Five taels for each blue devil's (sailor's) head.   Ten for each red devil's (soldier's) head.   I pay money down, and don't give notes payable in a moon, as some do.   I live in the street of the yellow girdle, overlooking the Temple of Agriculture.

"LAO-CHOW.

"Only fresh heads paid for.   None but white Fanquis paid for."

It will be seen that, in their desire to possess the heads of their enemies, the clever Chinese did not forget to advertise their business; indeed if we except the wealthy classes, who purchased the visages of enemies they dared not face in person, only a few of the city fathers indulged in such luxuries, and the articles thus obtained were exhibited as a lure to draw customers to their shops.

After a time Jerry was pushed on by the mob, and passed through the outer gate without even the semblance of a challenge.   It was a wonderful exodus, as nearly all the people were of the middle class, and had left their property protected only by bolts and looks, the secrets of which were known to every thief in the country; but the little notices had frightened them, and as Yeh did not care whether all the inhabitants left, provided his soldiers remained, the guards at the gates had secret orders to wink at the emigration, but to be very cautious not to admit disguised Fanquis into the city.   A proclamation like the one posted by Mr. Thompson would have shown weakness on the part of the governor, but he did not care a fig for the notices when they were once posted, although he raised a great disturbance upon finding one in his tobacco-pouch.

"What?   A Fanqui proclamation in my tobacco-pouch.   Treason, by Fo!   Send for my secretary ; send for the chief of the Tartar guard ; send for everybody ; send for my executioner ! " he cried.

"Gracious Yeh, why are you so disquieted ? " observed his physician, who at that moment entered the arpartment.   " Pray do not be annoyed by trifles."

" Trifles!   you withered old anatomy, you miserable compound of cunning and conceit, you—you go to—"

" Yes, your excellency ; but what is the trouble about ?   What has the usual serenity •f your most excellent excellency's mind been disturbed about ? " mildly inquired the patient and long-suffering " man of many remedies."

" Look at this !" cried the irascible governor, thrusting the offensive document under the nose of the last speaker, in a manner which totally prevented his reading it.   " Look at that.   Do—you—call that a trifle, eh ? "

Without taking notice of the offensive manner in which Yeh spoke and acted, the •ld fellow calmly re-adjusted his horn spectacles, scratched his shaven pate, and then delivered himself as follows :—

" My vision's not quite as good as it was sixty years ago, but from a casual inspection I judge this to be a prescription for the prevention of heart-burn, it being about the size of the papers I dispense for that disease."

" Hum ! and you're the official who has charge of my valuable person ?   Go, sir, you are dismissed ; I physic myself in future."

"Great Fo, hear him," cried the old fellow, falling upon his hands, and kow-towing before the now calmed governor.   " Oh, mighty Yeh, don't be angry with an old man. I confess I am almost blind, but believe me I am still possessing my other faculties. Who will prescribe for you when I am gone ?   Who knows your constitution as I do ? Oh, gracious governor, don't discharge me."

" Go, sir ! "

" Then I give thee a parting present, my lord ; for the day may come when you will wish me back.   Two at night before going to bed, and you'll never want another physician," saying which he handed Yeh a small bamboo-box, then kow-tow'd and having collected his treasures, made the best of his way towards the White Cloud Mountains.

" Two at night.   What does the fool mean ?   Two gold-leaf pills.   POISON ;   So he thinks these foreign barbarians may take me, does he ?   I'll keep them ; they may be useful if luck goes against me."

After much pushing and jostling, Thompson arrived at an open space where he deposited his buckets : and, walking away, mingled with the crowd, who were struggling towards the water's edge, where the boatmen were reaping a fine harvest by carrying passengers at about ten times the ordinary fare.   No one who could not pay was taken across ; and although a tremendous crowd was waiting, the calculating sampan men would not lower their demands a sapeck.

Finding his chances of obtaining a passage rather small, the shrewd sailor walked further down the river, and at length came to a place where a number of sampans were actually waiting for fares, and he without difficulty got one to take him across. Stepping into a boat steered by a pretty girl, he motioned her to pull him over to Honan.   When about half way he suddenly seized the girl from behind, and before she could offer much resistance, secured her hands and feet, and tied a cloth across her mouth, then taking the scull, propelled the sampan down the river in the direction of his ship.

It was just about daybreak when he got alongside, and having released and paid his boat-woman, was preparing to climb the ladder, when a surly marine looking over the gangway, told him to get into his boat again, as no one was allowed on board until the pipe went for breakfast.

"Hill! here! don't you see who it is?"

"You get back into your sampan, will ye?"

"James Hill, don't you see it's me—Mr. Thompson?" cried the now irritated acting boatswain. "Are you mad or drunk? can't you recognize an acting warrant-officer in disguise?"

Upon hearing this, the well-fed marine leaned over the gangway, until his cheeks became the colour of a cabbage rose,—then after surveying Thompson for several moments, he turned his head and called to the sergeant, who was chatting with the carpenter near the main hatchway.

"If you please, sir, here's a Chinee who reports he's the acting boatswain.

"Let him come aboard, then."

"You Chinee," whispered the sentry to the amused Jerry, "you ken come aboard, d'ye hear?"

"I hear, Hill; but who set up this main rigging?"

"I don't know, Chinee, Mi, ain't you a good un to talk English? Why, it's really Mr. Thompson! Lord, sir! how you do disgust yourself. I didn't know you."

There was a smile of satisfaction upon the acting boatswain's face when he walked aft, and reported himself to the officer of the watch, who, after assuring himself that it was actually Thompson, and not a Chinese, went below and informed the captain. Jerry looked round at the crew who were bringing aft the sand and holy stones preparatory to washing decks, but none of them recognized him; however, upon seeing one of the boys attempt to screw on a hose without the necessary implement, he cried, "You boy Arnold, get a spanner."

"Who are you a calling boy Arnold?" replied the youth.

At that moment the officer of the watch returned with orders for Mr. Thompson to go below to the captain's cabin, but when the disguised warrant-officer presented himself at the door, the sentry at first refused to let him pass; however, the captain hearing the altercation, came to his assistance.

"Well, Mr. Thompson, I'm exceedingly glad to see you back safe. Your disguise is perfect. I can only see in you the Chinaman who came on board at Foo-choo."

"I'm real proud to see you agin, sir; real proud, sir. I thought once or twice it was a gooser—beg yer pardon, all over with me, sir."

"How did you get through? Have you posted all the proclamations?"

"Every one of 'em, sir. The last I slipped into old Yeh's backker-pouch. They hauled me up to carry speccy, and I took the opportunity when he was a giving the supers fits, to drop my last paper into his pouch. He must find it when he goes to take a draw at his pipe."

The captain laughed at the account of his warrant-officer's adventures which followed, and having lavished many encomiums upon his daring and ability, dismissed Mr. Thompson to take a bath and rest as long as he felt inclined. As he left the cabin, Jerry stopped at the door, and after fidgetting about for a few moments, walked back to the place where Captain Woodward was seated, and begging he would excuse him for the liberty he was taking, asked if the captain had not such a thing as a wig among his baggage.

Woodward laughed when he heard the request, but upon sending for his servant, the required article was procured, and proved to be a theatrical wig of brilliant red hue, which the captain had once purchased for some amateur performance, and which had remained unheeded by him in his wardrobe ever since.

" You can take that and welcome, Mr. Thompson, but don't you think it will look rather odd ? "

" Well, sir, I'm used to old wigs. When I were on the stage I wore almost anything, and this is a star's wig, an' no mistake. It's as natural as life."

" Very well," replied the captain with a shrug. " After having sacrificed your growing crop for your country's good, I will allow you to wear even *that wig*, but shall order a darker one from Houg-Kong for you. I don't think that suits your complexion."

" Maybe it don't, sir, but it's a wig. I've a horror of being regarded as a Chinese by the men forward."

Mr. Thompson having secured the glowing head-dress, proceeded to his cabin, where he had not been long ensconced before Tom Clare found him out. Instead of going to sleep, after he had taken a bath and dressed himself once more in his warrant-officer's uniform, Thompson proceeded to give his friend a full account of his adventures when acting as bill-sticker in Canton.

" Well, Mr. Thompson, your mother says you're a genius, and she spoke true. How you could find courage enough to enter that ere city beats me."

" It wasn't courage."

" No ? "

" It was cheek—cheek, old friend, an article wot will carry a feller a deal further than genuwine courage. I don't say I'm afraid of much, but it wern't bravery as led me on,—it were cheek. Why, I consider my slipping that last proklemation into old Yeh's bakker-pouch the werry axme of cheek. I must ask the new paymaster to strike off a pictur of that. Old Yeh was a-blowing up his fellers like one o'clock, when sudden he backs upon me, and pointing to a pile of stuff says, ' You fools, you duffers, you thick-headed swine, that's not treasure, that's only make-believe silver; leave that in the treasury, you geese.' As he screamed this out, his bakker-pouch bobbed up agin me, and I slipped the proklemation into it."

" But didn't you feel afraid ? "

" Not much. I felt as if it were the gayest game in the world ; the only drawback on it was my being a scavenger. All the people bullied me to carry their rubbish ; which not being my little game, I were somewhat puzzled to refuse them ; but I felt glad when I got safe aboard agin, I can tell ye."

" I began to think you were never a-coming back. Three days away, and no signs of you when I turned in last night."

" By the way, Tom, it's Christmas-day. Don't you know it ? "

" Captain's compliments to Mr. Thompson, and will he dine with him this evening at six o'clock ? " said a voice outside the door.

" My respects to Captain Woodward, and I am werry much honoured by the inwite, and accept it with thanks," promptly replied the acting boatswain.

" Now you turn in, Jerry, and have a real good sleep, Why, what is that ? " said Tom, as his eye fell upon the bearing-pole which Thompson had brought on board with him.

" That's my pole wot I carried my buckets slung from."

" How did you get that rig, Jer—Mr. Thompson ? "

" Blow your politeness, Tom. When we're off duty call me Jerry. Mr. is a deal too civil. Well, old man, I were told to get a disguise, so I took the Chinese bum-boat, —old Chumpee's,—landed at the place where the scavengers shoot their rubbish into the tanks ready for floating down the river, and watched until I saw a feller all by himself. Well, having singled out my man, I grabbed hold of him, and when the bum-boat fellers had secured him, stripped off his clothes, put on a pair of old pants, and gave him in charge of Chumpee, who has him all right now, stowed away under the bottom boards of his boat. Well, I secured his pails, stick, and clothes, besides his pass, which was what I pertickler wanted, then come aboard and got my head shaved, arter which I went on shore in a sampan."

"Well, now go to sleep, Jerry; I'll wake you at eight bells in the afternoon watch."

Six o'clock arrived, and Mr. Thompson upon hearing the dinner bugle, marched aft in company with the gunner and carpenter, who were both well-educated men, and his very good friends. When they arrived at the cabin door, they were duly announced by the steward ; and, to the delight of the captain, the acting boatswain not only appeared in his red wig, but had painted eyebrows to correspond, his own having been shaven off, to complete his disguise when he visited the city. The operation was well done, but the effect was to give his face a slightly intoxicated appearance.

"Good-evening, gentlemen," exclaimed the commander. "Help yourselves to bitters."

In a short time the various officers invited upon the occasion made their appearance, and, to their surprise, found the acting boatswain not only well behaved, but positively au-fait in the courtesies of the table ; and after the novelty of his wig and eyebrows wore off a little, they took wine with him as gravely as with the others. It was a proud moment for Mr. Thompson when the captain challenged him, and he felt he was some one of importance, and half resented a kindly hint from the carpenter "not to empty his glass at every toast," particularly as that gentleman prefaced the remark by the familiar term "Jerry." The roast beef and turkey were splendid, the plum-pudding first rate, the champagne delicious, and everything grand, dazzling, and magnificent in the eyes of the acting warrant-officer. "Ain't it like a banquet in a play ?" he whispered to the gunner. "I can't believe it's real."

When dinner was over, the party adjourned to the upper deck, and the delighted fellow was again reminded of his new position, by the captain offering him a cigar. "Drink bitters with the captain ; dine in the cabin ; ax me to take wine with him, and now offers me a cigar to smoke on the quarter-deck. I must go aft and find out if it ain't all a dream," thought he. Finding, when he got aft, that he was not dreaming, his test being a question to Tom Clare, who was getting some boat's gear out of a locker abaft, Jerry proceeded to smoke his cigar, surrounded by those who, a few months ago, he thought as far above him as the masts from the deck. From that day Thompson became a more reserved man. He still retained his friendship for Clare, but held the crew at a distance ; and while always ready to oblige any of them off duty, treated them like men when on service, considering his position required a certain amount of respect from them, and consequently did not allow his former shipmates to take advantage of him. But the wig ! When he appeared on duty in it the day after, it created such a sensation among the men, that Woodward was obliged to send for the doctor, and consult with him as to the means of getting the acting boatswain to take it off. Wherever he went the eyes of the crew were upon him, and the Stingers virtually knocked off work to stare at Thompson's head.

"Did you ever see sich a fee-nomer-nile ?" observed the captain of the foretop. "Vy, it's a regler red-hot swab. Did he go ashore to av his edd dyed ?"

"No; he's got a wig on, can't ye see ? It's the capting's wig, wot the steward airs sometimes. It's a theatre wig."

"Pshaw ! Do you think the captain is agoin' to lend the acting bosun his 'ed dress Besides, whoever heerd of a captain in the Rile Navy wearin' a red wig ?"

These and similar observations caused the commander to seek the advice of the little surgeon, who thereupon sent for Mr. Thompson, and after a few preliminary remarks asked him why he wore a wig.

"Well, you see, sir, I don't like looking like a Chinaman on duty ; and as the captain has been good enough to lend me this, I wear it until I can get one more suited to me."

"That's right enough, but it is a very poisonous colour, and will ruin the growth of your hair. It would be a thousand pities to spoil that—"

Mr. Thompson looked at the doctor for a moment, but as no smile illuminated his face, Jerry concluded he was serious in his advice.

"But is it pisonous to wear for a few hours every day ? "

"Deadly. I can show you the picture of a case, if you like to step down to my surgery."

"No thankee, sir ; I don't like that place, with all politeness to you. I'll just take this wig back to the steward, as I don't care to pison my hair."

Mr. Thompson accordingly doffed his conspicuous adornment, and went about his duty with his uniform cap pulled tightly over his forehead, which gave him the appearance of having been bonneted.

The mail arrived that evening, and to his astonishment, Jerry received the following mysterious communication :

> " She who arth fix her art on the
> Wil alway tinder proav
> Wil dreme of yew by day or nite
> An treasure up your lov
> Think not tho ragin sees do part
> She wil beleaf your not untro
> Sheal wayt for the in spit of hawl
> Not dew as others dew."

"No name. No date. Portsmouth postmark. This is a rewiwer from Mary Ann," cried Thompson. "Well, if she waits until I get home, she'll have a warrant-officer instead of an able seaman for a husband. But I ain't pleased with her going into poetry ; besides, she don't mention my name. However, I'll write her a line by way of reply," saying which he proceeded to scrawl off the following :

> " Dear Mary Ann, I've got your poe-try ;
> Keep up your pluck and dry your eye ;
> I'll anchor alongside you by-and-by."

This elegant effusion he addressed—

> MISS MARY ANN ROSS,
>   Care of MRS. SHEVER,
>   Portsmouth.

And having posted it, turned his attention to official matters, and thought no more of his old flame.

Mrs. Shever, having written the stanzas, which Thompson supposed came from her sister, did not scruple to appropriate the reply to herself ; so Mary Ann never received this last love-offering from her old admirer, who was still in blissful ignorance of her being "his no more."

CHAPTER XXIV.

A few days before the combined attack of the allied forces upon Canton, the immense floating population moored off that city began to move towards Chow-chan. Boat by boat disappeared, until only a few sampans, manned by the most daring thieves on the river, remained, and these had a pretty lively time of it, as the sentries on board the war-ships would fire at them whenever they approached within a certain distance of those vessels. It seemed strange that those who had the best opportunity of judging what the western barbarians could do were the last to abandon their positions, the water population having been warned to leave ten days before. Mr. Thompson performed his celebrated feat of "bill-sticking under difficulties," yet it was not until the Cantonese came swarming out of the city that those who lived along the water's edge began to move their property out of the way of the barbarian's guns.

Yeh took matters very coolly, and seemed quite indifferent to the imposing force brought against him, so the watermen, who were a bold insolent set, composed of the dregs of the population, imagined he was right in his assertion, that the Fanquis would only talk and not fight; but the exodus of the merchants opened their eyes, and as all of them wanted to get under weigh at the same time, the waterside presented a more animated appearance than usual. Many of the merchants who owned wooden stores built upon piles near the water's edge, had tanks placed under those edifices at low tide, so that as the water rose it lifted the buildings clear, and huge stores were thus floated off, and towed away to a place of safety, in company with theatres, flower boats, restaurants, and the hundred and one other kinds of boats then common upon the river.

At one point so many houses were thus removed, that the outer wall of the city, usually hidden by a mass of buildings, was entirely exposed, offering a splendid target for the guns of H. M. S. Ruff, which was moored immediately opposite.

Canton is situated upon the river of that name, and opposite to the city is the Island of Honan, which, with other similar islands, divide the river into two parts—one to the left, running down towards Wampoa, and the other to the right, which flows past Chow-chan creek; these unite before they reach the Bocca Tigris, and both branches or sides are, in common, called the Canton River.

The Stinger was moored at the head of the left passage, while all along the front of the city French and English war-ships were anchored, each taking up its position as it arrived from Hong-Kong, without regard to nationality, the only care being to place the ships which drew most water where they could not well get on shore upon the numerous mud-banks with which the river abounded. About midway in the line of ships was a small island, where a fortification had formerly existed, but the year before, when the river was held by the foreigners, they had taken this fort, and turned its guns against the city. Upon their withdrawal, Yeh ordered the walls to be destroyed.

When the allied forces came to anchor off the city, the sailors again took possession of the island, and built a crows'-nest, or observatory, in a tree growing amid the ruins; from which lofty position the flags of the allies, side by side, waved defiance to Governor Yeh. At the same time the sailors cleared away the rubbish, and built a mortar battery in the centre of the island, from which shot and shell could be thrown as far as the outer wall at the back of the city.

The Island of Honan was partly in possession of the allied troops, there not being room enough for them on board the ships; the celebrated Buddhist temple was occupied as their head-quarters; and holy pigs, which could scarcely grunt—so fat were they—consecrated storks, and sacred gold fish, were ignominiously knocked upon the head, and converted into chowder by the sacrilegious invaders.   In vain the shaven-headed bonzes protested, and offered to procure good food, if they would only spare their respected swine and other live stock ; it was all without avail, and, in spite of fearful predictions as to the consequences which would ensue if they devoured the sacred grunters, the soldiers made many a hearty meal off their flesh.   Possibly, had they known the Chinese language, the warnings of the bonzes would have somewhat affected them ; but, as it was, they only patted the complainants on the back or kicked them out of their quarters, as fancy suggested.

The night before the attack a number of gun-boats arrived from Hong-Kong, and the allied forces became aware that at daybreak the bombardment was to commence. Considering the power of the invading force, Yeh took matters very philosophically, contenting himself with sending off a flag of truce at the last moment, and ordering the western barbarians "to leave the waters of Kwan-tung forthwith," under pain of immediate expulsion; to which amusing notice the allied commanders-in-chief replied by politely informing him that, as all hope of making terms was given up, they should proceed to bombard his palace at daybreak the next morning.

His wonderful indifference made the opposing forces imagine he had received large reinforcements since their last spies visited the city, little thinking that any person would show such composure, if he knew it was impossible to hold his ground.   Yeh was completely blinded by egotism, and probably none of his mandarins dared to tell him exactly how matters stood ; therefore, when Ho-qua and other merchants had urged him to make terms, he merely regarded their fears as mercantile ones, and treated them accordingly.   Besides, they were Chinese, not Tartars; they only had peddling ideas of trade and loss of goods ; whereas, he was a Tartar, who delighted in bloodshed, and knew if he were defeated, or if he yielded, it was all up with him at Pekin, so determined to stay where he was until everything went against him, and then—run away, as many a Tartar had done before.

At twelve o'clock that night Canton was as quiet as usual.   True, the look-out men perched up in the sentry-boxes built all along the walls, kept up a furious din with their bamboo rattles, to show they were awake and to frighten foul spirits away; and the ordinary watchmen made night hideous with their shrill cries.   However, their noises only occurred at intervals, and beyond that Canton was as silent as Pompeii, the streets being deserted, and not a soul abroad who was not on military duty.

Yeh slumbered until an hour before daybreak, when he arose and held a consultation with his officers.   At that time the city was hidden in a light fog, and it was imagined the western barbarians would delay their attack until sunrise, but to the governor's astonishment, as he was speaking, a shell came crashing into his ya-mun, and burst in the court-yard near the room in which they were assembled.   Hearing the explosion, he dismissed his officers, ordering them, as they valued their heads, to hold the walls till the last moment ; and then that learned scholar, great warrior, and plucky Tartar went into an inner apartment, and, ostrich-like, hid himself under a pile of cotton bags.

The mortar-battery commenced the attack, and at the same moment a signal was hoisted on the crows'-nest of the fort.   In a moment bang, bang went the guns of the various ships, and away tore hundreds of missiles into Canton.   Yeh's ya-mun was the principal object of attack at first, and the whole line of ships directed their guns upon that spot. Not a shot was fired by the Chinese in return, and their enemies had it all their own way. For several hours they continued firing with great precision, and in many places the outer wall was badly battered, large masses of it falling into the streets underneath, and completely filling them with rubbish.

About noon, the city being fired in many places by the shower of shell-rockets thrown in by the allies, it was determined to land the forces, while those left in charge of the ships were directed to keep up a steady fire upon the principal edifices. At times the shot went flying against strong-looking buildings, which in a few minutes would, as it were, reel and topple over; while the rockets, after striking against some obstruction, would rebound, and dart at it again, until they forced their way through, in most cases firing the structures they entered.

After the naval brigade, composed of all the men who could be spared from the Stinger, departed from that ship, those left in charge of Mr. Beauman did their best to damage the city as much as possible by firing at pagodas and watch-boxes, their exertions in that line being every now and then rewarded by seeing one of the objects incline and fall to the ground. The river thieves reaped a fine harvest, and looted to their heart's content, undisturbed by the missiles which flew over their heads, and ere night set in not one of them was left, as they had all loaded their sampans and departed in search of a mart in which to dispose of their plunder. At dusk the city was wrapped in flames from one end to the other, and all along the line of range palaces and hovels fell a prey to the devouring element.

When the Stingers left the ship they were conveyed to a point below the city, where the allied forces were preparing for the assault. Here, much to their chagrin, they were ordered to take charge of the landing-place; and it was with anything but satisfaction that they witnessed the departure of the forces selected to assault the heights. The Stingers were not relieved of their irksome charge until some days after, when they were marched into the city and quartered in a ya-mun.

Thus how Canton was taken and Yeh captured was a mystery to them; all they knew about the matter being that the wounded were brought down for embarkation, and that Yeh himself, amid the groans of the spectators, took boat from their wharf, when he was conveyed on board ship, preparatory to his removal to Calcutta. They heard that the French, after having agreed to assault the heights at a certain time, had, contrary to agreement, advanced an hour before, so as to boast of entering the city before their allies, but did not know any particulars of the attack; they also saw the body of one of the most esteemed captains in the service brought down, to be conveyed on board his ship; but beyond this, and hearing the guns, they knew little about the affair.

When they arrived in the city the place seemed quiet enough, and instead of plundering they were themselves fleeced by the inhabitants, who at once started a sort of market, and charged famine prices for everything they sold.

It was, no doubt, a wise regulation which forbade the Stingers looting or plundering, after the manner of the French, who searched everywhere, and not only ill-treated women and children, but often killed the inhabitants, when they could not satisfy them by producing treasure. There was not much exchange of courtesy betwixt the allies, and, indeed, upon several occasions the sailors belonging to the two nations came to open rupture.

Although the Stingers were strictly forbidden to loot, they had contrived to get hold of some very pretty things in the way of curiosities, purchased of the Chinese thieves; and, doubtless, now and then articles upon which it would puzzle them to prove payment had been made; but in justice be it said, they seldom annoyed the women, although they were not quite guiltless upon that head.

After they had been settled in their quarters a few days, they were repeatedly annoyed by the attacks of some zealous people who would assemble at night, and, under cover of the ruins near, fire rockets into the ya-mun. One evening, as the captain was inspecting his men, a shower of arrow-headed rockets flew into the court-yard, one of them passing through the body of a marine who was on duty at the door, so that he died shortly after of the wound. Woodward at once directed his men to assault the quarter from which the rockets proceeded, when they were met by a steady fire, killing two men and wounding several others. It will be seen from this, that although the allied forces held Canton, it was only in places; and at times the unruly Tartar soldiers would intoxicate themselves with rice spirit, and attack these little garrisons, when the invaders would retaliate upon the peaceable inhabitants who lived near their quarters.

Knowing it would not do to leave the ya-mun unprotected while he pursued the attacking party, Woodward sounded a retreat, and the next morning at daylight sent for assistance, which was at once forwarded by the commander-in-chief, whereupon they overhauled every nook and corner within a radius of a mile from the ya-mun, and Mr. Thompson was placed in charge of a party, who were directed to make a thorough search of a joss-house from which some of the rockets had been fired.

After a careful hunt, Jerry was about to recall his men, when he heard a sob proceeding from the gigantic image of the god Fo, which was placed at the end of the apartment he had just entered. As he noticed the robe thrown over the shoulders of the figure was composed of new silk of a very rich texture, he advanced to the god, and seizing the drapery, tore it from its fastenings, when lo! trembling beneath the bottom folds he discovered a girl, a pretty delicate Chinese, about nineteen years of age, quite speechless from fear. The acting boatswain glanced at her for a moment with quivering lip and flushed face, the girl resembling A-tae so strongly as to startle him.

"Open your eyes, pretty bird," he whispered in Chinese, but the poor fluttering little thing resolutely kept them shut.

"I'm your friend, and won't hurt you; look at me."

This had no effect upon the closely-contracted lids, so Jerry lifted the pretty face up to his own, and with a full heart, for he thought of his loving A-tae, tenderly and respectfully kissed her, upon which she opened her eyes—such bright ones, too, they were—and after looking at him for a moment half-timidly, she turned her head, then gave a scream, and fainted; four grinning sailors were standing in the doorway, and their appearance had caused her to faint from apprehension.

Mr. Thompson walked round to the back of the joss, opened a door (all of them are hollow, and have receptacles in the back), and gently depositing her inside, closed it, then turning round, ordered the sailors to quit the joss-house.

Now, the men were new hands who had lately joined the Stinger, and therefore did not know the temperament of the acting-warrant officer; besides, they were partly intoxicated, having discovered some rice spirit in one of the apartments, of which liquor they had partaken very freely. They advanced towards Jerry, evidently bent upon dragging the girl out of her hiding-place in spite of his orders.

Thompson placed his back against the door of the joss, and drawing his revolver, ordered the brutes out of the place.

"We wants that gal, and we means to have her. We chivied her here; she's *our* game," sulkily observed the ringleader.

"Yes, and we don't mean to give her up, in spite of you," chorussed the others.

"I'll give you three minutes to clear out, arter which I'll shoot the first man as moves," quietly replied the determined defender.

Hearing this, one of the men advanced as if to attack Jerry with his cutlass, when crack went the pistol, and the bully fell headlong at the feet of the brave fellow who had thus risked his life to defend a girl from worse than death. Upon seeing one of their number fall, the others made their escape, and Thompson, turning to the joss, opened the door, and assisted the trembling girl out of the building. When they had proceeded a few yards, she pointed to a door in a wall, saying, "That is my way;" then, chin-chinning him, was about to depart, when he caught her by the hand, and begged she would give him a small token of remembrance, at the same time pointing to a little image of Fo, worn instead of a button to fasten her jacket. Hastily tearing the same from her garment, she pressed it into his hand, and in another moment was out of sight.

Returning to the joss-house, Thompson found the bully sitting up, and complaining of a pain in his shoulder, upon hearing which he ordered him "to get up," and on arrival at the ya-mun took him to the doctor, who dressed the man's wound before he was placed under arrest. When the matter was reported to the captain, he ordered the other men to be put in irons and conveyed on board, where they were kept in confinement, until the ship arrived in Hong-Kong,

Mr. Thompson received many compliments for the gallantry he displayed upon this occasion; but his only reply was, "Now, do you think any man could ha' done otherwise?" He evidently thought very little about the service he had rendered the poor child, while she never forgot the good Fanqui who saved her from the fiends, who would have eaten her.

There was little to be seen in the city beyond the Chamber of Horrors and some very ancient buildings. In the former place a number of plaster groups, painted to resemble life, were ranged round the three sides of a chamber. Sawing men in halves, boiling in oil, impaling, breaking upon the wheel, decapitation, and many other horrible methods of putting criminals to death, were here represented with life-like fidelity; but no one cared to visit the place twice, although strangers were always taken there, as to a unique exhibition, which probably it was. Canton was comparatively deserted, and in many places in ruins, so the Stingers found their residence there rather dull work, after all.

When the city was first taken a provost-marshal was appointed, whose duty it was to arrest and flog every straggler he found when going his rounds; and as soldiers and sailors always will get astray more or less, that functionary often had his hands full. Sometimes he did not confine his operations to the Army and Navy, and on one or two occasions the sutlers fared rather badly at his hands, for which he was duly shown up in the "Hong-Kong Gong," a rival of that excellent newspaper, "The Friendly Shiner."

About the latter end of June the Stingers received orders to get ready to embark on board their ship, preparatory to leaving for Hong-Kong, and every one anxiously awaited the definite order to leave the ya-mun, when one morning three dirty-looking bonzes appeared at the outer gate, and humbly begged to be allowed an interview with the captain. Upon being shown into his presence, one of their number pulled forth a letter, or order, addressed to Captain Woodward, and signed by the commander-in-chief of the naval forces, which ran thus:—

" "SIR,—You are hereby directed to allow the three Chinese bonzes, who will hand you this, to pack up and take away all their property, which they may find left in the small Buddhist chapel situated in the grounds near the left wing of your ya-mun."

Upon reading this Captain Woodward sent for the first lieutenant, and asked him if he knew the building, and to what purpose it had been devoted. Also if any of the articles found in it remained. Upon which Lieutenant Russell, in his usual florid manner, politely informed his senior that, beyond its being used as a skittle alley, to the best of his belief it was unoccupied ; and as to the images, &c., probably they were there still.

" Let those men take all they want, and carry it away."

Hearing this speech, one of the bonzes, who spoke very fair Pigeon-English, requested permission for their porters to be admitted into the ya-mun, which was granted, and Mr. Thompson directed to see they took all they wanted ; whereupon he formed a procession, heading it himself, and marched towards the little joss-house, followed by the demure, mild-eyed bonzes, and about thirty carriers, who bore short bamboo ladders, he thinking all the time how foolish the Buddhists must be to imagine there was anything left that was worth carrying off.

Upon arriving at the door of the temple, the bonzes knelt, prostrated themselves, burnt three sticks of joss-stick, and repeated " o-mi-tu-fuh" for about a quarter of an hour, during which time the acting boatswain indulged in a pipe or joined in the chorus, as fancy led him ; while the irreverent bearers squatted upon the ground, and expressed a wish that the bonzes would hurry, as they did not like being so close to the " foreign devils."

When the " o-mis " were over, the most elderly bonze assumed a business air ; and directing the doors to be opened, ordered the bearers to bring in their ladders, which the three mild-eyed ones proceeded to lash together in a most artistic manner. Acrobats could not have done it better than did those meek individuals, who lashed, and chanted " o-mi-tu-fuh," until they had put together a set of ladders ; which upon being elevated reached to the highest rafters of the joss-house. When all was ready, the old boy of the party stripped off his loose jacket, and springing up the ladder was soon lost in the " dim religious gloom" overhead. Mr. Thompson looked on with a critical eye, and observed to a royal marine, who had wandered into the place, that he began to think that the old " bronzes " knowed what they was up to.

After a short time, during which the bonze up aloft had several times hailed his friends below to "look-out and stand from under," down came bundles of rich fur dresses, worth ever so many hundred dollars, then bales of silks, and at last bars of silver. Jerry looked at the bonzes, and then at the permit, but finding that correct allowed them to proceed, when in a short time the old man up aloft announced, with a grunt, that the place was cleared, after which he scrambled down the ladder, and assisted his companions to pack their property.

Having unrolled the fur dresses, they placed several bars of silver in each, then binding them up tightly, rapidly loaded the bearers, who seemed to take the proceeding very coolly, as though it were an every-day occurrence with them. When the last bale was packed, the elderly bonze turned to Mr. Thompson, and asked him how much he would give him for the ladders?

" A kick," replied the chagrined acting boatswain ; adding, " Come, clear out, old myty-few. You're a smart old dodger, you are ! "

" Fo ! " exclaimed the imperturbable old fellow. " He won't offer a sapeck. Well, I'll send for them to-morrow, chin-chin ; " saying which the old boy saluted Mr. Thompson, and trotted off after his companions, without bestowing a single glance at the prostrate forms of several small gods, which the sailors had been using instead of pins when they played skittles.

" Done, by Jove ! Hundreds of pounds of prize money swept clean out of our pockets," cried the enraged Jerry, "and we a gaping up with it almost in sight all the time. Pshaw, we ain't half as smart as them old *bronzes*, with all our cleverness. I'll back one of 'em agin two lawyers any day."

Loud were the growls of the men at what they termed their bad luck, but when Woodward heard of the affair, he only laughed, and declared the old fellows deserved all they got, for their coolness and sagacity.

That evening the mail arrived, and the captain received orders to embark his men at daylight; but long before that hour the Stingers were stirring. As they left the city they received a perfect ovation at every post they passed. "Going *home*, my boys! Going home!" Happy fellows! how proudly they marched along the narrow streets which had been the scenes of many incidents, both sad and amusing; past heaps of ruins caused by the shot from their guns; by Tartar guard houses, and dead walls, bearing still the proclamations so daringly posted by the acting boatswain,—with the fiddler scraping away at "Cheer, boys, Cheer," to which tune their happy voices joined in chorus. The first step from the ya-mun was one nearer home, and all of them felt delighted to think that in a few months they would see the faces of those who held them most dear. Tom Clare marched by the side of Mr. Thompson, and a happier face than the former's could not be found in the party.

"Jerry, old friend, in a little time I shall see her, and then won't I be happy?"

"Yes, old man, I daresay you will; but, 'pon my word, there ain't much pleasure for me to look forward to."

"Why, there's Mary Ann?"

"Yes, I know that; but she ain't A-tae. I never shall get another gal to love me, as she did."

"Come, Jerry, don't you be foolish. I used to be melancholy once, but look at me now," exclaimed the delighted fellow, as he joined in the refrain,

"Cheer, boys, cheer, no more of idle sorrow,
Courage, true hearts, shall bear us on our way;
Hope points before, and shows the bright to-morrow
Let us forget the darkness of to-day."

And so one friend cheered the other, until they arrived at the ship, where they were welcomed by Mr. Beauman, and in a short time got up their anchor and steamed down the river towards Hong-Kong.

Past well-remembered spots, where they had formerly landed and obtained supplies —through the barrier stakes without bumping aground, and by Yin-sin island, then guarded by H. M. gun-boat Stifler, the crew of which turned out to a man to cheer them as they steamed by; away they rattle right merrily, and the next day came to anchor in Hong-Kong harbour, where they remained until the twenty-fifth of July. During the interval they re-fitted the ship and prepared her for her long voyage home.

Mr. Thompson called upon his friends to bid them farewell, and during the evening Mrs. Mackay presented him with a gold call and chain, begging he would accept it as a small proof of her appreciation of his kindness to her. Before he left, his kind friends took him up-stairs, and there, calmly sleeping in its cradle, he saw their first-born, Jerry bent over the infant, and gently kissing it, observed, with a tear in his eye, that he hadn't been so near an angel for a long time; then, for the twentieth time solemnly shaking hands with the parents, bade them adieu.

"Mind you write us, Mr. Thompson, and don't forget to visit Mary Ann as soon as you arrive."

"Never fear, Miss; I'll write you, and if Mary Ann becomes Mrs. Thompson, she shall add a postscript."

13

.CHAPTER XXV.

A few days before the Stinger left the China station the P. and O. steamer Jowra arrived in harbour, and within an hour of her coming to anchor it was rumoured through the fleet that Captain Woodward and Lieutenant Russell were promoted. This news was received with great demonstration of delight by the Stingers; but when they heard that their good commander was to go home by the overland route, and that their first lieutenant had orders to take charge of H. M. S. Polecat, which had just arrived on the station, their pleasure gave way to regret. Woodward was exceedingly sorry to leave his men, but he wished to see his family, and a son and heir, born about two weeks after his departure from home, so he gave his steward orders to pack his clothes, and within six hours after he received the news was on his way to Singapore in the return P. and O. steamer. By this time a morose-looking individual, named Tortle, had read his commission, and taken charge of the Stinger.

As Woodward left the ship the men clustered round to bid him good-bye, and the tears trickled down some of their faces, when he stood up at the gangway, and exclaimed, "Good-bye, my brave fellows! God bless you all."

"There goes the best captain in the service, and it's a·black day for us."

" Why ? "

"Why, indeed! I knows, worse luck. We've been free under that gentleman, but bully Tortle will have the gratings rigged afore we have been at sea a week, see if he don't."

" Do you know him ? "

" Don't I ? I sailed in the old Spider with him, and a worse tempered man never wore uniform. He's all honey one day, and winneger the next."

Captain Tortle was what is called in the navy a disappointed man, never having been lucky enough to get promoted, according to what he considered his merits, and had done all sorts of naval drudgery for some years, but being ordered out to China as commander of the Stinger, was promised promotion upon his return in that ship ; so his only object was to get home as quickly as possible. Ill-natured people said he drank secretly ; and if an inflamed visage and generally bloated appearance are criterions, it may safely be said they were not far wrong in their assertions. Upon joining the ship he read his commission, said he was glad to see the ship was ready for sea, and then ordered the acting boatswain to pipe down.

Upon the following day Lieutenant Russell left the ship, and to the surprise of the officers and crew, " Nosey " Cravan made his appearance on board, and announced his appointment as first lieutenant.

After a few days' delay, during which about twenty of the best men in the ship volunteered to remain out upon the station, provided they were allowed to exchange into Captain Russell's vessel, which offer was at once accepted, and the same number of indifferent hands transferred to the Stinger, Captain Tortle received instructions to proceed to sea ; and upon the first of August the ship steamed slowly out of the harbour, amid hearty cheers from the crews of the ships at anchor. As they passed H. M. S. Polecat, their late first lieutenant stood upon the bridge and waved his cap, exclaiming, "There go the happy fellows; what a nice voyage they will have," little thinking how miserable they really were, and forgetting it was his humanity and Woodward's generous example which had raised them to what they were when he left the ship. The Stingers were sad at heart when they bade adieu to Hong-Kong, and the voyage which all had looked forward to as one of the happiest they could imagine, now seemed fraught with trouble and discomfort.

Cravan did not mince matters, but let the men know they were once more under the command of a tyrant, and all Russell's improvements and plans for their benefit were ruthlessly abolished. Three days after they left the harbour it came on to blow, and in directing part of the watch to perform some duty, upon their failing to carry out the order to his satisfaction, the first lieutenant swore at them so brutally, that the men, who were old hands on board, determined to wait upon the commander and endeavour to prevent such language being used towards them for the remainder of the voyage. So the next day the sailors who had been abused went aft, and respectfully submitted their case to Tortle, who was steadying himself against the capstan, evidently slightly the worse for liquor.

"What do you want, my men?"

"If you please, sir," said the spokesman, respectfully removing his cap, "yesterday the first lieutenant swore at us, and abused us in a way as we hasn't been used to: our last captain wouldn't allow no bad language, and we have kind of dropped it. Now, sir, will you be so kind as to speak to the first lieutenant, so as to prevent this in future? We are all ready and willin' to do our duty, but beg to be treated like men."

Now, the articles of war are very definite upon the matter of swearing, and they provide that any officer, seaman, or marine who shall be guilty of using profane language, shall be duly punished for the same; but, like many other admirable naval regulations, this only refers to officers upon paper, and is virtually a dead letter as far as they are concerned; so when the captain heard what the men had to say, he stared at them, and replied,

"You complain of Lieutenant Cravan swearing at you, do you?"

"Yes, sir."

"Is that all?"

"Yes, sir."

"Very well, that will do. You can go forward."

Tortle laughed until the tears trickled down his cheeks. "Oh, ha, ha, ha! Here's a crew—can't be sworn at. Oh, ha, ha, ha! I'm—ha, ha,—hanged—!" At that moment Cravan came up; and, seeing the commander laughing, joined in the merriment.

"What do you think, Cravan? Oh, ha, ha, ha! Those precious saints of Woodward's have actually had the cheek to come aft and—Oh, it's too much for me—to request I will be kind enough to ask you—Oh, ha, ha, ha!—it's too ridiculous—to leave off swearing."

"What did you tell them, sir?"

"What did I say? Why, I said—ha, ha!—go forward, which meant—go to the devil! I wonder what next. Why, they'll want to hold prayer-meetings, bless them!"

After this there was a marked difference in the behaviour of the crew, who exhibited a sullen, dogged manner, when going about their duty; and by the time they reached Singapore more than one man was reported for punishment; but, in spite of Cravan's endeavours, the commander did not flog them.

"I think that fellow deserves it, if ever a man did," observed the first lieutenant to Tortle, speaking of a fore-topman whom he had reported for some trivial offence.

"No doubt he does; all of them do, more or less. But the regulations are getting more severe; and if you flog for any less crime than mutiny you get a lot of bothering letters inquiring for particulars, and the newspapers take the matter up. I cannot flog the brutes for mere ordinary crimes; that time has passed, I am sorry to say. But if they only raise their voices in mutiny, I'll give them all they ask for—with the cat."

"You see, sir, Captain Woodward has spoilt the crew: taught them to believe they were of some importance, and given them ideas far above their position. It will be a very difficult matter to convince them they are liable to the lash now. Why, some of the fellows actually think, because you have not flogged the men I have reported to you within the last few days, that you have no power to punish them without a court-martial."

"Do they?" chuckled the captain, cracking the joints of his fingers as he passed one hand over the other. "Do they?" Only let them mutiny, Mr. Cravan, then they will find out if the lash is abolished. It never will be until there's an Act of Parliament passed for that purpose, as we can always find reasons enough for its use; and if we do not choose to give any explanation, who can interfere with us as long as we only use it to suppress mutiny?"

"But these are such a psalm-singing lot, that they won't mutiny."

"Then we wont flog them. Ha! ha! ha! Please, Cravan, don't swear at them. Have some regard for their feelings in future."

One night, when Thompson had retired to bed, he was suddenly awakened by the sick-bay man, who informed him that Tom Clare was in a fit, and in a few moments he was by the side of his friend, whom he found in a state of great prostration.

"What's the matter, Tom?"

Evidently the sufferer did not know who it was that addressed him, and soon after Thompson saw the poor fellow's head fall upon his chest, and he seemed to all appearance dead.

"Take him into my cabin! I'll look after him," said the acting boatswain, and the inanimate form of poor Clare was conveyed into Thompson's cabin, where the doctor did his best to bring him to consciousness.

As the surgeon stood by the man, with his fingers on his pulse, he observed, "It's one of his old attacks, Mr. Thompson. Don't you remember he has suffered from them about this time every year?"

"God bless us. What day of the month is this, sir?"

"The sixteenth of August—sure enough it's what he used to call his wife's day. Poor fellow, he won't enjoy her society long, his constitution is too much impaired."

"Don't you think it's flogging has brought this on, sir?"

"I cannot express an opinion, Thompson." the little doctor replied; but he knew full well that the lash was the cause of the poor fellow's trouble, although he could not say so.

"He ain't never been the same man since that cruel sentence was executed on him, sir. That and being separated from his wife has done it. See, he's reviving."

After a time he became sensible, and spoke quite rationally to those near him, but he steadily refused to speak about what he had seen.

"It's a horrid dream, a kind of nightmare, and I know it ain't real. Please, Jerry, don't ask me nothing more about it."

When the first lieutenant went his rounds the next morning, he observed Clare lying upon the bed in the acting boatswain's cabin, seeing which he sent for Mr. Thompson, and sneeringly remarked that he did not approve of the warrant-officers' cabins being turned into hospitals.

"If you please, sir, may poor Clare remain there for a day or two? I don't think he will last long anyhow."

"No, sir; let him go into the sick-bay, along with the rest of the men. It won't do to show favour. Why, they will want me to turn out of my cabin next."

"Never fear, sir."

"What do you mean by that reply, Mr. Thompson?" angrily demanded the bully.

"What I said, sir! No foremast hand would think of axing such a thing," coolly replied Jerry.

"Oh, very good. You must mind what you say. It will depend on me whether you are confirmed as boatswain or not, as Captain Tortle will be guided by my advice when he makes his report about you."

"I'll do my best to do my duty, sir; but maybe I shall never be a confirmed boatswain. I don't want to get it by unfair means, and I didn't ask for the rate, as you knows."

"Well, that will do, Thompson. I wish you well; but take my advice—don't show too much sympathy for your old associates. The time may soon come when you may be called upon to do your duty towards some of them, and it wont do to be too tenderhearted."

"You brute!" observed the acting warrant-officer, as the lieutenant vanished up the hatchway, "so that's your little game, is it? Well, if ever I lays a cat across a fellowcreature's back, may I never be happy afterward. Them's my sentiments;" saying which he walked aft to the doctor, and told him what the first lieutenant had said.

Clare was moved into the sick-bay, where he had a better chance of recovery than in the boatswain's cabin, that place being somewhat close and uncomfortable; but still to offer it showed Thompson's generous nature, and how willing he was to sacrifice any comfort to serve his friend. Tom mended apace, and when they left Singapore was able to get about; but the doctor kept him upon the sick-list, knowing that the slightest excitement might prove fatal to him.

Many of the crew returned to their old habits, and began to use bad language, doubtless encouraged by the example of Cravan, who worried and harrassed them nearly out of their senses.

One evening, when the watch below were as usual indulging in a song, he sent forward and ordered them to desist. Now, under ordinary circumstances the command would have been obeyed, but as this was the last of many petty vexatious orders, some of the men rebelled, and one of them continued singing. Upon hearing this Cravan put on his sword, and going forward, attempted to pull the man out from their midst; seeing which his shipmates threw a number of articles at the lieutenant, and compelled him to retreat aft.

"Come, chaps, let's rise and free ourselves," cried the excited sailor; and in a few moments several of the men had secured arms from the steerage, and were collected forward behind a barricade of clothes bags, &c., awaiting the return of the first lieutenant. At this time the watch on deck were at their duty, quite unconscious of the riot below, and, in spite of the bad treatment they had received, few of the original crew joined the disaffected party, although repeatedly urged to do so, and even being threatened when they refused to comply.

Cravan walked down to the captain's cabin, and found Tortle snoring upon a sofa.

"Captain Tortle, the men have mutinied."

" All right—let—'em—flog 'em—I'll do it," grunted the drowsy commander.

" But, sir, what shall I do ? "

" Fire among 'em ! put down the mutiny ! Don't bother me, sir, I'm sick," observed the captain in a dignified manner.

Finding he could not obtain the support of his superior, Cravan entered the ward-room and consulted with his brother officers, who advised him to reason with the men, when, as they were speaking, they heard the derisive cheers of the mutineers, who had succeeded in obtaining the arms belonging to the Royal Marines, and were shouting to them to come and take them back if they dared.

As matters were becoming serious, the first lieutenant requested the officers to put on their swords and go forward with him. When the mutineers saw Cravan they howled with rage, and swore they would serve him out.

Thompson arrived from the upper deck just then ; and seeing how matters stood, was stepping forward to speak to the foolish fellows, when a marline-spike, thrown by one of the malcontents, struck him, causing his right arm to drop powerless by his side. Without noticing this, the now disgusted acting boatswain rushed forward, and before the mutineers could understand what he was about, had seized the ringleader with his left hand, and dragged him aft to where the officers were standing, upon seeing which the rest of the men gave in, and sued for quarter.

" Put 'em all in irons, Mr. Thompson. You have behaved nobly, sir."

By the time five of the most prominent mutineers were secured, the others, who could not be readily identified, had mingled with their shipmates, and it was deemed best to let them alone. When the last of the malcontents was secured, Mr. Thompson repaired to the surgery, where the doctor examined his arm and pronounced it broken.

" How did you contrive to seize that big fellow with only one hand ? " demanded the surgeon.

" Well, doctor, you see I felt so mad with the fools, knowing they would never get their rights that way, and the sooner they come to their senses the better, that I rushes in and collars big Dick Henston, and afore I knew how much I was hurt, I had hustled him out ; but my arm's mighty painful now, I can tell ye, sir."

" You won't be able to punish the men when they are flogged," slyly observed the doctor.

" Thank goodness for that ! I'd rather have both my arms broken than use their strength in that way. I'm on the list, ain't I, sir ? "

" Yes ; you had better keep in your cabin for a day or two."

Thompson felt quite thankful for having been crippled by the mutineers, as he would most assuredly have refused to flog the men had he been so directed. His promotion was through the kindness of one who did not use the lash, and when he accepted the appointment, Jerry little imagined he would ever be called upon to perform such a brutal duty.

The morning after the disturbance the five prisoners were brought before the commander, who, after listening to the complaint of the first lieutenant, and refusing to hear more than a few words in explanation from the men, sentenced each of them to receive forty-eight lashes, directing the punishment to take place twenty-four hours after the sentence was passed. At the appointed time the gratings were rigged, and five foolish fellows were duly made more reckless than they were before. Thompson lay upon his bed and watched the countenance of Clare, who was seated by his side, and noticed that as the sailor heard the words " one! two! " his lips moved, and it was with great difficulty that he controlled himself.

"I thought all this devil's work were over in this ship, Jerry."

"So did I, chum, or I'd never ha' taken the warrant. Why, if any one 'ud have said to me, "Thompson, before the ship arrives in England the gratings will be rigged, and the cat laid across one of the Stingers' backs," I should have laughed at 'em."

"Jerry! did you hear that poor fellow cry out?"

"Hear him! Ay, Tom, and pity him. Poor devils, they put up with ill-treatment until flesh and blood could stand it no longer, and then, not knowing any better, they mutinied. Lieutenant Cravan worked 'em up to it, knowing he had only to keep on long enough, and they'd turn at last, but I was proud to see none of the old hands jined the foolish fellows—But—who are they flogging now? why, he groans awful!"

"That's Jack Jones. I can tell his voice. He ain't a bad man."

"He'll be a devil after this, though, Tom!"

"Gracious me! why, don't it seem strange, that here we've been for months and months, and never a lash laid on a man, when a few kind words kept all as orderly as possible; now nothing is heard but abuse, and the men gets the same sort of treatment as they did from Captain Puffeigh and Lieutenant Crushe? Well, it can't last long anyhow, that's one comfort."

Under the generous Woodward the good qualities of the men were developed, and all endeavoured to show how anxious they were to please him. Yet in a few weeks all this was changed, and his excellent work undone through the ignorance of two men, who were utterly unfitted to hold command. It may be said that even had the power to flog been out of their hands, they would probably have devised other methods of torture; and a brute will always find some means of revenging himself. But one thing is certain: were the iniquitous custom completely abolished, and the cat-of-nine-tails numbered with the rack and other things of the past, *no one would dare revive its use.* It is a cruel, savage punishment, degrading to all concerned in its infliction, and there is no excuse for it that man or demon can invent.

In the U. S. Navy this degrading practice exists no longer. Congress passed a law which for ever wiped the stain from the stars and stripes, it being therein enacted, "That in no case shall punishment by flogging be inflicted, nor shall any court-martial adjudge punishment by flogging."

When the Stinger came to anchor in Simon's Bay the men were kept close prisoners on board, and, in spite of having a large amount of pay and prize-money due, many of them deserted or attempted to do so, and were brought back.

After the ship had been in harbour a few days, Mr. Thompson went on shore, and paid a visit to some of his old friends. His first call was upon Miss Pferdscreptern, he not being aware she had entered the marriage state. Mrs. Schwartz was slumbering in a rocking-chair, while a small tow-headed, sleepy-eyed edition of herself sat blinking, and dozing upon a footstool by her side. The store presented about the same appearance as when he last saw it; but the lovely fraulein had so extended in latitude that the acting boatswain found he had quite lost his reckoning. Advancing with his cap respectfully doffed, Jerry politely inquired if the lady could inform him where Miss Wallbug Pferdscreptern lived.

Mrs. Schwartz turned her head and chuckled slightly, whereupon the rolls of fat forming her neck undulated like the folds of a flag when first agitated by the breeze; and opening one eye, she slowly replied,

"She tousant pe here at all now."

"Why, when did she die?"

"She tousant get tead."

"Where is she then?"

" For why does you ask ? "

" Well, you see, marm," replied the somewhat puzzled acting warrant-officer, " I knows a great friend of hers named Jerry Thompson, and he has axed me to look her up, and tell her all about him."

" No, you tousant know Sherry Thompson. He's tead, and his drue love marry ein odder man," observed the obese lady in a dreamy sort of manner.

" Well, never mind about his being dead ; I wants to see his old friend, so please mum, I'd thank ye kindly if you'll give me her directions."

" I'm vas Wallburg Pferdscreptern, but vas marry to Captain Schwartz."

" You—Wall—bug ? "

" Yaw, I'm vas her."

" Well, hang me if I can see a liniment of her face in yours, mum. I'm Jerry Thompson."

Mrs. Schwartz managed after a great effort to produce an incredulous sort of chuckle.

" Don't you believe it, mum ? "

Slightly roused, the lady bubbled off a laugh, which started in her throat and seemed to die away in her slippers, then turned her pumpkin-like visage towards him, and slowly ejaculated, " I tousant believe ein vord of vot you spoke."

" Well, mum, they says, absence makes the heart grow fonder, isle of beauty, fare thee well ; but I must observe that any little weakness as you may have felt for me I am happy to see is quite vanished. Good-day, mum."

" Stop, mine friend! vill you trink some schnapps ? "

Jerry was about to decline the offer, but, thinking it might be considered impolite, he seated himself upon a bag of coffee, and, knowing the lady objected to long sentences, nodded an assent to her proposition.

Having filled two glasses, Mrs. Schwartz motioned to Thompson to take one ; then, without more ceremony, observed, " My lofs to you," and in a moment set the glass down empty.

" God bless me !" ejaculated her visitor.

" Yaw, yaw ! Gott pless yon, mein friend ! "

Jerry advanced to the unwieldy form, and, holding out his hand, exclaimed—
" Well, I thought to find you altered, but 'pon my word, my dear marm, you puzzles me—and that 'ere little kid, I supposes it's yourn ? "

" Yaw, dat is mine kind."

" Well, mum, I must say adoo, and can't say I feels any sentiment of affection a-knocking in my bosom when I looks at you, but I'm Jerry Thompson, although you don't know me."

" Mine friend," replied the frau, in measured tones, " you tousant hombogs me like that. Scherry was ein handsome man, and ein deal petter-looking than ever you vos pe."

" Possible, mum, werry possible ; I never was considered striking in that line—adoo, mum—may you be happy," cheerfully remarked the unabashed fellow, who then left the store, muttering,

" From all such as she,
O Lord, deliver me ; "

and in a short time found one of his old acquaintances, who invited him to dine with him that evening. Mr. Tomson had made the acting boatswain's acquaintance when the latter was living on shore with his old commander, they having formed a sort of friendship on account of the similarity of their names, and since they last met both had prospered in the world. After strolling about the place until four o'clock, Thompson returned to his namesake's store, and shortly afterwards was driven by him to his residence, where he was welcomed by his friend's wife, and two charming children.

"We often used to talk about you, and were right sorry to hear you were killed," observed the lady.

"Thankee, mam, for your kind feelings—but really I didn't deserve them, as I have never written to you, although I promised to do so."

"Your old sweetheart is married! Do you know that?"

"Yes, mam, I called to see her this morning, and, would you believe it? she said I wasn't myself, and that Scherry Thompson (as if I were named arter sherry wine) were a deal handsomer man than ever I had been—ha l ha ! ha !"

"That was scarcely polite of her, Mr. Thompson."

"Well, she didn't know me, for she spoke very kindly about me, evidently thinking of me as dead."

Thompson amused his friends by relating some of his adventures, and they enjoyed his company immensely, when about ten o'clock a servant brought in a card, and saying it was for the sailor gentleman, and a gentleman was waiting for an answer, tittered and retired from the room.

Jerry, who who had just commenced a song, apologized to his friends, and perused the card, which ran thus:—

CAPTAIN MAX SCHWARTZ,

LATE

HANS JACOB PFERDSCREPTERN,

SHIP CHANDLER,

Licensed to sell Wine and Spirits wholesale and retail.

N. B. M. S. boards all the shipping upon their entrance into the harbour.

Having read the foregoing, Thompson glanced at his friends, who were laughing most immoderately, and observed,

"What does it mean?"

"Why, it's a visit from Max Schwartz," replied the lady, somewhat recovering from her merriment.

"Shall I ask him in?"

"Certainly, certainly. He is an honest sort of man, and very German."

Jerry walked into the hall, where he encountered the gigantic form of Captain Schwartz, who, looking at him in an absent manner, mildly demanded,

"Is you Scherry Thompson?"

"Yaw, yaw, mine-ear," bawled the acting boatswain, as if hailing some one in the attic. "What you want, mine-ear? Won't you come in?"

Captain Schwartz fumbled in his coat pocket, and bringing out another card, gravely handed it to him, and exclaimed,

"I schust vants zadisfaction."

"Satisfaction?"

"Yaw; zadisfaction! I sbeaks blain, doesn't I?"

At this juncture the host came forward and invited the captain to go into the parlour, and take a drink, but the gigantic Schwartz would not move, declaring he wanted satisfaction, and not schnapps.

" Well, what sort of satisfaction do you require, and what do you want it for ? "

" I vant zadisfaction for you to go und make love to mine vrow. Yah, dat ish vot I vonts zadisfaction for," observed the burly Teuton.

Upon hearing this Jerry burst out into a loud laugh, in which his friends joined, and for some time he could not reply to the imperturbable Schwartz, who gazed on the party in a most calm and indifferent manner. At last, however, his host addressed the man in German, and demanded to know why he had thus intruded upon their privacy and disturbed his guest; upon which the big one replied in a deep, monotonous voice,

" Vell, you see, mine friend, I vos ashleep in mine ped ven Hansen mine broder gomes in, and dells me tere vash un matrose make loves to mine vrow, so I gets up, and beeps between ein knot hole in mein store, and zees mein vrow trink schnapps mit der Scherry, und den I goes and takes a trink mit Hansen, and we talks it over until he tinks I must have zadisfaction, so I takes ein Doitch book and reads, tat I has to call upon mine enemy and temand zadisfaction, and so I vound him out and comes up here."

"Well, now you had better go back again," observed the acting boatswain in a jocular manner. "I'm laid up, can't you see, and don't want to fight about a woman who ain't nothing to me. Besides, you might get injured, which would be a pity."

The captain did not deign to reply : but drawing two ancient-looking flint-lock horse pistols from the depths of his capacious pocket, and producing a couple of bullets, and a tin canister of sporting powder, gravely placed them on a table near him, and waited for an answer to his challenge.

Seeing his host was about to interfere, Jerry begged to be allowed to settle the matter himself; and bidding his hostess not alarm herself, walked towards the table, and taking up one of the pistols between his finger and thumb, coolly inquired of the placid German if it were his property.

" Yah, it ish."

" Well, then," exclaimed the now annoyed acting warrant-officer, throwing the pistol through the window, and rapidly sending the other after it; " now, my lyebeer fryend, make sail, or with my friend's permission I'll put you off the premises."

Captain Schwartz gravely picked up the bullets and powder, which he carefully placed in one of his pockets, then advancing towards Mr. Thompson, held out his hand and said he " vas zadisfied." Hearing this, the master of the house invited him to take some liquid refreshment, which offer was promptly accepted.

When the husband of Walburg became a little animated by the good liquor he imbibed, Jerry again inquired what prompted him to bring the pistols, to which the captain replied,

" Vell, Scherry, mine friend, ven I looks in the Doitcher book, I vind it says ven a man vants zadisfaction, he pest get it by calling on his enemy und offering him schoice of arms, zo I kets down ter bistols of mine vrow's vater, und as I knowed, you see, der bistols vould be no goots mitout ter powder and balls, I shust brings tem, according to what is says in ter book ; and," added the captain, with a grave shake of the head, " ter book vas right, you see, for I've got zadisfaction ;" saying which he arose, and nodding solemnly to the party, stalked out of the room.

" Is that the Cape style of getting satisfaction, friend Tomson ? " demanded Jerry.

" Possibly," laughed his friend. " The captain is contented, and so you may laugh at him. But what is that ? Why, as I live, Schwartz is hunting for his pistols in our garden. Well, he's a harmless fellow, and evidently thought if he followed the book he would be doing the correct sort of thing under the circumstances."

Thompson bade his kind entertainers good-bye, and proceeded on board his ship, and the next day told Clare of his adventure; but by some means Tom seemed to imagine that Jerry had been up to his old tricks, and consequently Mr. Schwartz had good grounds for challenging him.

"I don't understand you, Jerry. First you say that the girl didn't know you, and then that her husband wanted to fight you because you made love to her."

"Them's the facts, Tom, old man."

"Why, how could he be jealous if she didn't know you?"

"Why, you see, this is how the case stands. Captain Schwartz is a man who wants a good deal of time to calculate in. Now, this matter wanted settling at once, so he consulted a book, and being in a hurry, took the wrong receipt, and werry near got a thrashing for his pains."

"Well, that may be so," replied Clare; "but I must say that my opinion is, you was both to blame, and I advise you to leave other men's wives alone, as no good never comes of it;" saying which Tom nodded to his friend and left his cabin.

"What a world this is, thought the acting boatswain. "I only call upon an old flame in a friendly sort of way, when I get into a row with her wooden-headed husband, and my motives are wrong understood by my chum. Now, had I gone in for a regular fashionable high and mighty first-class flirtation, and offered to elope with her, or some such thundering foolishness, no one would have said a word. 'Pon my soul, I believe the straiter one keeps the worser one's off. Well, never mind; in a few weeks this voyage will be over, and then I'll marry Mary Ann Ross, and settle down into a respectable member of society, for we single men always gets blamed when we're innocent."

CHAPTER XXVI.

A few days before the ship's departure for home, a rumour was circulated on board that some relatives of the commander were to embark as passengers, and the report was confirmed by the carpenters being directed to put up temporary sleeping accommodation in the captain's cabin for a lady and gentleman, their female servant, and two little girls.

The acting boatswain was delighted to hear that a lady was coming on board, thinking Captain Tortle would, under such circumstances, abstain from inflicting any severe punishment upon his crew, and he knew her presence would in many ways ameliorate the condition of the men. He also had some curiosity to see what sort of person the servant was; for it must be confessed that although Jerry had not forgotten A-tae, he was beginning to yearn after another affinity. We do not wish to imply by this that he desired to slight Mary Ann, although probably he did not feel particularly anxious to meet her. He knew that he had promised to make her his wife upon his return, so, thinking that without doubt she had waited for him, he was determined to keep his word ; but he somewhat resented what he called her silence, never imagining it resulted from his own inattention, and objected to her having written to him in poetry, "as if she couldn't write him a letter, instead of sending that stuff." It was in this spirit he anticipated the arrival of the female servant, and he determined to enjoy his freedom while he could, thinking that once Mary Ann was Mrs. Thompson all such luxuries as affinities would be simply out of the question. Jerry was fast returning to his former general devotion to the fair sex, and, as Clare observed, "would require a deal of looking arter for the future."

About nine o'clock on the morning of departure, Captain Tortle proceeded on shore to fetch the party, and it being rather a boisterous day, the lady was afraid to venture in the gig, so the captain politely brought her off in the pinnace, a boatswain's chair being slung from the main yard, in which she was safely lifted on board without having to climb the gangway ladder.

Mr. Thompson was standing by the starboard companion when the boat arrived alongside, and although on the sick-list, he gave an eye to the rigging of the chair. Everything being adjusted, and the lady comfortably lashed in the apparatus, a boatswain's mate piped "hoist away," and in a few moments the chair rose from the pinnace, freighted with a lady in whose lap was seated a most beautiful little girl, who, instead of betraying fear at her novel position, laughed and kicked her feet about, only seeming concerned when she found herself safely landed upon the deck. The lady being released from the chair, it was again hoisted up and lowered into the boat alongside, from which it once more emerged, bearing a smart-looking French bonne, who was tightly clutching a blue-eyed baby ; and although the latter did not cry, it evidently anything but enjoyed the hoisting process.

Mademoiselle Adèle, glanced timidly down upon the deck, and seeing Mr. Thompson with his arm in a sling, naturally supposed he was " un brave," and determined to captivate his heart, thinking how nice it would be to recline her head upon his manly bosom, and how all her friends would envy her the possession of " un officier de marine," but the young woman's thoughts were brought to a somewhat abrupt conclusion by the men at the fall slacking away too rapidly, and Adèle landed upon the deck with something very like a bump, which for a moment knocked all the romance out of her, and caused her charge to scream in energetic protest.

As the bonne was being released from the chair, her employer, Major Barron, walked over the gangway, followed by Captain Tortle, who went aft and welcomed the lady to his ship; and in a few moments they were all below, praising the accommodation, and thanking their relation for his kindness in giving up so much of his cabin for their comfort. The major had been out in Africa for some years, but, having lately inherited a large estate in Kent, was returning to live upon his property, as a country gentleman should. He had delayed his departure from Simon's Town, knowing that his cousin, Captain Tortle, would touch there in the Stinger on his way home from China, and under the circumstances the admiral had politely given him special permission to embark on board his relative's ship.

Mrs. Barron was a gentle being, thoroughly devoted to her husband and children, and beloved by all who knew her, while her eldest daughter, a little darling between three and four years of age, requires something more than a brief description. A most graceful child was Miss Barbara, with a dazzling complexion, which presented a charming contrast to her dark expressive eyes; the latter seeming to search into yours with mischievous intent, and to win your affection at a glance. Her dimpled cheeks, tinged with the healthy glow of childhood, were the admiration of every one who beheld her; while her pretty rosebud of a mouth was ever ready to pout in pretended seriousness, or arrange itself for the receipt of a kiss. These charms, crowned as they were by a mass of fair curly hair, in connection with a naturally naive manner, made this baby a being to be loved, and petted; and all the officers and crew were, upon beholding her, immediately converted into ardent admirers.

Having surveyed their new quarters, the major and his wife returned to the quarter-deck, and amused themselves by watching the arrival of their baggage. Mrs. Barron seated herself upon a chair brought up for her use, and took her youngest daughter in her lap, in order that Adèle, the bonne, might be free to direct which packages were required to be placed in the cabin, while Miss Barbara begged leave to be allowed to talk with Mr. Thompson, whom she termed, in her own charmingly-original language, "the man with the curly eye." As Jerry smiled upon her, and watched her every movement in a most admiring manner, Mrs. Barron gave the required permission, and the child walked half-way towards him, pretended to look shyly upon the deck, raised her bright eyes, lowered them again,—then, with a merry little laugh, rushed to the acting boatswain, who had knelt to receive her, and throwing her arms round his neck, hugged him as if he had been an old friend.

As the baggage was being moved about the deck, and it was possible the child might get in the way, Thompson took her upon his left arm and walked over to the port side, where he seated himself upon a shot-box. Having slid down upon his knee, the little pet carefully smoothed her ruffled garments; then, with a mingled expression of delight and coquetry, looked up in his face, and said, "How do you do, sir?"

"Werry well, thankee, miss. Why, you're as pretty as a pictur. What's your name, missy?"

The artful little monkey knew she had made an impression, so she bashfully inclined her head, and murmured "Cops."

"Cops, you beauty! Why, that ain't a name, is it?"

"No," exclaimed the cherub, shaking her head, as if to say, "Now, don't you want to know all about me?"

"It's a purser's name, ain't it pretty ?"

"No," continued the wide-awake one, not exactly knowing the meaning of the word, yet almost guessing its import. "I call my-self Cops."

"Do you, beauty ? Well, any name is nice that you are called by. But what is your regular name ?"

"Barbara Barron," demurely whispered the infant, playing with Mr. Thompson's gold chain as she spoke. "My name is Barbara Barron, but I call my-self Cops."

"You're the prettiest darling I ever saw," declared her admirer. You're as beautiful as a fairy. I'll do anything for you."

At this moment her papa came on deck, and seeing her seated upon Mr. Thompson's knee, pointed her out to the captain, observing, "There's Barbara captivating the boatswain; oh, that baby, never happy but when receiving attention from the other sex." But Tortle, who considered children rather a bore, merely observed that the boatswain would take good care of her, and took no further notice of the little darling.

Seeing her father, the young lady inquired if her parrot had come on board, upon which Thompson asked her what the bird was like.

Cops looked at him with a very serious air, as if about to impart a fearful secret, then taking his whiskers she tied them under his chin, untied them again, gazed earnestly into his eyes, and replied, "Ye-es. It's a grey one, with square blume eyes, pink nose, green feet, yellow tail, and gold ear-rings;" and added, her bright eyes extending with animation, "It will bite you off if you are a naughty boy, mamma says so."

"Will it, miss ? Now don't say so. I'll be a werry good boy, and then it will leave me alone. But where are you going to keep it ?"

"I don't know," helplessly replied his enchantress. "Won't you keep it in your house, and let it live with you, and I'll come and see it ?"

The bird was just then brought over the side, and Cops pointed it out to her friend.

"Is that your polly, darling ?"

"Ye-es. Oh, don't he shiver ? he's ill."

Thompson advanced, and told the sailor who was carrying it forward to take it down to his cabin, where, much to Miss Barbara's delight, it was duly installed in a place of honour just over the acting warrant-officer's table, from which elevated position it could throw its food and flirt its water over his head and down his neck as he sat at meals; but what cared he for that? to please such a child he would willingly have roomed with an alligator.

When the bird had been fed and received it's instructions from it's mistress, Cops ordered her slave to carry her up stairs, which he accordingly did in a most submissive manner: and upon their reaching the top of the ladder, were accosted by the bonne, who had evidently been searching for the child, and was somewhat out of temper.

"Oh, mon Dieu ! Mademoiselle que vous êtes nottcy !"

"No, she ain't naughty," replied Jerry, who was exceedingly indignant at the charge. "She's as good as gold."

"Eff you zay zo, sure, I it belief !" exclaimed the bonne, darting a look of unmistakable admiration at the last speaker. "You are trop good not to say vat is not ze trof;" saying which she bade the child kiss her hand to her good friend, and darting another killing glance at the acting boatswain, seized Miss Cops, said, "Good-bye, sare," upon her own account, and disappeared below with her charge.

"Oh," mused Jerry, "that's it, is it, Miss Polly-wo-frunkzay ? Well, I can't make love to you before such a beautiful angel as that baby is ; besides, I don't think it's right. Being an engaged man, it ain't correct for me to make love to French gals." It will be seen by this that Mr. Thompson changed his ideas, as some do their political opinions, to suit the circumstances of the case.

By noon, everything being quite ready, the Stinger saluted the admiral's flag, and, having steamed through False Bay, made sail for home, all bidding adieu to Africa without the slightest regret.

About five o'clock that evening the ship was howling along under close-reefed top-sails, and Mrs. Barron and Adèle were both confined to their cabins by sea-sickness, thus giving Miss Cops an opportunity of visiting her new friend, which probably she would not otherwise have enjoyed. Before she left the cabin the child fished out a toy-basket, which she had brought on board in her hand, and after giving it a good shake, to ascertain if its contents were safe, she knocked at the outer door of the cabin until the sentry heard her and let her out; then she proceeded into the steerage, and pre-sented herself at the door of the acting boatswain's cabin, which she found closed.

Mr. Thompson had invited his friend Clare to tea with him; and when Barbara arrived at the door they were busily discussing the merits of a tin of sardines, termed by them "Sardinians," and Jerry was in the midst of an explanation, when they heard a knock at the door, upon which Tom laid his hand upon his friend's sleeve, and said, "Hush! there's some one calling Jerry."

"I expect it's little Cops," replied Thompson, picking out a grain of Indian-corn which had just been dropped into the sardines by the parrot.

"Jer-ry!" again exclaimed the impatient child, who, now hearing her friend's voice, applied her boots to the pannel right vigorously, "I want to come in."

Thompson laid down his fork, slid the door back, and beheld his little friend, who, without more ceremony, walked into the cabin, climbed upon his knee, and, point-ing to Clare, asked "if he were his father?"

"No, Miss, he's my chum."

"I'm his old friend, Miss, and has got a little boy about your age," observed Tom, who had seen the child before.

Barbara pretended not to care about Clare's boy, yet asked a dozen questions con-cerning him; the fact was, Cops had a weakness for boys, whom she considered as being specially created for her amusement. So well known was she at the Cape, that none of her young gentlemen friends would submit to her tyrannical friendship, she regarding them as slaves, who were to be petted or slapped as the whim of the moment prompted her, a course of treatment many of her older friends submitted to with great equan-imity.

After partaking of some biscuit and sardines, the child produced her basket, and begging her friends not to tell any one about it, opened the lid, when out tumbled a much-ruffled monkey, seeing which Barbara laughed and clapped her hands, whereupon the animal sat up, stretched out one leg, scratched itself, and looked up at the beams, and when the attention of those present was attracted in that direction, quietly put his hind leg in the basin near him, and grasped a lump of sugar, which he deftly conveyed to his mouth, unobserved by any one but the child, who was perfectly frantic with de-light over his achievement.

When her merriment had somewhat abated, Cops, with wide-open eyes and ex-pressive action of forefinger, solemnly enjoined her friends not to tell "no one" about her monkey, as papa and mamma thought she had left it behind her.

"Is it such a dreadful secret, that the monkey can't go on deck?" observed Tom, who began to think his friend had enough live stock in his cabin, his hair being by that time pretty well decorated with rejected Indian corn rinds. "Don't you think it would be better to let him live in the pinnace, miss?"

" No," gravely replied the child, " it mustn't live not nowhere but here, or he'll die, and the blumo mouse will come for you."

Miss Barbara believed in a highly-decorative lot of bogeys, but was, while constantly threatening others with their visits, herself perfectly indifferent to them. Jerry listened to the child with rapt attention, and pretended to credit every word she uttered ; seeing which Cops enlarged upon the blue rodent question until Clare began to imagine she was slightly touched in the brain, he never having before met with an infant who possessed such wonderful imaginative power.

"Is she all right there ? " observed Tom, touching the back of her curly hair with his forefinger.

"Right! I should rather say she is," replied her champion. " Why, she's as smart as lightning ; and what you think is nonsense is real downright cleverness, a deal beyond the understanding of you and I. Why, she can speak French ; can't you, pretty ? "

" Oui monsieur," archly replied the young lady.

By this time the monkey began to revive, the sugar which it had freely purloined having acted as a powerful restorative ; and when the child declared she must go, it leaped upon her shoulder, and snicking its sharp little teeth, offered a determined resistance ; whereupon Clare cleverly manufactured a leathern belt, which he fastened round the animal's waist, and having secured it with the chain of Thompson's old call, he drove a nail in a beam ; then taking the wriggling creature from the child's shoulder, deposited it upon a shelf where Jerry usually kept his books and other treasures.

As the monkey landed overhead, the marine sentry on duty before the door of the captain's cabin left his post and walked forward, being directed by Tortle " to find out that child and to bring her aft ; " and hearing her voice in the boatswain's cabin, he put his head inside the door and told Cope " that her mar wanted her," upon which the pretty creature kissed Mr. Thompson, blew a similar favour to Clare and the monkey, and having heard her parrot say " Good-night," trotted aft, and was soon afterwards undressed by the drowsy Adèle, who was half-dead with sea-sickness.

After they had been at sea a few days the weather moderated, and the remainder of the voyage was remarkable for its uniformly fine weather. Miss Adèle recovered from her sea-sickness and managed to get about ; and the midshipmen took every opportunity of improving their knowledge of the French language by conversing with her. Now, although this flattered the bonne exceedingly, still it was not the attention she wanted ; and the sprightly girl was somewhat chagrined by her failure in regard to Mr. Thompson, who avoided her in every possible manner. At last, one afternoon, when the men were at cutlass-drill upon the quarter-deck, Miss Adèle sauntered forward to the acting boatswain's cabin, and seeing him engaged in examining a pair of trousers, boldly advanced, and addressed him.

" Monsieur Thompe-sonne, how you do you do to-day ? "

Jerry whistled softly, and pretended not to hear her, upon which she stood in his light, and, smiling on him, repeated the question.

" Ah ! how-de-do, may-dam-moselle ? "

" Monsieur Thompe-sonne, will you please be so kind as to tell me vare my malle-my tronke is? "

Jerry looked at his garment, then glanced at the speaker, as much as to imply that he thought her very bold to speak to him when he was engaged in such a business ; and, touching his injured arm, informed her that he was on the sick-list.

"Oh, are you sicke, poor theeng ? I am varrai sorry. Vill you allow me to attend to you ? I vill soon your arm make vell."

" Jerry got up, meditating a bolt forward, but the bonne was too clever for him ; as upon his rising she placed a hand upon each side of the door, and looking at him in a most affectionate manner, softly repeated, " I am varrai sorry."

Adèle was dressed in a most killing costume, and the effect of her speaking grey eyes upon his susceptible heart resembled that of the sun upon ice ; so Jerry stuffed the garment he was holding into his chest, and, approaching her politely, yet half reluctantly, begged she would withdraw, observing that ladies wern't allowed forward.

Seeing that he feared she would get herself in trouble with her mistress, the bonne altered her tactics, and with a sweet smile declared she had no intention of entering his cabin, but that all she required was the loan of a chair ; upon hearing which Mr. Thompson lifted out the best one he possessed, and having dusted it, motioned her to take it, after which he retired to his den.

Miss Adèle took out some knitting, and placing the chair exactly opposite the acting boatswain's cabin, worked away like a machine, much to the admiration of a group of marines, who were watching her proceedings with the greatest attention. The bonne did not lack admirers, as she well knew ; but the man she almost worshipped, " the charming Monsieur Thompesonne," was unkind to her.

Finding she meant to blockade him, Jerry turned his attention to cleaning the animals, when the quick eye of the French girl discovered the monkey, and she determined to thaw her cold idol by threatening him with exposing the child's secret ; so she started, and exclaimed with an affected little scream, " Oh, Monsieur Thompe-sonne ! vare deed you get zat monquai ? "

" It's mine, miss ; I've had it a long time," he coolly replied.

Adèle got up, walked to the cabin door, surveyed the animal with a slightly con-temptuous air, and observed, " Zat is Meece Barbe's monquai."

"Oh no, it ain't ; it ain't the little gal's ; it's mine."

"Oh no, Monsieur, I know zat monquai ; it my fingare bited too many times. Her papa zay it vas to be kill, but one leetle niggare boy he zave it, and now meece hide it here—I must tell her papa of it."

" For goodness' sake, don't do that ! " whispered the fellow, quite forgetting in his anxiety to shield his favourite from trouble, that probably her papa only deprived his child of her plaything because he thought it could not be accommodated on board. " Oh, please don't tell on the pretty baby."

" Adèle walked into the cabin, gazed almost fiercely in his face, and exclaimed, " Vy should I hold my tongue ? you do not care for me. Vy should I do so for ze meece ? "

" Phew ! " whistled Jerry, seeing in a moment what the girl meant. " Why, my dear may-dam-mosselle, I'll do anything to please you, if you won't split about the monkey."

" I do not vant to spleet ze monquai—mais I vant ze leetle politeness from yourself, Monsieur Thompe-sonne. Do you like me ? No ! Ees it zat I am zo uglee donc ! "

" Lord bless you, miss, I'm in a perfect fever about you. But please get out of my cabin, the engineers are a-looking over here, and making fun of us."

" Pah ! what you care for zengeneers ! If zey laugh, you can blow zem viz ze boxe ; you are brave. Vous etes un vrai Hercule ! "

" Anything you like, miss, if you'll only get out of my cabin."

" Monsieur Thompe-sonne," cried the girl, now thoroughly roused, and indifferent to any consequences to herself or the man she admired, " Ger-rrr-ai, do you lofe me ? "

" Lord bless you, miss, I adore you ; but do, if you please, get out of my cabin."

14

After much persuasion she finally left his presence, but not until she had extorted from him the word "yes," in reply to her inquiry, "Do you lofe me?" It appeared that she had, from some French novel, taken the idea that all the English law required was the repeating of the word "yes" on the part of the man; evidently the author must have taken a passage from the marriage service and introduced it in his story as "a manner and custom of the John Boule," as after Jerry had said that word she became as submissive as a slave, and that evening told her mistress, in great confidence, "zat she was going to be married to ze brave Monsieur Thompe-sonne as soon as zey arrived."

As the time passed Miss Barbara became known to all the crew, and it was a sight that would have moved a misanthrope to see the pretty infant tyrannizing over the men in her tiny way. As to Thompson, he was her slave, and poured out the choicest treasures he possessed for her amusement, it being nothing uncommon to see Cops sitting upon the image of the God Buddha, and nursing the God Fo, whom she called "a nice fat little boy," while an admiring crowd of sailors watched her footsteps, and removed every rope yarn from her path whenever she honoured them by extending her promenade round the forecastle.

Jerry was exceedingly particular how he treated the bonne; in fact, upon all occasions he what the Irish term "blarnied" her, in order that she might keep Miss Cop's secret; while she, imagining he was lawfully engaged to marry her according to English custom, gave him a little latitude, and overlooked many small offences which otherwise she would have resented.

"Upon my word, you get more beautiful every day," he observed to Adèle one morning when she brought Cops forward to feed her bird. "I wonder how it is you haven't got married before this?"

"Oh, cher Ger-r-r-r-ai, I vait for you. I know alway zat you live some-me-ware in ze world."

"Did you, miss? Ah! I see. You're one of them what's-his-names wot believe in having another of the opposite sex always a cruising about in search of them. I've never come across one of your specree before. How do you like it?"

"Oh, I lof you, Ger-r-r-r-ai, and vot do I vant more?" replied the girl, darting a sentimental glance at him over her shoulder as she walked away.

"A deal that you won't get, I reckon," quietly observed the acting warrant-officer, as he watched her across the steerage. "I'll keep on at this game until you lands, and then adoo to polly-woo-frunks; there's too much of the rile tiger about your style to suit me."

One afternoon, as the ship was running as upright as a dart, Cops was permitted to go forward as far as the booms, and of course was attended by her friend; and as this was to be his last day on the list, he had devoted nearly the whole of it to the child. After telling her some marvellous stories, which the clever "dot" perfectly understood, he told her what the guns said at Canton, and invented a new speech for each piece, Jerry being never tired of talking to her; when suddenly she declared she was weary, and made him sit down upon a shot box while she told him a story; seeing which a number of men who were lying upon the deck got up and watched the child, as if they could have worshipped her.

"Who is those men?" inquired the little autocrat, pointing to the sailors. "May I play with them?"

The captain and first lieutenant being below, and the men off watch, Thompson thought it would be no harm to indulge his idol, so the sailors were informed they might approach the child, upon which she assumed a severe expression of face and sent them all in the corner, while she plundered her attendant of his silk handkerchief, which she wrapped round a gun-chock and carefully nursed in her lap. After having amused herself for some time, she made them all sit in a circle, then with bated breath told them of the "blume" mouse.

The sailors looked at each other and laughed, upon which, thinking they were not sufficiently attentive, she ordered them all out of her house, and having sent her only love, Jerry, into the corner, drew the handkerchief more tightly round the gun-chock, and bade her baby go to sleep before the mouse came out of the gun. Thompson stood with his face to the ship's side, looking in Barbara's eyes, the very perfection of a naughty boy, when suddenly a hand was laid upon her shoulder, and she heard the voice of Captain Tortle, who roughly told her to go below, as mamma wanted her.

Now, Miss Barbara was an exceedingly dignified child; and Tortle having addressed her as youngster, she pretended not to have heard his speech, but proceeded to scold her naughty boy, who, unmindful of the commander's presence, was still "in the corner."

"Hush, sir!" she observed, when the captain again spoke to her, and added, looking up in his face,—her eyes dilated with excitement,—"Don't you see my baby is asleep? I'm samed of you!"

Hearing this, Tortle, who could not appreciate the pretty little comedy, rudely picked up the child, and carried her down to the cabin; and, upon stooping to ask her for a kiss, received a severe smack on the face from the indignant little lady, who immediately afterwards wisely sought refuge in the folds of her mamma's dress, where she indulged in a good cry.

Tortle rubbed his face with his handkerchief, and pretended to be amused, while he inwardly vowed he would never touch her again. Poor baby! 'twas very thoughtless of him to wake her so suddenly from her dream of pleasure, and he fully deserved the blow she gave him. Upon seeing her sister in tears, Marie, the younger one, joined in the out-burst, and cried "Go away" to the naughty captain, who thereupon beat a retreat to the upper deck.

When their grief was somewhat abated, their gentle mother, with solemn voice, told them how wrong it was for a little girl to do such a sad unladylike act as to smack the captain, and how she feared that Barbara would never become an angel if she did not alter her behaviour,—upon which the darling naively declared she would rather be Cops and smack him again than be an angel and not do it. This irreverent reply so shocked her mother that she reported the circumstance to her papa, who thereupon seized the infant, and smothered her in kisses; when the artful puss, finding him in a good humour, proceeded to tell him about her monkey, and how kind dear, dear Thompson had been. Adèle heard this, and did not feel pleased with the disclosure, but comforted herself with Jerry's having said yes, and looked forward to becoming "Mrs. Thompe-sonne" with as much confidence as ever.

The day after this Mrs. Barron had an opportunity of speaking to the acting boatswain, who, almost against the wish of the doctor, was now once more on duty, and after a little conversation she sounded him about Adèle.

"Why, bless your heart, mam, I don't mean anything to the young woman," and then he told her all about her threat of exposing the presence of the monkey, softening it down, however, as much as possible, and blaming his own dull head more than the girl's foolishness.

"You're not married, are you, Mr. Thompson?"

"Me, mam? what makes you think that?"

"Why, I have heard you mention your little boy."

"Do you know Clare, mam ? Tom, we calls him, Miss Cops knows him," he added, smiling at the child, who was seated on his arm. "Well, mam, that poor fellow has a wife and a child and I've a life-interest in their baby, that is, if poor Tom don't live, I shall help bring him up, as I knows if he dies his wife won't be long a follerin' of him, as they loves each other truly and dearly."

"Why, you cannot attend to the boy when you are at sea, can you, Mr. Thompson ? "

"I don't mean to foller the sea any longer. I've a poor old mother who is in an almshouse, and I'm going to take her out and stay by her in future ; and then if anything occurs to poor Tom and his wife, I can take the boy home with me."

"Where does your mother reside ? "

"At Nonnington, Kent, mam. I was born there."

"Why, that is near my husband's estate ; I must talk to him about you."

That evening the major sent for Mr. Thompson, having first obtained full particulars about the acting-warrant from the captain and doctor, the latter gentleman being a great friend of his. After putting a few questions to Jerry, he informed him that he had determined to pension off the steward now managing his estate, as he knew he was too old to agree with his ideas as to its future government, and that having observed Mr. Thompson was gifted with great tact and had a way which pleased him, he would give him a house and garden rent free, with coal and wood, and a salary of eighty pounds for the first year, if he would in return give all his time and best services to him as steward, adding, "I know you will quickly learn what is necessary, and will suit me far better than a man who has been brought up to the business."

Jerry stood quite dumbfounded for a moment, then in a few words thanked his benefactor, adding, as if that thought were uppermost, "I shall often be able to see your little daughter, which pleases me as much as anything."

Great was Miss Barbara's joy when she heard that her friend was to live near them on shore, and she immediately suggested to her papa the propriety of building a sugar-candy house for Mr. Thompson's mother, which proposition her father gravely promised to take into consideration.

Tom Clare was delighted with his friend's good fortune, little thinking that he intended to share it with him ; but when they chatted it over that evening, Jerry offered Tom a home in his house, saying, the country air and the society of his wife would soon bring him round. Visions of happy tea-parties under the trees in the orchard, for Thompson knew his future home well, and of little Tom learning to be a farmer, while Polly was to milk the cows, and Clare to see after the flower garden ; these pleasant thoughts busied the friends until they heard a cry along the decks of "light on our starboard bow," and they knew that they had once more arrived off their native land. Upon going on deck, they saw the Start light blinking across the water, and Jerry pressed his friend's thin hand, and laughingly observed that in a few days they would be on the right side of that light.

Clare soon after this went forward, and Mr. Thompson was left to his own thoughts, but in a few moments he became aware that Adèle was standing near him, and to his surprise found she was weeping.

"Oh, Monsieur Thompe-sonne, how could you trifle vith me like zat you have did ? I lofe you so mooche, and you say to madume you do *not* lofe *me*."

Thompson looked at the girl with astonishment, then desiring her to wait where she was for a moment, descended into his cabin. After a short delay he returned to the deck bearing in his hands a small box which he handed to the bonne, saying, "Addel-ly ! I knows you ladies are fond of gold chains. I knows, too, that I have been rather too soapy with you, but if you'll say you forgive me, as you knows I did it for the pretty one's sake, I'll give you that."

Adèle walked aft and descended to the cabin, where she examined the chain, which was of solid gold, and the one that Jerry had looted from the pirate Seh-wang. After carefully weighing it in her hands, and reflecting for a few moments, the bonne returned to the deck, and having found out the patient Thompson, informed him " that it was verray good, she vas content," and added in an undertone, " Je voudrais etre trompée, tous les jours à ce prix là !"

CHAPTER XXVII.

THOSE who have never been away from their native land, can hardly imagine the intense excitement which prevailed on board the Stinger, when the word was passed along the deck that the Start had been made. "Land ho!" shouted the boys who had remained up to get the first glimpse of the long-watched-for light. "Tumble out, chaps, and see the land." Hearing this, the ordinary seamen and boys of the watch below turned out and went on deck; while the older men of the crew, after vainly pretending not to care, at last followed their example. Under other circumstances the latter would have kept their beds until the time came for them to go on duty, but the Start light was to them a proof that they would shortly be free men again : and, leaving the snug shelter of their hammocks, they crawled on deck, and after gazing at the bright beam, fell to at discussion as eagerly as their more youthful shipmates.

"That ain't the Start light; it's the Shambles," growled an aged tar, who, wrapped up to the eyes in a lammy frock, strongly resembled a polar bear.

"I tell ye it's the Start," urged another speaker; "I was borned not far off it, and I ought to know."

"You was borned?" contemptuously observed the old man who had first spoken; "you, was borned? Well, I suppose every one has been borned as well as you. But I say it's the Shambles, and I don't care a button who says it isn't."

"There's the Portland light," cried another; and so they made out each beacon as it came in view, and yarned away the time utterly regardless of its being their watch below.

The "watch on deck" worked like lightning; and Tortle, who was on the bridge with Cravon, observed they were as smart a crew as he had ever commanded.

"Yes," sneered the first lieutenant, "they can move quick enough, the lubbers, now they smell the land; they are not as smart as this in a gale of wind."

Forward, the gun-ports of the forecastle were swarming with the watch below and idlers, and it was amusing to hear their ideas as to what they would do with their money when they were paid off; the opinions of the old petty officers being listened to with the utmost attention and respect by the boys, who believed their mess-bullies possessed the most profound knowledge of nautical human affairs.

"I say, Bill Farley, won't your old woman be in Portsmouth to meet you?" observed a leathern-visaged individual to a fat old boatswain's yeoman, who, with round figure and small head, looked like a turtle standing on its hind fins.

"She *will* be there, me hearty—trust her. My old gal has never missed a voyage but once, and then *I lost my way*, and by the time I reached her I had only a penny in my pocket. Ha, ha, ha!"

This being the signal for a laugh, the spectators joined in the roar, but the moral of the story was not lost on the boys, who whispered to each other, "Ah, old Bill's bin a gay one, ain't he?"

"How are you goin' to spend your whack, Joseph?" demanded another old salt, addressing a marine who was seated on the starboard side of the forecastle. "How are you a goin' to get rid of all your fen-pinners, chummy?"

"Me, old George? Why, I'm going to buy my discharge, and mean to emigrate to Awstraylea. I'm tired of soldiering."

"*Are* you, Joseph?" continued his friend somewhat sarcastically. "I know what sort of Stralia you'll reach. You'll go ashore, get a pint of beer, go up to the barracks, go to the canteen, treat a lot of fellers who is as greedy as sharks, get into a glorious state, have your furlough given you, go on a bender, be in a werry tight state for a week, wake up some mornin' to find you haven't got a mag, have a pint on tick, get histed out of the house and fetch up in barricks agin jest in time to larn your new drill. That'll be your Straylia. No, Joseph, you belongs to the sarvice, you don't know nothing outside of the sarvice, and the sarvice will keep you, mark me!"

The marine growled out a reply, saying that he sposed he weren't a born fool, and knowed what to do with his own; but the audience only shook their heads and looked pityingly upon him. Their oracle had spoken, and they firmly believed that Joseph would do exactly as George predicted.

Towards midnight some of the watchers began to get tired of looking out for the lights, and the more prudent went down below when the watch was called at eight bells; but many of them were far too much excited to go to sleep, so they kept on deck until the morning dawned, and the grey fog lifted and showed them the white cliffs. They believed that the hour of freedom was at hand; and although the "iron grasp" was light upon them, many of the lads determined never to let it close round them again. Unlike the marine, they were intelligent fellows, who having once felt what the tyranny of a man-of-war was like, knew too much to place themselves within its cruel power a second time; and although "continuous and general service men," many of them were, soon after the Stinger was paid off, ploughing the seas in merchant-ships bound for America or the colonies. It was this anticipation which excited them, and kept them on deck through that night. They remembered Clare's punishment, Dunstable's death, and the other atrocities which had been perpetrated on board by cruel men in command, and all their subsequent good treatment by Captain Woodward did not prevent them from thinking bitterly of their slavery, particularly as a tyrant had followed up his too brief term of strict but just command.

The Stinger steamed up the Channel, and in due time arrived at Spithead, where she saluted the admiral's flag, and having discharged her powder, entered Portsmouth harbour, preparatory to being paid off, and by five o'clock on Saturday evening was made fast to the wharf, upon which swarmed a crowd of relations and friends, ready to fall upon the crew, and, if not prevented by the police, to carry them off piecemeal

Major Barron had landed when the ship was at Spithead, and upon the Stinger arriving alongside the wharf was waiting with a carriage ready to take his family to the George Hotel. Great was the sensation when the mob beheld a lady led on shore by Captain Tortle, followed by a French bonne carrying a pretty blue-eyed baby; but when Cops made her appearance in the arms of Mr. Thompson—and that charming young lady kissed her hand to the crowd—all the mothers present, and there were not a few, cried "Bless her little heart?" and the spinsters, and other females, looked at the innocent face, thought of their own childhood, and, bad· as some of them were, said, "Pretty darling, aint she lovely?" the acting-boatswain by his looks almost resenting any encomiums passed by the latter speakers.

When Captain Tortle had landed her mamma into the carriage, he turned to Cops as if intending to take her from her friend, but she resolutely refused to allow him to touch her, upon seeing which the mob laughed and the women cried, "Well done, pretty dear!" Tortle's disposition being known to the people, who were well posted in the peculiarities of most naval officers of rank. Mr. Thompson having placed his tyrant in the carriage, was rewarded with a kiss, after which, to the further admiration of the crowd, the Major and Mrs. Barron shook hands with him, and the vehicle was driven away amid the deafening cheers of the mob, who considered such an act of condescension required a special mark of their approbation.

When the passengers had departed, Captain Tortle returned to his ship and informed the crew that, in consequence of some orders received from the Admiralty but a few moments before, it was decided that the ship was to proceed to Woolwich to pay off, and as it would prevent a great deal of trouble, the admiral had ordered that the men were not to have leave, as the ship was to start early on Monday morning, but from 8 o'clock A.M. until 8 o'clock P.M. the next day their friends and relations would be allowed to come on board to see them.

This information was anticipated by the crew, who were, upon the ship's arrival alongside the wharf, told of the facts by the mob, who seemed to know all about it. So upon receiving their letters and getting sundry presents from their friends, and a supply of beer on board, they kept tolerably quiet, and the dockyard police having cleared the wharf, by eight o'clock that night, the Stinger was as still as a graveyard.

At six o'clock the next morning the crew were turned out, and after they had scrubbed and washed decks, stowed their hammocks, put all the ornamental work round the wheel, capstan, and gangways, and generally decorated the ship, they were piped to church, and for the first time since the battle of Chow-chan received the benefit of the regular clergy, and as their thoughts wandered elsewhere, proved anything but a devotional flock. It is true under the generous Woodward the prayers of the Established Church were regularly read to them once a week, but "The Articles of War" having been substituted for religious service by Tortle, the crew had fallen into indifference, and the only affect produced by the clergyman was a tendency to doze on the part of the boys, while the men looked as if they were swearing instead of repeating the responses.

Church being over, the pipe went for breakfast, and various presents received from friends on shore were duly paraded in the messes. One old quarter-master produced a plum-pudding large and heavy enough to give an elephant a fit of indigestion; while another served out red herrings to all his less fortunate messmates who were unprovided with wives to send them off such delicacies. Some paraded fat pork sausages or handkerchiefs full of apples, while many a sly nip of grog, sent on board in skins secreted in the food, was swigged by the knowing ones, who imagined the nasty stuff to be nectar, because it was surreptitiously obtained. Every one was in good humour, and, taking it altogether, considered the admiralty order to stop their leave was a wise precaution.

About a quarter before eight o'clock all those who claimed to be the wives or relatives of the Stingers were let into the dockyard, and a mob of clamorous expectants swarmed upon the wharf, all eager to see their friends or to make friends with those they saw on board.

"Vy, Shack," screamed one gentleman, whose every-day occupation consisted in selling sham jewellery or ready-made clothes to half-intoxicated sailors. "Vy, Shack, ma poy, how are you?"

"Not much better for seeing of you, Peter," replied the man thus addressed. "I don't want no more of your tin watches and baggy trowsers this voyage;" hearing which, Peter turned his attention to another sailor.

A number of policemen now arrived, and having forced their way through the crowd, formed a half circle round the top of the gangway ladder, in order to keep the unruly among the mob from pouring on board the ship *en masse*.

Precisely as the dockyard bell struck eight the first lady was passed on board, and being rather short-sighted, she, much to her husband's annoyance, saluted the wrong sailor, which caused no little merriment among the others, and made her partner growl out, "I say, Peggy, when you've done with George Town per-haps you'll give me a buss."

"Ladies first," cried the sergeant of marines, who, with the ship's corporal, kept the girls from thrusting each other off the gangway into the water. "Just ease a little, mum, or you'll squeeze that ere infant's life out," he added, as one brazen-faced woman, who declared she was the wife of Mister Stebbings, A. B., pushed herself past him, and drove her way down the ladder.

Unfortunately for the creature, the sergeant laid hold of the child, and finding it was a dummy, rudely snatched it from her arms, whereupon the ladies on the wharf set up a howl of indignation.

"You brute!" cried one, "to serve a baby in that manner."

"The wretch!" shrieked another.

"Murder!" screamed the lady who was thus abruptly deprived of her *infant*.

The sergeant, after compelling the indignant woman to retrace her steps up the ladder, handed her over to the police, and proceeded to strip the wrappings off the dummy, which process at last brought to light a large-sized square bottle of "Hollands," seeing which the—*mother* swooned in the policeman's arms, and was carried to the dock gates, where they laid her outside to come to as best she might. We need scarcely say she recovered as soon as she found herself out of custody.

The sergeant's action was quite correct, for were women allowed to carry spirits on board a man-of-war the men would be simply unmanageable, and the most strict search has to be instituted to prevent liquor being thus introduced by disreputable characters, who as long as they can pillage the sailors do not hesitate to supply them with the most poisonous stuff.

In any cases the various friends were required to name their relatives before they were allowed on board, although it was not always possible to get them to speak, as among this disreputable mob were many genuine mothers, wives, and sweethearts, and some of those became so agitated at the sight of their relations, that they could not speak, but would point with their fingers to the loved ones, and with mute earnestness prove their claims were genuine.

There was much laughter when an old woman would frantically embrace her equally old man. The aged lovers in many cases joined in the roar; but now and then the faces of all, both on shore and on board, were saddened, as some poor creature would come forward and ask to see a husband whom she would never meet again in this world.

Just after the fictitious baby had been disposed of a respectably attired girl passed down the gangway ladder, and seeing Mr. Thompson, with whom she formerly had been acquainted, she laughingly asked him where her Jem was.

"Your Jem, mam? Jem what?"

"Why, don't you know me now you're promoted?" (She saw he was no longer a common sailor.) "Why, Jem Shaw," replied the woman, her mouth moving nervously, as if fearing to hear some ill tidings.

"God bless you, poor soul!—Come down into my cabin," said the sympathizing acting warrant.

The woman followed him as if in a dream; and when she reached the cabin, grasped his arm and demanded if her Jem were alive or not, bidding him out with it, and not kill her with waiting.

Thompson turned his face away, and in a husky voice told her that poor Jem was dead, and had been buried out in China.

"Oh! oh!" wailed the poor creature; "my poor Jem—oh, my poor dear man!" and then she fell fainting upon his arm.

Thompson called some women who were sitting happily by the side of their husbands, and told them to see to the helpless girl. Then, having directed them to give her a little brandy, the sympathetic fellow went on deck.

After a time the poor creature revived, and, sending for Mr. Thompson, was escorted by him to the dock gates, her eyes dry and tearless, and her heart feeling like a stone. Upon parting Jerry respectfully bade her good-bye, when she turned her wan face towards his, and, having thus mutely expressed her thankfulness, walked slowly away.

This was not the only case where poor women came to meet their relations, and found they were no more, and the scenes upon those occasions were most heart-rending. In this, as in all other phases of life, misery and happiness being side by side.

By noon the ship was completely crammed with the sailors' visitors, many persons suddenly finding relations of whose existence they had previously been unaware. Some of the boys had no less than seven uncles and aunts, and one old topman was claimed by five wives. These were, of course, exceptions, but upon an average the sailors had ten relatives a-piece, not less than five of these being well-known dealers in clothing, who showed their joy at meeting their "tear friends" by repeatedly measuring them for fashionable suits.

"Shest let me measure you round the vaist vonce again, Villiam, ma poy," urged the irrepressible Peter, who had somehow contrived to get on board. "I vant our verkmen to fit you like a glove, ma poy."

The sailor so addressed submitted to the measuring process for the fourth time, but, notwithstanding this, he had a suit of clothes sent to him at Woolwich, which would have fitted a man twice his size; but having foolishly paid for them beforehand, had no remedy, so he sold them to a gentleman who strongly resembled Peter, of whom he, sailor-like, ordered another suit.

Clare had received a short note from his wife, and a portrait of his boy, and the poor fellow was busily employed all the afternoon in writing a long letter to Polly, in which he communicated his friend's good fortune, and informed her of his intention of paying Jerry a visit when the latter should be settled in his new home.

Upon the day after they arrived in harbour Mr. Thompson received the following unsigned note; and, as he imagined that it came from Mary Ann, it somewhat revived his feeble attachment.

> "*No.* 34, *West Delacour Street,*
> "*Portsmouth.*
>
> "DEAR MR. THOMPSON,
>
> "We shall be pleased to see you to tea to-night, at five o'clock."

His heart now beat quickly, and a hundred little reminiscences of his old sweetheart came into his mind. "Well, she is right not to be too forward; she is a good girl," he thought; "so I'll go on shore and pop the question this evening, and if all goes smoothly she can join me at Woolwich, and we will get married. Then I shall be done for, and can start life ashore as a respectable individual."

About four o'clock Jerry, having dressed himself in his best uniform, left the ship in company with the carpenter and gunner, and after partaking of a friendly glass of ale, the trio parted, he to ascertain his fate, they to visit their friends and relations.

Mr. Thompson walked quickly to the street, which was in, to him, a new locality; and having peered at the numbers on one side of the way, was returning down the other when a door opened, and Mary Ann stepped forth, bearing in her arms a chubby-looking baby, who, seeing Jerry, crowed, kicked its little legs, and cried "Dad-da;" when, without waiting for a recognition from her, the excited fellow rushed forward, and catching Mary Ann round the waist, imprinted a hearty smack upon her lips, and cried, "Why, Mary Ann, my dear gal, how are you?"

"Gr-r-acious evengs! why, it's Jerry!" said the blushing girl. "Why—how—did —you—come— here?"

Hearing this a smartly-dressed young man stepped out upon the pavement, and seeing the visitor, coolly walked up to him, and taking his hand, said, "Welcome home, old chap, she's a waiting for you up-stairs."

By this time Mary Ann had somewhat recovered her composure; so, turning to her old flame, she welcomed him home; then, with a sly twinkle in her eyes, begged to introduce him to her husband, Mr. Joseph Jenkins.

"Why, d-d-dear me, if it ain't the carpenter!" cried the astonished acting-warrant; "and that little cheerup, is he or she your'n?"

Mary Ann nodded, and smilingly observed that they had another at home—a boy—older than that one, and they had named him Jerry, out of compliment to him, thinking he was dead.

"So you're married, and have got a family, and a good husband, have you, Mary Ann?"

"Yes, Mr. Thompson, as good a husband as ever a woman were blessed with."

"Being so, I can't marry you," he continued in a dreamy manner. "But, Mrs. Mary Ann, as I'm going to get married somehow, can you recommend me to a nice young gal; I feel mighty lonely now you're out of the way."

Mrs. Jenkins laughed, and having shaken hands with him, pointed to the sign over the shop before which they were standing, and observed, "There's a lady who will be proud to see you, Mr. Thompson;" then motioning to her husband to say good-bye, she passed up the street.

"Mrs. Shever, Dressmaker, Ladies' own materials made up," read the somewhat bewildered Thompson. "Well, she always was a kind-hearted one, so I'll call upon her and tell her how I am situated."

At that moment a smart servant-girl peeped forth as if to reconnoitre, but seeing Mr. Thompson withdrew again, and shut the door with a bang; upon which Jerry pulled the bell and lifted the knocker, directions to that effect being given over the handle of the former.

"After some delay the domestic appeared at the door, and, looking at the visitor as if she had never seen him in her life, sweetly murmured, "What do you want, sir?"

"Does Mrs. Shever live here?"

"Yes sir."

"Is she at home?"

"I don't know, sir. Will you please give me your card?"

Now, Jerry thought it rather a joke for Mrs. Shever to require her visitors to send up their cards, so, although he knew better, he pulled out an article bearing the name of "Edwin Lass, Bootmaker. Repairs neatly executed on the shortest notice." and having deposited it in a plated salver, which the girl produced from under her apron, was requested to walk in and wait in the "drawering room," until she found out if missis was at home.

Thompson seated himself on a sofa and laughed, as he thought how very stylish

Mrs. Shever had become, when all of a sudden the door was opened and in walked the boatswain's widow, who without more ado tottered towards him, uttered a little squeal, and fainted in his arms.

"Poor creature! why, it's too much for her," he cried. "Here, Mary—Eliza—what's your name? bring some vinegar and brown paper."

Finding the smart servant was out of hearing, and Mrs. Shever's rosy lips being in close proximity to his own, Mr. Thompson thoughtlessly imprinted a kiss upon them! and the first gentle pressure proving ineffectual, repeated the application until the lady found he began to weary, upon which she recovered from her faint, and allowed him to lead her to the sofa.

After passing her right hand several times across her forehead, as if recovering from a dream, the boatswain's widow suddenly ejaculated, "Am I awake?"

"I believe you are, my dear Mrs. S.," replied the somewhat amused sailor. "Would you like a little cold water sprinkled over your face?"

"Oh, dear me, no, Mr. Thompson," cried she, fearing he would spoil her dress. "I'm all right now; I fear I fainted."

"You went off like a shot, mum; but I'm glad you're all right, as I ain't up to this sort of performance. I were just a going to burn them things under your nose," cried he pointing to some peacock's feathers which ornamented a mirror hanging over the fireplace. "I've heard they are first-rate for lightstayricks."

"Can he be indifferent to me? No, surely he will be only too glad to marry me," thought the boatswain's widow, "but I'll be more distant, and draw him out."— "Would you like to have some music, Mr. Thompson?"

"Werry much indeed, mum. Have you a hand organ, or do that work by machinery?" inquired Jerry, pointing to a cottage piano, which stood on the other side of the room.

Mrs. Shever gave a peculiar little laugh, as if to hide her chagrin; then rising majestically, rustled to the piano, and having perpetrated some preliminary attempts, at last managed to finger her way through a simple air, although, in spite of her endeavours to check herself, she would every now and then audibly utter "one! two! three!" which caused Mr. Thompson to remark that she might just as well give him the whole of the words out loud, as he was fond of hearing a lady sing.

Having concluded the performance, which was the result of long study on her part, and much patience on that of her music mistress, the boatswain's widow returned to the sofa, and, notwithstanding the entreaty of her visitor, wisely declined to repeat what he called the ceremony.

"Now, Mrs. Shever wanted to bring Jerry to a declaration; and, as she had invited Mary Ann and her husband to return to supper, having no doubt but that Mr. Thompson would propose to her before they arrived, began to get a little fidgetty, so, in order to lead him on, she asked why he had called upon her.

"Well, you see, my dear Mrs. Shever, wot with that poor gal a fainting in my cabin this morning—"

"Oh, false man, false man!" murmured the lady, bashfully reclining her head upon his shoulder.

"No, marm, I were not false."

"I know that, I know that. You are too noble, too generous to be false. It was her own fault."

"No, it warn't. How could she help losing her husband?"

"Oh," cried Mrs. Shever, seeing she had made a mistake, "of course she couldn't help it, poor soul."

"Well, first that occurred, and made me feel as unhappy as if she had been my own wife."

"You ain't married, are you?" exclaimed the buxom widow, raising her head in alarm.

"Why, bless your kind heart, no. I've come here to ask your advice. I find Mary Ann hasn't kept; so, knowing you are a motherly sort of a soul, I come to ask you what you would advise me to do."

Mrs. Shever did not much relish the term "motherly sort of a soul;" but, relying upon her powers of entanglement, she let him run on.

"I'm young and have good prospects, and all I want is to meet with a girl who is honest and good, and who will be as true to me as I will be to her. I've got a first-rate berth on shore, and can afford to keep a wife, so I means to have one. I have loved a woman, who is now better off, in such a way as I shall never love again." Here Jerry's eye moistened a little. "But I promise that whoever I gets married to now I will stick to, and do my best to make her happy. But one thing I must bargain for. I must take care of my little boy, and she must be one as will look kindly on him."

"I'll forgive you that," cried the delighted widow. "Oh, Jerry, there ain't many men like you. The boy will not stand in the way."

"When his poor father dies—"

"I hope he'll be spared many years. Oh, Jerry, don't talk about dying upon such a happy occasion as this," cried the sympathetic woman, the tears streaming down her face.

"But, my dear creature, we must look forward to it; life is short, and we must prepare for such things;" saying which he drew forth his bandana, and gently wiped her eyes. "I've promised to be a father to poor little Tom, and I'll keep my word; and my wife must be a mother to him."

"She will, she will do that," sobbed the happy one through her tears, although she inwardly hoped the child was old enough to walk, as she hated babies.

"And now you knows how I am situated. Do, my dear Mrs. Shever, tell me what you think I ought to do; and if you knows a gal as will suit me, introduce me, and I'll be your everlasting debtor."

The boatswain's widow was somewhat nonpulsed by his obtuseness, but knowing it was "now or never," she motioned him to take a seat before her; then, averting her face, spoke as follows:—

"Je—hem! Mr. Thompson, I have long looked forward to this here day, and anticipated the pleasure of your society." (This was correctly delivered, all but the *here*, according to "The book of Etiquette for Modern society.") "I knowed" (here she forgot her text, but feeling equal to the occasion, spoke her own sentiments) "you were always a manly, beautiful-disposed, noble, generous, A 1, first-rate young feller, and I felt very much disgusted with some people when I found they didn't wait for you, and that it was throwing purl before swine for you to be constant to them."

"You're werry good, marm." Jerry winced a little at the last part of her remark.

"I thought, here is a generous heart wot will be chucked away on some good-for-nothing baggage as soon as he lands if I don't do my best for him."

"How kind of you!" murmured Jerry, looking at the averted face with a somewhat astonished air. "Go on, marm; go on. I can bear it."

"Well, my dear Je—Mr. Thompson, knowing, as I said before, that some one had, although I say it of my own sister, married a common carpenter, after she had been particular warned not to do so by—one who is worth a cart-load of sich—knowing all this, I felt for you, and determined to do everything in my power to make you happy on your return."

"You're werry, werry kind, marm, " mournfully observed her visitor.

"Yes, and, my dear Jerry—Forgive me calling you so."

"I forgive you. There, go on," cried the now wondering acting warrant, taking her hand by way of encouraging her to proceed.

"Well, my dear Jerry, when I looked around me, I wondered where I could find a virtuous, good-looking girl, suitable to your mind—"

"That's poetry, dear friend, ain't it?" put in her visitor.

"I saw painted faces, false figgers, flaunting airs, brazen-nosed impudence, and, nothing but sham—all—everywhere."

There ain't much sham about you," admiringly observed Thompson, glancing at her tightly-fitting silk dress, which set off her buxom figure to great advantage.

Mrs. Shever pretended not to hear this compliment, but continued—"Well, dear Jerry, I saw all this, and I said to myself, 'Now, I wonder if some good, kind, loving, devoted, amiable, not bad-looking, affectionate, well-to-do girl were to be willing—would he—make her a offer?'"

At this juncture the face of Thompson, who now began to what is vulgarly termed "smell a rat," assumed a roguish expression, and, quietly, pushing his finger into her side, he laughingly observed, "I say, Missis S., you don't mean to say *you* want to sacrifice yourself agin, do you?"

Mrs. Shever blushed violently, but being determined to carry it through, she fell into his arms, called him her own Jerry, and vowed he was a perfect "Dom Juam."

Thompson quietly unwound the somewhat impulsive lady, and having placed the table between them, was about to speak, when Mrs. Shever, finding her shots had fallen wide, and hearing Mary Ann's voice in the hall, suddenly assumed a severe air, and ordered him to leave the apartment.

"You quit, sir, and never dare insult me" (here the door was opened, and Mr. and Mrs. Jenkins looked wonderingly in) "in my own house again. Begone, false serpent, and lay your base snares for some other innocent heart! Villain, I scorn you! Clear out, or I send for a police to remove you from my premises."

"Wot's the row?" demanded the carpenter, looking at Jerry, as if he would like to challenge him to mortal combat.

"That base man has insulted me," screamed the boatswain's widow, who then pretended to faint, thinking the gentlemen would now settle the affair by an appeal to arms.

"Come, come, 'Melia, this won't do," put in Mary Ann; "you know Mr. Thompson don't care for you, and never did; and you've set your cap at him, and have been refused, and serve you right."

"Did you write this poetry to me, Mrs. Mary Ann?" demanded the acting warrant, producing Mrs. Shever's poetical effusion.

"No, Mr. Thompson, I didn't," emphatically replied the lady.

"Did you write this ere letter to me?" handing her the note which he had received that morning.

"No, Mr. Thompson, I'll swear I didn't. I don't write no letters to young men now I'm married."

Finding matters were going against her, and not wishing for any further explanation, Mrs. Shever got up from the sofa, dried her eyes, and walking to Mrs. Jenkins kissed her affectionately, and begged she would not say any more about it, as she had been very foolish, and now saw through her folly. Then, turning to Jerry, asked him, for the sake of old times, and him as was dead and gone, to forgive her, and forget she had been such a fool.

Thompson gladly made up matters, and explained to the still somewhat bewildered Jenkins that he felt the greatest admiration for both the ladies present,—one being still an out-and-out handsome woman, and as such to be admired by the opposite sex ; while the other was, to his mind, the werry *idle* of a comely mother.

This somewhat mixed compliment soothed the carpenter's irritated feelings, and after a general hand-shaking the party proceeded to the supper-table, where they attacked the good things in a most praiseworthy manner, and Jerry saw with no little amusement that her disappointment had not taken away the widow's appetite.

Mrs. Shever came out quite nobly, and pledged Mr. Thompson's health in a glass of sherry, wishing him speedily "a good partner;" while Jerry, not to be outdone, toasted "The fair widow, and may she soon agin be a happy wife." Of course there was no allusion to her little mistake, and the casual visitors who dropped in imagined it was "all right," and were a few days afterwards much astonished to hear that Mrs. Shever had changed her mind.

The buxom widow did not fret about her failure, but went into society, and turned men's heads with such success that in a few weeks the "Portsmouth Times" had the following announcement in its list of marriages :—

"On the 23rd instant, at Mount Hope Chapel, by the Rev. Mr. Barryl, Amelia, widow of the late Mr. Henry Shever, formerly of H. M. Royal Navy, to Orlando Huffers, an eminent retired grocer of this place."

Mr. Thompson walked down to his ship, pondering upon the vanity of all things, and of Mrs. Shever in particular ; and as he turned in that night vowed he would shun the sex in future, as there was no one in the world like A-tae, and he was tired of the women.

CHAPTER XXVIII.

According to Captain Tortle's instructions, about six o'clock on Monday morning the Stinger's warps were cast off, and she slowly left the wharf at Portsmouth, and steamed out of the harbour upon her way to Woolwich.

Early as was the hour, a number of people witnessed her departure; a few of the more persevering ones taking a waterman's boat and following in her wake across the harbour; as if imagining some unlucky sailor might fall overboard and be picked up by them, when they would have an opportunity of selling him a suit of clothes.

These gentry were loud in their denunciation of the Admiralty's decision, considering that as the Stinger fitted out at Woolwich, and their brothers had the glorious opportunity of swindling the crew upon that occasion, it would only be common justice for her to pay off at Portsmouth; and they looked at the retreating ship, and clawed their beards with rage, their feelings, no doubt, very much resembling those of an ardent angler, who, after having played with a fine trout for some time, sees his anticipated victim quietly wag its tail, and make the best of its way into deep water.

"Now, vot ish de use of us going to do expensh ov dish poat?" grumbled an unhappy-visaged young fellow, who sported a dog's-eared-looking suit of clothes, and smelt villainously of bad tobacco. "Vot ish do use of all dish foolishness?"

"Ma friend!" exclaimed a venerable old man, who was holding on to the seat, and apparently saying his "prayers at sea in a time of danger,"—"Ma friend, dish is a put op schob of Peter's, who sent us out here vile he starts for Voolvich—ve pay and he gets do penefit—so I votes ve leave *him* to settle vith de vaterman."

Upon hearing this observation the watermen ceased rowing, and demanded their fare; whereupon the passengers reluctantly drew forth their purses, and, under threat of "being chucked overboard if they did not pony up at once," after much squabbling among themselves, made up the sum required by the boatmen, who then leisurely proceeded to pull towards the landing-place.

In due time the Stinger reached Woolwich, where she was immediately taken into dock. The ship being what is termed "paid off all standing," beyond returning the running rigging into store, her crew had very little to do, and by noon on the day of arrival were cleaned and ready for inspection.

Cravan was all fuss and worry,—nothing went right,—and in his anxiety that the men should present a particularly smart appearance, had mustered and drilled them into a bad temper. The sailors knew there was no necessity for his absurd orders, and did not show much alacrity in obeying him.

About one o'clock a midshipman, who had been stationed in front of the superintendent's office, rushed down to the ship and announced that the expected visitors were coming, which news was immediately reported to the commander, who went on deck and proceeded to the gangway, where he awaited the arrival of the commodore and his staff.

As the party neared the ship, the crew, who were mustered for inspection, noticed their old commander Woodward was one of the number, and had they dared would have received him with a ringing cheer; as it was, they had to content themselves with smiling at him whenever they could catch his eye.

Mr. Thompson was in attendance at the gangway, and in his delight at beholding his favourite captain executed such an extraordinary "pipe," that Woodward could not avoid smiling; thus encouraged, Jerry redoubled his efforts, and finished off with a most artistic flourish.

After the various officers had been introduced to the commodore, and the ship had been officially inspected, the mustering of the crew commenced, Clare being one of the first men to answer to his name and pass in review before the venerable official.

Tom had replaced his cap and was again mingling with the men when Captain Woodward spoke to the commodore, and Clare was recalled and thus addressed by him :—

"Thomas Clare, captain's coxswain, I am directed by the Lords Commissioners of the Admiralty to express to you their lordships' appreciation of your gallant conduct upon the occasion when H.M.S. Stinger was threatened with destruction by fire-junks, and to hand you a gratuity of ten pounds. Your bravery has been especially brought before their notice by your late commander, Captain Woodward, and it is to his kindness you owe their recognition of your good services."

Upon hearing this speech the crew gave a hearty cheer, which was allowed to pass unnoticed by the worthy commodore.

Tom received the money, and respectfully thanked the giver; but the gathering of officers recalled his court-martial too forcibly to his memory, and although he knew he ought to feel pleased, the affair rather depressed him than otherwise.

Before the commodore left the ship Captain Woodward spoke to Mr. Thompson, but finding Jerry did not intend remaining in the service, asked him what he could do to serve him in any other way.

"Ask the commodore to give me leave to go home with Clare, sir; he wants looking after," begged the good-natured fellow.

Captain Woodward promised to speak for him; and although, usually, warrant-officers are not allowed to leave the ship until their stores are returned and examined, so powerful was Woodward's intercession, that the next day, before the men were paid off, Mr. Thompson received the required permission, with orders to return at the expiration of four days.

Inspection being over, the commodore took his departure, Captain Woodward remaining on board the ship.

After partaking of Captain Tortle's hospitality, Woodward went on the quarter-deck, and requested Cravan to send for Clare, and several other men. Obedient to the summons, the delighted sailors at once hurried aft, and each received a present from the generous captain. When Clare presented himself, Woodward held out his hand and kindly asked him if he had heard from his wife, and whether he had got over his old complaint.

Tom looked at his friend, and replied in a most animated manner, that he was all right, and hoped to see his wife the next day.

"There's a slight token of my esteem for you, Clare," said Woodward handing him a package containing a handsome silver watch and chain. "I beg you will accept this as a proof of my appreciation of your noble act. Is there anything I can do for you besides?"

"No, th—thank you, sir,—you're too good; I don't deserve this. I thank you very much indeed. My wife will be so proud of this. It makes me feel a man agin. I can hold up my head arter this."

15

Cravan, who stood near, sneered at the proceeding as openly as he dared ; but the malicious look was lost on Clare, who opened the parcel, and found the following engraved upon the back of the watch :

TO

THOMAS CLARE,

CAPTAIN'S COXSWAIN.

For Bravery.

He having at the risk of his life, single-handed, saved H.M.S. Stinger from destruction by fire-junks in the Canton River, on the——of——18—,

Presented to him as a mark of esteem,

by

CAPTAIN PAUL WOODWARD, R.N.

Captain Woodward further informed the happy fellow, that if at any time he wanted a friend, and would let him know, he would be delighted to do anything for him.

When Clare had left the captain's presence, the latter proceeded to the gangway for the purpose of leaving the ship, when his attention was attracted by a deputation of petty-officers, headed by the " re-constructed " Jemmy Spry, who after many salaams, addressed his old commander as follows :—

" Please, Captain Woodward, sir, would ye be so kind as to pardon our boldness—but—beg your pardon, sir, but the men forward, sir—wants to see—ye sir. We makes so bold as to ax if you will be so kind as to allow—us all to see you, sir."

Having consulted with Tortle, who was so " jolly " that he would have agreed to anything. Woodward returned to the quarter-deck, and the crew " laid aft " and heard him speak. After telling the old hands how glad he was to welcome them home, and having shaken hands with every one of them, he left the Stinger, amidst the cheers of the grateful fellows, who kept up their hurrahs until he was out of sight and hearing.

When the last " hip! hip! " had died away, the first lieutenant ordered them to be " piped down," and added, in an undertone, " You yahoos, I'd like to cheer some of you with the cat."

Cravan felt annoyed that the man who had once resented an insult from him, should be thus publicly complimented *upon the very spot where the outrage occurred.*

The next morning the Stingers were paid off, and in a few hours were on their way to their respective homes. When Clare left the ship with his friend many of the men went to the gangway to bid him good-bye, three cheers being given for Thompson, and hearty wishes expressed on all sides for his future prosperity.

"Good-bye, Mr. Thompson; good-bye, Jerry; good-bye, old ship."

It will be seen from this that the crew were very different men from those who manned the Stinger when she first fitted out. Captain Woodward had attracted some of the best sailors in the service to the ship, and, taking them as a body, they were as fine a crew as ever trod a deck.

Having bidden farewell to their old shipmates, Thompson and Clare walked out of the dockyard, and entering a cab were conveyed to the railway station.

As they left the dock gate Clare exclaimed, "Good-bye, prison ; good-bye slavery. Now for a *man's* life. Freedom and Polly."

" By-the-by, have you heard from her since you have been here ? " demanded Thompson.

Clare replied that he had not, but thought it probable that she had directed her letter to Portsmouth, and that one would arrive for him this evening after he left.

When they got to the station Tom gazed wistfully at the telegraph wires, and observed to his friend, " Do you think it would cost more than five shillings to send her a wire message ? I should so much like to let her know that I shall be home to-night."

Jerry said that he didn't know what the damage would be, but he'd soon find out, so they proceeded to the booking-office, and ascertained that they could send quite a long message for that sum.

Clare took a pen, and, after being assured by his friend that what he wrote would be transmitted word for word, proceeded to write as follows :—

" *H.M.S. Stinger. Dear Polly, We paid off this morning. I will be with you, my dear, to-night. Your affectionate husband, Tom Clare.*"

Tom handed this to Jerry, who paid the sum demanded, and returned the receipt to his friend.

" Do you think jist them words will go—Dear Polly ? Don't you think they will alter it ? "

" Lord bless your foolish old head ! why, if you wrote Chinee, them ere clerks would send it ; they're awful clever. Why, they sends French and German. Of course they put dear ! "

When they arrived at the London Bridge Station they transferred their baggage, and Thompson sought out the guard, who proved to be an old school-mate. To him Jerry delivered the parrot and monkey, with directions to leave them at the Sandwich station, where Maxted the carrier would take charge of and convey them to his mother ; and in order that the animals might not be neglected, he affixed the following notice to their cages :—

" *Live animals, with care. Give them a drink if they wants it, but don't blow them out with wittles.*"

The first part of their journey by the South Eastern Railway was a most pleasant one, as they made a number of acquaintances.

Sometimes Jerry would nurse a fractious baby for a weary-looking mother, or take charge of an old woman while her husband fetched in the baggage. Then a pretty face attracted his attention, and he would sit and watch it until the girl turned away her head, or he was called to order by Tom.

As they neared their journey's end, Clare became very much depressed, frequently asking the time, and fidgetting so, that Thompson had great difficulty in getting him to reply to his questions; however, at last he roused himself, and recognizing the places they were passing, became much more communicative.

" That's Sandwich ! " he observed, pointing out a Dutch-looking town, round which the railroad wound, as if fearing if it ran too close to the old place that it would wake up the Rip Van Winkle-like inhabitants.

" Oh, that's Sandwich, is it ? That's the original and only genuine ham, mustard, and bread-and-butter Sandwich, is it ? Well, let us get out and have a glass of ale, shall we, Tom ? "

" You won't find no ale nearer than the Three Coltses," observed a railway labourer, who had just entered the carriage. " There's no beer, no nothing in that place, 'cept dead and buried people. The whole town is gone to sleep, and nothing won't wake it but a 'lection."

Hearing this remark the passengers laughed, and the speaker finding Clare and his friend were sailors, generously proffered his tin bottle of beer, which was duly accepted by them.

" So you're a Kingsdown man, are you ? " said Tom, having entered into conversation with the navvy. " My wife lives at Kingsdown ; her name is Clare. I'm Tom Clare. Perhaps you've heard of me ? "

It so happened that, although the railway navvy looked a rough sort of a man, he was really very intelligent; and having heard of Tom, saw at a glance how matters stood, and replied, " Oh, yes, I have heard of you. I'm glad to see you back. You've got a fine little boy."

" When did you see Polly—my wife—last ? " excitedly demanded the sailor.

" Here's Deal ! " shouted the man, who thereupon searched under the seat for his tools, and stopped all further inquiry on Tom's part.

" De-al ! D'l ! D'l ! " bawled the porters, and the train stopped with a jerk, which nearly threw the occupants of the carriage off their feet.

In the confusion of arrival the navvy slipped away, and Clare was unable to get any more information.

Having engaged a fly, the friends proceeded to Kingsdown, Jerry evidently very much puzzled at the navvy's manner, yet unwilling to alarm Tom, who seemed to be utterly unconscious of anything but the approaching meeting with Polly.

When they arrived at the cottage it was twilight, and lights were gleaming from the front windows. Thompson paid the driver, and, taking the baggage, walked up the pathway after his friend, who had run ahead, and was loudly knocking at the door.

" Why, they don't seem to know we are here," gasped Clare.

At this instant the door was opened, and Tom saw his wife's father, who, with troubled face, exclaimed, " Glad to see you, poor fellow ! Here, little Tom, come, see your daddy."

Clare walked into the room, and seeing his wife's mother, who was seated on a chair by the fire, advanced to her, and taking her hand, quietly said, " Where's my dear Polly ? "

The poor creature, evidently too much overcome to speak, with trembling lips pointed to her husband, who was watching her with a pained expression of countenance.

" Wh—why—what *does* this mean ? Where is my wife. Mother, what makes you look so ? Surely she is—"

" Tom," cried the old man, " it ain't no good to deceive you *now*. Polly is *dead*. She died the sixteenth of August three year ago, and—God forgive us !—we have let you be in the dark all this time, fearin' it would be too much for you."

Hearing this, Clare staggered to a chair, and after passing his hand across his brow, exclaimed, " My— Polly—dead ? "

" Yes, poor soul ; she giv birth to this one in sorrow and anxiety, and never rallied. Tom, go to your father."

The little child did as he was bidden, though he seemed almost afraid of the scared face; but when he felt his father's fervent kiss all his fears vanished, and the boy hugged him, and called him "dear daddy," until Thompson, who was a sympathizing spectator of the proceeding, sobbed audibly.

The old woman had covered her face with her apron, and was weeping bitterly, while, in spite of his stoicism, the tears were rapidly coursing each other down her husband's wrinkled cheeks.

"Here's—her—sun-pictur," continued the old fisherman, taking a little case, containing a portrait of Polly, from the mantel-piece. "That's like her, poor soul! she looked—werry thin—afore she died."

Tom took the portrait, and holding it towards the candle, gazed on it with a face expressive of reverence and love.

"So that's—all there is left—of my—darling, is it?" he falteringly inquired.

"Yes, poor feller, that's all. She's gone to her last home."

As the old man uttered these words Clare lifted his little boy off his knee, and having gently kissed him, observed to Thompson, in a quiet, weary manner, "that he must be going." The words were scarcely uttered before the speaker's head dropped upon his chest, and he fell heavily forward.

Thompson sprang towards his friend, and, with the assistance of the old man, raised him from the ground. The agony of the woman was most painful. She threw her arms around the inanimate form, and uttered most heartrending cries. "O Tom, dear, dear feller! I've killed you! It's me that's done this. Oh, wicked woman that I am."

"Come—Fanny—don't—take—on—so,—it's—no—fault—of—your'n," observed her husband, sobbing between each word; but the poor creature did not hear his well-meant words of comfort, she having swooned from grief.

After in vain trying to restore Clare to consciousness, Thompson ran for a doctor, and when he returned with one, they found the room filled with neighbours.

"Turn these people out," directed the physician.

In a short time the gossips retired, taking with them the grief-stricken old woman, who, in spite of their endeavours to comfort her, blamed herself as the cause of Clare's sudden death.

While Thompson was clearing the apartment the doctor proceeded to examine Clare, who had been placed upon a sofa; and when the kindly sailor had seen the last person out, he hurried to his friend's side.

"The poor man is dead," sadly observed the doctor

"Ain't there no chance for him, sir?"

"No, none whatever. Is this the husband of Mary Clare?"

"Yes, your honour."

"Where is the child?"

Thompson searched about the room, and at length found little Tom fast asleep under a table, with his innocent face pillowed upon his dead father's jacket.

The gentle-mannered physician touched the child lightly, saying, "Poor baby, he knows nothing of his great loss;" then, having advised the old fisherman to look after his wife, and directed Thompson not to disturb the body until the inquest should be held, took his departure.

After a time the broken-hearted old woman returned, and taking the child in her arms, retired to rest. Thompson remained by the body of his friend all night, and as the clock ticked off the moments, could scarcely credit it was not all a dream.

"Poor old chap!" he murmured, passing his hand across Clare's brow. "Poor heart, so you saw her spirit arter all. Well, I can't understand it; it's beyond me, but

it may have been so. If you can hear me, old shipmate and brave heart, hear me
say I'll never let your little chap want as long as God gives me health and strength ; "
and having uttered these words, the kind-hearted sailor sat down beside the couch, and
placing his hands to his face, the man who had seen death gather many friends before,
wept like a woman.

There lay poor Tom, with the portrait of his loved wife tightly clutched in his hand.
True to her in life, and true in death ; and the wording of the telegram he had penned
that morning, which now lay open upon a table near, seemed prophetic—"*I will be
with you, my dear, to-night.*" We may hope he was with her, in a world of which we
can have no conception until our eyes are opened by the angel of death.

In the morning little Tom crept into the room, and with awe upon his face asked to
" see his dear daddy."

Jerry, unable to refuse the child's request, uncovered the calm face, which the little
one gazed upon with a sorrowful expression. Taking the poor orphan in his arms
Thompson carried him from the room, and leaving the child with a neighbour, walked
along the breezy downs to get rid of some of his miserable thoughts.

" What is life ? " he mused. " Here to-day and then gone, and nobody knows that
so insignificant a creature ever troubled the earth. What have we to live for ? Another world ? Yes, that must be it. We ain't created for nothing ; the God who made
us has power to do everything. I'll try and do better in future, and be more kinder
to others, and less selfish. This death of Tom has made me think. We've all got our
duty to do in this world, like we have got to do it in a man-of-war, and according as
we does it so we gets our reward."

Thus mused the sailor, who had probably seldom before given his future a thought.
Death made him think, as it does most of us, and the kind-hearted fellow, in his desire
to do better for the future, imagined he was one of the most miserable sinners in existence. It is thus with all men ; when the " dark shadow " envelopes their acquaintances,
they cry " mea culpa," and vow to be very good ; but it requires something more than
human philosophy to keep them in remembrance of their vows.

The inquest was held that day, and, in accordance with the custom in that part
of the country, the jurors returned a verdict, that Clare " Died from the visitation of
God."

After seeing to the arrangements for the funeral, and promising to return in time
to attend it, Thompson proceeded to Woolwich ; and his stores being found correct,
received his pay, and left H. M. service.

Finding Captain Woodward was still in the town, Jerry called upon him, and informed
him of Clare's death, which news much affected the good officer.

" Has he left any family, Thompson ? "

" Yes, sir ; one little boy."

" I'll get him into Greenwich School when he's old enough. Tell his relatives to
remember that, Mr. Thompson."

" God bless you, sir, for your good heart. Excuse me, but little Tom won't never
want. I'm going to be his father now, and, while much obliged to you for all your
kindness, I think I can manage to keep him until he can earn his own living. But I
won't forget your kind offer, sir."

As Thompson was taking his leave, Mrs. Woodward entered the room, and Jerry
had the inexpressible satisfaction of being presented to her. She heard his touching
story of Clare's death, and dropped a tear of pity to the memory of the unfortunate
lovers. Jerry left the house bearing several tokens of her sympathy for the orphan boy,
and, what pleased him beyond anything else, the gift of the captain's portrait, which

he proudly exhibits to this day, as the picture of a noble man, that was given him by an angel.

Clare was buried in the village churchyard, by the side of his faithful wife; and when the last spadeful of earth was heaped over the grave, Thompson proceeded to a stonemason's, of whom he purchased a suitable monument, which he ordered to be erected over the pair, and to bear this inscription:—

SACRED TO THE MEMORY

OF

MARY AND THOMAS CLARE.

True hearts. Parted in life, but now united in death.

18—.

This accomplished, Thompson returned to the fisherman's cottage, and told them his intentions towards the boy. At first the old couple would not listen to his proposal to adopt little Tom; but when he pointed out to them that it would be better for him to take the child at once, they yielded, and finally gave their consent; upon which the good-hearted fellow wrote to his mother, telling her that he should bring the boy home with him.

It was arranged that all poor Tom's pay and prize money should be placed in the Deal Bank until such time as the boy came of age, or it was wanted to start him in the world; and that, added to the money already there in his late mother's name, would form a very handsome sum by the time it would be required.

Before parting with the old folks, Jerry—without implying any reproach—asked them plainly why they did not write Tom about his wife's death? when they informed him that, fearing the blow would kill him, and that he would never see his child, they had enlisted the sympathy of a young girl who lived near, and all poor Tom's letters had been answered by her—always endeavoring to avoid positively false statements.

Thompson could not openly blame them, as they had evidently committed the error with a good intention; and after saying he was sorry they hadn't written him about it, bade them good-bye, and taking little Tom by the hand, led him away.

The child's parting with his relatives was of course a trial on both sides; but when he and Jerry were clear of the cottage, and seated in a conveyance on their way to Deal, the little fellow soon dried his tears, and by the time they arrived at their journey's end, had taken to his new protector most contentedly.

Having seen a lawyer, and settled the necessary business in connection with the property belonging to poor Clare, Thompson proceeded to an inn, and early the next morning hired a conveyance, by which he reached his native place about noon. Everybody seemed to expect him, and his progress from the entrance of the village to his mother's cottage was one continued ovation.

"Here's Jerry Thompson come back," giggled a girl, who, standing at the top of the garden steps, was shouting to her mother in the potato patch.

"Hallo, Jerry," roared a farm labourer, who had known the sailor at school, but who, save by the uniform, could not have recognized his old playfellow.

"Glad to see ye, master," cried the old men.

"Service to ye, Jerry," squeaked the old women, who were somewhat dazzled with the uniform, and didn't know whether to be polite or familiar.

"Hurrah! Hurrah!" screamed the children; and the ducks and geese flapped their wings, and scuttled about as if joining in the acclamation; and when Thompson arrived opposite Trotman's Charity, a saucy bantam, which had perched itself on the gate, tried to crow out a welcome. Ere it had fairly commenced it was swung off its legs by an apple-faced little girl, who, regardless of chanticleer, opened the gate with a vigorous swing, stood against it to keep it in its place, and with smiling, upturned face bobbed a courtsy to "Squire Jerry," she imagining that Mr. Thompson could not be less, as he came in a carriage, and everybody hurrahed.

When the vehicle stopped, Jerry leaped out over the door, being too impatient to allow the man time to open it, and, rushing up to his old mother, hugged and kissed her as only sailors do; and after thus demonstrating his affection for her, turned to a charming-looking girl, standing respectfully behind her, who had blushed a recognition to him as he alighted, and taking her round the waist, saluted her right lovingly, and inquired if she were his Cousin Nelly.

The girl coloured, and half-timidly endeavoured to withdraw from his grasp; but finding the old lady smiled upon her, she turned smartly round and replied, " Yes, I'm Nelly, and I suppose you call this a cousin's privilege ? "

Seeing the merry twinkle in her eye, Jerry repeated his attention, and then stepping forward, thus addressed his friends and relatives, who had gathered round the door to welcome him :—

" My dear ship—friends and kinsfolks, I'm mighty glad to see you. I've passed through many dangers since I left here a boy. But Jerry has always fallen upon his feet (cheers). I ain't got time to say much to you, only to tell you once more how glad I am to see you (voices—'So are we to see you, mate'). I've shipped—I mean I've got a billet as steward to as good a gentleman as ever owned a estate, and he's got the loveliest little girl *you* ever saw (more cheers). I am going to take my old mother out of this and make a lady of her, although she's always bin a good woman, and can't be improved upon anyhow (deafening cheers, and cries of 'Bless him!' from the women). I thanks all of you as ever has done her a good turn in my absence, and promise you, when I knows who you are, I'll do you a half-a-dozen in return " (loud uproar).

Having thus delivered himself, Jerry, forgetting he was no longer on board a man-of-war, seized his call and piped down; upon which his friends, thinking very correctly it was a sailor's way of dispersing a crowd, quietly drifted off to their homes, and before night had invented no end of stories of the sailor's adventures, of course all being told them by Jerry.

While Thompson was delivering his speech, little Tom had crept close to Ellen, who, taking him in her arms, entered the house, and seating herself upon a sofa, removed his hat, and stroking his brown hair whispered to him tenderly, " Will *you* be *my* boy ? "

" Oh, shouldn't I like to ? " he replied, his dark eyes sparkling with animation ; then looking up into the loving face bent over him, the child, who had never known a mother's care, placed his plump hands upon her cheeks, and fervently kissed the offered lips.

" You dear little fellow. Then you shall be my boy, and I'll be a mother to you," said the warm-hearted girl, her eyes suffusing with tears; and from that moment she took little Tom to her heart, from which he was never displaced.

When they got over their excitement a little, Jerry was taken into the next house to see his aunt, Mary Golder, that indignant old lady having refused to stir over her threshold until he first visited her; and although she could plainly hear all that was said in her sister's rooms, and was burning with curiosity to see her long-lost nephew, still her pride was so great that she wouldn't demean herself to beg favours, and vowed she would wait by her fireside until he came to see her, and not "go a-running arter him, like a foolish young colt as didn't know no manners."

However, when the sailor burst into the apartment, and had given her a dozen nautical hugs, she relented, and in spite of "rheumatiz" and sundry "spazims," managed to get out of her chair and visit her sister, where, considering she was an invalid, she greatly distinguished herself by eating more than any two persons at the tea-table.

So astonished was little Tom at the capacity of the dear "old girl" for tea, that he actually laid down his bread and butter, and gasped.

A few days after the sailor's return the Major arrived at Lee Park, and Thompson was sent for, and instructed to take possession of the Holt Lane farm house, to which he at once removed his relations, including his aunt Mary Golder; Miss Cops being expressly sent in a carriage to convey the old people to their new home. The young lady was unaccompanied, Adèle having returned to France.

Great was the excitement in the almshouses when Miss Barbara walked up the pathway, and, with the utmost self-possession, asked the silver-haired handsome old woman, "Is you Missis Jerry?"

"Yes, my pretty darling, I'm Jerry's mother," tremblingly replied the delighted Mrs. Thompson.

"Then you are to come with me to your barley-sugar-candy-house, returned Cops, who, catching sight of little Tom at that moment, exclaimed, "Dear boy!" and, without more ceremony, seized the astonished child and led him off to the carriage.

In a short time the party were all seated, with Jerry on the box beside the driver, and having waved a farewell to Trotman's Charity, they started for Holt Lane, amidst the sneers of the alms-house folks, and the cheers of all the other villagers.

When they arrived at the farm, Miss Cops loudly expressed her delight at the place, evidently oblivious of its not being a barley-sugar-candy building; and taking little Tom's hand, proceeded upon a tour of inspection, looking in her loveliness like a good fairy who had just bestowed the place upon some faithful friend.

After having gone through the house, she left the adults, and proceeded to show her protégé the surroundings; and when hunted out by her friend Jerry, was found busily engaged in instructing young Tom in the art of "making little pigs sing," her principle being to watch until they got close to the interstices of the sty, and then to seize their tails between her finger and thumb, which operation generally produced the much-admired musical sounds. It may be imagined that Miss Barbara required a course of soap and water before being sent home.

Major Barron, or "The Squire," as he was usually termed, found Thompson a very apt scholar, and in a few months, under his tuition during the day, and Ellen's in the evening, Jerry became quite expert at accounts.

It was very evident to all the good folks in the place that the steward was desperately in love with his cousin, yet when spoken to upon this subject he would shake his head and gravely deny it.

One night, after his aunt Golder and Ellen had retired, Jerry was seated in the chimney corner smoking his pipe, and watching the motion of his mother's knitting needles, when the old lady fixed her keen eyes upon his face, and demanded to know what ailed him.

"Ails me, mother!" he replied, with a forced laugh, "why, nothing as I know of; I'm hearty enough." Having said this, he heaved a deep sigh.

"Jerry, look at me. You're in love, I know you are. That puss Ellen has turned your head."

"Nonsense, mother."

" No, it ain't nonsense, that is, your loving a good girl like her ; that ain't no non-sense, my boy. Now, all your brothers and sisters are away in Ameriky and Australy, and I shall probably never see none of my children's children if you don't get married soon. It would do my old eyes good to see your little ones."

" All right, mother,' ejaculated Jerry with a depreciative wave of his long clay pipe " All right. Ease your steam, my dear. I ain't married yet, and ain't likely to be."

" Not all the while you keeps a shillyshallying about as you does. You ain't, that's true," somewhat warmly retorted the old lady.

Upon hearing this Thompson got up, and walking to his mother's chair leant over the back, and in a somewhat troubled manner made the following confession :

" My dear old mother, pardon me if I was hasty. My heart is full, and I want you to tell me what to do.'

" Go on, dearie,' replied the now mollified old lady, firing away at her knitting in order to give vent to her feelings.

" Well, mother, I love Cousin Nelly as I never loved a gal afore, only once, and she, poor thing, a Chinee."

" You was allus soft-hearted as a boy," put in the not at all astonished dame.

" Well, she is dead, and I hope in a better world along with poor Polly and Tom—little Tom's mother, you know."

" Oh, I know,' said the dame, working more furiously than ever at her knitting.

" When I came home I little thought, arter all the girls I've been soft over, that I should ever become so desperately fond of Cousin Nelly. But it's a ease, and but for you, I'd go to sea again, as I can't marry her."

" Can't marry her? why not, in the name of goodness ? "

Jerry informed his mother that he believed it was " agin the law for him to marry his cousin."

" Bless us, is that all ? " coolly observed his mother.

" That all! Well, I should think that's enough. I suppose you don't want me to break the law, do you, and be had up for bigamy ? "

" Bless your heart!" gasped the old lady. " Why, don't you know ? "

" Yes, I knows, mother. I've always heard that it ain't lawful for to marry your cousin. If I was in China I'm blest if I wouldn't. That's the best of China, there ain't no laws like that there."

Hearing this outburst, the old dame gave a hearty ringing laugh, which sounded most unkindly to her troubled son.

" Nay, mother, don't laugh. This is a big trouble for me.'

" Why, you stupid boy ? It's quite lawful, besides Ellen isn't your cousin at all."

" Not my cousin ? " screamed the almost frantic sailor ; " not my cousin ? Hurrah!" Then, darting out of the kitchen, he rushed up-stairs, loudly knocked at his aunt's bed-room door, and begged her to ask Nelly to come down, as his mother wanted to see her very badly.

In a few moments the girl, who had not retired to rest, but having noticed he was unhappy in her presence, had wisely left him to himself as much as possible, entered the room, upon which Jerry respectfully kissed her, and when she was seated, giving the log upon the hearth a kick, which made it blaze right merrily, begged his mother would go ahead with her yarn, when she spoke as follows :—

" Many years ago when I were a gal, in service up at the Hall, I had a friend named Mary Reynolds. She was a dear good girl, and were only out at service so as not to be a burden to her parents. Well, to make a long story short, she married a gentleman, and lived in good style for some years, until one day he lost all his property. They were then living in Canterbury, and I went to see her, poor thing, and I promised her if anything occurred to her, I'd take care of her little girl, Ellen here. You had then gone your first voyage in the "Royal Shepherdess," and when you came back Nelly was nine years old. Now she's twenty," said the old lady, fondly caressing the girl. "So you see there's no blood relationship betwixt you, although that wouldn't be an obstacle. But I'm tired. I'm going to bed. Good-night. God bless you *both*, my children."

"I'll say good-night, too, cou—Jerry," timidly added the girl.

Hearing this, her lover advanced, and leading her to a chair, begged she would stay, as he wished very particularly to speak to her.

When the last creak of the stairs announced that the old lady had reached her room, Thompson took a seat close to the agitated girl, and having gently placed his left arm round her waist, told her he loved her, and frankly asked her to be his wife.

For some moments Nelly hung her head, too much overcome with the revelation of the mother and the happiness of her position; but, being somewhat encouraged by the tender kiss which her lover imprinted upon her cheek, she at length turned her face towards him, and softly replied, " Yes."

He made no demonstration when he kissed her then, being too much in love to shout and dance as he had formerly done. They chatted over their prospects quietly, and before they separated it was determined that upon the eighteenth of February they would become man and wife.

The banns were duly put up, and upon the day appointed the gentle Nelly vowed to love and honour the now happy Thompson; while he, on his part, promised to cherish and protect her as long as Heaven permitted.

There was no idea of "co-partnership" between these lovers—they considered themselves bound in the bonds of holy matrimony, and believed the union so contracted was approved of by their Creator.

They were married in the parish church, the Squire giving away the bride, who, with her lovely complexion, looked like a peach-blossom. Four bridesmaids assisted at the ceremony, the principal one being the charming Cops; and as little Tom watched the party from the gallery, he wondered if the angels were more beautiful than that young lady and his adopted mother.

The villagers turned out in their best attire to witness the interesting ceremony, and the wedding breakfast was given in the big barn, and every one invited to be present.

A doubly proud woman was Mrs. Thompson that day; and when the Squire made a speech, and drank the health of the happy pair, the dear old lady cried for joy.

Many speeches followed, in one of which, a jolly old farmer, who was the only relation of the bride present, observed, that having such a flower as Nelly committed to his care, he hoped the late sailor would never prove a traitor to his trust; hearing which Jerry arose, and, in a brief speech, thanked his newly-found uncle for his *good wishes*, then amid loud acclamation re-seated himself by the side of his happy wife.

When the dinner was over the barn was cleared for dancing. The merry folks kept up the festivities until the morning dawned, and to this day the villagers speak of the splendid feast they had when *Muster* Thompson was married.

The sailor never forgot his friends in Hong-Kong, and, according to promise, wrote to Mrs. Mackay, saying, "I have married the best girl in the world, and if there is any victim in the case, it is not your happy friend, Jerry Thompson."

Nelly added a postscript.

*   *   *   *   *   *

Some years have elapsed since the foregoing, and Mr. Thompson is now the esteemed agent of the Squire, and farms a large estate upon his own account. He still retains his admiration for Miss Barbara, who has grown up into a beautiful woman; her word to him is law, and he makes it so to all under him.

Little Tom is at college, and promises to become a great scholar; he has ever cherished the most ardent affection for his adopted parents, who in return treat him as if he were their eldest son.

Several children have blessed the union of the pair, and if in a journey through Kent you pass Oakfield Farm, where Mr. Thompson now resides, you will probably see a blue-eyed Nelly and some black-eyed boys playing upon the lawn.

Jerry sometimes talks about his adventures when he was a blue jacket, but never reverts to the sad fate of the poor Chinese girl. He is happy in the society of his wife and friends; and though she is not forgotten, he has no desire to dwell upon the memory of "A-tae."

THE END.

www.ingramcontent.com/pod-product-compliance
Lightning Source LLC
Chambersburg PA
CBHW021959050726
47498CB00006BA/1948